The Last Sin

The Last Sin

A Detective Cancini Mystery

K.L. MURPHY

WITNESS

IMPULSE

An Imprint of HarperCollinsPublishers

This is a work of fiction. Names, characters, places, and incidents are products of the author's imagination or are used fictitiously and are not to be construed as real. Any resemblance to actual events, locales, organizations, or persons, living or dead, is entirely coincidental.

Excerpt from *Stay of Execution* copyright © 2016 by Kellie Murphy.

THE LAST SIN. Copyright © 2017 by Kellie Murphy. All rights reserved. Printed in the United States of America. No part of this book may be used or reproduced in any manner whatsoever without written permission except in the case of brief quotations embodied in critical articles and reviews. For information, address HarperCollins Publishers, 195 Broadway, New York, NY 10007.

Digital Edition MARCH 2017 ISBN: 978-0-06-249163-3
Print Edition ISBN: 978-0-06-249173-2

WITNESS logo and WITNESS IMPULSE are trademarks of HarperCollins Publishers in the United States of America.
HarperCollins is a registered trademark of HarperCollins Publishers in the United States of America and other countries.

FIRST EDITION

17 18 19 20 21   LSC   10 9 8 7 6 5 4 3 2 1

If you purchased this book without a cover, you should be aware that this book is stolen property. It was reported as "unsold and destroyed" to the publisher, and neither the author nor the publisher has received any payment for this "stripped book."

For the saints and sinners among us

...for the saints and sinners among us

Chapter One

Sunday, February 21: The Day of

THE SMELL OF incense lingered in the air, temporarily masking the odor of rotting wood. Father Matthew Holland inhaled. The bitter scent stung his nose. Three years had passed since he'd taken over the church, and nothing had changed. Even with the increased attendance and community outreach, the church offerings remained meager. Without offerings—without money—the parish church would die.

The priest sat down on the front pew, his robes gathered around his feet. His gaze shifted to the empty pulpit. Two large and colorful plants graced the altar, but they weren't enough to hide the worn carpet or faded paintings, nor could the soft candlelight make him forget the plywood that covered the cracked stained glass. There was so much to do, so much need. He sighed and looked to the cross over the altar. Not for the first time, he asked for forgiveness, for understanding. There would be money now—he'd made sure of that—but at what cost? He'd done it for the church. His pulse quickened and his stomach clenched. Bending forward, he forced himself to take one deep breath after another until the moment passed.

He loosened his clerical collar and yawned. The evening's Mass had been long and difficult. The drunks in the back of the church had refused to leave, in spite of the old deacon's best efforts.

"Gotta right to be here," the man with the long, stringy hair had slurred. He'd fallen forward as though he might topple straight into the next pew. "Worshippin' God," he'd said, although it had sounded like something else judging by the gasps from the congregation. The drunk had pointed a dirty hand toward the altar. "Here to see Father Holland. Tol' us to come anytime."

The drunk had swayed again, and his companion had reached out with a strong arm to catch him. Father Holland's mouth had gone dry at the sight of the tattoo on the man's forearm—a black dagger plunged into a white skull. Three drops of blood extended in a single line from the tip of the dagger to the man's wrist. He knew that tattoo, knew what it meant.

The awkward moment had passed, although not before Father Holland caught the disdain on the faces of the ladies in the choir. Still, none of the parishioners had said a word, all looking to him instead. He'd hidden his trembling hands in the folds of the heavy cassock and swallowed. "St. William is open to everyone, our members and our guests. However, since we are about to have communion, I would ask that everyone who is not singing remain quiet. Guests may come forward for a blessing, of course." He'd been careful to keep his voice steady. Thank the Lord it had been enough. The man with the oily hair had quieted down and then stumbled out during the Eucharist. His friend with the tattoo had stayed a moment longer, then followed.

Silence filled the sanctuary now. Father Holland rubbed his hands together and shivered. He could still feel the cold eyes of the tattooed man and the curious glances from the congregation. The man's presence at the evening Mass had been no accident and no drunken whim. The message had been clear.

After the church had emptied, Father Holland had walked to the corner market and made the call. He'd done the best he could. Money changed everything. It always did. He opened his hand and stared at the crumpled paper with the phone number. He was not a stupid man. Nothing came without a price. He murmured a prayer until his shoulders relaxed and the drumbeat of his heart slowed.

His stomach growled, the gurgling loud and rumbly, and he realized it had been hours since he'd eaten. Breaking the quiet, a sound came from the back of the church, a click and a swish as the heavy outer door swung open. He stood and smoothed his cassock. Dinner would have to wait. He strained to see, but the vestibule was dark. "Who's there?" he asked.

The door clanged shut and heavy steps sounded on the dingy marble floor. Father Holland replaced his collar and ran his fingers through his hair. There was only silence. The hair on the back of his neck prickled. "Is somebody there?" he asked again.

A figure shrouded in black stepped out of the dark.

Father Holland stiffened. "Why are you here?"

From the shadows, the eyes of the visitor glittered in the candlelight. "I'm a sinner, Father."

Father Holland's shoulders slumped. "We are all sinners in God's eyes."

"Some of us more so than others. Isn't that right, Father?"

His breath caught in his throat. "What do you mean?"

The visitor came forward, raising one arm, a shiny gun in hand. "I think you know what I mean."

Father Holland blinked. He took two steps backward and shook his head, his eyes shifting from the gun to the face in front of him. "You don't want to do this," he said. "It's not too late."

"You had your chance." The gun moved upward until the priest was looking directly into the blackness of the barrel. The visitor's face hardened. "People say you're a handsome man, Father. Did you know that?"

The priest staggered backward. Blood pounded through his veins and his breath was heavy in his chest.

"That's what they'll say. He was handsome once." Pale lips turned up in a sneer. "Before he wasn't."

Father Holland found his voice. "Please don't do this."

"Don't do what? Don't shoot you or don't shoot you in the face?" The visitor matched him step for step until the priest fell against the steps of the altar, his cassock under his feet. The crinkled slip of paper fell from his hand, landing at the bottom of the steps. "Well? Which is it, Father?"

"Both. Neither. Let's talk about this. We can pray together until we find a solution. This isn't the answer." He struggled to sit up. Under the robes, cold sweat dripped down his back.

The visitor snorted. "Why would God listen to you?"

"Please." The finger tightened on the trigger. Father Holland's heart slammed against his chest. "Not like this. You can't."

"I can. I'm a sinner. Just like you, Father."

Father Holland's body shook, knees knocking together. He knew it was over then. He would never refurbish the old church or rebuild the faith among the community. He would die like his mother, his own sins coming back to haunt him. He would meet his Maker. The priest brought his hands to the cross around his neck. His lips moved silently until his body became still and his breathing slowed.

When the shot sounded, it echoed through the turrets and the steeple, melding with high-pitched laughter. Blood leaked from the hole in Father Holland's head and spread across the carpet. Bits of bone and skull dotted the steps. The priest's hands remained clasped around the cross even in death. The visitor pocketed the paper at the bottom of the steps, crouched next to the dead man, and dipped one gloved finger in the blood. Rising, the visitor crossed to the altar and traced the figure of a cross on the snow-white cloth.

Sinking to the floor, the visitor whispered, "Let us pray."

Chapter Two

DETECTIVE MICHAEL CANCINI slowed the car and stuck his arm out the window, badge in hand. A uniformed officer waved him forward, directing him toward a small gravel lot.

"Guess this is it," Smitty said. He reached behind the seat for an umbrella.

Cancini glanced up at the dark sky. Rain-swollen clouds hung over the nation's capital, and thunder boomed somewhere in the distance. A cold wind blew open his jacket and rattled the limbs of the trees.

Smitty pulled up the collar of his camel-colored jacket. "It's gonna be a soaker."

"At least it's not snow," Cancini said, burying both hands in his pockets. He hunched his shoulders against the chill. "We'd better get started." A handful of gawkers hung back behind the police cars. Mostly elderly women, they clung to each other in the wind. He'd have someone get their statements before the day was over. "Who called it in?" he asked.

"Another priest. Found him this morning."

"Did someone take his statement?"

"Basics. Waiting to let you do the full." Smitty slowed, his eyes taking in the crumbling church. "Hard to believe people go here. It's kind of a dump, isn't it? For a church, I mean."

Cancini studied the building and grounds. St. William looked like so many other buildings and houses in this part of town; new and majestic once, ultimately falling into disrepair when large segments of the population migrated to the suburbs. Peeling paint hung in sheets from the white columns. A spiderweb of cracked and broken bricks served as a sidewalk. Still, the gravel parking lot and front lawn were devoid of trash, and cheerful wreaths decorated the heavy doors. Someone had made some effort.

Cancini ducked his head as the wind whipped up again. At the doors, he hesitated. He couldn't remember the last time he'd been inside a Catholic church, or any church for that matter. Raised Catholic, he'd fallen away from the church—from God—when his mother had been murdered in a convenience store robbery. His withdrawal from religion was just another way he'd managed to disappoint his father, but no more or less than any other. A homicide detective, Cancini preferred to put his faith in evidence and justice, things he understood. He drew in his breath and swung open the heavy door. Smitty followed. A pair of uniformed officers stood just past the vestibule and nodded when the detectives flashed their badges. Cancini slowed his steps, breathing through his nose. The odor of spilled blood permeated the chilly air.

A second cluster of uniformed officers loitered in a side aisle, their quiet conversation drifting over the pews. A precinct photographer snapped pictures and a forensic officer moved near the altar, dusting for prints. A pair of lights had been brought in to cut the darkness of the church.

Cancini's dark brows drew together. "There are too many people in here." He waved a hand. "Get everyone out but forensics and the photographer. We don't need some idiot contaminating something."

Smitty pointed a long finger at a man sitting in the middle of the church, head bowed. "What about him? Must be the priest that found the vic and called 911."

The man sat in the center of a pew, head bent, hands clasped in front of him. Freckles dotted his pink, balding scalp. Curly wisps of white-cotton hair ran from ear to ear. His thick neck bulged out over his clerical collar. Cancini looked away. He knew that head.

"He can stay."

Cancini waited as a half-dozen officers filed past him. The photographer finished, waved a hand, and followed. A tall woman from forensics dusted the pews, the candlesticks, and the altar. He watched as she covered every inch. When she appeared to be done, he walked down the center aisle until he drew parallel with the old priest. The man had dropped to his knees, his bulk squeezed between the pews, mouth moving in silent prayer. Cancini shook his head and looked up to the rafters. Damn.

"Cancini?" Smitty's voice was low and somber. "They're ready for you."

The forensic specialist locked her equipment case, nodded at him once, then left through the vestibule. He knew the rest of her work would be done in the lab. Snapping on a pair of gloves, he moved closer to the lifeless body sprawled across the steps. The old priest in the pews would have to wait.

The body lay supine, legs outstretched, face turned upward.

Cancini circled the dead man twice, careful to avoid the blood spatter on the carpet. He stopped near the man's feet, at the base of the steps. The priest's scuffed black shoes pointed to the sky, and the hem of his vestments had risen to his knees. "These are short steps."

"I noticed that," Smitty said. "Doesn't seem like a place he would be sitting, just waiting to be shot."

"Agreed. Most likely, he fell or stumbled backwards."

"Trying to back away from the shooter."

Cancini came down the steps again. He raised his right arm and pointed his finger at the dead priest. He glanced over at Smitty. "About like this."

"Makes sense."

Cancini dropped his hand and approached the body again. A kidney-shaped stain fanned out from one side of the dead priest's head as though his lifeblood had oozed from his right ear. The worn carpet around his head was dark and crusty. Cancini stepped around the sticky stain and crouched at the man's waist. The dead man's hands were clasped just below his neck. Cancini gently pried his fingers apart to find a golden cross. He closed the hands again and rocked back on his heels.

From a distance of only a foot or two, he studied the priest's face—or, more accurately, the part of his face not ripped apart by gunshot. The bullet had entered through the priest's right eye, obliterating the socket. Where his nose had been, there was a mash of broken bone. His forehead and skull had been split open. Splattered brain matter dotted the carpet and steps to the right of the body. The left eye, untouched, was closed as though in sleep. Cancini tipped his head up to his partner. "It was quick at least."

White-blond locks fell across Smitty's forehead. He looked at the dead man for no more than a few seconds, his face paler than usual. "Pretty brutal, shooting a priest that way."

Cancini said nothing. All murder was brutal. He rose and stepped back. "How long would you say he's been dead?"

Smitty's gaze skimmed over the body. "Several hours, maybe more."

Cancini nodded. The body was cold and stiff.

Smitty waved a hand in the direction of the uniformed officers at the back of the church. "I've been told there was a service here at five-thirty last night. So it had to be sometime after that."

"Mass is typically an hour. That gives us six-thirty as a starting point." Cancini climbed the steps again, drawn to the altar. The cross decorating the white cloth had not been stitched with red thread or stenciled from paint but had been drawn in blood. Measuring a foot in length, the dark and crusty image was narrow, the width of one finger—two at the most. He glanced back at the body and then again at the altar. Cancini sighed and stripped the rubber gloves from his hands. The press would have a field day, and they wouldn't be the only ones. He joined Smitty at the bottom of the steps. "Is the M.E. here?"

"Yeah. Waiting in the back."

"Who is it?"

"Will."

"Good. The sooner he and Kate can get the autopsy done, the sooner we might get some answers."

Smitty waved to Will, then shifted his attention to the man in the center pew. "What about him?" The man still knelt, as though in prayer. His shoulders sagged and his bald head glowed under the old yellow lights.

"His name is Father Joe Sweeney."

Smitty's eyes flicked over his partner. "Care to explain how you know that?"

Cancini shrugged. "He was our priest when I was a kid." He hesitated only a second before adding, "We still keep in touch."

Smitty looked back at the priest. "That going to be a problem?"

"Not for me." Both detectives watched as the assistant medical examiner tagged the body, careful to preserve evidence on and around it. "Does he have an alibi?"

"We're checking it out."

Father Joe had risen to his feet, his balance wobbly and his face wet. Cancini shivered, his skin clammy under the wool jacket. "Can you take him downtown? I want to talk to Will and have another look around."

"Whatever you say."

Smitty disappeared, and Cancini rubbed the back of his neck. He looked up at the shadows on the ceiling, his mind both charged and tired. It was going to be a long day. He stepped outside to get some air. Icy rain spit and swirled in the gusty wind. From the corner, he watched Smitty escort Father Joe Sweeney outside, one hand at the man's elbow. The priest was not a young man and carried more weight than he should. He walked purposefully and carefully. In spite of the weather, the small crowd still huddled on the other side of the yellow crime scene tape. A handful of reporters shouted questions that no one answered.

Halfway to the car, the old priest stopped, face turned toward the street. Following his gaze, Cancini saw a man. Tall and lean, he stood alone on the other side of the street. He wore a long, dark leather coat and held an umbrella in his right hand. His hair and eyes were hidden from view. A heavy beard covered the lower half of his face. The man dropped his head, stepped back, and vanished around the corner. Cancini ran a hand over his face, wiping away the rain dripping from his hair.

Lightning cracked across the sky, close and angry. A rumble of thunder followed and the rain came down harder, slashing against the church, and he ducked back inside. Church bells rang out, their chimes muted in the thunderstorm. He let out a long breath. The face of the dead priest flooded his mind and he could still smell the tinny odor of death clinging to his skin. He touched his hand to his head and without thinking, swept it across his chest in the sign of the cross. He waited but no prayer came. His hand dropped back to his side.

He walked back down the center aisle of the sanctuary to the altar. God couldn't stop death and murder, and he couldn't stop the news cycle. This case would be headlining the midday news and be featured again at five and eleven. The shooting of a priest—in his own church—guaranteed a story.

He moved past the assistant medical examiner, past the body, and up to the altar. Crouching, he leaned in, his long nose only inches from the cloth. The cross, already half dried, would be bagged and taken in. They would test for fingerprints and for DNA that might have mingled with the blood of their victim, but he didn't expect to find either. The cross wasn't a careless afterthought. He stood again, his bones cracking as he rose. The killer had shot the priest at close range. Even without DNA, without evidence, Cancini already knew the murder was a cold and calculated act. There'd been no panic. Instead, the killer had taken the time to paint the cross on the cloth using the dead man's own blood.

It had been years since Cancini had attended Mass, but he

hadn't forgotten everything he'd learned as an altar boy. The cross itself had many meanings. It represented the Holy Trinity: the Father, the Son, and the Holy Spirit. Different versions could symbolize the birth of Jesus, the resurrection, or the Christian faith. The lines around his mouth deepened, and the twisted knot of nerves between his shoulders hardened. The cross drawn on the cloth was not a celebration or a pronouncement of faith. It was crude and deliberate. Cancini recognized it for what is was. The bloody cross embodied the ultimate sacrifice. Death.

Chapter Three

THE VICTIM'S APARTMENT, neat and spare, smelled of aftershave and ripe bananas. A small television sat perched on a stand in a tiny living room furnished with only two chairs and an end table. A cluttered desk had been pushed into the corner. Cancini thumbed through a short stack of spiral notebooks but saw only handwritten drafts of sermons. Inside the refrigerator, he found milk, eggs, and a few other items, all still fresh. The closet held only robes, dark pants, and a handful of shirts. One pair of dress shoes and a pair of sneakers sat on the floor. Like most priests, this one lived on a fixed income. A laptop, a few years old, sat on a battered nightstand. Cancini made a note to get Landon from the forensic department to take a look at the hard drive. Nothing appeared out of place. After one final glance around the apartment, he pulled the door shut.

Striding across the church grounds, he turned his collar up against the wind and rain. He ducked under the yellow tape and entered through the sanctuary. The altar, now empty, was bathed in darkness. Only a pair of officers remained inside. He passed through to the Commons, stopped short and blinked, the canned fluorescents jarring after the dim lighting inside the church. An elderly man sat hunched on a bench, his face pale and somber.

"What've we got?" Cancini asked a third uniformed officer.

"Forensics is still in the vic's office. The photographer left a few minutes ago."

The detective gestured toward the man on the bench. "And him?"

"Janitor. Says he comes in every morning at nine. There was a secretary that showed up, too. When she heard about the priest, she broke down pretty bad. The guy with her took her home." He handed Cancini a piece of paper. "This is her name and number."

"Thanks." Cancini crossed the floor to the bench and sat down. He placed a card in the space between them. "I'm Detective Cancini."

The man drew a deep breath and lifted his head. Deep hollows under his cheekbones gave his face a skull-like appearance. With yellowed eyes, he glanced once at the card, then down at his knotted hands. "Tony Santos."

"I've been told you're the janitor here, Mr. Santos."

"Been coming every day at nine except for Sundays for fifty-eight years now. Never missed a day of work."

"Fifty-eight years. That's a long time."

The man grunted.

"How long had Father Holland been the priest here?"

Santos raised one bony shoulder. "Not long. A few years." He clucked his tongue. "This is gonna be bad for the church, really bad."

"Why do you say that, Mr. Santos?"

He ran his tongue over cracked lips. "Father Holland was the only thing keeping this place going. Before him, wasn't much work to do." His eyes took on a faraway look. "We used to have the best priests in town, you know, but they all moved out or got old. Big crowds for Mass every Sunday back then." He sighed. "We had some lean years for a while, but Father Holland, he was gonna change all that. He was changing it." He swallowed hard, and tears slid down his face.

A radiator rumbled to life and blew tepid air over Cancini's head. He let his gaze wander over the Commons. Old photos of bishops and cardinals hung on a pockmarked wall, and a dark hallway led toward the back of the building. The only furniture was the bench and a pair of worn chairs. "Tell me about how Father Holland was gonna change it."

"What's to tell? He got people to come back to the church. That's how." He gave a shake of his head. "It's not right." The tears flowed freely now.

Cancini waited. He shifted on the bench, turning toward the janitor. "I'm sorry for your loss. I know this is hard, but any help you can give me would be appreciated." Santos sniffled, his head bobbing up and down. "What can you tell me about Father Holland?"

"A good man," he said after a moment, wiping his eyes with a handkerchief. "Kind. Friendly." He hesitated. "Treated everybody like they was somebody, like they was worth something."

Cancini nodded. "Anything else?"

"He gave me sandwiches. This coat." The janitor held out his arm. "Always helping people, you know."

"How about some other folks who worked here at the church? Can you think of anyone else I can talk to about Father Holland?"

"Deacon Bob. Deacon Joe. They do Sunday at nine. Been here almost as long as me. They'll say the same. Everyone loved Father Holland."

Cancini wrote down the names and Santos rattled off a few more names of old-timers. "Anyone else? Maybe someone in the office?"

The old man picked at the fabric of his blue uniform. "Mrs. Harding. She works in the office."

Cancini recognized the name as the one belonging to the secretary. "Did anyone else work in the office I should talk to?"

Santos sucked in his cheeks, his lips pressed into a hard line. "Just her."

With a small staff, it wouldn't take long to interview those on the list. The congregation would take longer. Assuming there was no interference from the diocese, the secretary should be able to give him any contact information he needed. "What's Mrs. Harding like?"

The janitor pushed himself up to his feet. "Don't really know her," he mumbled, averting his eyes. Gnarled fingers fumbled at the buttons of his coat.

Cancini stood, too, the hair on his arms raised. "Didn't you see her every day?"

"I see lots of folks every day. Doesn't mean I know them."

"I understand," he said, tone gentle. "You're saying you knew Father Holland well but not Mrs. Harding."

"He was friendly. I told you that."

"I see." The man might not have come out and said he didn't

like the secretary, but his message was clear. "Father Holland and Mrs. Harding must have spent a lot of time together though."

The man's hand froze over the last button. "I wouldn't know. I'm just a janitor." Santos eyed the door. "Can I go now?"

Cancini stepped aside. At the door, the janitor looked over his shoulder. "Father Holland was a good man, Detective. A very good man."

Chapter Four

"Is HE A suspect?" Captain Martin stood next to Cancini, the toothpick in his mouth bobbing up and down with each word. "Doesn't look like the type, but you never know. I've seen stranger."

On the other side of the glass, Father Joe Sweeney sat at a wooden table, his hands wrapped around a Styrofoam cup of coffee. He stared straight ahead, eyes puffy and red. For a moment, Cancini was struck by how old he looked, how lost. Shaking off the thought, he glanced over at Martin. "He found the victim. Called it in."

The captain stepped closer to the glass until he was near enough to see his breath. Both men watched the old man sip the coffee. "That doesn't mean he didn't shoot the guy."

"He didn't."

Martin spun around. "Why? Because he's a priest? That's no get-out-of-jail card in my book. Plenty of sleazy priests out there."

Cancini faced the captain, his face stony. "He's not sleazy."

"Oka-ay." Martin dragged out the word. "He didn't shoot the guy and he's not sleazy." He flicked the chewed toothpick into the trash. "Either somebody got pretty cozy on the drive over here, or I'm guessing you got something you wanna tell me."

Cancini looked away. Grief lined Father Joe's face and was evident in the lethargic, heavy way he moved. "He's a friend. I've known him since I was a kid."

Martin's mud-brown eyes opened wide. "Wait a minute. Is that the same Father Joe Lola is always talking about? The one that helps take care of your dad?"

It was Cancini's turn to be surprised, though he didn't know why.

"He's a close friend of yours, right?"

Cancini hesitated. It would be just like his ex to spill details about his life to Martin, her new husband. She'd always been a talker, something he'd once thought made them a good pair. He didn't like to talk. Lola never quit. He hadn't counted on having to listen, or that she'd find someone else who would. The failure of his marriage came down to more than that, of course, and yet, for reasons he didn't quite understand, she still talked to his father regularly—probably more than he did. It was just another part of his life where he failed on a daily basis. He shifted his weight from one foot to the other. "Yeah. One and the same."

"Perfect." Martin shook his head. "The one witness we might have happens to be buddy-buddy with my top detective." Cancini was surprised again. It wasn't like Martin to offer compliments. "Shit. I sure as hell don't need this kind of complication after that friggin' shooting last month. IAB's already up my ass as it is. Christ."

Cancini tuned out, letting the captain rant. Behind the glass, Father Joe hunched over his coffee, stiff with sorrow. Cancini squared his shoulders. It wouldn't be easy, but he would have to put aside his sympathy for the old man. The victim deserved that at least. Martin jolted him from his thoughts.

"You're off the case."

"What?" Cancini's eyes flashed. It was just like Martin to be quick to the trigger. "Why?"

"Did we or did we not just establish you've known this guy practically your whole life?" He stepped closer to Cancini, spit flying from his mouth. "That's your damn reason. Not to mention Clark's on desk work for drunk and disorderly, and I don't need this crap." He paused, glancing once more at the man waiting on the other side of the glass. "I'm sorry about your friend. I am, but there can't be so much as a whiff of favoritism or anything else with this case. The press is gonna go bonkers with this story as it is and you know it." He laid a meaty hand on Cancini's shoulder. "It's better this way. You're off."

"Captain?" Smitty came in with a tray of coffee. "May I say that sounds like a wise decision?"

"Huh? Oh, yeah." Martin took a cup. "Thanks."

"Yeah, thanks," Cancini muttered.

"By the way," Smitty said, "initial reports show Father Sweeney is clean. No gunpowder residue on his hands, clothes, or hair."

"He could've changed his clothes."

"Good point, but unlikely in this case. He was dropped off at St. William at seven this morning by a friend he'd been visiting last night. That's been confirmed. He has an alibi for last night and this morning. He phoned the police less than five minutes after arriving at the church. Tough for him to change clothes and get rid of the gun in that amount of time."

Martin squinted. "So, you're saying he's not a suspect."

Smitty nodded. "Solid alibi. But better to be safe than sorry. No one can tell you how to run your department, Captain." Martin shot him a look, and the young detective smiled broadly back at the boss. "Bronson's available though. He and Jensen could take the case."

Martin snorted. "Christ. The Penguin and the Joker? Bronson couldn't find his own ass if you lit it on fire."

Cancini choked but kept quiet.

"They'll do better this time," Smitty said.

The captain paced the small room. "Is that all we've got?"

"Yes, sir."

"Shit."

Behind them, through the open door, file cabinets clanged and cell phones trilled. Voices rose and fell. Cancini remained silent.

"Shit," Martin said again. He dumped his cup. "Scrap what I said earlier. Cancini, you can stay, but I want Smitty taking lead with the priest. Bring Bronson and Jensen in, too. We need as many eyes and ears on this case as we can get. I want this thing closed yesterday. Got it?"

"Got it," the detectives said in unison.

"And make sure I get updated every couple of hours. No holding shit back." He frowned, eyeballing Cancini. "If there's even a hint your priest might be a suspect, even the tiniest bit, you're out." He didn't wait for a response, turning on Smitty next. "And don't think I don't know what you did."

Cancini watched the captain leave, heard him bark orders to the detectives at their desks, then slam his office door. Cancini gave his partner an approving nod. "Pretty damn slick."

"Thanks."

"But we're stuck with Bronson and Jensen."

"Doesn't matter," Smitty said.

"If you say so." Cancini filled Smitty in on his interview with the janitor and the search of the apartment. The secretary was expected later in the day. He gestured toward the glass. "What've you got so far?"

Smitty flipped open a notebook in his right hand. "This is from the statement given at the scene." He paused. "Father Sweeney was meeting the deceased for breakfast. Stayed with a friend last night, and that friend dropped him off in front of the church at seven. He went around back to the apartment where the deceased lives, but there was no answer. Went back to the church and found the body. Called 911. Claims he didn't touch the body or anything else."

"Then he didn't. What else?"

"That's it. Said he was done talking. Except for one thing. He asked for you."

Cancini sighed. The knot between his shoulders throbbed, and he rubbed the back of his neck. "Okay. Let's go."

After a vending machine stop, Cancini and Smitty entered the interview room. Cancini set a sandwich and napkin on the table and slid a fresh cup of coffee toward Father Joe.

"Thanks, Michael," the old priest said. His voice held only the trace of a tremor. Bloodshot eyes looked out of a pale, spotted face.

"I'm only here to observe," he told Father Joe. "Detective Smithson has some questions for you."

"Whatever you say, Michael."

Smitty took the seat across from the priest, and Cancini pulled out a chair at the far end of the table. He twisted in his chair and looked back at the glass. The captain, along with Bronson and Jensen, observed from the other side.

Smitty cleared his throat. "Thank you for coming in today,

Father Sweeney. I know this is hard for you." He paused a second. "I also know you already gave a brief statement, both to the officers at the church and to me earlier, but we're going to need you to do that again."

"Right." Father Joe's gaze drifted to the camera set up in the corner of the room. "Is that on?"

"Yes," Smitty said. "Is that a problem?"

The priest shook his head. "Not at all. Just making sure we only have to do this once. Your time is valuable."

Smitty shot Cancini a questioning glance.

"Father Joe's showing you his smartass side," Cancini said. "Saves it for his friends."

The young man's lips twitched. "Lucky me."

Father Joe walked them through his arrival at Father Holland's apartment and his discovery of the body at the church. "It was clear he was already dead, so I called 911. There was so much blood. It was horrible. I—I . . ." He shuddered and took a deep breath before he spoke again. "I was careful not to touch anything—other than the doors when I came in. I knew that could contaminate the crime scene."

Smitty sat forward, putting his elbows on the table. "Do you know a lot about crime scenes, Father Sweeney?"

Cancini caught himself before he could interrupt. He didn't like the implication, but if it weren't Father Joe, he would have asked the same thing. Smitty was only doing his job. He stared down at his notebook, well aware the old priest knew more than most about murder investigations. How many hours had they spent discussing George Vandenberg and the Coed Killer, to name just a few? The old man loved it and never failed to give his own perspective on guilt and justice.

"I read a lot of books. I watch those crime shows on TV, the ones that show all the evidence, like *CSI*. Guess we all think we know more than we do about these things." He half smiled, his lips trembling. "Hopefully, I did the right thing. And please call me Father Joe."

"You did fine, uh, Father Joe." Smitty shifted in his seat and stretched his long legs. "Do you normally meet Mr. Holland—I mean Father Holland—for breakfast?"

"Not usually for breakfast. We meet for lunch mostly. Just depends."

"On what?"

"Our schedules. Although Mass is at the same time, both of us are busy with meetings, church suppers, Bible studies, things like that."

Cancini made a few notes, watching the exchange. His respect for his young partner grew. Smitty had understood, without discussion, how important it was for Cancini to allow him to take the lead during the interview. Martin, for all his blustering, occasionally made a good decision. While Father Joe might gravitate to Cancini, their relationship could influence or impede the questions Cancini asked and the answers he got.

"When was the last time you'd seen Father Holland? Before this morning, I mean?"

The old man rubbed his chin with thick fingers. "Last week, I guess."

"Okay. So it's fair to say you and the deceased saw each other on a fairly regular basis."

"Yes."

"How would you characterize your relationship? Were you colleagues? Close friends?"

The priest looked past Smitty and wrapped his hands around the cup. He took a long, slow sip.

Smitty leaned forward. "Well, Father?"

The lines on the old man's face cracked and broke. Father Joe's chin sank to his chest, and his shoulders shook with quiet sobs. When he raised his head again, his eyes found Cancini's. He gave a single shake of his head, a shake of wonder and sorrow. "Like a son. He was like a son to me."

Chapter Five

2000

THE BOY SLIPPED around the corner, shoulders slouched, face hidden under an oversized hoodie. He scanned the street. Mr. Jones and Mr. Smalley sat in their green and white lawn chairs—like always—smoking and shooting the shit. His mama said they were like postmen. Nothing stopped 'em. Not rain or snow or anything. He didn't understand it. What could they have to talk about all day?

The rest of the street was quiet. He stuck his hands in his pockets, lowered his head, and strolled past the rotting row houses and boarded-up storefronts. He crossed to the far side of the street, opposite the old men. He didn't need his mama knowing he'd skipped school again.

Head hanging, he trudged down the broken sidewalk, careful to keep his pace casual. He passed the empty Popeye's. He exhaled when he got close to Barry Farm and the squat apartment buildings. Most of the project was close to being condemned, and his unit was no better. Sometimes there was no hot water or the lights didn't work. The whole place smelled like garbage, the ground littered with greasy food wrappers and used syringes. It was a hellhole, his mama said, but it was the only hellhole they could afford.

He ducked down an alley and climbed the rusty chain-link fence that marked the edge of Barry Farm. A cloud of dirt rose from the ground, and he stifled his cough. He stopped and listened. There was nothing but the usual—some kid crying and the sound of cars on Martin Luther King Boulevard. He stood up a little straighter.

"Where you goin', Li'l Matty?"

The boy froze. The voice was close. Twenty feet, thirty maybe. It was farther than that to his apartment, and he knew Juan could outrun him.

"Yeah, where ya goin'?" Big Rick stepped out from behind a concrete block. The boy took one step back. The older boys laughed, looking at each other.

"Kid looks scared, don't he?" Juan asked.

"He should be scared." Big Rick moved toward his partner. A baseball bat dangled from his fat hand. "Dab knows what you been doin'."

The boy shuffled his feet, inching closer to the fence. "I haven't been doing anything."

"C'mon, man. Dab trusted you." Juan's face was grim, his hands already balled into fists.

"I have his money." The boy reached into his pocket, feeling the large wad of bills. "I can pay you. Honest."

Big Rick waved the bat in the air. "That's not the problem, man, and you know it. You been sellin' on the other side of town, cuttin' the shit and holdin' Dab's profits. You shouldna been stealin' from Dab, kid."

The boy shifted his weight, body tensed.

"We gotta teach you a lesson, Li'l Matty. You know how it is. Dab can't let you be doin' shit like that." Juan's eyes were like marbles, cold and flat. "It looks bad."

Big Rick licked his lips. "Yeah, bad. But you're lucky, kid. Dab likes you. Tol' us not to touch your mama. See how good he is?"

While they talked, the boy kept moving, one foot at a time. He'd gained five feet, maybe six. Watching their faces, he knew he had only a few seconds, no more. When the two older boys looked at each other, he whipped around and sprinted the short distance to the fence, throwing himself over and rolling to the ground. He jumped to his feet and took off, his shoes pounding on the pavement. Behind him, Big Rick struggled to climb the fence, hurling curse words with the effort.

Big Rick had earned his nickname by the time he was twelve. His gut was as big as his shoulders were wide. Word on the street was he'd crushed a guy's head once between his bare hands. The boy didn't believe everything he heard, but he'd seen Big Rick pound a kid once, and it had been bad. Big Rick had ball-busting strength, but he was slow.

The boy ran harder, the sounds of Big Rick's wheezing fading already. Still, he dared not turn around. Juan wasn't big or strong, but he was fast and had a nasty mean streak. He'd beat him and enjoy every second of it. The boy ran faster, arms pumping, heart racing. He rounded the corner and ran straight toward St. Elizabeth Hospital. His sneakers slapped at the ground, and he hiked up his pants to lengthen his stride.

A handful of people—mostly nurses and orderlies for the

crazies inside—stood outside smoking and talking. He ran across the parking lot, weaving in and out of cars. He couldn't hear Big Rick anymore, but Juan's steps were close. His breath ragged, he ignored the cramp in his side. He ran straight toward the cluster of smokers outside the hospital doors. Fifty feet. The pounding steps behind him echoed in his ear. Thirty feet. Fingers grabbed his collar, yanking him backward. He stumbled before he landed hard on the pavement.

"Get up," Juan said, standing over him. His chest heaved and he waved a six-inch blade in front of the boy's face. It glittered in the late-afternoon sun, casting light across the lot.

A woman screamed. "He's got a knife."

"Hey, you there!" A security guard stepped out of the shadows of the hospital entrance.

Juan closed the knife, hiding it in his sleeve. He backed away from the boy, focused instead on the big man in the uniform.

The guard lumbered toward them. "Damn kids." His eyes bulged and his face flamed red. "I'm calling the cops."

The boy's skin went cold and he scrambled to his feet, running again. Within seconds, Juan was at his heels, the heavy chains he wore around his neck rattling with each step. The boy darted in front of one car and dodged another to reach the other side of the street. Horns blared, drowning out the pounding in his ears.

Sweat stung his eyes and he ran blindly, pushing through anyone who got in his way. There were angry shouts behind him. His lungs burned with every step. He pushed, but it didn't matter how fast he ran. Juan was faster. He passed row houses with crumbling steps and dirt yards. There was nowhere to go. Then he saw it. The church on the corner. He ran harder, ignoring the pain in his side and his screaming muscles. He ran up the steps, two at a time, hauling open the heavy wooden doors. He ran down the aisle to the altar, collapsing there, his face bathed in sweat. The door behind him opened again. He heard Juan stop, breathing heavily.

The boy lay still, suwcking in air, unable to move.

"Get up, you little shit. You think you're safe here?" Juan spat out the words.

"Everyone is safe here." The boy's head jerked up. A man in a black robe emerged from the shadows and moved between the boys, his head jutting forward. "Juan, is that you?"

The gold chains stopped jangling. "Uh, yes, Father. I didn't see you there."

"No, of course not. I was just coming in to pray." His voice was even, almost gentle. "Your grandmother was at Mass this morning."

"Oh."

"We've missed you this last year."

"Uh, yeah. I've been busy."

"I see. Well, you're here now." The boy shifted on the floor even as Juan took two steps back. "Would it be a good time for reconciliation?"

"Uh, no, Father. I've gotta go."

The heavy door slammed behind Juan, the sound echoing up to the rafters. The boy sat up. He blinked and looked around. There was a golden cross hanging from the wall in front of him and half-burned candles lit everywhere. He spotted colored windows and row after row of wooden benches. Sniffing the air, he breathed in a scent he didn't recognize.

The man in black stood over him, one hand outstretched. "Are you okay?"

The boy ignored the hand, getting to his feet. "Yeah, fine." He looked around, searching for any other exits.

"Other than the way you came in, the only way out is down the stairs over there. There's a door that leads to a back alley."

He hesitated. The stairs appeared shrouded in darkness even during the day. "Uh, thanks."

The priest placed a hand lightly on his narrow shoulder. "I wouldn't go just yet if I were you. Young Juan won't have gone far, and he won't be alone. Your best bet is to wait him out."

The boy bit his lip. He needed to pay the landlord before he tried to evict them again. His mom might not come home for days, but she had to have a place to sleep when she did.

He glanced at the dark stairwell again. The man was right. Big Rick would have caught up to Juan by now. They were probably covering the front and back doors. He'd run to the church for safety, but now he was trapped.

"I was planning to have a bowl of soup." The boy watched the priest glide down the steps, his black robes sweeping across the floor. "Why don't you have some while you wait?"

The boy's stomach growled. "Why not?" He followed the priest down a long hall to a tiny kitchen. The counters were crowded with boxes and cans of food, but it was clean. Even better, it didn't smell of rotting food or sour beer. He sat down at the table. The priest emptied two cans of soup into a pot and turned on the stove.

"It'll only take a few minutes." The priest gave the soup a stir, then sat across from the boy. "Everyone calls me Father Joe." His robes fanned out under him and he folded his hands in his lap. "What's your name, son?"

The boy stifled a groan. He knew a do-gooder when he saw one, and this guy was one for sure. After the soup, he was outta there. He didn't need some priest tracking him down. The lie was on the tip of his tongue, but for reasons he didn't understand then, it was the truth that spilled from his mouth. "Matthew," he said. "Matthew Holland."

Chapter Six

FATHER JOE STRAIGHTENED, hands spread on the table. "When I met him, he didn't have a father. His mom was . . ." The old man hesitated, shifting in the hard wooden chair. "Well, there's no easy way to put it. She was a junkie. She tried to hide it from Matthew, but he knew. For a while, she tried to hold down a job, but the heroin took hold. She spent the rent money, sold their food stamps, whatever it took." His eyes clouded. "As you can imagine, not a great environment for any kid. They lived at Barry Farm then, always under the threat of eviction. He did the best he could to keep them afloat. He loved his mother, in spite of everything. She was all he had."

Smitty rubbed his chin. "How did he, uh, keep them afloat?"

"I couldn't say specifically what he did, only that it probably wasn't legal if that's what you're wondering."

Smitty tapped his pen against the table. "I see."

"Do you really, Detective? Did you grow up in the projects surrounded by filth and gangs? Do you know what it's like to beg for food?" Father Joe's hands gripped the table, and his words came faster. "Did your mother have to prostitute herself to keep buying drugs?" He shook his head, his face flushed pink. "I don't think you see at all."

A silence fell over the room. Cancini had seen his share of junkie mothers, too messed up to know whether it was morning or night or when they'd last eaten. Taking care of a kid would be impossible for someone that strung out. The life the priest had described would be difficult for any child, especially one young enough to need her and still love her, but old enough to be aware.

"Sorry," the priest said, his skin pale again. "I didn't mean to get upset." His lower lip quivered. "This has been really hard."

Smitty nodded once. "Where is his mother now?"

Father Joe blinked hard. "Gone. She overdosed right after Matthew started high school. I wanted to take him in, but legally, it was impossible. He was a minor, and the church is not in the business of adoption." He picked up the paper napkin next to the untouched sandwich and crumpled it between his thick fingers. His voice dropped to a whisper. "I let him down." The old priest clutched the napkin in his hands, bowed his head, and wept.

Cancini lowered his gaze. His mind raced and he struggled to ignore a sudden and unexpected resentment. He'd never even heard of Father Holland before today. Father Joe had been a fixture in Cancini's life for more than two decades. How could Cancini not have known about someone so important to the old priest? The quiet sobs lasted no more than a couple of minutes, but it was long enough. Cancini breathed deep and raised his head.

"I'm sorry." The old man's hands trembled.

"Take your time," Smitty said, keeping his voice even. After the priest had calmed, he asked, "What happened to Father Holland after his mother died?"

Father Joe wiped at his nose. "I tried to help him, to find some family, any family, but there was none. Social services took him. They'd lined up a foster family for him. I never got the name, but it didn't matter anyway. The day he was scheduled to go to his first foster home, he disappeared."

Smitty looked up from his notes. "Disappeared?"

"Ran away. Matthew was fifteen then." The old man's shoulders sank lower into his chest. "I didn't see him again for three years."

Chapter Seven

2005

MATT TUCKED HIS hair behind his ears and pulled his hoodie over the battered baseball hat. Hunching his shoulders, he ducked behind the hedges. A man with short, dark hair came down the steps, his stride quick and purposeful. Matt crouched lower and watched the man walk down the path and around the church to the street. He heard the hum of a car engine. Even after the man pulled away, he remained still, his head cocked, listening. He stood slowly, uncoiling his body. The house behind the church was small but well maintained. Black shutters hung neatly against the bright white siding. A pair of bushes with pink flowers flanked the front entrance. He glanced back at the street but saw and heard nothing. He moved closer to the house, his eyes darting from side to side. He wiped his damp palms across low-slung jeans. He knocked once, twice.

Father Joe opened the door halfway, taking in the young man's dark hoodie and untied basketball shoes. "Yes? Can I help you?" His tone was wary although not unkind.

Matt couldn't speak, his tongue thick and dry in his mouth. What if coming was a mistake? He wasn't the boy he used to be, and maybe he'd misjudged the man. He appraised the priest from under the brim of his cap. The old man hadn't changed much. He wasn't wearing the robes, but he was still dressed in a button-down black shirt tucked into black pants. Black belt. Black shoes. The soft features of his face showed no fear, only curiosity.

Father Joe opened the door wider. "Can I help you, young man?" Matt let out a breath. He reached up and pulled off the cap. After only a moment, the priest's eyes grew round. He threw open the door and wrapped Matt in a tight hug. "I can't believe it," he said. He repeated the words twice more. Matt's arms hung at his sides, limp. After a few minutes, the priest let go and stepped back, waving his hand. "Come in. Come in."

"Thank you." Matt stepped inside to a small hall. On the left was what looked like an office or library. A computer sat on a desk surrounded by books. More books were stacked next to a chair near the window. Two coffee cups sat on an end table. To the right of the hall was another small room, this one a formal living room.

Father Joe steered him into the living room, offering the sofa. "Sit down. It's so good to see you." His smile widened. "After all this time, you're here. How are you, Matthew?"

"I'm fine," Matt said, the words clipped, short. It was true the priest seemed genuinely glad to see him, but that didn't mean anything. "Who was the cop, the one that just left?"

Father Joe started, his head turning toward the window. "What? Were you watching my house?"

"Who was he?"

"A friend."

"He's a cop."

"Yes, and a friend. I've known his family for years." The air in the room grew chilly as the afternoon sun waned. The priest sighed. "There hasn't been a day that's gone by that I haven't thought of you, prayed for you. When you ran away, I was so worried about you. You were just a boy."

"I can take care of myself." Matt didn't mean for the words to come out so hard, but maybe that was for the best. It wasn't that he hadn't expected the old man's kindness, but after seeing the cop, Matt needed to be sure he could trust him. Everything depended on it.

Father Joe met his gaze. "Yes, I can see that. And yet, you're here. Why?"

Matt repressed a smile. Father Joe was as feisty as ever. Good. "I need your help."

"I see."

"I'm eighteen now. I can't be put in foster care anymore, but I can't stay where I was." Matt paused. "I don't have anywhere else to go."

Father Joe rubbed his fingers across his brow. "What kind of help are we talking about?"

"I want a new life." The priest waited. "But no cops and no cop friends."

The lines between the old man's gray brows deepened. He sat quietly for a minute, two. "A new identity?" he asked.

Matt laughed. Father Joe had never been one to mince words. It was one of the things Matt had always liked about him. "Not the kind you think. I want to start over. I want to do things right this time." He watched the old man's face as he spoke. "I want to help people now. Like you." As he leaned forward, his eyes shone. "I want to be a priest."

Chapter Eight

"THE FIRST THING he did was get his GED." Father Joe blew on the coffee, watching the wisp of steam over the cup. "He was smart, and it didn't take long. I helped him the best I could. He got his undergraduate degree in religious studies at a small college in the Midwest, then finished up at seminary. That was followed by a year in a parish outside Boston. Matthew seemed happy, thrilled to be doing what he'd dreamed of. I even thought he might settle there." He put the cup down and sat back. "But he wanted to come home to D.C., to his old neighborhood."

Smitty lifted his head, pen poised over a notepad. "You didn't think that was a good idea?"

"I wanted him to escape his past. He'd had it rough. He turned his life around and made something of himself. Who doesn't want that for someone they love?"

"So if things were great in Boston, why come back?"

Father Joe's hands twisted in his lap. "I wish I knew. I still don't understand it entirely. He wanted to come home and make things better, make things right, he said. I think . . . I think maybe he blamed himself for his mother's death."

"You said she OD'd. Why would that be his fault?"

Smitty asked one question after another but with each answer, the old priest's eyes drifted back to Cancini.

"He was the man of the house. He felt like it was his duty to protect her. We never spoke about it, but I think he knew how hard it was for her to put food on the table, to pay the rent. She had trouble holding a steady job. Like I said before, she found other ways to make money. When she couldn't do it anymore, it fell on Matthew to find a way to pay the landlord."

Cancini sipped his coffee. Holland's mother wasn't the only junkie from the projects who sold herself for money and drugs, and Holland wasn't the only boy to grow up in that kind of household.

"And Father Holland knew about his mother's prostitution?"

The priest raised one heavy shoulder. "He never said so, but yes, I think he did. But he never would have blamed her. He loved her. There was nothing vindictive about his nature. That's why he wanted to come back, I think. He wanted to offer others like his mother forgiveness and a chance to come to God. He wanted to give them the chance he thought his mother never had."

"But surely they have drug users and prostitutes in Boston."

"That's what I said. As hard as it was to have him away, I thought he should stay there, build a new life. I begged him not to come back."

"Were you afraid for him?"

Cancini sat forward.

"Yes." Father Joe wrapped his hands around the coffee cup again. His chest heaved.

"Why?" Smitty kept his voice soft, questioning. There was no hint of accusation, only encouragement.

For a moment, there was only silence. "The neighborhood had changed. You know what it's like. The gangs. The drugs. It's all worse. But he wouldn't listen."

Cancini opened his mouth, then thought better of it. The old man's answer, while probably partly true, sounded like bullshit.

"So, he came back," Smitty said.

"It didn't take long. He'd done well in his first year, and when it came time to cast around for a more permanent home, he pushed hard to get placed at St. William."

"Was that difficult?"

"Not really. St. William was struggling to keep a regular priest. It's been falling apart for years. I helped out there when I could— same as I did when Matthew was young." He paused. "He was right when he said it was a parish in need. Membership had fallen steadily. There was no one to help with community outreach, no support. He told the diocese he wanted to help people, to give something back. He dreamed of growing the church, making it better. The diocese was thrilled. The fact that he knew the neighborhood was icing on the cake."

"And did he? Make it better?"

"The membership was up. There was more hope than there'd been in a long time. He worked very hard." Father Joe struggled to maintain his composure. "So yes, I think he did."

Chapter Nine

2005

FATHER JOE STOOD at the kitchen sink wiping the plates and silverware dry. Matt, fresh from the shower, watched from the doorway. His hair hung wet and heavy on his cheeks, and his skin smelled of strawberries and Irish Spring. He rocked on the balls of his feet, waiting. The priest set the dishes and towel on the counter and waved a hand toward the table. "Let's sit."

Matt nodded and laid his black backpack on the floor next to his chair.

"You've grown so tall," Father Joe said.

Matt grinned. He could see the old man reconciling the skinny teenager he'd known three years earlier with the six-foot man now sitting in his kitchen. "Thanks for letting me crash here, Padre." They exchanged smiles. "Feels like old times, saying that."

"I'm glad you're here, Matthew."

Matt tucked his damp hair behind his ears and cleared his throat. "You want to know about where I've been."

"If you want to tell me."

"I thought about looking for my real father once, but always seemed like if he'd wanted to be around, he would've been." Matt was quiet a moment. "I had to leave. I couldn't live with strangers, Padre. They didn't want me anyway. They just wanted the money."

"You don't know that."

"I do. I had to meet them first. The lady, the mother, she hovered all around me, touching me and stuff while the social worker was around, acting like she cared, but the minute the social worker left us alone, she had no interest in me." The hard lines around his mouth softened. "My mom may not have been the best, but I know she never faked it with me."

"Not all foster families are like that. There are some wonderful families out there."

"I didn't want another family. My mom was gone. She was my family. She didn't need me anymore, so what was the point of sticking around? I wanted to be alone."

Father Joe folded his hands in his lap. "So you ran away."

"Yep. And I'd do it again." Matt raised his chin as though challenging the priest, but he only nodded.

"Where did you go?" Father Joe asked.

Matt dropped his head. It was a logical question—one he'd been expecting. He'd been dead to the priest for three years. True, he'd had his reasons, but that was over now. Father Joe seemed sincere in his joy at seeing him again, but how would he look at Matt if he knew the truth? He'd done what he had to. He'd survived and he was alive. That was all he had to hold on to for now. In time, maybe. Matt shook his head. "You don't need to know that."

The priest sighed. "I tried to find you. Looked for months. No one knew where you were."

"But eventually, you gave up." The words were delivered without accusation, without rancor. "You stopped looking. Life moved on."

Father Joe's cheeks reddened. "Yes," he admitted, "I gave up." He unfolded his hands. "I guess I figured you didn't want to be found. But you were in my daily prayers and always will be. Just like your mother."

Matt blinked back tears. "I'm sorry I never thanked you for all you did for her. I know you tried to help, tried to get her a job."

"She was a good woman, Matthew. She just got lost along the way."

"Lost. Yeah, that's a good word for it." The young man stood, his chair scraping across the tile floor. "That's why I'm here."

The old priest craned his neck to look up at the young man. "What do you mean?"

Matt went to the sink, leaned over, and took deep breaths. It wasn't going to be easy. Matt knew what he wanted, what he needed to feel whole again. He wanted to help women like his mother, women who'd been beaten by drugs and surrounded by violence. He wanted to help kids so they wouldn't end up in rat-infested apartments and shitty foster homes. He wanted to give them a place, a home to believe in. He had faith, but he couldn't do it alone.

Matt faced the priest and drew himself up to his full height. "I want to be a priest like you and help people. A man of God. That's what I want."

"Such determination from someone so young."

Matt lifted his chin. "I can do it."

Father Joe stood, too. "You don't need to be a priest to help people, Matthew."

"You're wrong, Padre. I need to be a priest, more than anything." He reached out and clasped Father Joe's hands in his. "Will you help me?"

Chapter Ten

SMITTY SIFTED THROUGH a stack of printed pages. "Janie Holland was in her early thirties when she OD'd."

Cancini looked across his desk. "What else do we have on her?"

Smitty rolled his chair around the desk. "She was born and raised in Hazleton, Pennsylvania. According to her parents, she ran away when she was seventeen, her senior year of high school. The parents said she'd started staying out late, drinking, typical teenage stuff. They tried grounding her, taking away the car. They suspected she was sneaking out. Then one day, she didn't come home from school. They filed a missing person's report."

"This was when?"

"In 1986. The local police did what they could. They interviewed her friends, went to the high school."

"Boyfriend?"

"According to her friends there was, but no one had ever met him."

"We've got nothing on him at all?"

"Nope, but she did start skipping school. Wait a minute."

Smitty paused to read. "Here it is. She skipped school five times in the month before she disappeared, twice that week. Police wrote her off as a runaway, most likely with the boyfriend."

"Did the parents ever hear from her again?" Cancini asked.

"No. She turned up in D.C. a few years later with a kid. Registered him for kindergarten in the fall of '92."

"She would have needed a birth certificate."

"Already got a copy. Matthew Holland was born in Sioux Falls, Idaho, on May 15, 1987. No father on the birth certificate."

"And we don't know how she got to D.C.?"

"No. Fell off the grid. When she started him in school, she applied for food stamps. They moved from apartment to apartment, but the last several years before she died, they were in subsidized housing at Barry Farm. Her employment records are sparse. She was picked up a couple of times for prostitution, but they didn't keep her. She landed in an outpatient rehab once, but it didn't stick. Then she died."

Cancini ran a hand over the fresh stubble on his chin. "And that's when Holland pulled his own disappearing act."

"Yeah. Not right away though." He rolled back to his desk and picked up a manila folder. "According to social services, the kid said very little. They tried to track down his maternal grandparents, but either they were dead, had moved, or just didn't care. Your friend Father Joe was the only one who seemed to want to help him, but he didn't have guardian status and wasn't family, so the boy was set up to go to a foster family. That's when he checked out."

"Let me guess. They didn't look for him all that hard."

Smitty snorted. "You know it. They did a brief search, but according to social services, they've already got more needy kids than they can handle. They pushed it back on the police as a missing person, and they chalked it up as another runaway kid."

"Figures. So, we've got nothing on him from fifteen to when he turned up on Father Joe's doorstep at eighteen." He dumped his empty cup in the trash. Three missing teenage years didn't seem important, but Cancini was finding it difficult to fight his curiosity. Where had Holland been? How had he survived? This man meant a lot to Father Joe. And Cancini had never even heard of Holland until he turned up dead. Who was he?

Cancini stood, his chair sliding away from him. "Tell you what. I'll grab us a couple cups of coffee and we'll go over the interview list and make some calls. Holland's secretary is due in soon, right?"

Smitty checked his watch. "Yeah, in about an hour."

"Good."

"What are we going to do about Father Joe?" Cancini's shoulders tensed. "Do you think he knows something? That business about not wanting Holland to come back from Boston . . . seemed like there was more to the story than a bad neighborhood."

"Possibly," Cancini said after a moment, his voice quiet. His eyes wandered over the large precinct room. Pairs of desks were crammed together; partners facing off elementary school style. Phones rang and keyboards clacked. The large case board on the wall was filled, no detective unassigned. In bold letters, he saw their names and their case. HOLLAND. Pain pulsed at the base of his neck, the headache that came with each new investigation gathering strength. Lifting his chin, he swung back around and faced his partner. "That's what we're going to find out."

Chapter Eleven

"SHE DOESN'T LOOK like a church secretary." Smitty nodded toward the woman on the other side of the glass. "At least none I've ever seen."

The lines around Cancini's eyes crinkled. "Yeah? How many have you seen?"

"None," Smitty said with a laugh. "Still. She's a looker."

"Who's a looker?" Bronson ambled in from the break room, cinnamon bun crumbs on his upper lip and chin. A head shorter than Cancini, thick-waisted, and with a head full of slick-backed dark hair, he'd earned the nickname Penguin soon after joining the department. He stopped, let out a low whistle, and slapped Smitty on the shoulder. "I wouldn't mind taking the lead on this one," he said, a lopsided leer splitting his face. "If you know what I mean."

Cancini shot Bronson a dark look. "No, Detective. What do you mean?"

Bronson raised his pointy chin. "Geez, Cancini, why you gotta be that way? I don't mean nothin' by it. She's hot, that's all, like Smitty said."

"Hot or not, that woman's boss was just shot in the face at point-blank range. In case you hadn't noticed, she's wearing a wedding ring and praying. I don't think she needs you taking the lead, if you know what I mean."

Bronson frowned, thin lips turned down. "Whatever," he mumbled.

"I'll be handling the interview." Cancini glanced into the precinct room at the rows of desks. "Where's Jensen?"

"Went home sick."

"Figures." Cancini turned back to the glass. Smitty was right. The secretary was pretty in a West Coast, TV commercial kind of way. She had long ash-blond hair that fell in waves to the middle of her back. Perfect teeth, pert nose, almond eyes. She wasn't tall, but she wasn't short, either. Slim but curvy in ways her winter coat couldn't hide. It was true she didn't look like any church secretary he'd ever met before.

Behind the glass, she rose. Black mascara streaked her cheeks. She gripped the chair with both hands, swaying before she was able to steady herself. After a few moments, she resumed pacing.

"She's been working at the church for two years, which is about when she and her husband moved here," Smitty said. "Before that, they lived in Minnesota. They moved here for his job, one of those big building companies out in Tyson's Corner. She's thirty-one years old, no kids."

"How long have they been married?" Cancini asked.

"Almost ten years."

"Alibi?"

Bronson spun around. "You suspect her? The church secretary?"

Cancini's eyes cut to Bronson. "Until I have reason not to, I suspect anyone who knew the victim and had contact with him in the last few days. That includes the church secretary. It's called police work, Bronson. You should try it sometime."

Bronson flushed and pursed his lips. "I'm gonna call Jensen and check on him." He brushed by both detectives. "Asshole."

After he was gone, Smitty said, "Still making friends in the department?" He stood square to the window, watching the pacing secretary.

Cancini sighed. It was true Bronson got on his nerves, although Jensen was worse. "It's not my job to make friends. It's my job to find out who killed Father Holland."

Smitty was quiet a moment. "Well, like it or not, it's their job, too."

"Don't remind me."

The younger detective faced Cancini. "I don't have to. Martin will do plenty of that." He looked away briefly and took a deep breath. "Look, no one likes being told what to do or how they aren't great cops—even if it's true."

Cancini raised one eyebrow. Smitty had been his partner for more than a year, the longest he'd had a partner since he could remember. Smitty was smart, detailed, and a damn good cop. Cancini glimpsed Bronson hunched over his desk, speaking into the phone. It was true he'd been hard on the man, and it wasn't the first time. But it was also true the job didn't require him to make friends. It required him to find murderers as quickly as possible without making mistakes. Guys like Bronson and Jensen seemed to have trouble with both of those things. He sighed again and looked back at Smitty. "So, what you're saying is you agree with Bronson? I'm an asshole?"

A slow grin split Smitty's face. "Not exactly. Bronson definitely acts like an idiot, and you are absolutely an asshole."

Cancini laughed, some of the tension between his shoulders melting. "Good. Then we're all in agreement on that." He looked back at Smitty, and the smile left his face. "I'll try not to be such grade A jerk all the time."

His partner shrugged. "Maybe you could just tone it down once in a while. Bronson may be an idiot, but we need him."

"We do?"

"Yeah, we do."

Cancini nodded. His partner was right again. They had a lot of ground to cover, and with each passing hour, the trail would grow colder. The more manpower, the better. "Got it." He gestured to the glass. The secretary was sitting again, head cradled in her hands, and shoulders shaking with quiet sobs. "What about her alibi?"

"The husband and wife say they were both home all night."

"Anyone else able to back that up?"

"Not so far."

Cancini let it go. He knew it was more likely they were home together on a Sunday night than not. Still, it proved nothing. "The janitor didn't seem to like the lady much."

Smitty grinned. "Maybe she didn't give him any sandwiches."

Cancini gave a short laugh. "Yeah. Maybe." He watched through the glass another minute. "Ready?"

"Ready as I'll ever be."

"It can wait." Both detectives turned to find Martin clutching a pile of papers. "You need to see these e-mails first." The detectives exchanged glances. "We've got our guy."

Chapter Twelve

TERRY LANDON PUSHED his glasses up on his nose and turned the laptop toward Cancini. "These are all the dates your victim received e-mails from this particular address."

The dark-haired detective leaned forward. "That's more than three years."

"True, but they were sporadic until recently." The young man pointed at the screen. "Most of them were all sent in the last couple of weeks, sometimes more than one a day."

Cancini scanned the dates. Several e-mails had been sent in the days leading up to Holland's murder. He straightened. "So, what were the e-mails about?"

Landon held up a thick folder. "At first, they were kind of friendly, but real short. Stuff like 'good to know you're not dead' and 'don't be a stranger.' Nothing exciting. A couple of weeks ago, that changed."

Smitty took the e-mails from Landon and skimmed several. He paused, then read one out loud. "'Don't turn your back on me, Matty. We been through too much. Remember who was there for you when you had nowhere else to go.'" He flipped through a couple more, then read again. "Here's another one: 'Friends don't desert friends. I did you a favor. This is how you fucking repay me?'"

Cancini rubbed his hand over his face and considered the message. "Not sounding so friendly anymore."

"Right," Landon said, excitement in his voice. He handed Smitty another page. "This one's from a week ago."

Smitty read, "'I'm not playing around anymore. I don't give a shit what your reasons are. You know I don't do all that religion crap. Besides, I know the real you, and the guy I know sure as hell isn't some pussy priest. You've done plenty of sinning. If you don't do the right thing, you're going to need a whole lot more than dumbass prayers.'"

Martin spit a toothpick into the trash. "Get to the one from the day he was murdered."

Landon squinted at the trash can and wrinkled his nose. "Right."

Smitty took the paper from the forensic specialist and cleared his throat. "'Matty, time is up. Don't think I don't know you've gotten every single one of my e-mails. You have till tomorrow. I'm watching, so you'd better not be late or you're a fucking dead man. You got me? Bring the cash OR ELSE!!!! And keep your trap shut if you want to live.'" Smitty looked up. "Blackmail?"

"That's my take." Martin folded his arms across his chest. "The priest didn't pay up and got a bullet through the eye."

A heavy silence fell over the room.

Cancini took the copies from Landon, reading the words again. There was anger—probably over whatever wrong was done—and the threat of violence, but there was something more. There was an intimacy, a feeling the relationship was deep-rooted. Again, he found himself wondering about the missing teenage years.

"Did Father Holland respond to any of these e-mails?" Smitty asked.

"Not that I've found," the young man said.

"Good work, Landon." Martin clapped the young man on the back. "Let's pick this guy up."

Landon gathered the pages and shook his head. "Unfortunately, I can't trace this account. The e-mail service is free. I ran the name and the birth date on the profile, and this woman died twenty years ago."

"What about an IP address?" Smitty asked.

"Also no use. I haven't had time to go through every e-mail yet, but I've done about a quarter, and every one came from a public place like a coffee shop or library."

Cancini's head began to pound. "How many places so far?"

"Five or six. Maybe more. Whoever sent them moved around a lot."

"For Christ's sake, Landon," Martin said, voice raised. "What the hell can you tell us?"

The young man reddened and returned to his keyboard. After a moment, he looked at Cancini, ignoring Martin." All the e-mails I've checked so far are were sent from within a fifty-mile radius of the church where the priest was murdered. Some are in D.C., some in Maryland, and some in Virginia. That's all I've got for now."

Cancini stood up. "Thanks. It's a big help."

"What do you mean it's a big help?" Martin crossed his arms over his chest. "That's five million people."

Cancini knew the captain was right, but he had another idea.

"Maybe we can see if there's a pattern to the free wifi places he used. Landon, can you get me a copy of each e-mail and a list of the IP addresses. And can you sort them by date and time, too?"

Landon nodded. "I'm not done going through the victim's computer, though. There are thousands of e-mails, and I'm trying to put together a picture of all the sites he'd visited in the days before his murder."

"Good. What about a contact list?"

"I can get that now." The young man pushed his glasses up again. After a moment, the printer spit out several pages. He handed them to Cancini.

"Thanks."

Martin and Smitty headed out of the computer lab, but Cancini lagged behind. His fingers trailed down the contact list. "Landon, one more thing." He pointed at an address on the list. "Can you tell me how many e-mails Father Holland sent to this address?"

"Let me check." The room was silent except for the clicking of keys. "About one a week I'd say." He typed a little more. "Except for this last week, when there seem to be a few more." His voice dropped lower. "Three on the day he was killed."

Cancini blinked and turned his head away. Fresh pain radiated across his shoulders and up his neck.

"Detective?" The young man stared up at him. "Are you okay?"

"I need you to do me a favor." He folded the pages listing the e-mail contacts and slipped them in his pocket. "I need you to send me copies of those e-mails over with the others." Landon blinked, his head bobbing. "Make sure they're addressed to me." The young man nodded again.

Cancini left the lab, his head throbbing. He'd told Martin that

Father Joe wasn't involved. He'd been blindsided by the close relationship between the priests and now the e-mails. Why had Holland e-mailed Father Joe several times that week and three times the day he was murdered? Father Joe knew something. Cancini could feel it in his bones.

Chapter Thirteen

THE SECRETARY TWISTED the mascara-stained tissues into a ball. "I put together the bulletin, set up and maintained the Web site, answered the phones. Really, I did just about whatever Father Holland needed." Makeup wiped away, she looked no older than a college student or recent graduate. She plucked a fresh tissue from the box.

Cancini held his pen over his notebook. "Did he ask you to do anything unusual over the last few days? Did you answer any strange phone calls?"

"No. Everything was the same as always."

"Did Father Holland seem worried or preoccupied?"

Her brows drew together. "I don't think so. I mean, not any more than normal anyway."

"What would be normal for Father Holland to be worried about?"

She squeezed the wadded-up tissues. "Well, he was always worried about money. We all were. Lots more people were coming to church, but most of them were poor. The Sunday offerings hadn't grown as much as he'd hoped, and the diocese didn't want to increase the church funding."

Reminded of the e-mails Landon had discovered, Cancini wrote, *Money troubles?* in his notebook.

"The word was spreading about Father Holland and how kind he was and how he wanted to help the community. It's not that people didn't want to give. Everyone loved Father Holland." She sniffled and pressed a tissue to her nose. Cancini glanced over at Smitty, who stood against the wall, his arms crossed. "Sorry," she said. "I just can't believe it. He was doing such good work."

"But there wasn't enough money to keep doing that work?"

She sighed. "Well, no. There was just so much to do. The people he was helping, some of them were coming to church, and that was good. He was making their lives better. But a lot of those were single moms or prostitutes or, you know . . ." Her voice faded.

"Drug users?" Cancini filled in.

"Yes." She leaned forward, earnestness animating her face. "Father Holland was trying to help them, offer them a place to pray, to get closer to God, show them another way."

"And how was that working?"

"More were coming every Sunday. His message was getting out there."

"What exactly would he have done with more money if he had it?"

She sat back against the chair and ticked off a list. "Lots of things. He wanted to fix the stained glass windows, finish some of the repairs around the church. He wanted to grow his outreach for the drug users, help get them into programs. He wanted to increase the church donations to the poor in the community. He had a list he kept tacked to the bulletin board in his office."

"I saw that list. It was pretty long."

Her lips turned up in a wistful smile. "Father Holland dreamed big. He wanted to do everything and help everyone." The smile twitched and faded. "He was going to change the world."

Cancini paused over his notes. "You don't sound like you believed it."

Flushing, she looked down at her hands again. "I did. I wanted to. I guess I'm more realistic. I don't believe everyone wants to be helped. Some people are just looking for a handout and don't really want to change." He raised an eyebrow at the harder edge in her tone. "That sounds terrible, I know, but it's true," she added.

"Did you ever tell him that?"

She paled. "Of course not. That's not my place. Besides, compared to Father Holland, we're all pretty cynical." She reached up, fingers trembling, and smoothed her hair. The sleeve of her dress fell away, exposing the length of her slender arm. She pulled the sleeve back over her wrist, but not before Cancini saw the black and blue marks dotting her forearm.

"What happened to your arm?"

Her lips parted and she pulled her arms close to her side. "I banged it." She tossed her head and forced a laugh. "I'm a klutz, always tripping over something." She raised a hand to her head. "I'm sorry. I'm really tired. Do you think I could go home now?"

Cancini stood and slid his card across the table. "We'll have someone see you out."

After she was gone, Smitty asked, "What did you think?"

"The janitor was right. I wouldn't describe Mrs. Harding as overly friendly." He hesitated. "The list of things the church needs is extensive, though. Could be Holland's worry over money is somehow connected to the threatening e-mails."

"He got in with some bad people?"

"More likely someone while he was doing outreach or someone he knew before—maybe even from those years he disappeared. It would help if we could get a handle on where he was and what he was doing then."

Smitty shrugged. "I can keep looking. Maybe something will turn up."

Cancini picked up his notebook and read over the words he'd jotted on the page. "Did you notice the bruises on her arm?"

"I didn't have a great view."

Cancini frowned. "I could be wrong, but one of those bruises reminded me of a handprint, like someone grabbed her tight and just held on."

Smitty cocked his head. "Husband?"

"What do we know about him?"

"Not much other than the job and when they moved here. I've seen him, though. He's a big guy."

Cancini slid his notebook into his pocket. "Let's get Bronson to see what he can find out."

Smitty hesitated at the door, turning back to Cancini. "Do you think the bruises mean anything?"

Cancini didn't comment for a moment. He knew about Smitty's sister, about the ex who'd used her as a punching bag. He didn't want to jump to conclusions. "That's what we have to find out."

His young partner's shoulders seemed to loosen. "Sounds good."

Cancini watched him leave. Smitty's sister had lost her hearing in one ear and still wore long sleeves to cover the burn scars on her arms. His young partner blamed himself for not knowing, for not seeing it sooner. He wore that guilt like a mantle. Cancini didn't know if Erica Harding's husband had touched her. Maybe she was klutzy and had only fallen and someone—her husband— had caught her by the arm. It was a reasonable explanation. But if that was true, why lie?

Chapter Fourteen

CANCINI LIFTED THE glass to his lips, savoring the warmth of the scotch as it passed over his tongue and slid down his throat. His eyes flicked from the TV to his silent phone. He wrapped his hand around the cell phone, bringing it to life, then tossed it back on the bar.

"Who were you hoping to hear from?" Smitty lowered himself onto the stool next to Cancini.

"No one."

"Bullshit." Smitty raised a hand to the bartender.

Cancini looked back at the TV as *SportsCenter* counted down the top ten basketball plays of the weekend. He traced the rim of his empty glass, watching the screen, seeing nothing. Cancini rarely frequented the "cop" hangouts, preferring Monty's, with its minimal crowds and minimal conversation. He stayed away on most weekends when the loudmouths and drinkers took over. The music played louder, and the clientele got sloppier. It wasn't his scene. Smitty showed up occasionally when he needed to talk about a case, or sometimes for no reason at all.

"So, who was it you were hoping to hear from? Father Joe or Julia?"

Monty ambled over with a beer and another scotch. Smitty drank straight from the bottle and grabbed a handful of pretzels. Cancini sipped from his glass. "Father Joe."

"I figured." He pushed away the empty bowl. "Do you think he knows more than he's saying?"

"I do." Cancini ran a hand over his short, spiky hair. He hadn't yet read the e-mails Landon had sent over. "He's not going to make it easy, I can tell you that."

Smitty shifted on his stool. "What do you mean? He's a priest. Doesn't he have to tell the truth? Tell us whatever he knows?"

"It's not that simple."

"Sounds pretty simple to me."

Cancini reached for the bowl of peanuts that appeared in place of the pretzels. "It wouldn't be about lying so much as omitting the truth."

Lines creased the young man's forehead. "Isn't that the same thing?"

"Yes and no." Landon's e-mails came to mind. "Let's assume Father Holland told him why he wanted to meet Monday morning but asked him not to tell anyone. Father Joe would never knowingly violate that trust."

Smitty set his bottle back on the bar and faced Cancini. "I know I'm not Catholic and I don't get the whole confession thing, but this is just a conversation right? Not one of those things where you get forgiven for your sins. We just want to know what was bothering him."

Cancini sighed. "But what was bothering him could be part of some ongoing confession. If Father Joe felt free to tell us, he would have. It's not going to be easy to get him to open up if that's the case."

Smitty's light brows drew together. "But you can get him to, right?"

The old man was stubborn. "Probably," he said.

Onscreen, a red-haired sports analyst in a low-cut blouse interviewed a heavily muscled basketball player almost twice her size. She smiled up at him, her expression fixed throughout the exchange. The two men watched the TV in silence until the interview ended, neither hearing a word of it, each lost in his own thoughts. Cancini picked up his phone again. Nothing.

Smitty spoke then, his voice quiet. "How'd Julia take it when you told her you couldn't take her to the airport?"

Cancini tossed a handful of peanuts into his mouth, crunching. "Fine."

"Things good between you?"

It was a fair question, but he didn't know the answer. He liked Julia Manning—more than liked her—but he was in D.C. and she'd left for a story in New York. She said it was temporary, but it wasn't the first time. A relationship was hard enough for regular people, but considering what they both did for a living, he wondered if he wasn't better off being alone. He drained the rest of his scotch. "Fine," he repeated.

Smitty finished his beer, stood, and threw some bills on the bar. "I'd better get going."

Cancini nodded. He checked his phone a third time. What was she doing? He knew she was a night owl, often writing late into the night. Was she working? Was she alone? He wouldn't blame her if she weren't. He couldn't understand what she saw in him anyway. Julia drew people to her in the same way he repelled them. He loved the sun-kissed freckles that dotted her nose and the dimple that popped up on her left cheek when she grinned. He liked the way her ponytail bounced when she walked and the way her laugh made him smile even when he had no idea what was funny. He relaxed when he was with her. She made it easy. It was different than it had been with Lola. That was work. His breath quickened and he picked up the phone, punching the numbers before he changed his mind.

"Hi, Mike." He heard the sound of rustling sheets in the background, and his fingers tightened over the phone. "I didn't expect to hear from you tonight."

He let out a long breath. "I just wanted to make sure you got to New York safely. I feel bad about this morning. There were all those thunderstorms."

"It's okay. My flight was delayed, but it wasn't bad." He heard the hesitation in her voice. "Was it that priest that got shot?"

"Yeah."

"Do you want to talk about it?"

"No." Silence crackled over the line. "I'd rather hear about New York. The book."

"You don't have to do that, Mike." Her words were quiet, measured.

He cradled his glass in his hand and looked up to the ceiling. He didn't know the right things to say or when to say them. He didn't know how to do any of this. "I know I don't."

"Not that I wouldn't love to talk about the book or my work if that's what you really want." She laughed then and added, "But you might be on the phone way longer than you planned."

"Not going anywhere." His lips turned up as he listened to her talk. They'd met months earlier during the Coed Killer case. She'd been assigned to the story when Leo Spradlin had been granted a writ of innocence after more than two decades in prison. Cancini, the arresting officer in the original case, had been drawn back into the investigation and the small town where—following Spradlin's release—the murders began again. Emotionally and physically wrung out after the case, she'd quit the paper, quit her doomed marriage. She'd freelanced for a while but wanted a fresh start. She claimed writing this new book about a fifteen-year-old unsolved Manhattan murder was just what she needed. He hadn't wanted her to go to New York, but she hadn't asked, and he hadn't stopped her. It was her life. He understood what it was like to come out of a failed marriage. He wouldn't pressure her.

"The families," she said. "Bringing it up is like living through it all over again for them. Even though it's been years, it's still raw. They lost their loved ones. It's not a story or a book to them. It's real."

He heard the doubt in her voice. "You'll figure out a way. They probably just need you to listen, show compassion."

"Wow." She laughed again. "Is that the official advice of the tough D.C. detective?"

He hesitated. Was that what she thought, that he was tough? He didn't feel so tough most of the time. Working homicide was a maze of dead bodies, ruined lives, and devastated families. Shootings, stabbings, beatings. He'd seen them all. Cancini recognized it could desensitize a man, harden him to tragedy. He'd seen it happen. But homicide hadn't made him tough. It had softened him, and he knew it. With each new investigation, he found things weren't always as black and white as they appeared. He believed in justice, he believed in the law, but he wasn't tough. He lost a piece of himself with every case, but he didn't know how to do anything else. She laughed again, and the moment was gone. "I think I like this side of you, Detective."

"Good to know."

"I'm glad you called." The words came faster. "I should be honest. I wasn't mad this morning, but I was annoyed."

The text he'd sent her had been short, no explanation. "I should have told you why I couldn't take you to the airport. I'm not very good at this sometimes."

A few seconds ticked by. "I'm not looking for 'good at this,' Mike. I had that once. It didn't work out."

Her voice, tinged with sadness, washed over him, and he swallowed the lump in his throat. He took a deep breath. What the hell? "I miss you."

"You're full of surprises tonight, Detective."

"Hope that's a good thing."

"It is." She paused. "I miss you, too."

He sucked in his breath, and the lightness in his stomach made him smile again. "Talk to you tomorrow?"

"Sounds good."

He laid the phone back on the bar. Monty refilled his glass and wiped the counter in one motion.

Cancini hadn't expected to care about a woman again. After Lola had traded him in for Martin, he'd been happy to have her gone, happy to let her take it all. Her absence had left a trail of quiet, a legacy of solitude. He'd socialized little, dated even less. He'd worn that solitude like a cloak, armor on the job and in his personal life. It was easier that way. But Julia had come along and made him wonder. For better or for worse, Julia had slipped under his skin.

He pushed the scotch away and slid off the stool.

"Gonna call it a night?" Monty asked.

"Yeah. Long day tomorrow." The bartender picked up the empty glass and waved a hand. Cancini slid off the stool. The phone on the bar vibrated. He snatched it up and read the glowing screen. A text from an unidentified number lit up the screen.

Follow the money.

Chapter Fifteen

PAPERS AND PICTURES covered the surface of the long table. Smitty pointed to a photocopy of Holland's wish list, the one that had been pinned to the bulletin board outside his office. "Stained glass. Landscaping. Steeple. Paint. Basement. And that's just the beginning." He paused and whistled softly. "That's quite a list.

Father Joe ignored the paper. "Matthew had big goals. It is also true that the church needed a lot in the way of renovations."

"And the other stuff on the list?"

From the corner of the room, Cancini appraised the old man. If possible, Father Joe looked worse than he had he day before. A weary voice, pallid complexion, and red-rimmed eyes suggested he'd spent a long and restless night.

"Matthew was not only interested in the physical problems of the church. That was one thing," Father Joe explained. "But more, he wanted to increase attendance, get people back in the church, show them faith and give them hope. He created outreach programs and Bible groups and support groups."

Smitty uncrossed his long legs. "And did he? Give them hope?"

"I think so, but I'm not sure he thought it was good enough or fast enough. Matthew had a tendency toward impatience. He wanted to get the windows fixed right away. He wanted the pews to be filled every Sunday." Father Joe looked down at his hands. "Most of all, he wanted to help those he considered lost—and he didn't want to wait."

"How noble," Smitty said.

Father Joe stiffened.

"All those repairs, the stained glass, getting people in the church, that takes money, right?"

Father Joe looked up, moon-shaped crevices between his brows. "Yes."

"A helluva lot of money that St. William didn't have. Am I right?"

Father Joe sighed. "Yes, Detective Smithson, you're right. St. William has needed money for a long time. Matthew was frustrated by that, but it's not uncommon in the poorer churches. I have several friends in similar situations, but they aren't dead because of it. What exactly are you getting at?"

Smitty put down his pen and notebook and slid his chair closer to the table. He leaned forward, his voice even. "What I'm getting at is that we know money was an issue and we know Father Holland was anxious about it. As you said, he had a tendency toward impatience." Smitty paused and waved a hand in the air. "I'm asking if Father Holland might have taken a few shortcuts."

"Shortcuts?"

"Let's call it nonstandard methods of acquiring funds."

Father Joe's face turned pink. "You mean illegal, don't you?"

"A loan at a very high interest rate, then?"

"Do you know how ridiculous that sounds? Matthew was a

good man. He was a man of his word." He placed both hands on the table, his voice rising with each word. "He wouldn't go to a—a loan shark or anything else like you're suggesting. It's absurd." He took several deep breaths and ran a trembling hand over his bald head. "He was a good man," he said again.

Smitty pushed copies of the threatening e-mails across the table. "What about these, then? Someone was angry enough to threaten him." Father Joe stared at the e-mails. "Go ahead. Read them."

Five long minutes passed as Father Joe read one e-mail after another. His complexion, already ghostlike, paled, and the shadows under his eyes darkened. He laid the papers back on the table. "I didn't know about these."

"Do you know who wrote them?"

"I just told you I didn't know about them."

Cancini sat up straighter in his chair.

"Let's try this, then. Do you have any idea who might have hated Father Holland enough to send those e-mails?"

"I could think about it, I suppose." He looked around, licking his lips. "Could I get some water?"

Cancini's head pounded. Father Joe might not have known about the e-mails before that moment, but Cancini didn't believe for a minute he had no idea who might have sent them. He stood up, drawing both men's attention. "Father Joe, I know this is hard. Losing someone you care about is difficult no matter how it happens." His back itched and he sensed Martin's eyes burning behind the glass. Cancini had done exactly the opposite of what Martin told him to do and inserted himself in the interview. Too bad. "Just a few more questions."

The old man's face sagged. "I do want to help."

"I know you do." He pulled out a chair close to the priest. "We've looked through all of Father Holland's e-mails—including the ones he sent you—and according to those, the two of you did meet on a regular basis, for lunch on Wednesdays."

"Not always. Sometimes one of us had a funeral or special Mass."

"But most of the time it was a Wednesday, and yesterday was a Monday. Also, you were seeing him for breakfast instead of lunch. Was there a reason you couldn't meet this week at your usual time?"

Father Joe looked at his hands again. "Not that I know of. He didn't say. Just e-mailed me and asked me to meet him Monday morning."

"E-mailed you on Sunday?"

"Yes, between the noon and five o'clock Masses."

"He e-mailed you three times in two hours."

"I guess he did. I didn't answer the first two because I hadn't checked my e-mail yet, so he sent another. As I said, Matthew was often impatient."

"Did you think it was strange that he wanted to meet on Monday?"

"Unusual but not strange." Father Joe touched the collar at his neck. "Is there a point to this?"

"Why didn't he just call you? Or text you?"

"Matthew didn't like talking on the phone, and you know how I feel about texting." He held up thick fingers. "My fingers don't work so well all the time."

Cancini leaned in, his face close to Father Joe's. "Impatient or not, sending three e-mails in two hours seems excessive. What was so important that it couldn't wait until Wednesday?"

The priest pressed his lips together. "The e-mails didn't say."

"But you knew?"

Father Joe shifted in his chair, eyes still downcast. "I knew he wanted to meet for breakfast. I like breakfast, so I said yes."

Cancini frowned. More evasion, truth without truth. He glanced at Smitty and shook his head. It was the best he could do.

Understanding they wouldn't get anything more, no matter how many questions they asked, Smitty wrapped up the interview. "Father Joe, why don't we get someone to take you home? We'll let you know if we have any more questions."

Martin burst into the room the minute the priest had gone. "Goddammit, Cancini! I told you to stay out of it. Are you trying to screw up this case? Smitty had him ready to tell us who might have had it in for the guy, and you start talking about a couple of random e-mails. What the hell were you doing? Why did you let him go?"

Cancini exhaled slowly. "We let him go because he isn't a suspect."

"I don't give a shit if he's a suspect or not. We need information and you let him walk out."

"He's an old man. He was tired."

"He was tired? For Christ's sake. Should we let every suspect we interview leave when they get tired?"

"He's not a suspect," Cancini said again.

"I told you I don't give a shit. Pull one more stunt like that and you're off the case," he said, and stormed out of the room.

Smitty returned to the conference room, pale lips pressed together. "I think you were right. That e-mail about the breakfast Monday meant something. Father Holland was worried."

"Not only that," Cancini said, his heart heavy, "whatever it was, Father Joe knew about it. He's in this up to his neck."

Chapter Sixteen

2005

"I GOT ACCEPTED." Matt waved the letter in the air, a broad smile creeping across his face.

Father Joe grinned and hugged the young man. "I knew you would."

"I couldn't have done it without you," Matt said. The old man reddened, but his smile deepened. Matt hugged him again. It was true. The priest had given him a place to sleep, food, and a place to study. He'd breezed through his high school equivalency exam and sent off applications to three small Christian colleges. All accepted him.

"I'm so proud of you, Matthew."

The young man shrugged his shoulders and then let out a whoop. It was the first step and he'd done it! If only his mother could see him now.

Father Joe poured two cups of tea. "Well, which one is it going to be?"

"This one." Matt held up the letter in his hand. "Assumption." Father Joe lowered his eyes, and he understood in an instant. Assumption was in Massachusetts, the farthest of the three schools.

"That's a good school."

"It's the best one," Matt answered.

"It's also the most expensive."

"I've got money."

"Ah." Father Joe picked up his cup and saucer and blew gently on the steaming tea.

The old man wouldn't look at him, but the young man heard the questions in his mind anyway. Where did the money come from? Was the money how he'd survived? Where had he spent the last three years? He'd discouraged questions up to now, easily steering the conversations back to the present, but he knew the old man's concerns would not go away.

"Padre."

Father Joe looked up. "Yes?"

"You seem upset. Aren't you happy for me?"

The priest offered a resigned smile. "Of course I am. I'm sad because Assumption is so far away. You just got back, and I feel like I'm losing you again. But I'm extremely happy for you."

Matt leaned forward, his face serious. "I want to be far away. Not from you," he added quickly, "but away from other people here, other stuff."

"Running away won't solve your problems," Father Joe cautioned.

"I know that." Matt stood up and went to the window. Sunlight poured through, wrapping him in white light, and he shivered under the warmth. He'd run away at fifteen and he'd run away a second time—this time to Father Joe. He swung around, his eyes flat. "But leaving gives me time."

"Time for what exactly?"

Matt shoved his hands in the front pockets of his jeans, pushing up the hooded sweatshirt. "Lots of things. Time to think. Time to fix things. Time to change my life."

The corners of Father Joe's mouth turned up for a moment before the smile faded. "You've really thought this through."

"Yes."

"When will you leave?"

"Tomorrow."

Father's Joe's head shot up. "Why so soon?"

Matt looked at the floor, then back out the window. When he spoke, the pride and excitement that had tinged his earlier words was gone, resignation in its place. "I can't stay here any longer. It's not safe. For me or for you."

"What do you mean, not safe?"

The color had drained from the old man's face, and Matt felt a pang of guilt. "Someone's looking for me. At least I think they are." Maybe they'd given up, but he couldn't take the chance any longer. "I need to leave before they find me or figure out I've been here."

"Who, Matthew?"

The young man admired how quickly the old man had recovered. If he was afraid, he hid it well. "I don't want to get you involved."

"It's too late for that."

Matt winced at the rebuke. Father Joe was right. The minute he'd entered the old man's house, Father Joe had been involved. He wouldn't have brought Father Joe into it if he'd had any choice.

Maybe it was time to tell him the truth, tell him everything. The silence stretched out for several minutes, then he rose and stood before the priest. He fell to his knees.

Father Joe took Matthew's hands in his. "What is it, son?"

"Bless me, Father, for I have sinned." He whispered the words, his head bowed. "It's been three years and eighty-nine days since my last confession."

Chapter Seventeen

"Just got the word from Landon. The text came from a burner. No way to trace it." Jensen handed Cancini his cell phone and stepped back. He wiped his forehead with a handkerchief.

"Damn." Cancini shook his head, unsure why he was so upset. The chances it could have been traced were slim at best. He slipped the phone in his pocket and circled his desk, stopping in front of a large rolling board. On the left side of the board, he'd written their victim's name, Father Holland, in the middle. Circles and names spread out in a fan from the center. With a marker, he drew a dollar sign on the board and connected it to the deceased. After a moment, he added a question mark. He stepped back, turning his attention to the map pinned to the right side of the board. Push pins marked each location where the threatening e-mails to Father Holland had originated. The dates for each e-mail were listed on a printout next to the map. No matter how many times he studied the map, he couldn't find a pattern. Three e-mails from a Starbucks in Arlington within one month, not again for a year. Six times from the public library in

Northwest, spread over several months. The time of day varied. Without a consistent pattern, he couldn't interview cashiers or librarians. Who would remember an occasional patron with a laptop? The origin of the e-mails was untraceable, like the text. His head pounded. "Can someone get me some goddamn coffee?"

"I got it," Jensen said, scurrying to the break room.

Smitty watched the man go, then plopped down on the corner of his desk. "Jesus, Cancini. What'd you say to the guy this morning? He's practically jumping out of his skin."

Cancini shrugged. "Not much." He let his fingers trace the list of dates and times again. Jensen had a nasty habit of catching colds and missing work. Cancini had simply told Jensen if he was out sick during this investigation, he'd call the man's wife to ask how he was feeling. Jensen had blanched, his thick lips blubbering, but before he could get a word out, Cancini had walked away. He didn't care about the man's gambling problem or that he hid it from his wife. He cared about finding Father Holland's killer. As long as Jensen toed the line, kept his nose clean, and did his job, Cancini had nothing to say.

"You sure? He hasn't even told any of his stupid jokes this morning. At this rate, we're going to have to stop calling him Joker."

Cancini rolled his eyes. Jensen wasn't a stupid cop, but he was awkward. The bad jokes didn't help. Cancini had always thought the man would be more comfortable balancing a ledger or working at a computer than hoofing it as a homicide detective. He just lacked the nose for it.

Jensen returned with four cups of coffee, Bronson at his heels.

"Glad you could make it today," Cancini said, the words directed at Bronson.

"Sorry. Overslept."

"Don't let it happen again. You can sleep when the case is closed." Bronson and Jensen exchanged glances. "We've got a lot to do today." Cancini looked at his partner. "When do we get ballistics?"

"Today. Also, Kate has the preliminary autopsy results. She'll be ready for us in an hour."

They expected no surprises about the cause of death, but there could be other details in the autopsy that were relevant. "Jensen," Cancini said, "Landon is going to meet you at the church office in an hour to start going through the financial records of the church. We've also got a request pending for copies of Father Holland's personal records. I want to know about anything, and I mean anything, that looks odd. Do you think you can handle that?"

"I got it. Go through all the records." His head bobbed up and down with every word. "How far back do you want me to go?"

"Start at the present and work your way backward—all the way to when Father Holland took over at St. William."

The man blinked. "Isn't that more than three years?"

"Good to know you can add, Jensen. That's why you got the job." He shifted his attention to Bronson. "Where are we on the interviews with the parishioners from the evening Mass?"

Bronson cleared his throat, pulled out his phone, and scrolled through his notes. "I've spoken to about ten so far plus the deacons, and all said the same thing. Father Holland seemed fine. What's weird is all the ladies had a thing for him. It was like he was George Clooney and Ben Affleck and Denzel Washington all rolled into one. They went on and on about him."

An eight-by-ten picture of Holland was pinned to the rolling board. Taken outside on the steps of the church, it showed him dressed in his black robes and smiling, one hand raised. His sandy hair fell in a soft wave over his forehead. Golden-brown eyes, Roman nose, chiseled chin. The only thing missing was the dimple. Movie star looks wrapped in black cloth. Bronson's report didn't surprise him. Cancini guessed Holland was the kind of guy women swooned over—or would if he wasn't a priest. Aloud, he said, "Anything else?"

"Yeah. A couple of the ladies looked for him after Mass Sunday night but couldn't find him."

He thought about the Masses he'd attended as a boy and shrugged it off. "That's not too unusual. The priest usually leaves the sanctuary during the recessional. He might have gone to his office or back to his apartment. Why were they looking for him?"

Bronson consulted his phone again. "There were a couple of drunks that came in right before communion. They were loud and obnoxious—the ladies' words, not mine. According to them, Father Holland handled it."

"How'd he do that?" Smitty asked.

"They said he invited the men to stay, that everyone was welcome. Then he explained communion and offered to bless any guests. They said it quieted the men down and they left."

Cancini sat down and took a long swig of the office sludge they called coffee. "If Father Holland handled it, what did the ladies want to talk to him about? Were they worried?"

"I think so. It was that bit where Father Holland said everyone was welcome. They didn't really like that. That's what they wanted to talk to him about."

"Maybe they didn't want drunks at their church," Smitty suggested. "I guess I can understand that, but it doesn't sound very Christian."

Bronson shook his head. "No, that wasn't it. Supposedly, Father Holland wanted everyone in the church to act as missionaries, teach the faith, offer forgiveness. The ladies worked with addicts, the homeless, lots of people. Father Holland called it Catholic Outreach for the People Eternal, or COPE for short." Bronson looked up from his phone. "And the ladies said even though they lost a few parishioners, they got new ones over time. Folks were buying in."

Cancini leaned back, his gaze wandering up to the ceiling. COPE. It sounded familiar. Hadn't he heard Father Joe talk about a Catholic program in the city not long ago, one that was targeting the roughest neighborhoods? Maybe he should've paid more attention. "So what was the problem?"

"It was one of the drunks. He'd come in wearing a leather jacket, but took it off. Underneath, he wore a T-shirt, so they could see his arms. On his right arm was a tattoo."

Drunks with tattoos. Cancini thought Mass must have changed a lot since he'd been a kid. "What kind of tattoo?"

Bronson pulled a page from inside his coat pocket and held it up in the air. The drawing was crude but clear. Cold fingers prickled at Cancini's neck, and goose bumps rose on his arms. A sword through a skull, and three drops of blood. He knew that tattoo. They all did. It was the mark of a killer.

Chapter Eighteen

DR. KATE STEVENSON smoothed her white lab coat and spread her hands on the desk, her face grim. "I know time is important, Detective, so I'll get right to it. The victim died of a single gunshot wound delivered at very close range, possibly a .22 with a hollow-point. Ballistics should be able to confirm that." Her red-stained lips were drawn into a line. "The right side of the victim's face was severely damaged by the impact. The bullet appears to have entered through the right eye or just below it, and lodged in the brain. He died almost instantly."

Smitty brushed his hair from his forehead. "A .22 isn't a big gun."

"No, it isn't. But it wouldn't have to be if it was fired at close range."

"And it's easier to hide," Cancini observed. "How close was the shot?"

"Five feet, give or take a few inches."

Cancini extended his right arm, holding it straight. He looked back at the medical examiner. "Just far enough away to be out of reach."

"Probably. It's not definite, but based on the temperature inside the church and the rigor mortis in the body, I'd put the time of death between approximately seven and nine p.m."

"Thanks, Kate. It's a start." Cancini wrote the time in his notebook. "Anything else?"

The medical examiner touched the folder in front of her and opened it to several photos. "Looking at the crime scene photos combined with the angle of the gunshot entry, I'd say the victim was lying on the steps with his head tipped back slightly and looking up at the shooter."

"That's about what we figured." Cancini shifted in his chair. "Any fibers or hair?"

"Nothing. His hands were clean. Other than the shot to the face, there were no bruises or anything to indicate he fought off his attacker. Overall, I'd say he was in good health." She paused. "Based on the man's bone structure, I'd say your victim was a very handsome man."

"We've heard that," Cancini said.

Her fingers plucked at the edges of the manila folder. "There is one other thing." Cancini heard the hesitation in her voice, and his hands tightened on the arms of the hardback chair. "It's only preliminary. We'll have the full tox screen results later in the week, but one drug did pop up in the victim's system. Ativan."

"Ativan? Is that prescription?" Smitty asked.

"Yes. Do you know anything about it?" Both detectives shrugged. "Typically it's used to alleviate symptoms of anxiety. Most doctors don't prescribe it long-term as it has a risk of being addictive and can have some serious side effects, including headaches, dizziness, trouble concentrating, and depression."

Cancini's body stilled. They had threatening e-mails and possible worries about money. "The victim was taking pills for anxiety?"

"That's right."

"Short-term?"

"Right again. Someone with long-term anxiety issues or a history of panic attacks wouldn't be a great candidate for this drug. At least not usually."

"My sister takes an antidepressant," Smitty said, his voice quiet.

"It's not the same," Kate answered. "Lots of people take those, but that doesn't mean they feel anxious. Of course, it's not uncommon for someone to have symptoms of both, but I didn't find any evidence of an antidepressant or any other drug in the victim's system during the preliminary tox screen. Not even an aspirin."

Cancini sat back. Whatever was going on with Holland, he'd been feeling the pressure. What were the chances Father Joe knew about that, too? He got to his feet. "Thanks, Kate. I think we have a doctor to visit."

Chapter Nineteen

"Christ," Martin said, his head in his hands. "It's not as if this case isn't already a fucking pain in my ass. Press is making this guy out to be some kind of hero already. Putting him up for sainthood. Have you seen the front page today? Can you imagine how the crazies would respond if it got out about that little calling card painted in the victim's blood?"

Cancini bristled. He had no intention of reading the paper. He was more concerned with solving the case, gathering evidence.

Martin tossed the papers on the desk. "Now, you're telling me our sainted victim is depressed. That just adds to the guy's appeal. It's like a friggin' soap opera."

"Not depressed," Smitty said. "Anxious."

"Whatever." He fingered the bowl of toothpicks on his desk, his eyes drifting to a framed photo of his wife. "All right. Let's go over this again." He took a deep breath. "We've got a priest shot down in his own church. We've got the e-mails, but don't know who's been sending them. We've got an anonymous text about money that we can't trace. We've got pills and—what was it you said earlier? We've got a gang member showing up at the church and scaring all the ladies." He shook his head. "You can't make this stuff up."

Cancini felt a moment of sympathy for the man. He wasn't a fan of Martin—he had personal and professional reasons—but he was grateful that it was the captain who took the heat with the brass and the press. The captain might have been a plodding investigator at best, but that plodding mentality made him a natural administrator.

"I need something," the captain said. "What about the e-mails? Anything new?"

While Smitty talked, Cancini's attention wandered to the array of pictures on the wall. Martin appeared in every picture, grinning, arms looped over the shoulder of whoever happened to be closest. Lola was the newest addition to the wall. It was bad enough everyone knew she'd dumped Cancini for the captain. He'd seen it in their eyes, in the way they'd moved past him with a quick nod. He'd preferred it that way then. He hadn't wanted questions or false sympathy. He'd just wanted it to be over.

In the picture, Lola smiled up at Martin with red lips, her head thrown back as though whatever he'd said was incredibly funny. Cancini sincerely doubted that. The picture, framed in silver, highlighted Lola's shiny blond hair and golden skin. No man with blood coursing through his veins could fail to see her beauty. It had always baffled him that a woman who looked like that would marry a man like him. Now it baffled him that losing her didn't bother him more than it did.

"What about that money thing?" Martin asked.

"Jensen is working with Landon to get through all the bank statements and ledgers," Smitty said.

Martin rolled his eyes. "Jensen's slow as molasses. The case'll be cold before he finds anything."

"He has a business degree, Captain. Landon called and said they found what looks like a donation to the church in the last few weeks. Could be something. They'll find it if there's anything there."

The captain reluctantly agreed. "But get some more eyes on those statements if this turns into a marathon." He shifted his focus to Cancini. "Where are we on this pill thing?"

"I've got an appointment with his physician this afternoon. I don't know what he'll tell us, but he should be able to verify the prescription at the least. The dosage in his system was consistent with treatment for anxiety according to Kate."

The captain fiddled with the toothpicks in the bowl, touching them one by one. "And the man at the church with the tattoo? What gang is that?"

"It's not really a gang," Cancini said, his tone dry.

"Then what the hell would you call it?"

"I'd call it what it is—a death squad."

The captain sat back and folded his arms across his chest. "That's just a name to make them seem more powerful than they are."

"Yes and no. The Death Squad is part of a larger group, the Eastside Gang, but that's only at arm's length." Cancini recited the little he'd learned. "They call themselves The Squad for short. I've heard there are only a few of them. The tattoo, the one Bronson got the sketch of, that's their sign."

"And?"

"And they're more mercenary than thug. No drug organization, no pimping, no intimidation in the neighborhood. For the most part, they stay outta sight unless they're needed." Cancini rolled his shoulders, the cluster of knots tightening the longer he sat in the chair. "They've been around for a few years, but have stayed under the radar for the most part. It's only been in the past few months that the FBI has even been able to find out anything. They still don't know a lot, but they suspect members have specialized training, maybe even former military."

Martin uncrossed his arms. "Military? Why?"

"The name isn't just for fun. It's not for street cred. It's real. That's what they do. They kill people for hire."

"Shit." He fell back against the soft leather of his high-backed chair. "Hired hands."

"Looks that way, but we don't know who the man with the tattoo was or why he was at the service. It could have been a threat. It fits the M.O. of the group, but for right now, we don't have enough to go on."

"Fine. I want you—"

Bronson burst into the office, his roundish frame filling the doorway. Sweat dripped from his temple.

"What is it, Bronson?" the captain asked.

Cancini rose, cold fingers stealing up his spine.

"An incident was just called in over near St. Ignatius." Bronson's voice dropped, his pinball eyes on Cancini. "It's your priest friend. He's been shot."

Chapter Twenty

Cancini flashed his badge and rushed past the nurse at the front desk. His shirt clung to his skin under his coat and he stopped short, struggling to catch his breath. Empty gurneys were pushed up against another nurses' station, and smaller, cubicle-like rooms lined each long wall. Heavy curtains marked occupied spaces.

"Hey," a man yelled from behind. "You can't go in there."

Without turning, Cancini raised the badge again. He pulled aside the curtain at the first room on his right, letting it drop just as quickly. Not Father Joe. Two more cubicles. Still not him. The next two rooms stood empty. He looked to his left, and a strong hand caught him by the shoulder, spinning him around. A heavy-set man in a dark uniform glared. "You can't just come barging in here." Cancini held up his badge a third time, and the security man's eyes flickered over it and back to the detective's face. He stood close to the detective, imposing his bulk. "You're supposed to follow procedure," he said. "There are patients here."

Cancini looked over his shoulder. Four rooms on the left were occupied. He considered brushing by the man, but thought better of it. "I'm looking for one of those patients. Gunshot wound."

"Yeah?" His expression was unchanged. "We get a lot of those."

"This one's a priest."

The security guard's face changed, his eyes registering surprise. Shit. Maybe he should've just pushed by the man. Martin would have a field day if the press caught wind of a second priest shooting.

"Older guy?"

"Yes."

The man pointed to the last room on the left and stepped out of the way. "He came in about an hour ago."

Cancini's pulse quickened. He slipped his badge back in his pocket, saying, "I may need to talk to you. Can you wait?"

The man straightened his shoulders, thumbs tucked in his waistband. "I'll be at the front desk, right outside."

"Thanks." He crossed the floor to the last room and pulled back the privacy curtain. Father Joe lay on a rolling bed, tubes protruding from both arms. White as a sheet, the old man looked more dead than alive.

A woman in blue scrubs stood near the bed, writing in a chart. She looked at him, eyebrows raised. "And you are?"

"Detective Mike Cancini." He pulled out his badge one more time and held it up. She leaned in but said nothing. "How is he?"

"He got lucky—just a flesh wound in his thigh. No major damage, but he won't be running any races anytime soon." The words were spoken in an impassive monotone, the voice of a woman who'd seen far worse and would again. "The bullet went clean through. We gave him a sedative and he's on an antibiotic drip. Monitoring his vitals. He'll be moved upstairs soon, but for now, we're letting him sleep."

Relief washed over him. His chin fell to his chest, and he let out a ragged breath.

"Detective, if you'll excuse me, I have other patients." She closed the chart and hung it from the end of the bed.

As she moved past Cancini, he caught her arm. "Wait. Did he say anything about the shooting? Anything at all?"

"Not to me," she said. "I think he was in shock. You might ask the paramedics who brought him in."

"Do you know—"

"You'll have to ask at the front desk." Over her shoulder, she said, "Good luck," and pulled the curtain closed again.

Cancini sank into the guest chair, his head in his hands. A flesh wound. Not fatal. The blinking monitor beeped. He looked up, forehead furrowed, and studied the numbers. Again, he felt a sense of overwhelming relief. All the old man's vitals appeared normal. For another minute, he watched the rise and fall of Father Joe's chest. Even in sleep, deep lines ran across the old man's broad forehead, and heavy jowls framed his square chin. His normally pink skin had the appearance of chalk, dusty and dry. Cancini reached out and took one of the man's hands in his own. The soft flesh was warm to the touch. He bowed his head and held on.

Chapter Twenty-one

2013

THE WAITER PICKED up the bottle of wine. He glanced at the clerical collars they wore and hesitated. "Would you like a refill?"

"Not for the old man," Matt said, face somber. "His liver can't take it."

Father Joe lowered his head, hiding his smile. The waiter made a quick exit, and Matt burst out laughing. "I couldn't help it. He doesn't know what to make of us now." Still chuckling, he took the bottle and filled his mentor's glass. "You're not mad, are you?"

"That I will never be able to drink a glass of wine in this restaurant again? No, why should I be?"

Matt's smile faded. "I was only kidding."

"So was I." Father Joe smiled and raised his glass. "To you, Matthew. Your first year as a priest. You've achieved exactly what you hoped, and I'm so proud of you."

Matt grinned again, his face both proud and sheepish. "I couldn't have done it without your support." He lifted his own glass. "I mean that. You were there for me, even when I didn't believe you were."

The old priest blinked away tears and drank. "Enough of that. Have you received your permanent assignment?"

"I have." Matt set his glass back on the table and wiped his mouth with his napkin. Father Joe waited. "It's an old church with lots of history, but it's run down. The neighborhood's bad. It's not exactly packed on Sundays. The truth is, I think attendance is at an all-time low. There's not much money in the coffers." With each word, Matt saw the old man's expression change, turn wary. The pride and anticipation he'd witnessed moments earlier were replaced by furrowed brows and a downturned mouth. Matt knew the old man suspected, but he kept talking anyway. "I'll be mostly on my own with some help coming in weekly. The diocese was against it at first, but I insisted. It's exactly what I wanted."

Father Joe pushed his glass away. Seconds ticked by. When he spoke, his voice shook. "And where is this parish, Matthew?"

Matt held his gaze. "Here in D.C. At St. William." The old priest's mouth closed and he looked away. "I know what you're thinking, Padre, but I can bring that church back to life. I know I can." He paused, adding, "It's where we met. You were filling in that day." He pressed his palms against the table. "Remember?"

"I remember a scared boy running from a thug."

"I wasn't that scared."

The old man raised a single silver eyebrow.

"Okay, I was. But that's why I want to come back, and you know it. You found me, and it's because of you that I'm a priest today. I could be dead, but I've made it. I want that opportunity. I want to do that for someone else."

"It's not the same, Matt. In the years since you lived at Barry

Farm, the neighborhood has gotten worse. And the church is no better. St. William has fallen into further disrepair. The weekly offerings are so small, I heard talk in the diocese about closing the parish. It's barely hanging on."

"Exactly."

"You're just being nostalgic, Matt."

"It's not nostalgia. It's payback."

"Ah." Father Joe cocked his head, his expression stern. "An eye for an eye?"

Matt threw back his head and laughed. "You should see yourself, Padre. So serious." Still smiling, he looked at his mentor, the lines around his eyes softening. "Not that kind of payback. What I meant was, this is the neighborhood that killed my mother, that kills so many. I've been given so much these last few years. Now is my chance to turn the neighborhood around, to stop all of it, to give the hopeless hope." He opened his palms. "How does the saying go? Fight with love, or something like that?"

"That's an honorable dream." He held up a hand at Matt's protest. "But it's still a dream. I don't think you understand what you're getting yourself into there. I've heard talk the church might be combined with St. Anthony's."

"I've heard that, too," Matt acknowledged. "But they're willing to let me give it a shot." His golden-brown eyes glowed under the restaurant's soft lighting. "St. William will be beautiful again," he said, his tone wistful. "Can't you just see it, Padre? The stained glass windows sparkling, the pews polished and full of people. It'll be gorgeous, just like it used to be." He raised his glass again, and his face split into a toothy smile. "C'mon, Padre. We're here to celebrate." Matt tipped his glass and swallowed the rest of his wine. He sat back, satisfied. "It's all gonna happen, Padre. I promise."

Father Joe smiled, but his eyes remained doubtful.

Matt sighed. "What is it? What's bothering you?"

The old man's finger trailed the rim of this glass. He licked his lips. "It's not just that the church is old and the neighborhood is more crime-ridden than ever. That's all true, but returning to D.C., do you think that's a good idea?" He paused and lowered his voice. "He'll know you're back."

Matt didn't answer right away. They both knew whom the old man was referring to. Once he'd confessed to Father Joe, he'd held nothing back but a few details the old man was better off not knowing. Father Joe's concerns were valid, but Matt had vowed not to let his fear change what he wanted to do with his life, what he needed to do. He wasn't afraid—at least not the way Father Joe was. He'd seen what he'd seen and never gone to the police. Hadn't enough time passed? He shrugged. "It's the only way." He picked up the knife and turned it over on the plate. "I can't run away anymore. I'm doing the right thing here."

Father Joe didn't agree, worry on his face and in his voice. "He has a lot of people around him now, a lot of bad people."

Matt scratched at his chin. "And how would you know that, Padre? Have you been hanging around the old neighborhood? Infiltrating gangs?"

The old man blushed. "Of course not. You know I volunteer at St. William once a month. I keep my ear to the ground. I hear things."

The young man's mouth opened and closed. It would do no good to brush aside Father Joe's concerns. Besides, what he knew could prove useful. "You never fail to surprise me, Padre." He gave a shake of his head. "Tell me, what have you learned?"

"He's more dangerous now."

Matt laughed again, but this time, the sound was bitter. "I'm not afraid, Padre. If I was, I wouldn't be here."

"He'll find out you're back." Father Joe spoke softly, but Matt could hear the concern in his voice.

"He already knows."

Father Joe's pink skin blanched. "How?"

Matt lifted his chin, gaze steady. A vein throbbed at his temple. "I told him."

Chapter Twenty-two

"IS FATHER JOE OKAY?"

Cancini could hear the concern in Julia's voice, a concern he shared. She'd met Father Joe once and liked him immediately. Still, Cancini didn't want to worry her. "He will be. It's not serious. Probably go home soon."

"It is serious, Mike. He was shot."

Cancini dumped three aspirin on his desk. "You're right. I just meant he's going to be fine."

"And after he's home? Will he be safe?"

He tipped his head back and swallowed the aspirin. Covering one ear to block out the battery of noise in the precinct, he spoke softly. "Why would you ask that?"

"He was shot, wasn't he? It's only been two days since that other priest was murdered. What if someone's going around targeting priests?"

He hesitated. So far, there was nothing to link the shootings other than the priest's professions and the fact that they knew each other. Father Joe had been shot in what looked like a drive-by. The nature of that kind of crime was different from the cold-blooded murder of Holland. Until they had evidence otherwise, he'd been informed the shootings would be treated as separate crimes. He didn't completely agree, but it wasn't his call. "I don't know yet. We've just begun the investigation."

"But you'll make sure he's okay?"

"Yes."

"How's your dad? Does he know?"

"I haven't told him."

"Can you speak up?" Julia asked. "I can't hear you."

Around him, phones trilled and the booming voices rose and fell in waves. He spoke louder. "I don't want to worry him." Since the discovery of Holland's body, he'd only been able to call his dad twice, both times speaking to the day nurse. Somehow, the man kept defying the odds, kept hanging on. Father Joe called it a small miracle. Cancini wasn't convinced miracles had anything to do with it, but he, too, wondered where his old man got the fight. "He's been really tired."

Smitty approached, caught Cancini's look, and nodded. "Going for some coffee. Be back in five."

Cancini mouthed his thanks. "Julia, I've got to go." He hung up with a promise he'd keep her posted and walked over to the whiteboard dotted with lines and circles and magnets. With his finger, he traced the line from Father Holland to Father Joe. Two shootings. Two priests. Less than forty-eight hours. Coincidence? It didn't feel right, and the hammer in his skull pounded harder. He whirled around at the hand that landed on his shoulder.

Captain Martin stood over him, a thick file folder in his hand. "In my office. Now." He pointed at Smitty. "You too."

"Word got out about the shooting of your friend Sweeney." Martin's lips pursed as he spoke. "Some ambitious reporter is trying to call it a serial attack on priests."

"Shit," Smitty said.

"No kidding. I need to make a statement, and fast. What have we got?"

Cancini opened his notebook and read from the notes he'd already called in. "Paramedics arrived within twelve minutes after the 911 call. A neighbor called it in after hearing the gunshot. That same neighbor said they heard a car take off down the street immediately after the shot. I did a check on the area and there were two other shootings in that neighborhood in the last year. One was a domestic. The second shooting was a confirmed drive-by."

Martin sat forward. "We know all that already. Is there anything new?"

"No."

"Fine. That's how we're going to play it then. An unrelated drive-by. Are we clear?"

Cancini slumped down in the chair, his arms crossed.

Smitty cocked his head at his partner. "What is it?"

"I don't know." Cancini thought about his conversation with Julia. There was no real evidence that Father Joe had been targeted, and yet . . . . "We have one dead priest and another injured. Both shootings. The priests happen to be friends. They're planning to meet for breakfast the morning the first is shot. Two days later, the second priest is shot. Sounds like an awfully big coincidence to me."

Martin scowled at Cancini. "With that kind of talk, we'll have reporters crawling all over this story."

Smitty raised a hand. "Coincidences aside, there are too many inconsistencies to link the shootings without knowing more." Cancini watched his young partner tick through his fingers one by one. "First of all, Father Holland was shot at close range in an empty church. Somebody knew he was alone. Father Joe was shot on an open street in the middle of the day. Second, although we can't know this for sure, it's probable that whoever shot Father Holland knew him or was hired by someone who knew him. We can't make those assumptions with Father Joe. Drive-bys are not unheard of in that neighborhood. Third, Father Holland was shot at close range, no question to kill. In Father Joe's case, the shooter fired from some distance we haven't yet determined and hit him in the thigh, hardly fatal."

"Good." Pleased, Martin made notes. "I can use that."

Cancini stared down at the floor. Everything his partner said made sense, but his stomach churned.

"And there's the cross," Smitty said.

Cancini frowned. "What about it?"

"Assuming the killer painted it as a calling card, the murder had to be personal, like a message."

Martin seized on Smitty's theory. "That's right. The shooting of your friend looks random. No calling card. No message. Not connected."

"Just because it's not obvious doesn't mean there's no message."

Martin snorted. "We're not looking for messages. At least not ones that need to be shared outside this office. I agree with Smitty. For now, we stick to the assumption the shootings are unrelated. That's how we'll play it at the press conference. Understood?" Both detectives agreed. "One more thing," the captain said. "Have they found the bullet that hit your friend yet?"

Cancini shook his head. "Not yet. We've got a team searching the perimeter of the church, the trees, the fence, anywhere the bullet could've lodged. Maybe we'll get lucky."

"Keep me posted," the captain ordered.

Walking out of the captain's office, Smitty said, "Mrs. Harding is here for her second interview. Are you ready?"

Cancini ran his fingers over his head, brushing up the short dark hair. "Ready as I'll ever be."

Erica blinked when they entered, her hand rising to her throat. A box of tissues and a Coke sat in the middle of the table. Neither had been touched.

"Thanks for coming in, Mrs. Harding. Hope you haven't been waiting long," Cancini said.

"Not too long. I left work a little early." She bit her lower lip, her heart-shaped chin quivering. "I don't know what else I can tell you, but if there's any way I can help . . ."

Cancini asked a few basic questions, studying her from under his lashes. Even under heavy makeup, dark circles hung under her eyes. An unnatural pink color on her cheeks only accentuated her pallid skin. She wore a long skirt and a turtleneck that rose to her chin. Matronly pearl earrings were clipped at her ears. Her ash-blond hair fell across one eye, partially hiding the left side of her face. It reminded him of a pinup from the World War II era. He turned the questioning to the church's finances.

"I think the church used an outside accountant for the big stuff." She touched one large pearl. "Mr. Henderson is on the church financial council. He's a parishioner and works at a bank. The council met once a month and went over stuff. I usually took notes and typed the minutes."

Cancini opened the file he'd placed on the table. "Do you remember last week's meeting?"

"Yes."

"Good. Do you recall Father Holland's explanation for funding the stained glass window repairs?"

Her hand moved up to her hair, touching it where it fell over her face. "I think he said something about a donation. Is that a problem?"

Cancini avoided the question. "Why didn't you tell us about the donation yesterday?"

"I didn't know it was important."

"You told us he was worried about money. Were you lying, Mrs. Harding?"

She sucked in her breath. "No. He was always worried about money. At least I thought he still was."

"Father Holland was also looking to get quotes from landscapers, wasn't he?"

Her chin tilted higher. "The property grounds hadn't been cared for in years."

"Do you remember him asking for an estimate to get the steeple refurbished?"

She twisted her ring faster and licked her lips. "I think he did."

Cancini pulled out an income statement from the previous month and placed it on the table. "Did you think it was odd that one day the church was in financial straits and the next, it had an anonymous donation?"

"I—I don't know."

"Did you have any idea who the anonymous donor might be?" Cancini asked.

She shook her head slowly. "Should I?"

He smiled at the woman. "I'd gotten the impression you were sort of his right-hand woman, Mrs. Harding. Several people have told me how much he relied on you."

"That's true, I guess."

"So I thought he might've confided in you."

Her lips turned down. "We did work closely together, Detective, but not on church finances. I helped with the administrative details of running the parish. I helped him stay organized. He struggled with that a bit. I created and maintained the church Web site. I told you this yesterday."

"But surely you were curious? At least a little?"

Her skin darkened, cheeks flushed. "I—I might've been a little curious, but I didn't ask. I would never do that."

Cancini considered the woman across the table. Rising, he faced the one-way glass. He'd asked Bronson to observe, see if he could pick up on anything, and it couldn't hurt for her to know someone was watching. "Mrs. Harding, how much do you know about Father Holland's past?"

"His past? You mean before he came to St. William?"

"Yes. Anything about his youth, schooling, friends."

The pinched lines around her mouth eased. "He grew up here in D.C. Never knew his dad." She recounted his early youth, the shabby apartments, the poverty, his mother's growing addiction. "I heard him say once that after his mother died, he lived on the streets." Cancini and Smitty exchanged a glance. This would have been when Father Joe lost touch with him. "Can you imagine how horrible that must have been? I think that's why he cared so much about helping the people in the community. He was one of them." Her voice cracked and her body seemed to fold into itself. Clutching a wadded-up tissue in her hands, she rocked gently in the chair. After a few moments, her shoulders stilled. "I'm sorry."

Cancini cleared his throat. "Take your time. Just a few more questions, if you don't mind." She nodded. "One thing we've been wondering about is whether or not Father Holland had any friends."

"Friends? I've never thought about it." Her brows screwed up. "I guess most of the regular members of the parish were friends. He was invited every week to someone's house for dinner. Priests don't really earn a lot of money, you know, and they spend their lives serving church and God. They get housing usually and a small salary, but every little bit helps."

Cancini paced the room. He knew Father Joe relied on the generosity of parishioners, too. He enjoyed the meals, but he also called it outreach. Getting to know his parishioners was one of his favorite aspects of his service. "Did he ever mention any other friends outside of parishioners?"

"Not really. I know he was friendly with another priest. I met him a few times when he came by the church to visit. His name is Father Sweeney."

"Any of his old friends from his childhood ever stop by? Did he ever mention anyone?"

"No. I don't think so." Her eyes widened. "Wait. There was someone who called once—definitely not a parishioner from St. William. He didn't ask for Father Holland. He asked for Matty. I remember that. I'd never heard anyone call Father Holland Matty before. I asked what it was about and he said, 'old times.' His name was Charlie or Carl or something that started with a C. I—I might have overheard Father Holland tell him not to call again." She blushed and explained, "Normally, I wouldn't have been listening. I'm not an eavesdropper. It's just that he'd seemed mad when I told him about the man on the phone. Father Holland never got mad. It was just so odd to me." She angled her head, recounting the call. "He picked up the extension in his office and I heard him tell the man never to call again. He didn't even say hello. I think he knew I could hear him then because he got up and shut the door. After that, I didn't hear anything." She looked back at the detectives, face sheepish. "I did ask him about it later, who the man was, but all he would say was it was someone he knew a long time ago. That was it."

Smitty's pen hovered over his notebook. "Did this person ever call again?"

"Not that I know of. Do you think it means anything?"

Cancini ignored the question, asking his own. "When did this man call? How long ago?"

She sat up a little straighter in her chair. "Two weeks. Three. I'm so sorry. It really didn't seem important at the time."

"It's fine. We can check the phone records. Did Father Holland say or do anything unusual after he hung up?"

Erica frowned. "Now that I think about it, he did go out for coffee as soon as he came out of his office."

"Did he say where?"

"No."

"How long was he on the phone?"

"A couple of minutes maybe."

"Did he seem agitated or upset when he went out?"

"I don't think so." She looked at both of them, apologizing again. "I'm sorry. I really don't remember."

"It's okay," Smitty said. "You've been very helpful."

Her lips trembled. "Really? I'm glad."

Cancini helped her to her feet. "That's all for today, Mrs. Harding. If we have any more questions, we'll let you know."

She hooked her purse over her shoulder. "My husband is waiting for me."

Heads turned as she walked to the front desk, her hips swaying gently under the knee-length black skirt. She slowed when a large man held out his hand. She took it, bowed her head, and pressed into him. He placed his large hands on the small of her back and buried his head in her hair.

"Big guy," Cancini commented after they'd gone. "Looks strong enough to hurt someone."

"Did you notice the bruise on the lady's face, the one near her temple?" Bronson asked, coming up behind them.

Cancini had and said so. "Yeah. Good observation."

"Still buy the klutzy excuse?" Smitty asked, voice strained.

Nothing about Erica Harding seemed klutzy. If anything, she moved with the grace of a former dancer. Cancini's forehead creased. The purple marks on her arm. The fresh bruise at her temple. Cancini frowned. "What do you think?"

He shook his head and walked to the whiteboard, eyeing the line connecting Father Holland to Erica Harding. His head throbbed. He drew a new line to the outer loop, one that extended to Erica's husband, Sonny Harding.

Chapter Twenty-three

"You sure you don't want me to come in?" Smitty stood with his long legs spread apart, his hands thrust in his pockets.

Cancini glanced down the hall at the closed door. A uniformed cop stood just outside the room, his arms folded across his chest. Martin had reluctantly agreed to the guard, but Cancini knew Father Joe would be unprotected outside the hospital. His stomach knotted. "I need a few minutes on my own."

"Martin won't like it."

Cancini's head jerked around. "I don't need a babysitter."

Pink spots appeared on Smitty's pale cheeks, but his even tone never wavered. "I didn't say I was. I'm your partner. We're both on this investigation. You're the lead, but we have to stick together."

Cancini looked away. Smitty was right and he was only doing his job, but Cancini had his own line of questions for the old man that had nothing to do with the murder or the shooting. There were still things he didn't understand, couldn't get his mind around. *He was like a son to me.* If Holland was like a son to Father Joe, what was Cancini? His stomach lurched and he faced his partner. "I need to see him alone. Just for a few minutes."

Smitty held his gaze. If he could read the open need behind Cancini's insistence, he didn't let on. "Five minutes, then I'm coming in."

"Fifteen."

"Ten. That's all. I have to be there when you question him. It's not about Martin. It's about the investigation." Smitty's voice softened. "It's what you would say to me if the situation were reversed."

Cancini nodded once, his shoulders loosening. Ten minutes would have to do. Cancini glanced over at the nurses behind the long desk. A young brunette, hands moving slowly across a keyboard, watched them from under her lashes. He jerked a thumb toward the brunette. "You should make good use of the ten minutes. That nurse over there's been watching you."

"Maybe she's been watching you . . ." Smitty said, even as he raised a hand in her direction.

"Sure she has," he scoffed. "Not unless she has a thing for cranky cops old enough to be her father." He left Smitty with a smile on his face.

Father Joe lay propped up in bed, his face turned toward the night sky. His round belly rose and fell under the crisp white sheet. The monitor next to the bed glowed in the dimly lit room. Cancini pulled a chair close to the bed. He reached out, took one of the old man's hands, and covered it with his. Father Joe stirred, his eyelids fluttering. The priest mumbled and licked his lips, the last of the drug-induced sleep falling away.

"Hey," Father Joe said. "You're here."

Cancini squeezed his hand. "Can't get rid of me that easily."

The priest attempted to sit up, but grimaced. "Oomph," he grunted.

"Are you okay?" Cancini asked, leaning in close. "Do you want me to get the nurse?"

"No, no. It's fine. Just moving is a little difficult." He touched a hand to his leg. "They tell me I was lucky. Nothing major hit. A flesh wound really." He smiled. "For once, it's a good thing I have some extra flesh."

Cancini sat back and returned the old man's smile. Typical of the old man to make light of his gunshot wound. Still, it didn't change the fact that he'd been shot. Recovery might be long and difficult for a man his age. He took Father Joe's hand again, the smile gone, his face somber. "I was worried when they told me you'd been brought in."

Father Joe's eyes fell on him, soft and sad. "So was I, but here I am."

Cancini searched the old man's face. "Father Joe, I need to ask you some questions."

"I can't tell you much. I didn't see anything."

"No. Smitty will come in for that. It's something else." His chest and face felt hot and he lowered his gaze. "I don't really know how to begin."

"Ah. Maybe I do the." The priest patted Cancini's hand. "You want to know why I never told you about Matthew."

The air went out of Cancini. As a boy, Cancini had turned to the priest for comfort, for guidance, for friendship. It had never occurred to him that another boy could have done the same or that their relationship wasn't special and unique. The bond, both paternal and familial, had given him strength through the most difficult of times. *He was like a son to me.* The words bounced around his head. It was as though the old man had deliberately kept his friendship with Father Holland a secret. Why? He sighed and raised his head. "Yes, I do."

"He asked me not to." The old man's head fell back on the pillow. He stared up at the ceiling, deep lines etched into his cheeks and forehead. "He saw you once, when he first came back, before he went away to college. He recognized you were a police-man and he asked me why you were there. I told him you were my very close friend. He asked me not to mention his existence at all. I promised." He reached out and touched Cancini's shoulder. "My relationship with Matt was different than with you." He paused. "When your mother was murdered, I ached for you and your father. Her loss touched us all, but none more than your father." He held up a hand. "I don't mean you didn't feel the loss or hurt any less. I only mean it was almost as though something in him died that day, too." Cancini blinked hard. "With your father's, uh, absence in your life, I was grateful to be there for you. I could not have known then that I would come to value our friendship so much, that I would be the one who needed you." He was quiet a moment, seeming to gather his thoughts. "Matthew and I were not friends in the same way. When he was just a boy, I tried to help him stay off the streets. Then I helped him get to college and seminary. I supported him in his quest to help his community. But I must be honest. I didn't always agree with everything he did or everything he was. He often acted impetuously or without thought for the consequences. There were times when he might have bent the definition of right and wrong." Cancini raised one eyebrow. "We had arguments, and in fairness, sometimes he lis-tened, sometimes he didn't. In his heart, though, he was a good man." His voice caught and he whispered, "I'm going to miss him very much." A single tear slipped from his eye.

Cancini held the priest's hand tight and remained silent. What had the old man meant when he said Matt acted without thought for the consequences? How exactly did he bend what was right and wrong? Most parishioners wanted to believe their priest was a saint, close to God. It was a common—although flawed—sentiment. Perhaps Father Holland was turning out to be a more complex person than he'd first realized.

"You still have questions?"

Cancini glanced at the closed door. "Yes." Holland's doctor had verified he'd written a prescription for Ativan; however, he'd refused to speak about Holland's anxiety, saying only that Matt insisted he had someone he could talk to about his problems. Cancini suspected the doctor was right. "He confided in you."

"He did."

"It could help me in the investigation into his murder."

"Possibly, it could. I can't say either way, but it doesn't matter. I'm afraid I'm going to disappoint you." A deep sadness tinged his words. "I wish I could change some of my choices—I do." He let out a long, shaky breath. "I can't tell you what we talked about because I wasn't just his mentor. I was also his confessor."

Chapter Twenty-four

2013

MATT PICKED AT the lint on his pants and leaned his head against the screen of the confessional. "Things had already been going downhill. We weren't talking much anymore. I never should have gone that night." He shuddered at the memory. "I just stood there, doing nothing . . ." His chest heaved with each breath. "I'm sorry if that disappoints you, Padre."

"It's not about disappointing me, Matthew."

"Isn't it?" He heard Father Joe sigh. "I know, I know. You don't have to say it." Matt leaned back against the chair and folded his arms in close. He swallowed the lump in his throat. "It's just that no matter how many times I talk about this with you, I still feel guilty, like maybe I could have done something differently."

"Matthew, are you sure you want to keep telling me these things?"

It was an old conversation, and Matt knew that Father Joe would never judge, but sometimes he wondered. Even so, there was no mistaking the love and concern in the old man's voice. It was unfair to continuously put the man in this awkward position, but it couldn't be helped. And in a way, the older priest had asked for it.

He closed his eyes, the past as close as the present. Barely in his teens, he hadn't yet understood the power of reconciliation. Father Joe had taken him to religious education classes, but his mind had drifted. It was something about confessing your sins and God was supposed to forgive you just like that. He'd snorted out loud when he'd heard that one. That's not how the real world worked. If he confessed even a little of what he'd done, he'd be locked up in juvie. The whole thing seemed stupid. And why did Father Joe sit behind that screen, as though they both didn't know who was on the other side?

His first time, he'd folded his arms across his chest.

"Is someone there?" Father Joe had asked.

"Yeah, it's me."

Father Joe had explained again how it worked. Then Father Joe had told him to be honest and everything would be all right. The old man meant well. But could he trust him? He'd decided to test him, see where it went.

"I stole money from the collection plate," he'd said.

The silence had been brief. "How much did you steal?"

"Ten dollars."

"Do you want to say why?"

"Do I have to?"

"No."

"Then I'm done." Father Joe had given him his penance, blessed him, and he'd left. On the next Sunday, he was asked to assist with the collection. At his next confession, he asked, "Did you tell anyone about me stealing money from the collection plate?"

"No, Matthew. God has forgiven you, and what's said in the confessional cannot leave here."

"What if I told you I stole again this Sunday?"

"You would be forgiven, but I don't think you did."

"How do you know I didn't?"

"I don't know. I just don't believe you did."

The boy had frowned. "So, let me get this straight. No matter what I tell you, no matter how bad, you won't tell anyone."

"If you come to make reconciliation, I am bound by the sacrament. I cannot tell anyone."

"Even if you wanted to?"

"Even then."

Wide-eyed, he'd sat dumbfounded. Then it had dawned on him. Going to confession was like a code, like a street code. Father Joe couldn't rat him out. It was against the rules. Instead, he offered forgiveness. Matt didn't know why, but he felt better, lighter.

"Matthew, are you still there?"

Father Holland blinked and the past receded. "Sorry, I was thinking about what you said." The memory gone, he felt the burden of unconfessed sins. They both knew he could find someone else, but he wouldn't. The confessional was where he went to cleanse, to feel whole again. And it had to be with Father Joe, the man who knew who he was and where he'd come from. It saved time. "I need to do this and I need it to be you. It's the only way for me."

He heard the priest sigh again. "Are you ready for your penance?"

Matt clasped his hands together. "Yes, Father."

Chapter Twenty-five

SMITTY FOCUSED ON the road, silent, lips pressed together. He turned the car and they sped past a dozen boarded-up row houses that rose like shadows from under the streetlamps. After a few blocks, the row houses gave way to short, squat apartment buildings with small, rectangular windows. Ahead, an illuminated Washington Monument pierced the skyline. Lines creased Smitty's brow, and the long fingers of his hands opened and closed over the steering wheel.

Cancini stared unseeing out the window. He understood Smitty's frustration, shared it even. Father Joe had been able to tell them very little about the shooting. He'd seen nothing and heard nothing until the shot rang out. His leg had buckled and he'd fallen. He'd looked up to see a dark sedan speeding down the street, but he couldn't tell them the make or model. His face had been blank when they'd asked if he'd caught any of the license plate.

Smitty pulled into the precinct lot and slammed the gear into park. He made no move to get out of the car. His fingers tapped the steering wheel.

"Spit it out," Cancini said.

"He told you something before I came in the room, didn't he? Are you going to tell what it is?"

"You think I'm holding something back."

The words hung in the air. Smitty rubbed the tips of his long fingers with his thumb. "Are you?"

The older detective let out his breath. He didn't know anything that changed the evidence they had. He didn't have any new leads. All he'd learned was that their victim was having regular confession sessions with Father Joe. Without a more intimate knowledge of those conversations, he couldn't justify betraying Father Joe's confidence. "Not the way you mean."

Smitty faced Cancini. "You didn't say a word when I questioned him about the shooting."

"You were doing a good job. I had nothing to add."

"Or you already knew everything he was going to say." Smitty shook the hair from his forehead. His blue eyes fixed on Cancini. "I have to ask you. What did you talk about before I came in?"

"We talked about his relationship with Father Holland. He told me they were close, but we already knew that."

"Anything else?"

"Nothing important. They're going to keep him another night to watch his blood pressure."

"That's all?"

Cancini was quiet a moment. The old man had always been devout and had always been stubborn. Being shot had not changed that. "You can't ask me about his confessions, Michael," he'd said, hands clasped across his belly. "I won't tell you anything. I will not break my vows."

"Even if it could help us find his murderer?" Cancini had asked.

The old man had blinked only once. "Even then."

Cancini had been disappointed but not surprised. There were things about the Catholic faith he would never understand but was forced to accept. Father Joe, for better or for worse, would never break his word.

The priest had shivered under his sheet. "I must ask a favor of you now."

Cancini had rubbed Father Joe's hands, warming the old man's flesh. "Let me guess. You'd rather I not mention the confessions at all."

"It wouldn't change anything. All priests go to confession. I go to confession. But there are some who would not understand, who might misinterpret that even priests have sins to confess." Cancini had pulled back. "You don't like it?"

"No, Father, I don't. I'm not going to promise you I won't say anything. If it seems important, I won't have any choice. He may have told you something, especially recently, that could be the break we need in our investigation."

The old man had shrugged. "I couldn't say. You will find his murderer, Michael. I have faith in you."

"I hope you haven't misplaced it this time, Father."

"Never." Father Joe tipped his chin toward the door. "When do you expect your partner?"

"Any minute. I know you're tired. I'm sorry."

"There is nothing to apologize for." He'd laid his head back again, and white tufts of hair fanned across the pillow. "It is sometimes a terrible world we live in. Good men are gunned down and lives are lost. It makes me sad." He looked out the window into the darkness, words of the past spilling out. "When Matthew came home, after he finished seminary, he was disappointed to see that his neighborhood had gotten even worse. The drugs, the prostitutes. I tried to warn him, but he would not be dissuaded. He felt it was his mission from God, no matter the consequences."

Cancini had frowned. It seemed the consequences were high, and Holland's mission had left him dead. Was that what the old man had feared all along?

Smitty cleared his throat, and Cancini was jolted back to the present. He considered his young partner. There was nothing to be gained by sharing the knowledge of the confessions without their substance. Father Joe was right. All priests went to confession, and Holland was no exception. As evidence, it meant nothing. "That's all. He didn't tell me anything we can use." He paused and added, "But I wish like hell he had."

Chapter Twenty-six

"I GOTTA TELL you, Captain. This guy, he might've been a priest, but he had a way with the ladies, if you know what I mean . . ." Bronson raised his eyebrows.

"Don't be an ass, Bronson," Martin said.

Cancini stifled a grin and peeked at his watch. Martin loved meetings—the more participants the better—counting the time as hands-on involvement in the investigation. For fun, he liked to call them at seven in the morning. While Cancini didn't mind, Bronson looked like he could use an entire pot of coffee on an IV drip.

Bronson shifted in his chair, red splotches erupting on his fleshy cheeks. "For one thing, since Holland took over as permanent priest, membership has doubled."

"So?"

"Almost eighty percent of those were women. All ages, too. They all wanted to come and see the good-looking priest. One guy said it was turning into St. Wilhelmina Church." He chuckled once.

Martin's forehead creased. "I get it. What else?"

Bronson's smile faded. "It wasn't just at the services. They started a ladies' Bible study on Wednesday mornings. Holland would come in at the end, have coffee and such. Got pretty popular according to a couple of the regulars." He cleared his throat. "The secretary was there, too."

Martin's voice grew strained. "So the guy was good-looking and the ladies' Bible study was popular? Where the hell are you going with this, Bronson?"

Bronson stuck out his chin. "The husband. That's where I'm going with this."

"What husband?" the captain asked.

"I think he means the secretary's husband." Cancini leaned forward as he spoke. "Sonny Harding."

"Yeah." Bronson twitched, his voice a whine. "You told me to watch him, let you know if anything seemed weird, so . . ."

Martin's head swiveled around to Cancini. "Why is Bronson watching this man and why is this the first I've heard of it?"

Cancini ignored Martin, his focus on Bronson. "And did something seem weird?"

"Not at first." Bronson shifted in his seat, his eyes darting between the captain and Cancini. "He takes the wife to work, picks her up every day. Lotta guys do that. Then I saw he drives her to the grocery store and waits. Same with the hairdresser. Then I heard about the Bible study." He paused and licked his lips. "On Wednesdays, he brings her to work like always. At ten, the Bible study starts. A couple of the ladies who went said the husband started showing up, waiting for his wife. When she comes out of the meeting, they talk, then he leaves."

Cancini made a few notes. "What time does he drop her off in the mornings?"

"Eight-thirty."

"Maybe he just stuck around on Wednesdays."

"Nah. The other ladies said he wasn't there when they would go into the meeting, but he was standing right at the door when they came out."

"So he would wait for his wife, talk, and then leave. Anyone say if he seemed angry? Anything unusual?"

Bronson shook his head. "But I did hear more than once that maybe the husband wasn't too fond of the deceased."

Martin leaned forward, irritation forgotten. "In what way?"

"The ladies said Father Holland tried to talk to him a couple of times, but the husband wouldn't look at him and barely said a word. They thought it looked like the secretary might've been embarrassed. A couple people told me she seemed nervous about everyone watching. She would take him out of the church, they'd talk, and he'd leave. Every week for the last couple of months."

Cancini made a few more notes, then looked over at Smitty. "Do we know if Mrs. Harding has a driver's license?"

"She does," Smitty said.

"How many cars do they own?"

"Just one, but St. William is only a short walk from the metro and about the same distance from their house."

"Technically, she doesn't need a ride to work?"

"Not technically, no."

Cancini closed his notebook and stood up. Martin stood with him. "Why don't you do a little more digging into Mr. Harding's background?"

"Got it," Bronson said, and left the conference room.

"Hold on a minute." Martin raised a hand when Cancini stood. "I'm curious. Why did you have Bronson watching the husband?"

"The wife seems to have a lot of injuries." Cancini knew he might have misjudged what he'd seen, but something about the lady felt off, felt like she was hiding something from them.

The captain's face was blank. "What does that mean?"

"She has a lot of bruises that don't seem to be explained. She's not a big woman and works in a church. It's not a physically demanding job. Her husband is big, muscular. She's either awfully accident-prone or . . ."

Martin chewed his lower lip, turning the words over in his mind. "You think this guy is using his wife as a punching bag?"

"Maybe."

"We just heard the husband didn't like our victim. Are you thinking maybe he's hitting his wife because he's jealous? Of a priest?"

"I don't know, Captain. That's what we're trying to find out."

"Just when you think you've heard it all . . ." Martin shook his head as he spoke. "Fine. Check the guy out." He pointed a finger at the detectives. "But I don't want you wasting a lot of time on this theory if you can't tie him to the e-mails. The guy who sent those, he's our killer." He swept his folder under his arm. "I'll expect an update at the end of the day."

The door swung shut behind him. Cancini's stomach rumbled and burned. The captain wasn't wrong. With the e-mails, they had evidence of threats and a relationship that appeared to have gone from mildly unfriendly to outright hostile in a hurry. *Follow the money.* The sudden increase in funds at the church was a giant red flag, too. Could Holland have been playing fast and loose with church money? Either way, neither the e-mails nor the church funds could be tied to Harding. At least not yet.

Chapter Twenty-seven

2013

CARLOS VEGA SLIPPED into the booth. "I'm here."

Matt inhaled and sat back against the hard plastic of the bench seat. Goose bumps rose on the back of his neck. It had been close to a decade since he'd seen his former friend. A single gold rope glittered against the dark hair that peeked out over the collar of his shirt. His hair, shiny with oil, was tucked behind his ears. A thin white line ran from his cheek to his chin, and tattoos decorated the insides of his muscular forearms.

Carlos looked around the diner, one heavy eyebrow arched. "I still don't know why you dragged me out to the middle of nowhere. We're city boys, Matty."

A waitress in a pair of stretch pants and a T-shirt set a cup and saucer on the table. Matt waited. She poured Carlos's coffee, refilled Matt's cup, and tossed two menus on the table. When she was out of earshot, Matt said, "I wanted to talk to you alone, without anyone around."

"Shit. You coulda just come to my crib for that." Carlos dumped three packets of sugar into his coffee. "My guys coulda waited outside."

Matt glanced out the window at the black Escalade with the tinted windows. How many others were with Carlos? Two? Three? He pulled his baseball hat lower. "I didn't want other guys around, even outside."

Carlos's eyes narrowed to slits. "Yeah? It's been a long time since you split. You in some kinda trouble, man?"

Matt shook his head. "No, nothing like that." He pulled aside the collar of his jacket, exposing the stiff clerical collar. "I'm a priest now."

His former friend flopped back against the bench. "Get the fuck outta here."

"No, it's true," Matt said with a sheepish grin. "Kinda surprised myself, actually."

"A priest? For real?"

"Yep. That's where I've been these last few years. Studying at seminary."

Carlos shook his head. "You mean like you went to school for that shit?"

Matt smiled. Carlos had always missed more school than most, his job on the streets requiring his presence, even as a teen. He had no use for the kind of education the teachers were giving. "Yeah. I went to school."

"Shit," Carlos said again, drinking his coffee. "You comin' back to the hood?"

"That's why I wanted to talk to you."

They sat in silence for a moment. Carlos, friendly one moment, was suddenly all business, expression wary. "What do you want?"

"Nothing."

"Fuck that, man. Everybody wants somethin'. You didn't haul my ass to this shithole after I haven't laid eyes on you in who knows how many years 'cause you don't want nothin'." His face hardened with each word.

Matt nodded. He did want something. "Fair enough." He licked his lips and let out a long breath. "I want to be left alone."

Pink crept across Carlos's dark skin. "What the fuck does that mean?"

Matt flinched, but pressed forward, keeping his voice low. "It means I'm going to be taking over at St. William. That's my assignment. I'm the new pastor there." He paused, watching Carlos's face. "It means I can't go back to my old life."

"Or your old friends." Carlos spoke through a clenched jaw, his words clipped. "You too good for me now? What you really want is for me stay away, act like we don't know each other so I won't mess with your priest image." He shook his head again. "Fuck. You think you know a guy." He pushed the cup and saucer across the table, the black liquid spilling over the sides. "I thought we were friends. Wasn't I there when your mama took the pipe? Didn't I help you pay the rent? Didn't I stick around even when that priest wanted to put you in a foster home?" Carlos's words came faster. The white of his scar glowed against his skin. "Who the hell gave you a place to live and a job? It was me, you shithead. I don't give a fuck if you're a priest. Now you want me to act like we don't know each other? Is that the fuckin' reason you brought me out here?"

Matt held Carlos's gaze until the other man threw up his hands and slid out of the booth. Matt reached in his pocket and pulled out an envelope. He laid it on the table, smoothed out the creases, and slid it toward Carlos. "I want you to take this."

Carlos sat down again, black eyes guarded. He picked up the envelope and turned it over between his thick fingers. "This some kind of trick?"

"No trick."

Tearing open the envelope, Carlos pulled out a check. "What the hell is this?"

"It's all I have left," Matt said. "You're right. You were there for me. Helped me stay alive, brought me into the business."

"It's my business now."

"I heard."

The sharp lines of Carlos's face softened. "We had good times didn't we, Matty? We were small-time, but it was fun, right? Good weed, hot ladies." He laughed loudly, drawing the attention of the waitress.

"Yeah, good times," Matt said, voice quiet, head turned away. It had been good for a while, but that was a long time ago in another life. There'd been weed and girls, but they were mostly Carlos's idea and Carlos's problem. He'd never noticed Matt slipping out the door, Matt disappearing until the party was over, or Matt cleaning up the mess after. Carlos had embraced the life they made on the streets. Matt remembered doing what he had to do. He nodded at the check in Carlos's hand. "I used what I needed for seminary, but the rest is for you." He hesitated a moment, touching the collar at his neck. "I don't need that now."

Carlos read the numbers on the check a second time. "How'd you have so much left, man?"

"I invested some of it when I turned eighteen."

"You invested some of it?" He flopped back against the seat. "Man, you're just full of surprises, ain't you? First the priest shit, and then you're some kinda stockbroker?" Matt raised one eyebrow. "Yeah, I know what a stockbroker is. I got one a couple o' years ago. Seen too many guys blow it all."

Matt nodded. He wasn't surprised. Carlos played the part, talked the part, but he'd never been stupid. He played hard and he worked hard. "Glad you're doing well," Matt said, and he meant it.

"I'm doing fuckin' great." Carlos grinned and twisted a shiny gold watch on his wrist. He tossed the check on the table. "I don't need this. But you already knew that." His smile faded. "Can't erase who you are, Matt, or what you done. You can't get clean by givin' it away."

Matt's head bowed. "I can try."

"Won't work." Carlos slid from the booth and stood over his old friend. "Invest it. Use it for somethin' good if it makes you feel better." He tossed a hundred-dollar bill on the table. "I'll leave you alone if you want, but only if you give me your word."

Matt raised his head, pulse racing. "My word?"

"You keep your mouth shut."

Matt breathed in and out. Wayne, the crew boss back in the day, hadn't been pushed out. He'd been forced out when his blood had been emptied in the backroom of that crappy bar. Matt had thought it was just another handoff, but Carlos had always been ambitious. Matt lifted his napkin and swiped at the beads of sweat dotting his upper lip. "I never said anything."

"Yeah? You left me hangin', Matty. How the fuck was I s'posed to know what you would say after you skipped out on the job, skipped out on me? You ran, left town when the shit hit the fan. Things got hot and you just disappeared. Poof. Police start comin' around. Asking questions." All trace of nostalgia had faded from his voice. He paused, then picked up the envelope and pocketed the check. "On second thought, I think I'll hold on to this for insurance." His lips turned up, the corner of his mouth twisting the scar. "And I better not ever hear you ratted me out, man. Being a priest ain't gonna save you." Carlos leaned close until his breath brushed against Matt's ear. "You do, man, and you're fuckin' dead."

THE LAST SIN D.

Chapter Twenty-eight

"TAKE ME THROUGH it again." Cancini squinted and pinched the bridge of his nose with his fingertips.

"Maybe this will help." Landon tapped the keys and pulled up a spreadsheet. "This is a list of all Holland's accounts and current balances."

Cancini struggled to understand what he was seeing. There were five accounts in all, each with a string of numbers. A column to the right listed the current balance in each one. He shook his head. "I don't know what you're trying to show me. I don't see any money."

"That's right," Landon said, nodding fervently. "Because there is no money." He looked at Cancini, eyes wide and expectant. "It's gone."

Cancini pulled out a chair. "I don't understand. I get an anonymous text telling me to follow the money. Then you tell me Holland was planning to pay for repairs at the church, but now you're saying there isn't any money."

"He moved it." Terry tapped the keys again. Another page

came up with a ten-digit account number across the top. This one did have a balance, a six-digit balance. "This is a foundation set up by Father Holland a few weeks ago." The forensic accountant spun his chair around to face the detective. "Wanna guess where it came from?"

A dull pain gathered at the base of Cancini's neck. He hated guessing games. "No, Terry. Just tell me. Where did the money come from?"

The words tumbled out of Landon's mouth as he described a long history of accounts and large deposits and equally large withdrawals. The young man's excitement rolled off him in waves. When he finished, Cancini sat still, unsure he'd heard the young man correctly. "Hold on. I need a minute to think." He stood. "Is there coffee around here?"

Landon pointed to the break room.

Cancini filled a Styrofoam cup and drank as much as he could stand without burning the roof of his mouth. He topped off the cup and sat down again. "What you're describing sounds an awful lot like money laundering."

Landon's triumphant smile filled his young face. "Exactly. This account, the 2144 account, was used to funnel the money. There's no other possible explanation."

"Jensen?"

"I think Landon's right. I've worked a couple of fraud cases, and the cash in and out is the same."

Cancini didn't know if it was the coffee or the dull ache at the base of his skull making his head buzz, but he knew it had been a long time since he'd been this blindsided. "Let's assume for now you're right. This 2144 account was used for money laundering. The balance is zero now, right?"

"Right. Actually, that account is closed now, but the money for the foundation came from this account."

Cancini's head pounded. "How much did Father Holland transfer to this foundation?"

"About a half-million dollars."

Jensen whistled. Landon nodded. "There's more. The 2144 account was opened on his eighteenth birthday. That first deposit was five thousand dollars. All in cash. Not really enough to raise eyebrows but unusual, right?"

Landon clicked on another page, and Cancini squinted at the screen. "Go on."

"Over the next month, he added to it each week, always less than five thousand at a time, but after a few months, the balance stood at $33,824." He pointed at the screen. "These two accounts. These are investment accounts. They also started at five thousand dollars each."

"Investment accounts?"

"Stocks. Holland did pretty well. Took some risks. Some not so great, but the ones that hit, hit big. He made money. Those profits he transferred back into the original account, the 2144. It grew steadily, and the only withdrawals during those next few years went to the college and seminary school he attended. After graduation, around the time he came back to D.C., the balance had dropped to just over eight thousand dollars."

Cancini looked at the dates. They coincided with the time Father Holland showed up on Father Joe's doorstep. He'd never asked the old man how Father Holland had paid for school. How had an eighteen-year-old kid come up with tens of thousands of dollars in cash? What had he been doing? "What else?"

"When he first returned to D.C., the 2144 account sat dormant, the balance unchanged outside of interest and fees. He opened another account at a branch closer to St. William." Landon touched the screen. "Any money he earned at St. William went into that account and paid his expenses. The balance was rarely over a couple thousand dollars." He changed the screen again. "Then two years ago there was a series of cash deposits to the 2144 account. Again, nothing that would send up alarms but adding up. Usually when it got close to a half million, the money went back out."

Cancini read the series of deposits and withdrawals. "Where did it go?"

"A security company based in Germany. Limited liability." Cancini raised an eyebrow. "It looks like all the transactions were done online. The company in Germany has an address but no phone. When I try to find it on Google Maps, this is what I get." He tapped the keys, bringing up a screenshot of an empty parking lot. "The company is a shell as far as I can tell."

Cancini rubbed his hand over his head again. Why would a priest be sending money to a shell company in Germany? And where the hell was the money coming from in the first place? He ignored the pounding in his head and clapped Landon on the back. "Thanks, Terry. Good stuff."

"You might not want to thank me yet."

Cancini's stomach flipped.

The young man at the computer flushed, his open face a light pink. "Father Holland's will. We found a copy in his safe deposit box." The sinking feeling in Cancini's belly grew. "In the event of his death, the foundation he created was to be managed by a single executor. There would be other trustees, but the executor would have the power of attorney to manage the money . . ." Landon looked at the floor. "Father Joe Sweeney."

Landon handed the copy to Cancini. The detective scanned the document and flipped to the last page. It had been witnessed and signed by a notary, Erica Harding. He looked again at the screen and the endless lines of numbers. Too many questions. Too many secrets. "Jensen," he said, "tell Smitty to pick up Erica Harding."

"What about Father Sweeney? Do you want me to bring him in, too?"

The old man was still weak, his blood pressure still too high. He needed to rest, but he wasn't just a witness anymore. Cancini swallowed. "Yes. And tell him to call his lawyer."

Chapter Twenty-nine

"I ALREADY TOLD you I don't know anything about the church's finances," Erica Harding said.

Cancini locked eyes with the secretary. "Or Father Holland's?"

"Or Father Holland's."

"I don't believe you."

"Believe what you like." She tossed her head and turned away. He studied her profile. The bruise at her temple had faded. She'd pulled her hair back into a high ponytail, elongating her graceful neck. One hand lay on the table next to a glass of water. Her left arm was pulled in close, held against her side.

Cancini pushed a manila file across the table. "Open it."

Her eyes went from him to the file. "What for?"

"You might find it interesting reading."

She huffed but reached out with her right hand. Minutes ticked by as she scanned the first page and then the remaining pages. Her fingers trembled when she reached the financials. Closing the file, she tried to feign indifference. "So?"

"You notarized these documents for Father Holland when he created his foundation."

"I'm a notary. That's one of the reasons I got the job. You never know when you're going to need one, and that gave me an advantage over the other applicants."

"What do you know about the foundation?"

"I know he named it after his mother." Her face softened. "That's one of the things the foundation was supposed to be for, women like his mother. He wanted to help them get clean, get them off the streets. Father Holland had been doing good work. He took food to people every day and gave out blankets in the winter. He would sit with folks when they were sick. Everyone knew what a good man he was. But he needed more money. There were so many people in need."

"What else do you know about the foundation?"

"That's it. He never talked about it again after I notarized the documents. I just assumed everything was okay." She looked from one detective to the other. "Was that wrong?"

Cancini cocked his head as though suddenly curious. "Did you know the anonymous donation of funds came from the foundation?"

The color drained from her face. "Should I have? I only notarized the last page for him. He asked me to do it. He asked me . . ." Her pink lips quivered as her voice faded.

"How many documents did you notarize for him?"

She stared down at the table, her right hand dropping into her lap. When she looked up, her eyes shone with tears. "A few I guess."

"Did you notarize his will?"

"I might have." She took a shaky breath. "I don't remember."

She glanced over at Smitty, who sat at the far end of the conference table. "I'm sorry."

Cancini ran his fingers along the edge of the table. "Larry Henderson handled the funds for the church. Is that right?"

"Yes."

"Were he and Father Holland close?"

She flushed again. "I wouldn't say they were close."

"Did they dislike each other?"

She brushed away the stray hair that had fallen from her ponytail. "Father Holland liked everyone." She hesitated a brief moment. "I guess sometimes they had disagreements, though."

"What kind of disagreements?"

She sighed. "Larry wanted every major expenditure approved by the financial committee. He's like that—a stickler for procedure. And he's always talking about building up a cushion for emergencies before spending money on the windows or the parking lot."

Cancini sat forward, his pen poised. "Mrs. Harding, you told us you took the notes at those meetings, but I didn't see anything about any disagreements in those minutes."

"I didn't think it was necessary."

"But Mr. Henderson and Father Holland did argue?"

"Sometimes, I guess."

"Did it ever get heated?"

She dropped her gaze, folding her arms in tight across her belly and chest. "Maybe once or twice."

Cancini's heart skipped a beat. "Recently?"

She nodded again. "Last week. There was that anonymous donation Father Holland talked about, the one he wanted to use to fix the stained glass."

"But Mr. Henderson didn't?"

"Oh, no, and he was thrilled with the money. He just thought there were more important things to fix first, like the heating system. I couldn't really blame him. It's pretty old, and to tell you the truth, it's really cold in there sometimes. But Father Holland wouldn't listen. Everyone knew he dreamed of making St. William beautiful again. Larry said it didn't matter if the church was beautiful if no one came because it was freezing cold inside. Father Holland laughed at that and . . . and Larry stormed out."

"Is it possible he could have been mad enough to want to kill Father Holland?"

Her hand fluttered to her neck, fingers wrapping around the gold cross that hung just below the hollow of her throat. She shook her head. "No, not Larry. He would never do anything like that. He does get angry, but it never lasts."

Cancini glanced over his shoulder at the one-way glass. He hoped whoever stood on the other side was already gathering some background on the angry Larry Henderson.

"Mrs. Harding, do you have a list of names of everyone who has served on that committee since Father Holland came to St. William?"

"Yes." Her voice shook as she spoke.

"Good. I'd like to get a copy of that."

Cancini scratched out a few more notes. A blanket of silence fell over the room while he reread the words he'd written. His image of the young priest kept shifting and changing. He didn't know what to think about the man. Where did the money come from? If he was laundering money, why? It didn't jibe with Father Joe's description or the one he was getting from Erica Harding.

Why did he really come back to the neighborhood that killed his mother? To do good or to do something else?

He cleared his throat and raised his head. "Mrs. Harding, one more thing." Cancini tapped his pen against his notepad. "Do you think it's fair to say Mr. Henderson didn't know the anonymous donation actually came from a foundation set up by Father Holland?"

"Yes, that's fair. Nobody knew."

Father Holland had been less than honest with his own committee. What else had he been less than honest about? "Is it also fair to say that Mr. Henderson might not have liked it?"

She let out a breath, the words soft as air. "Yes."

Chapter Thirty

The lawyer set his briefcase on the table with a thump. He took out a notebook, a black pen, and a bottle of water. After closing the briefcase, he placed it on the floor. "Gentlemen, my name is Ben Harvey. I've been retained by the diocese to represent Father Joseph Sweeney."

Father Joe hobbled to the table, juggling a pair of crutches as he dropped into a chair. Breathing more heavily than he should have, his face flushed pink and his forehead shone with perspiration.

The lawyer glanced down at his client. "Are you okay?" Father Joe nodded. "Good. Are we ready?"

Cancini retreated to the far end of the table. Although his presence had initially been discouraged, it was now thought he might be needed to coax a more complete response from the witness. And although he didn't really believe Father Joe would be any more forthcoming whether he was there or not, he did think the man needed to see a friendly face. It wouldn't be enough to know he was on the other side of a large pane of one-way glass.

Smitty sat across from the lawyer and the priest. Jensen,

Martin's idea of insurance, sat to his left. The video camera in the corner recorded every word.

"Thanks for coming in, Father Sweeney," Smitty said.

Harvey answered. "As I understand it, Detective Smithson, my client has already been very cooperative—without the benefit of my presence. He exercised poor judgment when he agreed to speak without the benefit of an attorney." The lawyer shot a stern look at Father Joe. "The diocese has determined that a lawyer should be present for all future interviews, if there are any."

Father Joe lowered his head, but not before Cancini caught a flash of irritation in the old man's face.

"Right," Smitty said, his tone neutral. He opened a file and pushed it across the table. Both Father Joe and the lawyer leaned in. "Have you ever seen this document before, Father Sweeney?"

The priest reached out and touched the first page. "No."

"A will?" Harvey asked.

"Father Holland's will," Smitty said. "Take a look."

The gray-haired lawyer picked it up, flipping page after page. When the lawyer got to the last page and the estimated value of the foundation, his lips twitched. Harvey turned away from the detectives, whispering in his client's ear. Father Joe's head jerked up, his eyes wide. The two men exchanged a few words until the lawyer dropped the document back on the table.

"Jog your memory?" Smitty pressed.

"He said he'd never seen it." Cancini watched Father Joe. His knuckles whitened as he held on to the table in front of him. "It's unusual, I'll agree," the lawyer continued, "but Father Sweeney would not be the first to be unaware he has been named in a will."

"Father Holland never spoke of this with you? Seems like he

would have," Smitty said, keeping his expression bland and his tone just south of accusatory.

Harvey rose and laid a bony hand on the priest's shoulder. "He already told you he didn't know about it. Do you doubt this man's word?"

Cancini watched the old man. His bulk seemed to sway in the chair, shifting under his lawyer's hand. Cancini went to him, kneeling at his feet. "Father Joe? Are you okay?" He took Father Joe's hands in his, rubbing them back and forth. After a moment, the priest blinked and looked around. "Are you okay?" Slow and dazed, Father Joe shook his head once. Cancini looked over at Jensen. "Can you get him a glass of water?"

A silence fell over the room until Jensen returned. When he brought in the glass, Cancini took it and brought it to the old man's lips. Father Joe sipped, then wrapped his hands around the cup and drank. He set the empty cup back on the table and looked up at Cancini. "Thank you."

"Are you all right?"

Father Joe nodded. "I will be. I just need a minute." He looked around the room. "I'm sorry."

The lawyer patted him on the shoulder. "As I'm sure you can gather by Father Sweeney's reaction, this news has taken both of us by surprise. Of course, he would like to cooperate, but I don't know what else he can do to help."

Smitty shifted in his seat and cleared his throat. "Like it or not, Mr. Harvey, that document could be thought of as providing motive."

"Motive?" The lawyer snorted. "Motive for what? The man has an alibi and he knew nothing about the will. Being named executor of a foundation isn't a crime."

"That may be, but right now, it's as good as anything else, and we only have your word he didn't know about the will."

The lawyer did not try to hide his skepticism. "You have got to be kidding. This has gone on long enough. If you need—"

"I didn't know about the will," Father Joe said, his voice weary, his skin ashen. "If I had, I would have insisted I be taken out of it."

Cancini coughed.

Smitty hesitated. "Let's say I believe you. What about the foundation?" Smitty leaned forward with each word. "Did you know Father Holland had this kind of money? Do you know where it came from?"

Father Joe held the young detective's gaze for only a moment, then looked briefly at Cancini before dropping his head. The lawyer whispered again in the old man's ear, then leaned over and picked up his briefcase.

Smitty battered him with questions. "Did you know about the money going in and out of his accounts for nearly two years? Did you know that's how he started this foundation?"

Shielding Father Joe with both his body and his words, the lawyer gave Smitty a stern look. "Gentlemen, that's it for today. Father Sweeney is extremely tired, and he is recovering from a gunshot wound." Harvey helped the priest to his feet and handed him his crutches. "Please contact me if you wish to speak with my client again." Jensen held the door and escorted them out.

After they were gone, Smitty gathered up the will and his notes. "He knew about the money."

Cancini sighed. Father Joe's non-answer was the same as an acknowledgment. "Yes, I think he probably did."

"What about the money laundering? Where the money came from in the first place?"

The same questions had already occurred to Cancini. Whatever was going on with the money was far from legal. The more he learned about Father Joe's relationship with Father Holland, the more he feared for him. "It's hard to say."

Smitty shook his head. "I'd feel better about it if he would tell us what he knows."

"He won't." Cancini didn't like it any better than his partner, but the old man would never knowingly break a vow.

"The shooting . . ." Smitty hesitated. "I'm starting to think maybe it wasn't so random after all."

Cancini understood the logic. If Holland had been involved in money laundering, he might have been involved with some unscrupulous people. Cancini's mind jumped from one theory to another, but without facts, they were only guesses. Even without facts, he had to wonder if the money was the reason Holland was murdered. And if Father Joe did know about the money laundering . . . Cancini shook the thought from his head.

"We might want to keep an eye on him," Smitty said. "Maybe talk to Martin about protection."

Cancini nodded, his blood running cold. The image of Holland, clad in his black robes and his blood spilled across the steps, sent a shiver up his spine. "I'll talk to him," Cancini said, finally.

Chapter Thirty-one

LARRY HENDERSON WIPED his forehead with a wadded-up hand-kerchief and pushed silver-framed glasses up on his nose. "I don't really know how I can help you." He shot worried looks at the tellers watching on the other side of the glass.

"Are you okay, Mr. Henderson?" Cancini asked. "You seem nervous."

The man shook his head. "No, I just don't know why you're here. I'm trying to run a bank here. There are customers . . ."

Smitty waved a hand and smiled. "No reason to worry. This won't take long. We just have a few questions," he said. "We're speaking to several St. William members who'd seen Father Holland in the few days before his death on Sunday."

"Oh. I guess that makes sense."

Smitty looked down at the notebook in his lap. "I've been told you had a finance council meeting at the church last week. Both you and Father Holland were there."

"That's true. There were six of us that morning, I think. We usually meet once a month or so, unless something unusual comes up."

"Unusual?"

"Like a heater breaking or flooding or something that requires a big expenditure."

Smitty pointed at two pictures that sat on the bookshelf behind Henderson. The faces of three children seated on colored blocks—the kind you saw at Sears or Penney's—stared back out from a large frame. A smaller picture sat next to the larger one, this one of a middle-aged woman with short dark hair, hands folded primly in her lap. "That your family?"

Henderson turned briefly. Cancini watched the man as he talked. His face changed, lightened. "My wife, Carmen, and my kids." What remained of his hair was combed straight back on his head, making him look older than his forty-three years. He was slim, with long, thin arms, and wore an inexpensive suit. The frayed cuffs of his shirt stuck out from the sleeves of his dark gray suit jacket. The desk was clear except for matching in boxes that contained neatly stacked papers.

"Looks like they keep you pretty busy," Smitty said.

Henderson smiled. "Oh, they do." He jerked his thumb at the picture of his kids. "That's an old photo, but it's one of my favorites. My wife keeps giving me new ones. I like that one though."

"How old are they now?" Smitty asked.

"My oldest is in high school and about to get his license. My wife's not happy about having to share a car, but you know how it is," he said with a shrug of his shoulder. "The girls are in middle school, full of drama." He chuckled. "It's no wonder I like the old picture so much, right?"

Cancini leaned forward, his face unsmiling. "I'm told you didn't like Father Holland much. Is that true?"

Henderson's laugh faded. He glanced at Smitty. "I don't know what you mean."

Cancini cocked his head to his shoulder. "I think you do, Mr. Henderson."

Looking away, the man bit his lip. After a moment, he raised his head. "It's not true that I didn't like Father Holland. I did. I do." He picked at the frayed cuff of his shirt. "When he came to St. William, he brought an excitement, an energy the church hadn't seen in a long time. You could feel it. We were all so thrilled to have him." He paused and took a breath. "I've been going to St. William since I was a boy. The neighborhood . . . it wasn't always so rough. There were good people there. My mother still lives just a few blocks from the church. Even with the crime and drugs, you can't pry her out of that place. I've tried to get her to move in with us, but she says she's lived in that house for almost fifty years, and she's not leaving unless it's with her feet in the air." He shook his head. "So we drive into town every Sunday to St. William. It makes Mom happy."

"What about you, Mr. Henderson? Does it make you happy?" Cancini asked.

He blinked, then spoke slowly. "Yes, most of the time anyway. Being a part of St. William is kind of like going home. And like I said, when Father Holland arrived, we all got excited again. He had such great visions for the church. He wanted to renovate. He wanted to do outreach. He wanted to fill the church. It was contagious."

Cancini sat back. "So you volunteered to serve on the finance committee."

"It made sense at the time. I'm in banking, and I wanted to help. For a long time, I was glad to do it."

"Not anymore?"

"Lately, I was struggling with my role."

"Because you weren't getting along with Father Holland?"

Henderson sighed and resumed picking at his thumb. "It wasn't the way you're making it sound. Father Holland was good for the church in so many ways, but he was also a dreamer. We all bought into that dream, but the reality was that everything he wanted cost money—money the church didn't have. And there were other issues. The heating system was barely hanging on."

Cancini raised one eyebrow. "As I understand it, there had been some money recently, from an anonymous donor. Shouldn't that have eliminated your worries?"

"No, and that's exactly my point. An anonymous donation is one thing, but it wasn't enough to cover the things Father Holland had in mind. He was soliciting estimates for windows and land-scaping and I don't know what else. To count on more . . ." Doubt crept into his eyes. "Where was it coming from? Who was this anonymous donor?" His voice rose with each word. "I didn't like it, and I told Father Holland that."

"And what did he say?"

Henderson frowned. "Say? He didn't say anything. He laughed at me and told me not to worry so much. Be grateful to God is what he said."

"And you didn't like that?"

"The truth is, I don't think God had anything to do with it."

"Oh?" Cancini's shoulders tensed. "What exactly do you mean by that, Mr. Henderson?"

The banker rose, moving to the glass wall. "We work with nonprofits all the time. I've seen anonymous donations, but they're typically a one-time deal. I couldn't understand how he could be sure the money wouldn't run out." He turned back to face the detectives. He licked his lips and gave one shake of his head as though making a decision. "I wanted to replace the windows, too, but at what cost? It wasn't right."

"What wasn't right, Mr. Henderson?"

"The anonymous donations." His voice dropped to a whisper. "The money. I think it was dirty."

Chapter Thirty-two

Friday, January 22: One Month Before the Day of

MATT PULLED OFF his collar and tossed it on the bed. He flopped down and stretched out his legs. It had been a long day. He held the collar up in the air and turned it over in his hands. How long had he been at St. William? Not long enough to accomplish what he wanted. He knew that. But other days, he thought maybe it was too long. Maybe he wasn't really cut out for this job.

He closed his eyes. There were days when it was hard to keep his vows, hold steady in his resolve. He was a man, after all. He had feelings. Yet he'd voluntarily signed up for this, for the very idea that his feelings were to be sacrificed. So far, he'd been able to do it, to keep the faith. But lately, it was getting harder. Her beauty was hard to ignore. And she was always there, wide-eyed, devoted. He sat up. There must be some secret, some way to ignore women and stay true that they'd forgotten to teach him in seminary. It shouldn't be this hard.

He shook off the thoughts. He had a bigger problem. Carlos. He should have known he couldn't trust Carlos to leave him alone.

Matt had asked him nicely, and still he'd broken his word. Sure, he'd stayed away from the church, stayed away from Matt physically, but he'd done something much worse. It must have been the check. How could Matt have been so stupid? He shouldn't have given it to Carlos, should have just handed him cash, but it never occurred to him that Carlos would hack his account. Matt didn't know exactly how he'd done it—Carlos had never been that good with computers. It didn't matter how, though. Carlos had somehow been able to make deposits and withdrawals in Matt's name. The bed creaked when Matt rolled over and opened the drawer of his nightstand. He pulled out a stack of bank statements and scanned the numbers and dates. Almost two years of transactions. The amount of money was obscene. He groaned. He couldn't go to the police now. It didn't matter that he hadn't known about it initially. Ignorance couldn't protect him.

Hiding his anger and shock hadn't been easy in front of the bank manager, but he was glad now. At first, the banker couldn't understand why he needed the statements. "But we've been sending you online statements. Is there a problem with your online banking services?"

"No, no," he'd answered. Matt had gone on to assure the banker it only a matter of printer problems and he needed the financial statements that day. Relieved, the banker had printed the statements without another question.

If only the man had really known who was using those services. Things might not have been so pleasant. Not that it mattered now. Matt looked at the latest balance. It wasn't much. Still, if the last several months were a good indication, there would be a hefty deposit hitting the account in the next three days, then another, and then another. Things would be different this time. He was ready. He'd asked Carlos nicely. Now he was done being nice.

Chapter Thirty-three

CANCINI DROPPED A heavy file folder on the table. "Bronson, tell me what you've got."

The slick-haired detective pursed his lips. "Not anything that helps."

"Tell me anyway."

The detective lifted a rounded shoulder. "I checked out Henderson like you asked. He's not rich, but no big debts or problems I could find. Alibi's solid. Picked up his mother for Sunday dinner at five and drove her home at nine. Stayed and had a cup of coffee. Left at nine-thirty. Home by ten. There all night until about seven-thirty the next morning when his kids left for school. He drove straight to work and was there a few minutes before eight a.m."

"Any chance he slipped away from dinner and got back in time to take his mother home at nine?"

"Nah. The neighbor came by and joined them for dessert. Plenty of witnesses." He licked his lips. "I can look some more if you think I need to . . ."

Cancini shot him a look. "Do you think you need to?"

"No."

"Neither do I." Smitty cleared his throat, and Cancini looked up to see him nodding once in Bronson's direction. Bronson and Jensen were actually doing passable work, but wasn't that their job? Did they need gold stars, too? Cancini ignored his partner and plucked a report from the file. "Let's move on. This is the transcript from the secretary's last interview. I've also taken a look at the tape from that session and the others. As we discussed, the lady seems to be a little accident-prone. Did you talk to any neighbors or friends?"

Bronson pulled out his notes. "They live in a town house over in Arlington. It's one of those old neighborhoods that's trying to be new again. Mostly young couples like the Hardings. I talked to the neighbors on each side. The lady in the end unit said she didn't really know the Hardings at all. She works nights and sleeps during the day so she has a different schedule. The ones on the other side—"

"Wait," Cancini interrupted. "They're in a town house so they share walls, right?"

"Right. On the other side is a couple like the Hardings, no kids, about the same age. Now those neighbors, they were more than a little curious about why I was asking questions."

"Why's that?" Smitty asked.

"Seems they've tried to be friendly with the Hardings, but while the Hardings are polite, they pretty much give 'em the brush-off. They came to the neighborhood picnic but kept to themselves. Mrs. Harding, she talked a little more, but when she did, her husband stayed close. The neighbor told me that her husband called him the bodyguard."

"The bodyguard, huh?" This was consistent with the way he waited for her after Bible study or meetings or when she finished work. Seemed she was rarely out of his sight. "Had they noticed anything unusual?"

"You mean like bruises and stuff? Nah. Nothing like that, but sometimes there was yelling or what she said sounded like something being thrown against the wall."

Lines creased Cancini's forehead and he wrote two words in his notebook—*Domestic violence*? "Did she call the police?"

"No, she said it only happened a few times and it didn't last long. By the time she thought maybe she should, whatever was going on over there was over."

"No proof anything abusive going on, then?"

"Not anything specific. Do you want me to drop it?"

Smitty pushed back his chair, his long fingers twitching at his side. "I don't like it."

"Neither do I." Cancini watched his young partner pace the small room. Three steps forward. Three steps back. "But that isn't the case we've been assigned."

"It's still not right."

Cancini understood Smitty's discomfort, but he couldn't allow that to be a factor in the investigation. Still, Mrs. Harding was very close to their victim, and if Mr. Harding was as overprotective and jealous as he seemed to be, it could mean something. "Good work, Bronson," he said, instantly hoping he wouldn't regret it.

Bronson's face brightened. "Thanks, boss. I don't know if it matters, but there is one more thing. Mrs. Harding is off most Tuesdays. Most of the time on those days, her husband goes to work and she's home alone—except when she isn't."

Cancini's patience wore thin and he snapped at the detective. "For Pete's sake, Bronson, get to the point."

"Okay, okay. The neighbor lady I talked to works from home. She sets up her computer at the front window so she can see what's going on in the neighborhood. Kind of a nosy Nellie if you know what I mean."

"Now, Bronson."

"The last three Tuesdays Mrs. Harding had off, she had a visitor, a male visitor, for lunch. Anyone want to take a guess who that was?" Cancini and Smitty exchanged glances. "Yep. Father Matt Holland."

Chapter Thirty-four

Friday, February 5: Two Weeks Before the Day of

MATT SAT IN the back of the coffee shop, eyes glued to the bank across the street. The sun shone down and the glass front shimmered under the bright sun. Carlos had been inside two minutes, maybe three. His bodyguard stood at the front door, a cigarette dangling from his lips. Matt had emptied the account an hour earlier, transferring the entire balance to the foundation he'd set up only the week before. He shook his head. The amount of money boggled his mind. As soon as the transaction had been confirmed, he'd closed the bank account permanently. Carlos had been forced to visit the branch when he couldn't complete his own transfer online. Matt had timed his transfer to occur before Carlos could move the money out. He breathed out, his heart clattering like a locomotive. It appeared he hadn't been wrong.

Another long minute passed, and the bodyguard flipped his cigarette butt onto the street. Matt sucked in his breath when

Carlos flew through the doors, his brown leather coat flying up behind him. The bodyguard scurried to get the car door open, and Matt caught a glimpse of Carlos's face through the glass. His former friend had grown a heavy beard in the years since they'd met at the diner in Maryland. While it covered the white moon-shaped scar that marked his chin, it couldn't mask the venomous expression he wore. Tires screeched as the silver car tore down the street.

Matt's phone vibrated and skipped forward on the table. He read the screen—unknown number—and the blood rushed to his head.

"Hello."

"You and me. We got a problem, my old friend."

Matt swallowed. "We don't have any problems."

"The fuck we don't. You stole my fuckin' money, you asshole. You think I'm gonna let you get away with that shit? I left you alone like you asked and this is how you fuckin' thank me?"

Matt wanted to scream into the phone. Carlos hadn't left him alone. He'd played him, used him like a pawn. Matt clutched the phone and counted to ten. "I don't know what you're talking about. We had a deal. I kept my part of the bargain. So, no problems, right?"

"Fuckin' bullshit." Matt held the phone away from his ear. Carlos yelled and cursed, his words turning to threats. Matt's fingers shook. It wasn't too late to give the money back, but he knew he wouldn't do that. He couldn't.

When the screaming faded to a loud bluster, he brought the phone back to his ear. "Hey, hey, calm down." He forced concern into his tone. "Whatever it is that's bothering you, I'm really sorry, but I don't know how I can help you."

"The hell you don't."

"I don't. Why don't you tell me what's wrong? I know we're not friends anymore, and I can't be involved in your, uh, business, but I can listen. We have hours most afternoons."

"You mean for fuckin' confession?"

"Yes. What else would I mean?"

"No way. That shit's for my mother, not for me."

"That shit, as you say, is for everyone." He paused. It was time to plant the seed, do his best to buy some time. "You seem upset, Carlos. I know how it is, all those people working for you, depending on you. Some wanting a bigger piece of the pie. Are there problems with the business?"

Carlos didn't say anything for a moment. When he spoke again, Matt heard the suspicion in his voice. "What makes you think I would have any problems in my business? How would you fuckin' know anything about it?"

"I hear things, Carlos." The words rolled off his tongue. "Your operation has grown quite large, I believe. Management becomes more difficult. It's the same in the church hierarchy. Employees get disgruntled. They talk. Lots of moving parts. People you think you can trust want a little more of the action. Sometimes they aren't so patient . . ."

Matt heard the sharp intake of breath, the mumbled curse words. After a moment, Carlos said, "Yeah, well, I ain't got no problems you need to worry about."

"If you say so. Don't forget my offer."

"I ain't goin' to no fuckin' confession."

"That's up to you."

"Sure is. So long, Matty."

Matt laid the phone on the table. He breathed in and out. He had no idea how long it would work, but for today at least, he'd pointed Carlos in another direction. Carlos would look inside to find who'd taken the money, starting with the savviest technical man in the organization. Carlos wouldn't find anything, or maybe he would, but eventually it would come back to Matt. God help him.

Chapter Thirty-five

THE HEAVY DOORS thudded closed and the voices faded to a whisper. One by one, heads turned toward the four priests coming up the aisle, the gleaming coffin balanced on their shoulders.

"Here they come," Smitty said.

Cancini heard the edge of anticipation in his partner's voice. Just the hour before he'd explained the service.

"So the priest gets two funerals?" Smitty had asked.

"Not exactly. The first one is called the Mass of Transferal. It's basically how it sounds. The body is transferred from the funeral home to the church where the priest has worked. The next day is the Funeral Mass and the burial." Cancini had repeated what he'd learned from Father Joe. "When a priest dies, he is honored with two Masses, but they're technically different. That doesn't really matter though. The main thing is to be at both."

Smitty had raised an eyebrow. "To see who shows up."

"Exactly."

Cancini's gaze fell on the crowded pews. As he'd expected, the Mass of Transferal was heavily attended, the church filled.

Parishioners huddled together, alternately looking backward and whispering. Curiosity seekers craned to see, and the few reporters who'd sneaked in the back wrote feverishly in their notepads. Martin, Bronson, and Jensen stood in the back watching.

Behind the altar, large and small arrangements of bright flowers filled the empty space on the floor. Burning candles cast a soft glow. The archbishop stood waiting, his hands clasped among the folds of his cassock. A snow-white vestment hung around his neck. Father Joe, positioned between a half-dozen local priests, balanced his injured leg with a cane. His face, pale and somber, was a mask. Only his eyes, focused on the slow processional in the aisle, betrayed the swirling emotions he must be feeling. Cancini sighed and shifted his attention back to the pews.

Near the front row, he spotted the Hardings. Erica leaned heavily on her husband, tears shimmering. Sonny Harding, stone-faced, ignored the priests and the coffin as it drew parallel to them. She clutched at his arm and he bent toward her, whispering in her ear. Cancini glanced back at Bronson and nodded once. They'd agreed the younger detective would watch the couple as they entered and exited the service. He would watch them again during the Funeral Mass the next day.

The priests climbed the steps and lifted the casket from their shoulders, placing it in position behind the altar. A fifth priest draped an array of flowers across the coffin. A low murmur rose among the mourners. Cancini heard the whispers around him.

"The casket is closed. It's not supposed to be like that."

"I heard they couldn't have an open casket."

"So, it's true then? He was shot in the face?" Cancini heard the horror in the elderly woman's voice. They'd kept the details out of the paper, but he understood the rumors would escalate now.

"Must be. Why else?"

The archbishop stepped forward, his voice rising and falling throughout the service. Cancini moved to the rear of the sanctuary. Weeping ladies and somber-faced men bowed their heads in a final prayer. Larry Henderson hurried down the aisle, his arm draped protectively around the shoulders of a gray-haired woman. His wife followed closely behind. As mourners moved into the Commons, Cancini slipped out through the vestibule.

Outside the church, the street and parking lot were filled with cars and black-clad mourners. Pockets of men and women dotted the lawn and sidewalk. Evening had settled over the city, and a chilly wind gusted. Henderson came down the steps with his mother, her thin arm looped through his elbow. The banker paused and scanned the crowd. He froze, his face ghostly under the lights. Cancini searched the street, but saw only the figure of a man helping a woman into a car. The woman slid behind the wheel, waved, and pulled away. Henderson ignored the car, focused only on the man. Cancini squinted, straining to see the man in the dusky light. He pushed through the clusters of grievers. The man walked away from St. William, stopping once to light a cigarette. Cancini walked faster, closing the gap. One hundred yards. Fifty yards. The man reached the corner and stopped again, staying just out of the glow of the streetlamp. A car pulled up, and the passenger door opened. The man ducked under the light and got in the car. Cancini straightened, and his breath caught in his throat. It was the man with the beard and the brown leather coat—the same one he'd seen the morning of Father Holland's murder.

Chapter Thirty-six

"I'M COMING HOME for the weekend."

Cancini muted the TV and pressed the phone closer to his ear. "Really?"

"Well, not the weekend exactly, but Saturday. I'm taking the train home. I have a few things to take care of and then I'll be taking the train back on Sunday. One of my sources can meet with me Sunday night so I have to get back."

"Uh-huh." A few things to take care of, and all in less than twenty-four hours. He figured he got the message. "Well, hope it goes well."

"Mike."

"Yeah?"

"Can I see you? It would have to be late, but maybe dinner?"

As quickly as his heart leaped, it sank again. "Dinner would be good, but . . ." Cancini started, then stopped. What was wrong with him? Two minutes earlier he was disappointed, annoyed even that she wouldn't be available. Now she wanted to see him and he was hedging. He felt like a teenager. "The truth is, I want to see you. It's the case."

"Oh, I forgot." She laughed at herself. "Only a few days in New York, and I'm already out of the loop. The priest, Father Holland, right?"

"That's the one."

"Not much progress then?"

"Not really. Tonight was the Mass of Transferal."

"That sounds kind of weird. How was it?"

It was a good question. He leaned back against the headboard. A ceiling fan whirred over his head. The Mass was the first Catholic service he'd attended in longer than he could remember, and while he'd expected it to feel foreign, it was surprisingly familiar. The candles. The words. Even the music sounded the same. Maybe that's what people liked about it. But it wasn't the service he'd been interested in. The church had been filled, and he expected the same at the funeral the next day. The Hardings. Henderson. The man in the brown leather coat. Who was he and would he be there? "It was like every other Mass, I guess. Father Joe was there, on the altar with the other priests."

"How is he?"

"Better, I guess. Using a cane now. But . . ."

He heard only the hum of the long distance for several seconds. He pictured her face, light red brows knitted over crystal-blue eyes. Her voice was gentle. "What are you worried about, Mike?"

"He's taking it pretty hard. He'd known Father Holland since he was a kid."

"Like you?"

His fingers gripped the phone. He'd told her only the basics about his mother's murder, his father's withdrawal, Father Joe.

He'd told her how grateful he'd been for the priest, but stopped short of telling her how he'd cried himself to sleep for months, how he'd craved and needed the steadiness, the dependability Father Joe gave, how he'd learned to love the man.

"Sort of. Father Joe was more of a mentor to him, helped him become a priest, but it was more than that, I think." Cancini swallowed. "Like a father and son relationship. Even had disagreements just like a father and son." It struck him then that maybe the father-son dynamic was his problem. He'd missed out on that. His relationship with his own father was better now, but it didn't change the years when it wasn't. He sighed. "I think Father Joe is really having a hard time with all of it."

"That only makes sense." He heard the hesitation in her voice. "Was he able to tell you anything about the shooting?"

"Not really. He says he doesn't know anything."

"You sound like you don't believe him."

He did and he didn't. Cancini had no doubt the priest knew more than he was willing to tell, but he couldn't be sure how much. The foundation. The money. Throw in the confessions, and Father Joe was right in the middle of it. He sighed. "I can't really talk about it."

She laughed then. "We're a pair, aren't we? Both of us have jobs where we can't talk about anything. I have sources. You have evidence. Crazy. Maybe later, after the case is over, you can tell me."

"Maybe." He yawned. "Saturday then?"

"Saturday."

He slid under the covers, a slow smile spreading across his face. Maybe things weren't so bad after all.

Chapter Thirty-seven

CANCINI CHECKED HIS watch and tapped his foot on the linoleum floor. The funeral for Father Holland was set to begin in less than two hours. His eyes itched and a dull ache had taken up permanent residence at the base of his neck. He swallowed the last of his coffee and turned his attention back toward Landon. "I'm not following. You've traced the money to the shell company—we know where it went—but we still have no idea where it came from in the first place?"

"Technically, that's true." Landon's head bobbed up and down. "All the deposits into the bank account were wire transfers from an account that lists St. William as the owner."

Cancini leaned back against his chair, his head throbbing with any movement. "Are you saying the money that went into Holland's account came from the church?"

"Yes and no. The account owner name is St. William but the nonprofit ID doesn't match the one listed on their tax forms. Also, the church accountant said he'd never seen the account before."

"It's a fake account?"

"Right."

Cancini ran his hands through his hair and glanced at his partner. Smitty's brows drew together and he shrugged. Cancini had only three accounts: checking, savings, and his pension, and he had trouble keeping track of those. Even so, he knew they required paperwork. "How could someone set up a fake church account?"

"There are lots of ways, really, and it's not like banks are in the business of turning away money. Actually, the church status made it a perfect vehicle. Who's going to question that?"

"But they had to do it in person, right?"

"Not necessarily. You could do it by phone or online if everything looked legit. From what I can tell, there was a weekly deposit of cash in the overnight drop. That's easily explained as collections."

Cancini took a deep breath. "So, someone sets up a fake account and makes regular cash deposits. Then that money was wired to Holland's account from there."

"Exactly."

He shook his head. *Follow the money.* It sounded easier said than done. "How long did this go on?"

"Close to two years. I've got the dates and amounts right here." He handed copies to Martin and Cancini.

The captain whistled as he read the numbers. "That's a lot of dough. Gotta be drug money, right?"

Cancini's instincts were telling him the same thing, but he didn't comment.

Martin announced his theory. "Maybe someone was on to him and he was being blackmailed."

"I don't think so." Landon kept his eyes on Cancini. "Holland's account, the 2144 I told you about, was dormant for a couple of years, no money coming in or out. Like I said the other day, it was used to pay college expenses, but when he lived in Boston and the first year he moved back to D.C., there was no activity at all. He opened accounts close to the churches where he worked. He used those. It was like he forgot about the other account."

Martin snorted. "People don't forget about this kind of money."

"Right about the time the deposits started, someone switched all the statements and notifications to online," Landon said, voice quieter.

Cancini raised an eyebrow. "What are you trying to tell us, Landon?"

"I think it's possible Father Holland's bank account was hijacked."

"You're thinking someone hacked this account to funnel money?"

"Yes."

Martin snorted again, but Cancini leaned forward. "Why?"

Landon cleared his throat. "Well, for one thing, Holland didn't use online banking for any of his other accounts. He had one credit card and he sent paper checks to pay the bill. Same with his cell phone bill. I mean, who does that anymore?" His voice grew stronger as he spoke. "About two years ago, just before the first deposit, someone opted into online banking. They set up passwords using Holland's personal data and social security. By switching to online banking, that someone was able to transfer large sums in and out without ever speaking to or seeing anyone. There was no reason for the bank or Father Holland to suspect anything."

"This still sounds funny to me," Martin said. "We know he

used money from the account to set up the foundation, so he must have known what was going on."

Smitty spoke up. "Not necessarily. I went by the branch where the account was originally opened and I talked to the manager there. Father Holland came in a little more than a month ago to ask why he wasn't getting any paper statements. Like Terry said, the manager told him he'd opted out of them when he selected online bank statements and transactions. Father Holland asked him when he did that and the manager told him it had been almost two years."

Cancini addressed Smitty. "Did the manager say he seemed surprised?"

His partner nodded once. "He thought maybe he was, but apparently, Father Holland tried not to let on. The manager said he just sat there for a minute, then asked if he could have a copy of the statements for the last few years. Told the manager his printer was broken or he'd do it himself."

"Clever," Cancini said.

"Yep. And that was it. He left, and the manager didn't see him again until he shut down the account."

"When was that?"

"Two weeks ago."

Landon pointed to the report. "If you look at the dates just before Holland shut down the account, you'll see three large deposits. The total was close to a half-million dollars. And if you look at the pattern over the last two years, a transfer to Germany would have happened that same day. But the account was closed before that could happen."

Cancini turned the pages one by one. If he was understanding Landon's theory, Holland had found the pattern. Three deposits over about a month, followed by a total transfer. A couple of months later, it would start again.

"Holland requested that last transfer in person," Smitty said. "The manager told me he came in and personally submitted the paperwork. He waited, and when it was done, he made a call, then said it was verified."

"Can we get his phone records for that date?" Cancini asked.

"The request is already in," Smitty told him.

"How much did he transfer exactly?"

"It was $488,599."

Cancini looked out the window, then back down at the transactions listed. He added the deposits in his head. Over the course of two years, millions of dollars had been funneled through the dead priest's account. And if Landon was right, shortly before his murder, Holland had stolen nearly a half million from that someone. That wasn't small potatoes in anyone's book.

"After the transfer, Holland asked the branch manager to close the account permanently. And according to the manager, he wouldn't leave until it was done." Smitty paused. "That's not all. Later that morning, a guy came in, upset that he couldn't access his account. It was Holland's closed account. The manager got suspicious and asked the man for identification. The man left before the manager could find out anything else."

"Do we have this man on camera?

"No. He ducked the cameras from every angle. About all we've got so far is a brief description. Six feet, one hundred eighty pounds, dark hair, beard, brown leather coat."

Cancini blinked. "Did you say brown leather coat?"

Smitty nodded. "Yeah. Mean something?"

"There was a guy at the service last night in a coat like that," he said, dark brows furrowed. "I think Henderson was spooked by him. And I may have seen him the morning Holland was found—on the sidewalk across the street."

Martin perked up. "Did you get a look at him?"

"Not really. He was with a woman last night, though. I'm guessing a parishioner. It was too dark to get a good look at her or the plate on her car."

Martin stood. "Can we get a sketch artist to meet with that bank manager?"

"Already put in for it," Smitty said.

"Good." Cancini handed the pages back to Landon. "Is there anything else about these accounts we should know?"

"Not yet, sir."

"What about any evidence he used the money personally?"

"No, sir. Only for the church."

Cancini gave a single shake of his head. "If any of this turns out to be right, Father Holland was stealing from someone engaged in money laundering, and trying to use that same money for good. It's like he was a modern-day—"

Martin raised his palms. "Don't say it. The press would have a field day."

"Don't say what?" Landon asked, his young face upturned.

"Robin Hood," Cancini said. The pain in his neck radiated to his skull. "A modern-day Robin Hood."

Chapter Thirty-eight

Saturday, February 13: One Week Before the Day of

MATT'S STOMACH TURNED over and his hands shook. The black car was there again. Inside, a lone man sat smoking. If the man slept, if he ate, if he left the block, Matt didn't know about it. He thought about the flimsy locks on the windows and doors of his apartment, but realized if Carlos got serious, the locks would be worthless anyway. His hand rose to the cross around his neck. He wouldn't be able to avoid his former friend for much longer. He hadn't left the apartment except to attend to church business in two days. It had to stop soon.

Dusk fell over the city, and the streetlamp on the corner came to life. A handful of cars filled the gravel parking lot. He quickened his step. His parishioners waited. Inside the church, he exhaled and made his way to the reconciliation room.

An hour later, he rose from his chair, his book in his hand. The door opened again and he hesitated. The hour was up, but it wouldn't be the first time he'd made allowances. He sat down again. The wooden chair on the other side of the confessional creaked and a man sighed heavily.

"How can I help you?" Matt heard a clicking noise followed by silence. The odor of cigarette smoke drifted through the screen. "I'm sorry. You can't smoke in the church." he said.

"I don't think you're in a position to tell me anything, Father." The guttural voice echoed in the small space.

Matt froze. He didn't recognize the voice attached to the invisible body. "Are you the man who's been sitting in the car on the street for two days?"

The man chuckled and blew smoke through the screen. "I like you, Father. You got guts. I'll give you that." His voice changed, got hard. "So listen good. Your friend doesn't like what you've done and he wants his money back. You have one week."

"I don't have his money."

The stranger clucked his tongue. "Yeah, you got guts, but don't be stupid. One week. Or else."

Matt shivered under the heavy cassock. "Or else what?"

"Believe me, you don't want to know."

"I could call the police."

The man laughed, the sound loud and high-pitched, as grating as the screeching of a mewling cat. When the sound died, Matt liked the silence less. After a moment, he heard the man shift and the sizzle of the cigarette being extinguished. "You won't call the police," he said. "They can't help you."

Chapter Thirty-nine

MARTIN SLAMMED THE door behind Cancini. "Sit down." The captain moved behind his desk but remained standing. "God-dammit, Cancini. Sweeney must know something. Hell, even I can figure that out."

Cancini slumped in the chair, his mind on the funeral, the voice of the captain droning in his ear. Again, the church had been filled to capacity, and again, he'd scanned the parishioners for anyone out of place, anything unusual. The Hardings, Henderson, the old ladies. All there as expected. Missing was the man in the brown leather coat.

"Are you listening, Cancini?" Martin slammed his palm against the desk, and Cancini flinched. He sat up straighter. The captain looked down at Cancini and gestured toward the men in the precinct. "All these detectives devoting hours to this case, and the answer could be right in front of us." His face grew redder with each word. "The media is having a field day with this priest thing, and the brass is breathing down my neck. I don't need these headaches. Your priest friend knows something and we need to know what it is!"

Cancini bristled under the captain's glare but knew the captain was right. Father Joe did know something, but it wasn't that simple. He couldn't avoid the subject of the confessions any longer. "He won't talk."

"That's unacceptable. Lawyer or no lawyer, I want you to get him in here as soon as possible. That's not a request."

Tired and aching, Cancini struggled to keep his irritation in check. The captain was unusually ticked off, but they were all under pressure. Aloud, he said, "I can get him in here, but he still won't tell us anything."

Martin leaned forward over his desk. "Then threaten him with obstruction of justice, whatever it takes. Get a friggin' warrant to search his house."

Cancini shook his head. "It won't work."

The captain's mouth fell open. "Are you defending him? I don't give a damn about your relationship, Cancini, or about the big-deal lawyer. I've had it with the games. Holland was one of their own. They should be happy to help."

"He would if he could."

Martin gaped at him. "What the hell does that mean?"

"In the simplest of terms, it means he's bound by his position as a priest to never reveal what was told to him in confidence." Martin cocked his head, deep lines creasing his brow. "Do you know what confession is?"

"Isn't that where a person goes in and tells the priest about his sins like how many times he told a lie or cheated on his taxes or some other stupid thing?"

"More or less. The priest hears the confession, offers penance, and then forgiveness. Father Joe acted as Father Holland's confessor. Apparently, this is something he'd been doing since Father Holland was just a teenager."

"So what? I don't care if he smoked some weed or stole some beer when he was a kid. We only need to ask him what Holland told him about those bank accounts."

"He can't tell us." He kept talking before the captain could interrupt. "It's like the doctor-patient privilege, but more serious."

The captain dropped into his seat. He reached for a toothpick and stuck it in his mouth. "We've found ways around that. We can find ways around this, too."

Cancini shook his head. "There aren't any ways around it. It's called the sacramental seal, and it's unbreakable."

"Nothing is unbreakable."

"This is. According to papal law, the sacrament of reconciliation is absolute. If someone comes in to confess their sins, they have to know that nothing they say will ever leave the confessional."

"This is different. It's a murder investigation. There must be exceptions."

"No."

Martin's face flushed pink. "We can subpoena him."

"It won't matter."

"This is bullshit."

Cancini understood the captain's confusion. "Look, let's say someone walks into the confessional and tells the priest he is planning to kill his wife that day. He tells him everything, how he's going to do it, when he's going to do it, even why he's going to do it. The priest can try to talk the man out of it. He can try to get the man to go to the police. But he can never tell a soul. The best he can do is alert the police that the woman might be in danger, and even that can be tricky."

"That's crazy. He'd have an obligation to tell the police, wouldn't he?"

"No. His obligation is to uphold the sacrament. You can't reveal anything you've ever heard, even ten years, twenty years later."

Martin shook his head. "It doesn't make sense."

Cancini shrugged. "Maybe not, but that's the way it is. If people thought priests were allowed to reveal what they confessed, even small things, they'd never tell a priest anything."

"This is different." Martin tossed the gnawed toothpick into the trash. "Maybe priests can't say anything while a person is alive, but Holland is dead now. What difference does it make?"

"Still not allowed." Cancini brushed his spiky hair with his hand. He had his own reasons for wanting to bring Father Joe in again. "I'll have him come in, but I can't promise anything." He got to his feet. "That's the best I can do."

The captain stood and shoved his hands in his pockets. "That's not good enough. It's been four days and you don't have diddly. No suspect. No forensic evidence. You've got a trail of money and no clue where it leads. The brass is breathing down my neck. The press is going crazy and the archbishop of something or other is calling the mayor every day." Desperation crept into his voice. "Find something . . . anything."

Chapter Forty

FBI Agent Derek Talbot stifled a yawn and nodded toward the stately grandfather clock. "It's Saturday, Mike. Don't you ever sleep?"

"Not unless I have to." Cancini gestured toward his young partner. "This is my Smitty."

Talbot reached across his desk and shook the young man's hand. "Heard about you. You're a brave man to partner with an asshole like Cancini."

"So I've been told," Smitty said. "He's not all bad, though."

"You haven't worked with him long enough." Talbot waved a hand at the guest chairs. "Mike, it's good to see you."

"It hasn't been that long, Derek."

Talbot glanced at Smitty and spoke in a voice mimicking the older detective. "Good to see you, too, Derek. How've you been? How's the family? Thanks for coming in at the crack of dawn on your day off." Talbot's eyes crinkled as he spoke. "You haven't changed a bit, Mike."

Smitty laughed out loud.

"Are you done yet?" Cancini asked, but there was no resentment in his voice. Talbot was an old friend and they'd recently worked the Coed Killer case together. "How are you, Derek? How's the family?"

"They're fine. Girls are good and Allison says hi." He winked at Smitty. "See. Not so hard." He turned back to Cancini. "And you? How's your dad?"

"As well as can be expected." Cancini's hands tightened around the file in his lap. "Did you get the sketch?"

Talbot opened the folder on his desk. "I got it. His name is Carlos Vega. Twenty-nine years old." His lips turned down in a frown. "Reportedly, he's the leader of the Eastside Gang."

Cancini nodded once and pulled out a pen to take notes. "What can you tell me about him?"

"Most of what we know about Vega is vague. He started as a runner as far we can tell, probably thirteen or fourteen at the time. He delivered drugs, collected the money, and got paid a few bucks by the Dragons. That was before they joined with the Eastside Gang. He was arrested at fifteen for possession, but as a juvenile, got a month and probation. A few years after that, the captain of the Dragons—a guy named Wayne Johnson—went missing. He turned up stabbed to death. Wayne's girlfriend came forward and named Carlos as the murderer. Claimed there was another witness, but we never found him. She OD'd before the police could bring charges." Talbot paused.

Cancini remembered the case. Another drug dealer dead by his mid-twenties. It had barely made any waves. No witnesses. No evidence. No case. "Who was the other witness?"

"Another runner, kid who'd worked for Wayne. Matty was his name. Good-looking, she said."

Cancini's skin tingled. Good-looking? Matty? Holland would have been about seventeen or eighteen then. "You never found him?"

"Vanished. The timeline's a little hazy after that, but we do know Vega became the head of the Dragons, and when they merged with Eastside, he was still at the top."

"I'm guessing you don't have anything on him or he wouldn't be on the streets."

"That's right. He never moves without a bodyguard, and technically, he's clean. He owns four Chicken del Rey franchises. He purchased the first one with a bank loan cosigned by his mother. He pays his taxes. He lives alone in a two-bedroom house at the edge of Georgetown. He drives a Ford SUV. There are no red flags."

Cancini looked up from his notes. "Something tells me there's a 'but.'"

"Oh, there's a 'but,' all right. You and I both know the history of gangs in this city. The police, the FBI, we do what we can, and we were making some headway, but not anymore. Vega's organization is tight, the tightest I've ever seen. Runs it like a mafia."

Smitty frowned. "What do you mean?"

"Rumor is that Vega has strict rules. According to one source, he's forbidden anyone close to him to buy a mansion, drive a car that costs more than sixty thousand dollars, or throw money around like a fool. One story says he had a man shot on his boat after his girlfriend flashed a gigantic pink diamond ring. The girl was shot, too, and the third finger on her left hand was gone. The ring was never found."

"I remember that one," Cancini said. "Wasn't that up in Annapolis?"

"Yep. The gun used to kill them was left on the boat. No prints.

No way to trace it or tie it back to Vega. Still unsolved." He paused, shaking his head. "He doesn't like attention. He's been under surveillance for a couple of years now and we've got nothing. That's why his operation is so hard to pin down."

"How big is it?"

"It's hard to say. There are dozens of gangs in the city and more in the suburbs. Most are small-time, neighborhood gangs. Eastside is different. They started small, but Vega branched out, pulling a lot of the gangs under his wing. Each of the smaller gangs still sports their own colors, has their own territory. Eastside is like the holding company and the small gangs all report to them. I'm not sure how many Vega controls, but for all intents and purposes, Vega runs the largest drug trade in the city. He dabbles in prostitution and gambling, but from what we can tell, he focuses on the money business."

"Drugs."

Talbot tossed the folder back on the desk. "There's more. Vega is tough, but he's also very protective of his men. When one of his guys is arrested, he gets him a lawyer, usually one just good enough to get him a decent plea deal. When the guy gets out, his reward for keeping his mouth shut is a legitimate job. It keeps the probation officer happy and no one is the wiser."

"How is it you can't prove what he's up to?"

"He's careful. He changes phones on a regular basis. He likes women, but he never spends more than one night with them. His inner circle is small. It used to be easy to spot the gang leaders. They would flash rolls of cash, load up on jewelry and cars. Vega doesn't fit the mold. He has an expensive watch but just one. He stays away from his product. He shows up at his franchise stores on a regular basis. We've tried bugging the bathrooms, the dining room, even had an undercover kid working the fryer in his Southeast store. Nothing."

"But if you're right and he's running an organization that big, he has to talk to people, meet with people."

"He does, but none of our usual surveillance methods have yielded anything. He frequents clubs, but he sticks to one or two drinks. He takes women to hotels, never to his home. He runs every day, always with someone we've marked as part of the organization, but short of running alongside them, you can't hear the conversation."

"What about setting up microphones along the route he runs?" Smitty asked.

Talbot shook his head. "He runs several different routes a week—mixing it up—making it unpredictable. Even if we could do all of them, he has someone running the route ahead of him and someone else behind. Not only does it keep anyone from getting close to him, they act as scouts."

"Shit," Smitty said. "The guy is something else."

Talbot nodded. "I agree. He's also smart enough to keep his nose clean. Like I said, he keeps his expenditures in line with his claimed earnings. He pays every cent in taxes. He pays his mortgage on time."

Cancini rubbed his forehead. Frown lines appeared at the corners of his mouth. "What about his financials?"

"That's where we're looking now, but so far, the accounts we can find are clean."

"The accounts you can find," Smitty repeated.

"He uses a local accounting firm for his personal and franchise businesses. But there is one guy in his circle we've been watching. He runs with him at least once a week."

"Who is it?" Cancini asked.

"Justin Blackwood. Grew up in the neighborhood like most of his circle, but he was tagged gifted as a kid. He made it into one of those charter schools and then got a full ride to Dartmouth. Double majored in computer science and accounting. He got his master's in finance at Harvard. Following graduation, he came home to D.C., and according to some sources, to act as CFO for Vega."

Cancini stroked his chin. A man with a talent for computers and a balance sheet would be able to hack a priest's bank account in no time at all. He could set up a shell company and transfer funds with a few pecks at a keyboard. For the first time in days, the pounding in Cancini's head eased. Out loud, he said, "A guy like that would be smart enough to know how to launder money."

"Agreed, if we could prove it, but Vega doesn't make many mistakes."

"Maybe not," the detective admitted, and pointed at the sketch of Vega. "But he may have made one now."

Chapter Forty-one

Tuesday, February 16: Five Days Before the Day of

MATT SCROLLED THROUGH the e-mails, the lump in his gut growing. Less than a week and Carlos would make good on his threat. He'd bought some time, gotten a few things done, but it wasn't enough. St. William needed him, needed more than a paint job and new stained glass windows. He didn't ask for the money. He didn't seek it out, but there it was with his name on it. Technically, he didn't steal it, but he knew better. That money didn't belong to him. Still, it didn't really belong to Carlos, either. That money came at the expense of a lot of good people. That money came from the drugs he sold, the same drugs that left people too stoned to see how lost they were, and too wasted to do anything about it. That money came from the high-heel-wearing teenagers who earned a living on their backs. It came from the gambling addicts who couldn't stop themselves from spending the diaper money on a game of blackjack or craps. In a way, Carlos had stolen the money from these people. He'd taken advantage of them, used them. In much the same way, Matt reasoned, Matt had used Carlos's bank account for his own gains.

Had Matt done the right thing? No matter. It was done now. He'd created the necessary legal documents to set up the foundation. He'd funded it and already funneled some of the money into the church. He needed trustees in addition to himself and had already named Father Joe. He had a lawyer, too, but there was one more he needed. If she said yes, the money would be untouchable. It was risky, but if it worked, Carlos would never hurt him. He couldn't. They were different, but they were brothers. Still, he wasn't taking any chances. He needed to talk to Father Joe. He needed him to understand. He already knew Joe didn't approve, didn't believe that two wrongs could make a right, but Father Joe hadn't grown up in the projects. He hadn't sold bags of weed or pills on the street to buy crappy food and pay for a rodent-infested apartment. He'd never needed to hide from social services or walk the streets wondering if he was going to get hauled away to some group home. He looked up to the sky. Sometimes the ends did justify the means.

His leg twitched and his foot swung back and forth. The pills the doctor had prescribed helped but couldn't do for him what Father Joe could. He rose, stretched out on the sofa, and crossed his arms behind his head. It wasn't just the money. Father Joe knew his difficulties with the secretary, knew the untenable situation. Matt knew what Joe would say. He would tell Matt to remember his vows, remember his faith. It wasn't always that easy. Matt kept breathing until the pounding in his chest slowed. She was expecting him. He was going to have to do something soon, but he didn't want to. She'd touched him more than he cared to admit. Not for the first time, he wondered if he was cut out to be a priest after all.

Chapter Forty-two

SMITTY LAID OUT the money laundering trail, Father Holland's actions at the branch, and Vega's run-in with the branch manager. "The sketch is practically a photograph."

Talbot agreed. "Pretty convincing, but as far as I can tell, you don't have proof Vega did anything illegal."

Cancini watched the interchange with a sinking feeling.

"What about trying to access another person's account?" Smitty asked. "Isn't that fraud?"

"But he didn't access anything. If called on it, he could deny that's the account number he gave or say he must have transposed numbers." Talbot's answer was apologetic. "I'm sorry, but even the eyewitness testimony can't be corroborated. The cameras show a man, nothing more. He didn't speak to anyone else or draw attention. He was in the branch for only a few minutes."

"Talbot is right," Cancini said. "But even if we can't prove Vega was the man behind the money laundering, we now have a pretty good idea who was behind those e-mails."

Talbot leaned forward. "What e-mails?"

Cancini handed the FBI man a paper-clipped stack of pages. "Turn to the ones with the sticky notes."

The FBI man read, flipping page after page. When he got to the final marked e-mail, he read out loud. "'Matty, time is up. Don't think I don't know you've gotten every single one of my e-mails. You have till tomorrow. I'm watching, so you'd better not be late or you're a fucking dead man. You got me? Bring the cash OR ELSE!!!! And keep your trap shut if you want to live.'" Talbot stopped and looked up. "This was written Sunday, the day Holland was murdered."

"Right," Cancini said. "Holland died with one eye gone and the other wide open."

"He didn't wait until Monday. Instead, he went inside the church and shot the man."

Cancini's brows creased and he gave a shake of his head. "Or someone did." Cancini plucked another page from the file. "We have at least a dozen witnesses who were at the evening Mass who saw a man with a skull tattoo in the pews. He wasn't there long and left before Mass was over, but we all know what that man does for a living." Cancini handed Talbot another sheet with a drawing of the tattoo.

"Death Squad. A bunch of mercenaries." Talbot looked up again. "You think Vega used one of these guys to do the hit on the priest?"

Cancini lifted both shoulders, knots in his back tightening. "It seems logical, but sending the Death Squad either means he'd already recovered the money and he was tying up loose ends, or he'd been forced to let it go."

Talbot shook his head. "Vega would never let it go. It's not about the money for someone like him. From what I know about Vega, no one could be allowed to steal from him and get away with it. There would be hell to pay, and it wouldn't be pretty."

"But he didn't get the money. We've verified it's still sitting in a foundation account designated for the church." *Follow the money.* Cancini picked at the file with his fingers, his mind flitting through unconnected bits of information. "I think Vega was there the morning the body was discovered, on the street in the crowd. I couldn't see his face clearly under the umbrella, but he had a beard and was wearing a long brown leather coat. And again at the service the other night."

Smitty's face scrunched up in confusion. "Vega's a bad guy, and money laundering—even murder—are normal for him. Holland is a do-gooder. He hands out food and clothes. He volunteers at clinics. From everything we've heard, the man lived for St. William. I don't get it. How does a priest get involved with a guy like Vega in the first place?"

"I might be able to answer that one," Talbot said. "They grew up in the same low-income housing, Barry Farm, before it was condemned. They even went to the same high school until Holland's mother died and Holland disappeared. My guess is they stayed in touch."

Cancini brushed his fingers over the file. He pictured Holland and Vega, scrawny teens growing up in rat-infested apartments, slogging through low-budget schools that couldn't keep track of the numbers of kids skipping, and the never-ending presence of dealers and users. Maybe they were good friends once. Maybe Vega knew where Holland was during the years he was missing. Someone had helped him before he suddenly appeared on Father Joe's doorstep at age eighteen. "It makes sense they knew each other," he said. Cancini stood and pumped Talbot's hand. "Thanks, Derek. You've been a big help. Carlos Vega just jumped to the top of the suspect list."

Chapter Forty-three

Julia sipped her wine and cocked her head. "So, tell me something about Mike Cancini that I might not know."

Before he could answer, a waiter dressed in a black T-shirt and black pants whisked away their plates. A single candle glowed on the table. Wax cascaded down the green glass bottle and dripped onto the tablecloth. The golden light cast soft shadows across her face.

"Not much to tell," he said after the waiter was gone. "I'm really not that interesting."

"I disagree." She smiled. "But if it makes it any easier, I'll tell you something first."

He grinned, intrigued. "Shoot."

She lifted her shoulders, sitting taller. "I'm really good at fly fishing."

"What?"

"Fly fishing. Have you heard of it?"

He tried to think, fumbling to remember where he'd heard it or seen it. "Uh, I think I saw a movie once with that."

She laughed. "That's what most people say. *A River Runs Through It*. Brad Pitt."

"That's the one. It looks hard."

"It is," she told him. "My dad taught me. We used to go to Wyoming every summer when I was a kid. I have an uncle and some cousins there. Would you be interested in learning sometime?"

"Around here?"

"There are a couple of places not far away."

He thought about the movie. The men waded into the rushing waters to cast their rods. Behind them, tall trees reached up to a clear blue sky, and time stretched endlessly. It was as far from the life of a D.C. homicide detective as he could imagine. "I think I'd like that." She beamed, and a warmth spread through him. "Sounds like fun."

"Good." She sipped her wine again and pointed at him. "Now you."

"Okay, okay. Let me think." He rubbed his chin. His face grew warm. "Uh, there is one thing. I took a cooking class once."

"No way." She sat back, considering. "Wait. I thought you said you couldn't cook."

"I can't. I actually failed the class. Or I would have if I hadn't dropped out." He finished his scotch and shook his head. "The teacher said she'd never met anyone who couldn't even boil water. I was so hopeless, she even wanted to give me my money back. I couldn't take it, though. It wasn't her fault." He watched Julia giggling, and he smiled again. "That's why I stick to takeout and toast now."

"I can't believe you even took the class. It seems so unlike you."

"Yeah, well . . ." His smile faded. "Lola signed us up. I think she thought—well, I don't know what she thought."

She was quiet a moment. "You look tired, Mike." She pushed

her hair behind her ears and rested her chin in her hand. "Are you all right?"

He drank in the sight of her. Auburn hair shot through with gold, cinnamon freckles, cerulean-blue eyes. He was better than all right. "I'm good," he told her, and meant it.

"How's Father Joe?"

He put his napkin on the table. "Better. Still using a cane, but still plans to say Mass tomorrow." Cancini clucked his tongue. "Won't rest at all. Stubborn."

"Is that where you get it from?" A dimple popped out on her cheek when she smiled. "Your stubbornness?"

"Am I?"

She pinched two fingers together. "Maybe a little. You could use some rest, Mike."

"Probably," he said, but knew he wouldn't. Images of Vega, skull tattoos, and Holland lying across the steps to the altar kept intruding on his thoughts.

"Are you worried about him?"

Cancini looked around for the waiter. Most of the tables were already empty and the hour was late. "We should probably get going. It looks like they're trying to close."

She reached out and placed her hand over his. "They can wait. You didn't answer the question."

He sighed. "Ballistics didn't match. The shooting being a drive-by isn't just a theory anymore. It's official."

"You're unhappy about that."

He was, but he wasn't sure he could explain. The old man wasn't going to die. There was no evidence he'd been targeted specifically and yet . . . Two shootings. Two priests. What if Holland was the missing witness called Matty? He was never found. Another coincidence? Cancini just didn't think he could buy it. What if Father Joe wasn't the victim of a random drive-by, but was targeted? If that was true, the shooter didn't miss when he got the old man in the thigh, and it wasn't an accident. Someone had issued a warning.

"I guess I am."

She took a deep breath. "Then do something about it. You're the police, aren't you? Can't you protect him?"

The department was stretched thin, and Martin had already made it clear they couldn't afford police protection for the old man. "It's complicated."

She clucked her tongue. "Don't tell me. Money."

"Partly."

She tapped the table with her fingernails. "Could you have someone stay with him? So he won't be alone?"

"I tried that. He refused." He threw his napkin on the table. Father Joe had scorned the idea of protection.

"I don't need a babysitter, Michael," he'd said, his voice stern. "It's completely unnecessary, and as you can see, I'm fine." He'd pointed at his cane. "I'm getting around better every day. Even you said so earlier."

"That may be true, but you still look terrible. What did the doctor say?"

The old man had sighed. "I have to keep taking those pills for a while, maybe forever."

"For your blood pressure?"

Father Joe had shrugged, looking down into his coffee. "I guess."

Cancini's heart had fluttered. "What aren't you telling me?"

"Nothing important. Just some follow-up appointments next week."

A follow-up appointment wasn't out of the ordinary, but something in the old man's voice had made Cancini sit forward. "What kind of appointments?"

Father Joe had set his cup aside. "You have enough on your plate right now. Enough about me." Cancini had tried to protest, but the old man would have none of it, mouth set in a firm line. "You have far more important things to worry about than me, Michael."

Cancini looked back at Julia. "I think he might be sick." She waited, face grave. "When I was visiting him in the hospital, a cardiologist came to see him. I thought it was just routine, but now I don't know. He admitted he has a bunch of appointments next week, but didn't want to worry me."

"You think he's having heart trouble?"

Father Joe was not a young man, and his weight had blossomed in recent years. "It wouldn't surprise me."

"I'm sorry. I wish there was something I could do."

Piano music floated over their heads, the sound tinkling and the tune bubbly. A lump formed in his throat, and he dropped his head. He hoped he was wrong, but even if he wasn't, he had more immediate worries. How much did Father Joe really know about Father Holland's money issues? What did he know about Vega? Cancini's gut and the ache in his head told him the old man was hiding more than medical issues. He couldn't shake the feeling that the gunshot to the old man's thigh was more than it appeared.

"Promise me you'll take care of him." Her soft voice made him look up.

Julia was right. The old man was stubborn, and he wouldn't take care of himself. Cancini nodded once. "I promise."

Chapter Forty-four

"Someone should stay with you for a few days." Cancini leaned forward, his hands folded in his lap.

"We talked about this." Father Joe couldn't hide the irritation in his voice.

The detective hesitated. "What if that shot at you wasn't an accident?"

"Well, a drive-by is hardly an accident, is it? Only who gets hit is an accident." Father Joe lifted his injured leg and laid it on the ottoman. A cup of coffee teetered on the arm of the overstuffed chair. "Is there something I should know?"

"No. Just a precaution."

Father Joe sighed. "I don't need protection, Michael. You worry too much."

Cancini rose, took the cup, and placed it on a table overflowing with books. He glanced at Smitty leaning against the doorway to the tiny office. "Father, worry has nothing to do with it. Whether you like it or not, you're a material witness in a homicide investigation." Father Joe opened his mouth to protest, but Cancini raised his hand. "We're not taking any chances."

"You mean you're not taking any chances. I don't want a stranger in my house." The priest's lips closed tight in a hard, thin line. He tipped his chin up a fraction of an inch. Cancini sighed. He knew the look all too well, and it would do no good to argue with the man. He'd let it go—for now.

Cancini nodded at Smitty. "Since we're here, I wondered if we could ask you a few questions." The priest arched his silver brows. "Unless you want to call the lawyer."

Father Joe sank back into the chair. "You know better than that. Ask, and I'll answer if I can."

Smitty cleared his throat. "Father, have you ever met a man named Carlos Vega?"

"Yes, several times. His mother was a member of St. William when I was a visiting priest. Still is, as far as I know."

Cancini made notes as Smitty asked questions. "Did Mr. Vega attend St. William?"

Father Joe scratched at his chin. "I doubt it. I know he went when he was a young boy. I officiated at his first communion at the request of his mother. She's a lovely woman. Very devout. He stopped coming to Mass around the time he entered his teens. I know it broke his mother's heart, but I tried to tell her to have faith. I've told other parents the same." He hesitated. "Many times those who fall away from the church come back when they need it."

Cancini looked up to find the old man's eyes on him. He kept his voice neutral. "Did he come back, Father? Did he find God and return to the church?"

The priest shook his head once. "No, I don't believe he did." He picked at a loose thread unraveling on the arm of his chair.

He spoke slowly. "I hear things from time to time. It seems Carlos may have chosen a different path in life—one that has taken him away from God."

"Unlike Father Holland, who found God."

The old priest blinked. He looked from one detective to the other. "What is it you want to ask me? Spit it out."

"All right." Cancini crossed the room and sat down across from the old man. "How long had Vega and Father Holland been friends?"

"I don't know that they were friends anymore."

"But they were once."

"I suppose." Father Joe looked out the window. He twisted his hands in his lap, turning them over and over. "They went to school together when they were young." He drew out the words as though forming his thoughts one by one. "Matt left for college and then seminary. He was gone from the city for many years. I don't think they had anything in common when he returned to take over St. William."

"Are you sure, Father?" Cancini leaned forward. "Maybe something from when they were young, some bond between them still . . ."

The priest shrugged his shoulders. "Anything's possible."

"Were they enemies? Had their friendship turned into something else?"

Father Joe looked back at Cancini. "I really couldn't say." He swung his leg to the floor and pulled his bulk from the chair. He reached for the knotted-pine cane. "Gentlemen, I'm sorry to cut this short, but I'm due at the church for a council meeting." He held up the cane. "And as you can imagine, it's taking me a little longer to walk over than it usually does."

Cancini stood. "I'll walk with you."

The priest shot him a look. "That's not necessary. I'm perfectly capable, and you have business to attend to."

Cancini looked at his young partner. "Smitty, since our friend here refuses help, what are the chances we can at least have someone come over here to check on things every hour?"

The lanky detective shrugged. They both knew the department budget. "Maybe every couple of hours."

"Can we get a car outside at night?"

"I doubt it."

Father Joe clucked his tongue. "I don't need a car and I don't need someone to watch over me." He leaned on his cane and smiled weakly. "I'll be fine, Michael. You'll see."

Chapter Forty-five

Wednesday, February 17: Four Days Before the Day of

MATT PULLED OFF his coat and threw it on an empty chair. "They say confession is good for the soul, right? Isn't that what we want people to believe?" He picked up his menu.

"Whose soul?" asked Father Joe, his lips turned down in a frown. "You're twisting the purpose."

Matt set the menu down again. "Are you mad at me, Padre?"

"You're damn right I am."

Matt laughed out loud. He was still laughing when the waitress took their orders. Father Joe folded his arms across his chest. "I'm glad you find this all so amusing, Matthew."

The younger man wiped his eyes. "Oh, I do. I really do." The waitress returned, filling their coffee cups. "I'm sorry, Padre. I didn't mean to upset you."

"Yes, you did." He cut off Matt's protests. "You knew perfectly well how I would react to your confession. How would you react if the situation were reversed?"

Matt smiled again. "That would never happen."

"That's beside the point. Matthew, confessing to me, what do you think it accomplishes? I don't believe you're only looking for absolution or you would go to someone else. You want me to know." Father Joe paused, his face flushed. Matt said nothing. The old priest sighed. "Look, Matthew, I'm not just an anonymous confessor. I know you. I know Carlos. These threats are not going to go away."

Matt was quiet. Although he'd kept the e-mails to himself, Father Joe knew Carlos had made threats. "You're right. They won't go away unless I make them go away."

Father Joe shook his head. "I don't see how you can do that unless—"

"Unless I give him what he wants."

"Yes."

"I'm not going to do that. It doesn't belong to him, and it never did." Matt clenched his fists once under the table and took a breath. "He knows why."

"Matthew, you're being stubborn. It doesn't matter why. He's not a boy anymore, and neither are you. He has men with guns. I'm worried about you. I'm afraid you've made a choice that will hurt you and . . ." His voice dipped low, and the young priest leaned forward to hear. "And maybe that will hurt other people. Can you really live with that?"

"I don't have any choice."

"You do have a choice. Matthew, I have a friend who might be able to help. He's—"

"I'm not returning the money. That's final." He looked away from the naked fear he saw in the old man's face. Father Joe didn't understand, couldn't understand. They sat in silence until the waitress returned with two burgers and fries. Father Joe looked down at his plate, then pushed it away. Matt raised an eyebrow. "No appetite?"

"What will you do then?"

"I'm going to try talking to him, try to reason with him," Matt said between bites.

The old priest gaped. "What makes you think he'll listen?"

Matt put down his napkin. "At first, he'll listen because he wants the money. After that, I don't know. But I do have an idea that might work."

"What idea?"

Matt reached for the salt and a knife. "I can't tell you." He took a large bite of his burger and washed it down with coffee. He smiled at his mentor. "Do you have faith in me, Padre?"

Chapter Forty-six

BRONSON BRUSHED BY Smitty and tossed a typed report on Cancini's desk. He rocked back and forth on his feet. Cancini eyed the report. "Okay, I'll bite. What've you got?"

"Sonny Harding. You were right."

Smitty's head jerked up. "Hitting his wife?"

"Don't know about that, but he does have a temper." Bronson grabbed a chair and plopped down. "I got one incident at the company where he works—Mankin Construction. They build large office buildings and stuff like that. A lot of their work is out near Dulles."

"I've heard of it," Cancini said. The Dulles corridor, close to the airport, was populated by glass buildings, an expo center, and large corporations. The extended metro line contributed to the building boom.

"I interviewed some of his coworkers, and a couple things came up."

"Such as?"

"The first time was on the job. He threw a hammer at some guy because he said he screwed up. According to one guy—his name was Tucker—it was a minor issue and could have been fixed easily. Not so with the hammer. The guy ducked and the hammer missed him, but it was thrown so hard it smashed through the new drywall and it all had to be redone."

"What happened to the guy who screwed up?"

"Fired."

"Anyone else back up this guy Tucker's story?"

"Nah. No one wanted to say much. Think they might be worried about getting fired, too. I got a tip to talk to the bartender at Joe's Tavern, though. I showed him a picture of Harding, and he recognized him right away. Said Harding got in a fight with some other guy. Bunch of glasses got smashed and the other guy ended up with a shiner. According to the bartender, Harding felt bad after. He paid for the damages, bought the guy a drink, and left. Hasn't been back since."

Cancini flicked through the report. Harding had demonstrated a quick temper. After, he'd shown what appeared to be genuine remorse. Cancini knew it was a common pattern for some abusers. "Did he know what the fight was about?"

"Couldn't be sure, but the bartender thought it was over Harding's wife. Something about how the guy needed to keep his mouth shut and 'Stay away from my wife' and jealous shit like that."

Cancini scratched at his late-day stubble. Bad temper. Possessive behavior. "It could be something."

Smitty said, "It helps establish motive."

"I agree, but it's still a long ways from a bar fight to cold-blooded murder."

"Not if something was going on between the Mrs. and the priest." Bronson's thin lips puckered. "Harding coulda blown a gasket."

"Maybe she was just confiding in the priest," Smitty suggested. "Maybe she was telling him about her husband beating her up—"

"Allegedly beating her up," Cancini interrupted.

Smitty frowned but let it go. "They already work together. She said they were close. I know he was a priest, but it makes a weird kind of sense."

Cancini got to his feet, his knees cracking in protest. He crossed to the large whiteboard and followed the line he'd drawn between Erica Harding and Father Holland. The theory did make sense, and all other explanations bothered him. Was it his Catholic upbringing, or was it just the idea that the young priest might have been breaking his vows that bothered him? Cancini turned to the timeline he'd scratched across the bottom of the board. The murder had taken place Sunday evening when both Hardings claimed to be home together. "Even if we have motive, we don't have opportunity. We can't make a wife testify against her husband, and if we can't prove he wasn't home, we've got nothing."

"I might be able to help with that," Bronson volunteered.

"Go ahead." Cancini crossed his arms over his chest.

"Like I said earlier, I asked a couple of the guys if they knew what Harding did outside of work. Other than the occasional drink on Thursday evenings, most of them had no idea. Except one guy thought Harding might've had a small gambling problem. Said Harding is a huge NBA fan. Watches a lot of games at Wild Wingos in Roslyn and usually has a wager down. I checked last Sunday's schedule. There was a Wizards game that didn't end until after seven-thirty because it went into overtime."

"Now that is interesting," Cancini said. If Harding was at a bar, he wasn't home with his wife. "Have you checked with—what was it?—Wild Wingos?"

Bronson shook his head. "No confirmation yet. The manager recognized Harding's face, said he's been in before, but the manager didn't work that night. He thought the bartender might remember, but he's been out of town. He comes in at eight tonight, so that's where I'll be."

Cancini nodded. His gaze returned to the board, following the line that connected Father Holland to Erica Harding to Sonny Harding. He nodded at the young detective. "Good work, Bronson."

Chapter Forty-seven

"Why are we bothering with the secretary's husband?" Martin asked. "I thought Vega was the primary suspect."

Cancini kept his voice noncommittal. "He is, but it's still speculation at this point. Even if we can prove Vega is behind the threatening e-mails, it's circumstantial if we can't tie him to the weapon or place him at the scene."

Martin spit a shredded toothpick in the trash. As he reached for another, his hand froze over the bowl of fresh toothpicks. "Damn." He shook his head and reached in his desk for a pack of gum. Face sheepish, he said, "Lola doesn't like the toothpicks." Martin shoved the gum in his mouth and chewed hard, his jaw in constant motion. Cancini looked away, the man's chewing giving him a headache.

"Bronson's on his way to meet with the bartender now. If Harding was at the bar, he was lying about being home with his wife."

"Watching a game at a bar doesn't make him a murderer." His lips smacked together as he talked and chewed. "I briefed the brass this afternoon, and I don't mind saying, everyone—including the mayor—would like to see Vega off the streets. If we can get first-degree murder and money laundering charges to stick, it would be a coup for this department."

Cancini swallowed a groan. He understood the pressure Martin was under, but he wouldn't let it dictate how he ran the investigation. "I appreciate that everyone wants to nail Vega for the murder, but I've got to follow the evidence—all the evidence. Tonight, that means checking out Sonny Harding."

The two men stared at each other. Cancini knew full well Martin only tolerated him. They would never be friends, but for better or for worse, the captain's recent marriage to Cancini's ex had actually bought him some rope. After a moment, the captain waved a hand. "Fine. But after you rule out Harding, I want everyone assigned to this case working on Vega." He leaned forward, the wad of gum visible on his tongue. "Do we understand each other?"

"Perfectly." Outside the office, Cancini added, "Asshole."

"Is that our captain you're talking about?" Cancini's head whipped around to find Smitty laughing. "What did he do now?"

After Cancini repeated the conversation, Smitty whistled low under his breath. "Well, he's not going to be any happier after you hear what Bronson found out."

"Harding was at the bar?"

"Yep. Got there during the first quarter."

"How long did he stay?"

"Well, the bartender said Harding got a call on his cell. He didn't say much, just listened. Then he threw some bills on the bar and left. That was at six-fifteen, six-thirty at the latest."

"He's sure about the time?"

"Yeah, because another bartender clocked in at six-thirty, and by the time she came on, Harding was gone."

"It could have been his wife on the phone. He could have gone home."

"True."

Cancini frowned. Harding had motive and maybe opportunity, but Martin was right. There was no reason to assume Harding had penned those threatening e-mails or had any knowledge of the money. Vega had motive and wouldn't hesitate to gun down a priest in cold blood. He was the logical suspect, but Harding nagged at him anyway. "I want Bronson to stay on this, see if he can track Harding's movements, find out if any neighbors saw him return home that night. Might be good to get Mrs. Harding back in here, too."

"I'll call Bronson right now." Smitty yawned and picked up his phone.

"Good. Then I want you to go home. Get some sleep." Cancini shut down his computer. "I have a feeling it's going to be a long day tomorrow."

"What about you?"

"Headed to Father Joe's. Gonna swing by my place for a toothbrush, pick up some food, and call it a night."

"Thought he didn't want you to stay? He seemed pretty dead set against it."

"Yeah, that's what he said, wasn't it." Cancini pulled on his faded leather jacket and grinned. "But since when do I listen?"

Chapter Forty-eight

Thursday, February 18: Three Days Before the Day of

MATT PULLED THE lockbox off the shelf. He inserted the key and turned until the lid popped open. He sifted through the contents: letters from Father Joe, his birth certificate, social security card, a handful of papers. After a moment, he pulled out a photo and placed the rest of the contents back inside the box. He held the picture up to the light. In the picture, he stood awkwardly, Carlos's arm draped over his narrow shoulder. It was faded now, but the recollections of the day he'd run away from social services still burned in his memory.

He'd woken at five, eyes snapping open in the dark. Around him, the other boys in the group home had snored and snorted in their sleep. He'd sat up, careful not to make a sound when his feet hit the floor. He'd pulled on his sweatshirt and slipped into the beat-up high-tops he kept under the bed. He'd pushed the pillow and the rest of his clothes under the sheet and thin blanket, pressing it with his hands to resemble the rough shape of a teenage boy.

He'd known it wouldn't pass close inspection but might buy him a few extra minutes.

Social services had been scheduled for nine. It was the day he was supposed to officially move in with the foster family. He'd stood up straight, swallowing the bile that rose up in his throat. No way would he ever live with those leeches. He was no fool. He could see through their phony smiles and stupid words. It was bullshit. It was all about the money—just like everything else in the world.

Reaching into his pocket, he'd pulled out a few crumpled dollar bills. It was all he had, but it was enough to get him across town where he'd be safe.

He'd pulled his baseball cap low and tiptoed around the beds. Pulling a stolen credit card from his pocket, he'd taken one more look around the room. No one had stirred. The boys were sound asleep, probably dreaming of a better place, a place that didn't exist and never had. Too bad they were too naive to know it. With deft hands, he'd slipped the card between the door and the lock, tripping it on the first attempt. Quiet as a mouse, he'd slipped through the door, down the hall, and out into the darkness. He was free.

Matt sighed. He'd gone straight to Barry Farm, hiding in the shadows until he saw Carlos's mom leave for work. Carlos had answered the door on the third knock, bare-chested and drowsy with sleep. He'd blinked, wrapped his thin arms around his old friend, and pulled him inside, slamming the door. Carlos had done everything for him for three years. He'd helped him hide, brought him food. After enough time had passed, and they both knew no one was looking for Matt, he'd given Matt a job. Carlos had worked for Wayne then and he'd brought Matt in to help.

Matt had kept track of supply and demand, kept lists, packed bags. The money was good.

When Matt had turned eighteen, he'd known it was time to go. He'd grown tired of the life and tired of hiding. He'd wanted more, but he'd owed Carlos. He'd promised one more job. Carlos had said he needed a backup, but it had been more than that. Matt's skin went cold remembering Wayne's blood shooting across the room, the knife slicing a second time, a third. Wayne's hand had reached too late for his pistol. Matt had seen the cold ambition in Carlos's eyes. Matt had left that night without a word, disappearing as easily as though he'd never been there at all. They'd been friends, but that was a long time ago and they were on different sides now. He held the picture between his fingers and lit a match. He watched the picture blacken until it curled and shriveled, and he dropped it in the trash.

Matt sat down and took a deep breath. He couldn't change the past, but he could try to influence the future. Carlos had lost patience with him. It was time to be honest with his old friend. He wouldn't return the money. The best he could do was explain and help Carlos understand. Would it be enough? He couldn't be sure, but he had no choice. Either he'd live or he'd die.

Chapter Forty-nine

FATHER JOE WIPED his mouth with a napkin and placed the wooden chopsticks on the plate. "Thank you, Michael. I do love that spicy chicken and fried rice." He smiled. "You are so good to remember."

"It's the least I could do since you're putting me up for the night."

The old priest's smile faded. "You don't need to stay here. Nothing is going to happen."

Cancini pushed away from the table and cleared the plates. "You might be willing to take that chance, but I'm not." Father Joe started to get up, and Cancini laid a hand on his shoulder. "Sit. I've got it," he said, tidying the small kitchen while he talked. "Dad said to tell you hello."

"You saw him tonight?"

"Called. Jada said he was tired and getting ready to turn in. She takes good care of him."

"She's a good woman."

Cancini wiped the table and poured two cups of coffee. "In case you're wondering, I didn't tell him about you being shot."

Father Joe let out his breath. "Thank you. How's he doing?"

"He has good days and bad." The relationship between father and son might not have been traditional, maybe not even particularly good, but it was still difficult for Cancini to see his father so frail, so afraid. "The rainy weather we've had doesn't help his breathing, and he can't really go outside."

"Isn't he using oxygen?"

"Most of the time, but he fights it." Cancini set the cups on the table and sat down. "He hates the oxygen. Doesn't think he needs it, but without it, you can see him struggling." He shook his head. "Stubborn." In his head, he heard Julia's voice. Hadn't she said the same about him?

"Mmm. Like father like son."

Cancini looked at him sharply. "We are not alike, Father."

The priest picked up his cup. "It's true you are different, but you are alike in one way. Neither of you listen—even when someone asks you nicely."

"That's not going to work, Father. I'm not being stubborn. I'm doing my job. If we had available manpower, someone else would be here, but we don't." He grinned. "Lucky you."

Father Joe returned his smile. He reached out and patted the younger man's hand. "I'm always glad to spend time with you, Michael. Just because I don't think I need a babysitter doesn't mean I don't enjoy the company." He sipped his tea. "I also know you still have questions, although I don't know how much help I can be."

Cancini nodded. The sacrament bound the old man, forced him to keep the secrets of every man, woman, and child who entered the confessional. Cancini had been one of those children once. The decades had gone by, but he couldn't forget the words he'd once spoken in confession.

"I hate my father," he'd said, his voice trembling.

"'Hate' is a very strong word."

"It's true," he'd insisted. "I wish he'd died instead of my mother." He'd stumbled over the words, choking back sobs as he spoke. "I wish he was dead."

Cancini shook away the memory. That was a long time ago, and he'd been young, just a boy grieving for his lost mother and the father who couldn't or wouldn't fill the void.

"You asked me earlier about Carlos," Father Joe said. "He never left the neighborhood. He was probably Matt's closest friend when he was just a boy, but that was a long time ago."

"What about Carlos's mother? Could she tell us anything?"

The priest shook his head. "I doubt it. She's a good woman. Quiet. She doesn't live far from her old apartment in Barry Farm. The new one is nicer, of course, but still small. When Carlos was very young, his grandmother lived with them, too. She didn't speak much English, but she went to Mass at St. William every day, rain or shine."

"What do you think his mother knows about Carlos's business?"

"The chicken business?"

"No. His other business."

"Honestly? Probably nothing. Carlos's father died when he was five. Like many young boys, he felt it was his responsibility to take care of his mother and grandmother. Unlike most of them, he never outgrew that feeling."

"He kept her out of his business then?"

"That would be my guess. She knows about the chicken stores, of course, but I honestly doubt she knows about the gangs or the drugs or the rest . . ." His voice trailed off.

Cancini rubbed his fingers across the table, back and forth.

He agreed with Father Joe. The mother was probably a dead end. "Let's talk about something else then."

"Such as?"

"How about women?"

"I'm no authority as you know, but happy to listen." The lines in his forehead seemed to ease, and his shoulders settled into his chest. His lips turned up in a half smile and he raised his cup. "How is Julia?"

Cancini sat back and crossed one leg over the other. "She's fine. Says hello."

"Please say hello back."

"My question isn't about Julia. It's about the relationship between Father Holland and Erica Harding."

Father Joe set his cup on the table, hand steady. "She worked for Matt as the church secretary. I understand she was very good at her job."

"What I mean is what kind of relationship did they have?" He hesitated. "Beyond employer/employee. Friends outside of the office? More than friends?" The old man's faded eyes flickered, drifted away for a second, then locked on his again. Cancini let out a breath.

"I don't know what you mean."

"I think you do, Father. Erica Harding is an attractive woman. They spent a lot of time together."

The old man frowned and looked away. His face took on a far-off expression. "Matt took his vows very seriously."

"I'm not saying he didn't, but one thing I've learned about Father Holland was that he wasn't an ordinary priest. He was a complicated man."

Father Joe rose from his chair. He reached for the cane leaning against the table. Taking his cup to the sink, he balanced his weight against the counter. "We are all complicated, Michael. It's just a matter of degree."

"That doesn't change the fact that there was something. I haven't been able to put my finger on it exactly, but I don't think Mr. Harding liked it too much."

Father Joe refused to be baited. "You're only speculating."

"Really? I'm not speculating when I tell you Sonny Harding has a bad temper. I'm not speculating when I say he's an extremely possessive husband." He hesitated. "Sonny Harding beats his wife."

The old priest remained still, face placid. "I don't know that to be fact, and neither do you."

"I think Father Holland believed it. Maybe Harding didn't like all the time his wife spent with another man, priest or not. Maybe he found out the good Father Holland was making house calls while he was at work."

Father Joe shook his head. "You don't know what you're talking about."

"Don't I?" Father Joe's lips pursed. Cancini could almost see the uncertainty, the confusion. Had the young priest confided his attraction to his mentor? Or had he confided something more?

After a minute, Father Joe spoke again, any possibility of doubt wiped away. "A priest is not born asexual, Michael. He is a man who has committed himself to serving God. He makes the sacrifices required of him by choice." He sighed. "I will not speak for Matt on this matter ever again, except to say this. He may have been a man with a man's weaknesses, but he was also a man who swore his allegiance to God until his death." His shoulders slumped with his last words. "Those are my final thoughts on the matter." He turned back to the sink, washed his cup, and set it in the drying rack. "I'm turning in. If you still feel like you need to stay, I've set some bedding on the sofa in the living room. Sorry it isn't more."

"It's all I need." He stood, hugged Father Joe, and watched him hobble out of the kitchen. Cancini sat watching the old man's retreating back. What had the priest really told him? Nothing concrete, of course, but it occurred to Cancini that it didn't matter what actually happened between Erica Harding and Father Holland. It only mattered what her husband believed had happened. He sighed. It would be another long night.

In the living room, he sat in the dark, his head in his hands. His mind jumped from closed bank accounts to jealous husbands to skull tattoos. He couldn't decide if Father Holland was complicated or just plain crazy. Stealing from Vega? How did he think he was going to get away with it? Cancini raised his head and ran his fingers through his hair. It was almost like the guy had a death wish.

He stripped down to his T-shirt and laid his gun and cell phone next to him on the coffee table. Ignoring the bedding, he stretched out on the sofa, folding his arms over his chest. One hour stretched into two, and his mind refused to stop. Father Holland had an edge and a crazy streak, but he also had courage. He'd turned his back on the street life, the only life he'd really known. More amazing, the man had returned on a mission to make life better for those he'd left behind. He hadn't been able to save his mother, but somehow, he'd tried to make it up to her. Cancini understood.

He rolled his head to the side and yawned. A flicker of light caught his eye. He blinked. There it was again—the flicker. He leaped to his feet, hand finding the gun on the table. He crept to the large window and peered around the heavy drapes. In the immediate yard, he saw nothing. He looked to the right, at the dark building that dominated the property. Orange and yellow flames jumped and rose almost to the roofline. The church was on fire.

Chapter Fifty

RUNNING OUT THE door, Cancini shoved his gun in his waistband with one hand and dialed 911 with the other. Close to the church, hot flames forced him back. The fire climbed up the stone wall, gathering strength with each passing minute. Smoke billowed above the rooftop.

Cancini raced to the front of the church, searching in every direction. Most of the houses sat in darkness. A few cars lined the street, a few more sat in driveways. Sirens approached from the south. He looked up and down the street. Except for the siren and the crackle of the fire, he saw and heard nothing. The hair on the back of his neck rose, and he spun on his heels. Someone was watching him. There. The second house from the end of the block. The curtains on the upstairs window swung gently, as though whoever had been standing there had suddenly stepped away.

Twin fire engines rumbled down the block, sirens blaring. Lights went on up and down the street. He sprinted back to the small apartment, the heat from the fire swelling and hitting him in waves. He stopped short. Father Joe stood on the steps, leaning heavily against the doorway. Tears streamed down his cheeks. "Why?" he asked. "Why?"

"Come on," Cancini said. "Hang on to me. We need to get out to the street." He wrapped his arm around the old man's shoulder, pulling him forward. Father Joe limped alongside him until they reached the sidewalk. Breathing heavily, the old man sagged. Uniformed police arrived and blocked both ends of the street. "Everybody, get back," shouted a fireman. Along with the police, firemen herded them down the block. The minutes ticked by and the firemen alternately yelled, blasted water, and yelled again. Several residents clustered on the sidewalk, clutching their robes or coats and shaking their heads. Father Joe's lips moved in prayer. Black and white smoke rose into the night sky. The air smelled of charred timber and wet ash.

Cancini looked at Father Joe. "Will you be okay for a few minutes?"

"Are you leaving?"

"No. I just want to talk to whoever's in charge." He nodded in the direction of the fire trucks.

Father Joe stood up straighter. "I'll be fine." Cancini glanced back once. The old man was already surrounded by his neighbors, his parishioners.

"You need to stay back," said a young officer, holding out his arm.

"Detective Cancini. I called 911. I don't have my badge handy."

The young man caught sight of the handgun tucked into his waistband. Barefoot, Cancini wore only a plain T-shirt and pants. The officer's voice took on a wary tone. "I don't care who you are. You need to stay behind the line."

"Let him through, Johnson," came another voice. Fire Chief

Zeke Howell walked over. "He's with Homicide." The young man looked him over one more time, then backed away.

Howell pulled Cancini to the side. "Did I just hear you say you called this in?"

"Yeah." He pointed in the direction of the apartment. "I was staying the night with a friend and saw the fire from the front window."

The fire chief looked from the apartment to the church. "Well, you can count yourself a hero tonight."

Cancini eyed the blackened walls at the back of the church. "Doesn't look too bad. You guys are the heroes."

Howell shook his head. "No, you don't understand. That shouting you heard. There's a gas line just on the other side of that wall. Another ten minutes, maybe less, and the whole damn church might've blown."

Chapter Fifty-one

"CHRIST. WHAT A goddamn mess." Martin paced the small conference room. He whirled around to Cancini. "Any chance that fire was an accident?"

"I'm afraid not, Captain. Preliminary reports show it was deliberately set. And if the fire had gotten to that gas line . . ."

"Shit."

The room was quiet. Jensen stared at his shoes. Bronson twisted his pen in his hand. Smitty sat hunched over, his arms resting on his long legs. The implication was there. If Cancini hadn't been on the couch, if he hadn't been awake, if he hadn't seen the flickering light of the fire, the church, the apartment, and some of the block would have exploded into flames. Father Joe and Cancini might not have made it out alive. No one commented on the shortage of manpower. No one commented on the captain's insistence that the shooting of Father Joe had been an unrelated drive-by. No one hinted at his reluctance to request extra men. But everyone in the room knew. And they understood.

The fire had amped up the spotlight on Vega. Even though Cancini accepted that Father Joe would never break the sacrament of confession, he had to presume Vega was not convinced. He had to know they'd found the money, seen the trail of withdrawals and deposits. The drive-by had been a warning. Was the fire meant to be another warning or something more sinister?

"What's done is done," the captain said, his words resigned. "From here on out, we have twenty-four-hour surveillance on the priest." He looked at Cancini. "Where is he now?"

"I put him at my place."

"Fine. I want a uniformed guard outside the door until this investigation is closed."

"Already done, Captain."

Martin's head whipped around. He opened his mouth, closed it again. With deliberate slowness, he fished a toothpick out of his pocket and unwrapped the cellophane. He chomped a minute, then said, "What I want to know is, can we tie the fire to Vega?"

Smitty shook his head. "Not yet. I met with forensics this morning. Cancini is right. The fire was deliberate, but it was set with stuff you can get at any hardware store or gas station in the city. What's left is so charred, there's no chance of finding any fingerprints."

"What about witnesses?" the captain asked.

"It was close to two in the morning when the fire was set, so most of the residents on the street were asleep," Cancini said.

"So, another dead end."

"Well, maybe not. I talked to a woman named Cora Adkins. She lives across from the church, a couple of houses down, and her bedroom window faces the street. Suffers from insomnia and was awake. She had the TV on and thought she saw the glare of headlights come down the street and stop. She got up and went to the window, but it was dark and there were no headlights on. She got back in bed, kept the TV on but turned down the sound. Then she heard a car door slam. She got up again. This time, she saw the taillights of a car heading south."

"Why didn't she call the police?" Jensen asked.

"What was she going to report? That she saw a car driving down the street at two in the morning?"

"What about the fire?" Jensen whined. "She coulda reported that."

Cancini spoke through clenched teeth. "She couldn't see the back corner of the church from her bedroom window."

Martin shot a look at Jensen, whose gaze returned to his shoes. Bronson kept his mouth shut. "So she saw the car. Assuming the driver is our arsonist, can she tell us anything about the car? Make? Model?"

Cancini flipped open his notebook. "According to Mrs. Adkins, the car was a dark blue or black 1959 Chevrolet El Camino."

Jensen looked up from his shoes. "How could she know that? It had to be pitch black out there."

Cancini grinned. "True, but the 1959 El Camino has very distinctive taillights. If you see them, you'll notice."

"You're telling me she identified a car from nothing but the taillights."

"Yes, I am."

"C'mon," Jensen said, scowling. "Isn't she like eighty-five years old? She's probably half blind. How the hell would an old lady know an El Camino from a Camaro or a Monte Carlo?"

"She's eighty-one. She was wearing both her glasses and her hearing aid at the time. So my guess is she can see and hear better than you on your best day." He turned his back on Jensen. "The reason Mrs. Adkins is so positive is she drove an El Camino for most of her life. Her husband was a huge car buff, and while they had other cars, they kept that one. She sold it to a collector after he died." He dropped a picture of the car on the table. "See how the taillights have that long, curved shape? You can see how you might remember them—especially in the dark."

Martin picked up the photo, then passed it around the room. "Let's say she's not only right, she's credible, which is all we have to go on right now. There can't be that many of those old cars around. It should be easy enough to get a list of owners."

"I've already put in a request with the DMV."

"Good. Let's expand that to all the counties within fifty miles of the city. It still shouldn't be a long list. Maybe, just maybe, we'll get lucky." Martin looked at his watch and stood. "I've gotta brief the chief before the press conference." Cancini started to speak, but Martin held up his hand. "I got it." He looked around the room. "The El Camino will not be part of the briefing, and is not to be shared outside of this room." Cancini exhaled and nodded. "Officially, as far as the fire is concerned, we're investigating all possible leads. End of statement." He paused. "I want every available man on Vega. I don't care how many rocks we have to dig under or how many people we have to interview. Let's get that asshole." He headed for the door, then stopped short and bowed his head. "Cancini, sorry about your friend being involved. We'll do what it takes to keep him alive."

Chapter Fifty-two

"FATHER JOE OKAY?" Smitty asked, and swiveled his chair to stretch his long legs.

"Yeah. Complaining, but okay." Cancini half smiled. "More worried about having had to move today's Mass to another parish than about himself. Typical." He glanced up to find Bronson standing close. The young detective shifted from one foot to the other. "What is it, Bronson?"

"Well, after the fire and everything, and what Martin said . . ."

"Spit it out."

"Harding. I'd planned to see if I could track his movements the night of Holland's murder, see if he went straight home or somewhere else. Might be nothing and maybe I should be on Vega . . ."

Cancini tapped his pencil in his hand. "But?"

The man dipped his head and licked his lips. "But I'd kinda like to see it through."

Looking over the man's shoulder at the whiteboard, Cancini found the line connecting Harding and Holland. It was a tenuous connection, speculative at best. A jealous husband with a bad temper? And jealous of a priest? It would be almost laughable if it didn't seem oddly possible. Men had killed over less.

He nodded at Bronson. "Talbot's sending over some financials from Vega's restaurants. Jensen can handle those with Landon. In the meantime, see what else you can find on Harding."

"And the captain?"

"Will see how hard you're working."

Bronson smiled and moved away. "Thanks, boss."

Cancini studied the board, eyebrows furrowed. Sensing Smitty behind him, he turned. "What is it?"

The blond shrugged one shoulder. "Just wondering what that was all about. I thought we were focused on Vega."

"We are, but Bronson's showing some work ethic for a change. Besides, Harding has a temper. We've both seen his wife's bruises."

Smitty frowned. "Nobody wants Harding to get what he deserves more than I do." He paused and slowed his breathing. "But the fact that he's a wife beater doesn't make him a murderer or an arsonist."

Cancini sat forward. Even though Smitty had good reason to dislike Harding, he was willing to hold off and focus on Vega. As the lead detective, he recognized it was the right call. He just wasn't sure he could do that yet. "He lied to us about where he was when Father Holland was murdered."

"Again, that doesn't make him guilty. Everything points to Vega. Follow the money. Remember?"

"Yeah, I remember." Vega—or more likely someone working for Vega—was the logical suspect in the murder, the shooting, and the arson. But that didn't stop Cancini from wanting to tie up loose ends, and right now, Harding was a loose end. "Where are we on the car?"

"The DMV has a listing for four '59 El Caminos in the district, one in Alexandria, two in Great Falls, and three in Potomac." Smitty handed Cancini a copy of the printout.

"Ten total?"

"Yep. Probably more if we expanded, but it's a good start."

Cancini scanned the list. "This gives us names and addresses. What about ages, sex, anything else?"

"I've already started looking into it. The first name is John McGinty. He's sixty-three and a CFO in some design firm. Lives in Georgetown and owns three other cars from the fifties, as well as a two-year-old Aston Martin. I'm guessing he's a collector."

"Okay. You take the top five on the list and I'll take the bottom five."

An hour later, his cell phone buzzed. Seeing it was Bronson, Cancini picked up the line. "Yeah?"

"I don't know whether it's something or not, boss, but Harding is definitely a suspicious guy."

Cancini sat down and slugged back a cup of lukewarm coffee. "Get to the point, Bronson."

"I just got to Harding's building and he came out for lunch, so I followed him. He met with some guy at a deli. There was some kind of an exchange."

"An exchange?"

"Yeah. Looked like they swapped envelopes. Not only that, but Harding seemed angry. He got in the guy's face and had his finger in his chest. People were looking."

Cancini put the cup back on the desk and gestured to Smitty. "What happened after that?"

"Harding left. I figured he was headed back to work, so I followed the other guy. He made a couple of stops—dry cleaner, drugstore—then went back to his office. I waited about ten minutes, then ducked inside. Only three names on the sign inside: a real estate guy, an accountant, and a private detective. My money's on the private detective."

"Did you get a name?"

"Yeah. Hank Goins."

Cancini made notes and held them up to Smitty. "Has he left the office since?"

"Not yet. I'm parked close to his building so I can see if he leaves, but I thought I should check with you first, see what you wanted me to do next."

"Good work. Hang on a sec." He covered the cell phone with his hand and nodded at Smitty. "Can you run a check on this guy Hank Goins? Supposed to be a private detective."

"I'll make some calls, see what I can find."

Cancini took his hand off the phone. To Bronson, he said, "Hang tight, Bronson. Stay where you are until I call you back. If he leaves the building, let me know."

"You got it, boss."

Cancini looked over at Smitty, already on the phone and typing on his keyboard. Assuming Bronson was right, why would Harding hire a private detective? To follow his wife? Cancini rubbed a hand across his head, then reached into the top drawer for a large bottle of ibuprofen.

Smitty hung up. "Goins is a former cop. He was in vice for fifteen years, then took an early retirement." Cancini arched one eyebrow. "Yeah. Story is he might have been sampling the wares. There were a couple of accusations and rumors, but he resigned before it got any further." His blond hair flopped over his forehead as he read from his computer screen. "Until the last six months or so before he quit, he had a clean record." Smitty looked up again. "I reached out to a friend that used to work Vice. Said Goins was an okay cop, 'passable' was his word."

"'Passable' is not an endorsement."

Smitty grinned. "I knew you'd say that. According to my friend, Goins got caught up in a bad situation. Things were tough at home, divorce, custody, the whole works."

Cancini had heard similar stories for years. The job took its toll on a lot of marriages, a lot of families. "Anything else?"

"He set up the private business about a year ago. His Web site says he specializes in domestic cases."

Cancini glanced across the room at Martin's office. The door was closed. Around him, the focus was Vega. Everything Vega touched and everyone he knew was being scrutinized more than once. Martin was working on getting warrants, but their case was flimsy. Vega had a problem with Holland. Vega wanted his money back. Vega had motive. Vega had connections to the Death Squad. Vega had opportunity. Cancini didn't doubt that Vega was more than capable of ordering the murder of a priest, and he was not above burning down a church. They just had to prove it. "Can you handle going through the rest of the names on the list until I get back?" Smitty nodded and raised one eyebrow. Cancini stood up and slipped on his jacket. An image of Erica's bruised temple crossed his mind. "I need to have a little chat with Mr. Hank Goins."

Chapter Fifty-three

Saturday, February 20: One Day Before the Day of

"THANK YOU FOR staying after today, Sophia. I hope I'm not keeping you from anything." The late-afternoon Mass had ended and the parishioners had gone. "I promise I won't keep you long."

"It's no problem, Father Holland." She sat on the hardback chair, hands folded in her lap. Her dark hair, speckled with gray, had been swept into a tidy bun at the base of her neck. Her only makeup was a subtle color on her lips.

"I asked you here to thank you."

Twin lines appeared between her brows. "Thank me? For what?"

"For everything you did for me when I was a boy."

She waved a hand in the air. "It wasn't me. It was Carlos." She smiled at him. "Did you know I didn't even know you were staying with us for the longest time?" She frowned. "The truth is, I don't remember you being there all that much."

"I spent a lot of time out when you weren't at work. I didn't want to be a burden."

"Oh, you could never be that." Her face brightened. "And look at you now. A priest." She hesitated, then said in a soft voice, "I think your mother would have been proud of you. I didn't know her well, but I know she loved you."

Tears pricked at his eyes, and he bowed his head. "Thank you." After a moment, he raised his head. "Sophia, I want to give you something." Her lips parted, surprised. "Before you say you can't accept it, let me tell you it's not a gift—not exactly." Her mouth closed. He bent his head and took a breath. "It's more of a favor actually."

"I'll help if I can."

"Thank you." He smiled. "As you know, we've been working very hard to rebuild this old church." He waved a hand around the office. "We've also been working to bring in more parishioners and grow our outreach program to help people who are unable to help themselves."

"And you've been doing a marvelous job, Father Holland. Everyone says so."

"You're a good woman, Sophia." He reached over to the coffee table and picked up a large manila envelope. "I'd like to give this to you."

She stared but did not take it. "What is it?"

He smiled again. "It's something I hope we can work on together." He pushed it gently into her hands. He nodded at the envelope. "St. William has had some good news. We have a very generous benefactor, someone who believes in this church and our mission. This person—who chooses to remain anonymous—has set up a foundation to help fund the renovation and our other projects."

"That's wonderful." Her surprise melted into confusion. "But I don't understand. What does this have to do with me?"

His smile widened. "The donor has designated you to serve as one of the trustees. I am also a trustee. There are three more, an attorney, a bishop from the diocese, and Father Sweeney. Originally, I was the only trustee, but I believe a larger committee is better. Don't you agree?"

"Yes, but I still don't understand. Why me?"

He squeezed her hand. "I hope you'll forgive me. It was my idea. I wanted someone who had been a member of this church for a long time. I also wanted someone who understood the challenges of living in this neighborhood, in this community. It's getting better. I believe that, but we still have a long way to go." Again, he smiled and held her hands in his. "I also know what an honest and giving woman you are. You've always been kind to me. It would be an honor to have you as one of our trustees."

"Well"—she bowed her head—"I don't know what to say."

"Say yes."

Her eyes rose to meet his. "Yes."

Chapter Fifty-four

CANCINI EYED THE darkening sky. Thick clouds heavy with rain hung overhead. He walked faster, dodging fat raindrops. Huddled under the overhang, Bronson waited outside the P.I.'s building.

"He's still in there," Bronson said as Cancini joined him. "On the third floor."

"Is there a secretary?"

"Not that I've seen."

Cancini scanned the street. Most of the buildings on the block were old. Some looked as though they could be abandoned, and traffic was almost nonexistent. "Not exactly in the best part of town, is it?"

Bronson snorted. "That's for sure. I've only seen three people go in this building all day, and one of 'em was Goins."

The dark-haired detective looked up and down the street one more time and pushed open the door. "Let's go."

Bronson entered the outer office first. A single desk—empty—took up most of the space. A metal file cabinet pushed in the corner was topped by a dusty, vinelike plant with curling, brown leaves. A silent phone sat on the bare desktop. Cancini nodded his head toward the door behind the empty desk. Bronson followed.

In the doorway, Cancini held a finger to his lips. The shorter detective nodded, careful to step in quietly. Hank Goins lay stretched out on a sofa, his feet hanging over the arm, nearly touching the floor. A newspaper over his face rose and fell with every breath, occasionally interrupted by short spurts of snoring. Low voices came from a TV perched on a battered credenza. Cancini moved to the desk, where the rest of the newspaper covered the surface. There was no sign of an envelope. He nodded once at Bronson, then slammed the door closed, rattling the hinges.

"Wh-what?" Goins shot up off the sofa. The newspaper rustled and floated to the floor. "Hey. Who are you?"

"I'm Detective Bronson, and this is Detective Cancini." Bronson jerked his thumb at Cancini. "We were hoping you could answer a few questions."

Small and wiry, Goins scurried across the room, flipping on the lamp and clearing the papers from his desk. He looked at both detectives, his close-set eyes coming to rest on Cancini. "You know, I used to be on the job, too, before this . . ." Goins's voice drifted away. He waved a hand at the two chairs. "Have a seat." He dropped into the chair behind his desk. "What can I help you with?"

"I want to know about your client Sonny Harding," Cancini said.

"Former client, you mean." Goins's top lip curled. "Asshole fired me today."

"Why'd he fire you?"

"Just wasn't working out, you know."

"No. I don't know. Why don't you tell me?"

The small man's foot swung under the desk, and his hands fluttered over the desk. "Nothing to tell really," Goins said. "Domestic case—that's my specialty—but just wasn't going anywhere."

"Your client—excuse me—former client has a bit of a temper and is a little on the possessive side when it comes to his wife."

Goins straightened a pile of paper clips. "I don't know about that, but his wife is a looker."

"Yes. Mrs. Harding is very pretty." Cancini watched the P.I.'s face as he spoke. "Maybe even pretty enough to attract a priest."

Goins's mouth fell open. "You know about that?"

"Yes, I know about that."

"I guess I shoulda come forward before, but Harding is my client." His foot swung back and forth. "I mean, was my client."

"Come forward about what exactly?"

"Nothing really. It's just, you know, the priest . . . he's dead now." He stared at the floor, lips closed tight.

"Harding had you following his wife, right? That's how you discovered the relationship between Mrs. Harding and Father Holland. You saw him visit her at the Harding's home while Mr. Harding wasn't there. Is that right?"

Goins blinked. "Yes, that's right."

"And like any good private detective, you gave that information to your client."

"He hired me to watch her. I had to tell him."

"Because he was paying you." The man nodded. "And you were still watching her."

Goins picked at a scratch on the desk. "He didn't trust her."

"But he fired you anyway."

"Yeah. I gave him a written report and he paid me."

Cancini tapped his pen against his notepad. "You said he didn't trust her. You reported on her activities, right?"

"Yeah?" Goins cocked his head, his tone wary. "I guess he thought he'd learned enough. Plus the priest was, uh, dead."

"Right. But you didn't say the case was closed. You said he fired you."

"'Fired' might be a bit strong."

"Did he think you weren't doing your job?"

Goins face flamed. "I did my job."

"But he fired you anyway?"

"It wasn't my fault his wife gave me the slip."

Cancini and Bronson exchanged glances. "What do you mean gave you the slip?"

The private detective looked away. "The asshole blamed me. She probably knew he was having her followed. He wanted to know everything she did. For Christ's sake, I think he would've had me follow her into the bathroom if it was possible. I mean, I've worked with some weirdos, but I'm telling you, this guy's obsessed with his wife."

Cancini didn't like it. In his experience, even the most banal obsessions could grow into something sinister. They already suspected domestic violence. How far would Harding go? "How'd she evade surveillance?"

"He was out. I don't know where." Goins shrugged. "I was parked halfway down the block, and I saw her leave the house in a cab. I followed until the driver dropped her off at Ballston in front of Macy's. The cab pulled over to the loading zone to wait. I parked as quick as I could and waited, too. It was just before six, and the stores were getting ready to close, so I figured she was picking something up. She never came out."

Cancini's fingers tightened around the pen in his hand. "What about the cab?"

"It left at six-fifteen without her. That's when I knew I'd been had. I called Harding as soon as I realized it."

"Where do you think she went?"

"Hopped on the metro is my guess. Don't know after that."

"When did this happen?"

Goins mouth screwed up in thought. "A week ago Sunday."

"Shit," Bronson said. "That's the night Holland was—"

Cancini glared. "How did Harding respond when you called him?"

Goins's forehead scrunched, and his eyes seemed to grow closer together. "Hey, you don't think this has anything to do with the priest's murder, do you?"

Cancini ignored the question, asking his own. "What did Harding say when you told him you lost his wife?"

"He didn't say anything at first. He was pissed—like I knew he would be. But then he just said he had to go. That's all." His gaze shifted between the two detectives. "He didn't say anything else. I swear. Do you think it means anything?"

"Doubtful," Cancini said. He sighed and pasted a disappointed expression on his face. "Think you might have been right about Harding after all. Just a weirdo."

"Yeah, but—"

Cancini stood and stuck out his hand. "So sorry to have wasted your time. Thanks anyway." Cancini left the office, Bronson trailing after him. He remained silent until they reached the street. Heavy rain came down in sheets. Rivers of water dotted with trash flowed down the gutters on the silent street. The dreary sky matched his mood.

"Bronson, I want you to dig deeper. See if you can track Harding's movements Sunday night, and go back further if you can. I want to know everything there is to know about Sonny Harding."

"So, that bit about it being nothing? That was just for Goins's benefit?"

"You're learning."

"What about the wife? You want me to find out about her?"

Cancini paused. On Monday morning, Erica Harding had been distraught, weeping, and she'd been recently struck. Was that for sneaking out or for something else? "Yeah. Her, too." Cold rain dripped under the collar of his coat. He started to walk away, then stopped short. "And Bronson?"

"Yeah, boss?"

"Don't interrupt me during a questioning again. Ever."

Chapter Fifty-five

"START OVER," CANCINI SAID.

Smitty tossed a stack of papers on his desk. Dark smudges under his eyes gave his face a haunted look. "What's the point?" his partner asked. "I've spent the whole damn day on this, and nothing. I can't see any of these owners having anything to do with Vega."

"It won't be obvious," Cancini said. He kept his voice neutral in spite of his disappointment, in spite of the pounding at the back of his skull. "Let's start with the collector. Tell me one by one about every owner, how long they've had the car, how many drivers in the household. I want to know if they've ever had any brush with the law, even a speeding ticket." Smitty lowered his gaze to the motor vehicle report. His narrow shoulders drooped. Cancini's own body felt like he'd been in an NFL game. They'd all been working too many hours. "Tell you what. Let's duck out for a half hour. Grab a sandwich and some decent coffee for a change. Then we'll get at it."

Smitty looked up and exhaled. "Yeah. That would be good."

Cancini's cell phone buzzed. He looked down at the caller ID. "Give me a minute. I'll meet you downstairs." Smitty nodded, already pulling on his coat.

"Father Joe?" The tired muscles in his body tensed. "Everything all right?"

"Fine, Michael. Fine."

"You're okay, then?" The priest, at Cancini's apartment since the fire, was being guarded twenty-four hours a day. He didn't like it, but Cancini had given him no choice.

"Of course, I'm okay. But if you must know the details, food was delivered an hour ago so I won't starve. Your officer won't let me go anywhere. He won't leave the front door—not even to use the bathroom or get a drink of water. Apparently, he's under strict orders." Father Joe did not hide his annoyance. "So I'm good if you don't count not being able to leave or go to Mass or do any of the things I'm supposed to be doing."

Cancini sighed. He sat down again and stretched his legs. "It's only temporary."

"Well, I hope so. We have a shortage of priests in the city already, in case you've forgotten. The diocese is scrambling to find replacements on such short notice."

"I'm not going to apologize."

"Wasn't expecting you to."

Cancini spotted Martin coming out of his office with his suit coat clutched in his hand. The captain stomped down the hall and down the stairs. "What's that all about?" he muttered.

"What? Michael, did you say something?"

"Nothing," Cancini said. "You called me. Did you need something?"

"I wanted to run something by you."

"What's that?"

"Sophia Vega called me today."

Cancini inhaled and his shoulders straightened. "Carlos's mother."

"Yes. She said she wanted to talk to me about the foundation Matt started. She said it was very important that she talk to me and me only."

"How did she know about it?"

"I asked her that. She said she'd rather not say on the phone. She wants to meet."

"I don't like it."

"I'm not worried about Sophia Vega. That's not why I told you."

"Well, I am. Her son could be using her as a pawn."

"No. She doesn't have anything to do with his illegal activities. I'm sure of it."

"You're too trusting."

"And you're too suspicious."

Cancini raised his eyes to the ceiling. "You asked my opinion."

"No, I didn't. I said I wanted to run something by you. I told her I would meet with her, but I don't want her coming here with the guard outside. I don't want her to be uncomfortable."

"Now who's being suspicious?"

Father Joe ignored the comment. "Can you get your man to disappear just long enough for her to meet with me? An hour. That's all I'm asking."

Cancini sat forward, bending his knees again. Sophia Vega might be the closest link they had to Carlos. If they were to approach his mother for any reason, Carlos would be alerted. If her coming to them was as innocent as Father Joe believed, then it might not raise any alarm bells. "Maybe. When does she want to meet?"

"Tomorrow morning. At eleven."

It wasn't much time, but it would have to do. "Call her back and tell her to meet you then."

"No guard?"

"No guard."

"Thank you, Michael."

Cancini hung up and joined Smitty at the bottom of the stairs.

"Everything okay?" Smitty asked.

"Yeah," Cancini said. "I might need your help on something tomorrow."

The men ducked out of the building, both bracing against the wind. Smitty pulled on his gloves. "Do you think this car thing could be a dead end? A waste of time?"

Walking faster to match Smitty's long stride, Cancini considered the question. He shoved his hands far into his pockets, rolling his shoulders into a hunch against the bitter wind. Darkness had fallen over the city like a blanket, covering the ugliness of the day. Was it possible Mrs. Adkins was wrong about the make and model after all? He dismissed the idea. She was too sure, too definite. The lady was old, but she was more together than many young people he knew. "No," he said finally. "There's something there. We'll find it."

Chapter Fifty-six

"DID I WAKE you?" she asked, her voice soft and hesitant.

"No. What time is it?" Cancini sat up on the sofa, hanging his pounding head. He glanced toward his bedroom. The door was closed. He'd insisted Father Joe take the bed, arguing he often slept on the sofa. It wasn't entirely true, but he did spend many a sleepless night on the sofa, abandoning the bed for hours at a time. "Never mind. I don't want to know."

Julia gave a short laugh. "Can't sleep again, huh?"

"Nope." He stood, padded to the kitchen, and pulled an ice-pack from the freezer. "Father Joe is staying with me."

"Really? Why?" He gave a brief rundown on the prior evening's events, leaving out the details of the investigation. "That's terrible," she said. "How's Father Joe doing?"

"He's fine. As bossy as ever." Julia laughed, low and husky with exhaustion, and he was suddenly overcome with the desire to see her, touch her. Biting back on the words he felt, he asked, "How about you? Anything as exciting as church fires going on up in the Big Apple?"

"No, can't say that there is, but things are definitely happening with the story." She paused. "Do you want to hear about it?"

It was the reason she'd called and he recognized it, recognized the need to share, to have someone else learn what you've learned. He knew little about her assignment beyond research into the unsolved murder case in Manhattan. Theories had been swirling that the murder had ties to New York money and politics, but so far, nothing had been proven, and the body had never been found. The woman, a young beauty queen who'd worked her way into New York society, had disappeared on the eve of her engagement to the governor's son. The story had been big news, and with the discovery of some new evidence, could be once again. But it wasn't the story that would make him say yes. He just wanted her to keep talking. "Tell me," he said.

He settled down into the sofa, letting the icepack numb his head. Whenever she paused, he made the appropriate comment, but mostly, he listened. When she finished, he was impressed and told her so. "That's pretty damn good investigating, Ms. Manning. Maybe you should be a detective."

She laughed again. "Thank you. I don't have everything I need yet, but I'm getting there." Her tone changed. "How do we look for Saturday?"

He hesitated. He wanted to tell her they looked good. He wanted to tell her he wanted nothing more than to wrap his arms around her and hold her. But he knew he couldn't. After marriage to an unfaithful husband, she was sensitive to promises, and he knew better than to make them. "Still the same. I'm trying."

Cancini heard her soft breath through the line. "I know you are."

After she hung up, he remained on the sofa, the ice no longer cold and his head throbbing just a little less. The last date had been better than he'd hoped, more than he deserved. He was trying. They were both were. But what exactly were they trying for?

Chapter Fifty-seven

"I TOOK YOUR advice," Smitty said, handing Cancini a steaming cup of coffee. "I included family information, jobs, locations, anything I could find."

"And?"

"And I think I've got one." He read from his computer screen. "Gerald Ketchum, age sixty-two, lives in Potomac and works as CFO of Anderson Analytics. His office is on M Street."

"A collector like the others?"

"Looks like it. He owns five cars; three are classics. He's married to Evelyn Ketchum and they have two children, a daughter who lives in Florida and a son—also Gerald—who lives here in D.C."

Cancini took a sip, grimacing when the coffee scalded his tongue. He blew on it once, then sipped again. "Does the son live at home?"

"No. He's twenty-nine and lives alone in an apartment in Georgetown. He's a part-time student with no obvious means of income. Looks like Dad pays the rent."

"This sounds like there's a 'but' in there somewhere."

"Oh, there is. The son dropped out of college when he was twenty-one. Joined the marines. Served seven years"—Smitty paused and cocked his head—"before he was dishonorably discharged."

"Ah." Cancini set his cup on the desk. "What did he do?"

"During a tour in Afghanistan, he belonged to an elite unit that specialized in terrorist kills. He's an expert shot and trained in explosives."

"And the dishonorable discharge?"

"Punched a superior. Had a little trouble with authority."

"I see." Cancini fingered the files piled up on his desk. "And how long has he been back in the city?"

"He's been in the apartment for about six months."

Cancini stood and walked over to the large whiteboard. It was covered in lines and names and dates. Taped to the corner was a drawing, a crude reproduction of the skull and knife tattoo. He pulled it down and turned back to Smitty. "Let's pay Mr. Ketchum Senior a visit."

"I already made an appointment. He's expecting us in twenty minutes."

"Good."

"Cancini. I need to talk to you." Martin's voice carried across the precinct.

Cancini looked up and muttered, "What is it now?"

Martin crossed the floor in three quick strides. "Please tell me you and Bronson are not wasting time chasing after that secretary's husband. I specifically told you to put every man on Vega." Out of the corner of his eye, Cancini caught Jensen making a quick exit down the stairs. Spit flew from Martin's mouth with each word. As he grew louder, the room grew quieter and eyes looked anywhere but at the captain or Cancini. "Let me say this again. Harding is not our prime suspect here. He has an alibi. Vega is our prime suspect; therefore, he is our focus. Have I made myself clear?"

Cancini let several seconds pass. He clenched and unclenched his fists until the immediate tension drained. "Actually, Captain, we've been working the Vega investigation, and we've got a promising lead."

"Really?" Martin scowled. "What kind of lead?"

"The '59 El Camino." Smitty held up the file and waved it in the air. Cancini grabbed his coat off his chair and slipped it on. He looked at his watch. "We've got an appointment about it right now." He nodded at Smitty, and they skirted desks, heading for the stairs.

"Keep me posted," Martin said, the bluster faded from his voice.

Smitty and Cancini crossed the parking lot. Looking over the car, Smitty said, "Martin was pretty pissed."

Cancini frowned. The captain wasn't entirely wrong. Their focus should be Vega. The money was motive enough. The long-standing relationship. The e-mails and threats. All of that was real—although circumstantial. They just needed to prove it. But Harding bothered him. Was it the bruises? Was it the possessiveness? Was it the suggestive relationship between the secretary and the priest? He didn't know—only that he couldn't let it rest until he knew the answer. He waved a hand and ducked into the car. "He'll get over it. Just blowing smoke like always."

Chapter Fifty-eight

Sunday, February 21: The Day of

HE WATCHED THE couple as they left the pew. The Hardings followed the crowd, waiting in line for communion. She would come to him as she always did, reaching up with the fingers of her cupped hand, touching his for a second, maybe even less. Did her husband notice? He guessed the man did. He guessed the man noticed a lot of things she did.

As usual, she dressed conservatively. This Sunday, she wore a heavy wool skirt that fell to mid-calf, hiding her knees but not long enough to hide the shapely legs underneath. A turtleneck covered her arms and neck, although he could still see the purple bruises peeking out near her hairline. It had been risky, but he was glad he'd gone to see her. Mr. Harding hadn't been home, and it was her day off. At the church, he couldn't approach her without risking being interrupted. Outside of church, her husband was always there. Even at the church, the husband followed every move she made.

She'd been working for him for months before he'd really noticed her. He worked so hard, took almost no time off, and he had a mission, one he held close. He couldn't say how it had started exactly. Maybe it was a whiff of perfume. Maybe it was the way her brows knitted together when she concentrated. Maybe it was the way she hobbled around on a sprained ankle. He couldn't really place it. Only that her nearness was something he knew was wrong, and yet he wanted it anyway. She jumped when he called for her. She covered her body with clothing that somehow revealed luscious curves.

He knew he was a handsome man. His mama had told him when he was a boy. "My little Matt's gonna be a heartbreaker," she used to say to her friends. "The ladies are gonna swarm around him like bees to a honeypot, I tell you." More than one had offered to "break him in" but his mama had shooed them away. "You wait," she'd told him. "Make it mean somethin'. Not like it is around here." She hadn't elaborated, but he'd known what she meant. His mama had done things he didn't want to know about. It wasn't her fault, though. It was the drugs. He'd stayed away from the ladies, not because he wasn't eager to test his manhood, but because he was afraid. He saw the life around him for what it was. Death disguised as living. He hadn't wanted that then, and he didn't want it now.

But Erica wasn't like those women. She wasn't cheap or the type to go looking for one-night stands. He'd known she was special. The visits hadn't relieved his anxiety as he'd hoped, though. Did he feel better or worse? He didn't know. As she approached the front of the line, she kept her head down, hands pressed together in prayer. She came closer and closer still.

He held the wafer in his hand and placed it into the palm of her cupped hands. "The body of Christ," he said.

"Amen." She turned away and placed the wafer in her mouth.

He repeated the communion words and handed the next wafer to Erica's husband. The man stood still, holding up the line. Matt was forced to look at the man, look into his face. "Amen, Father," he said, eyes hard as stones.

Matt exhaled. It was only then he realized she hadn't touched him, hadn't brushed his fingers with her own. For better or worse, something had changed.

Chapter Fifty-nine

GERALD KETCHUM LED them to a five-car garage. It stood thirty yards behind the house, nearly invisible from the street. Cancini and Smitty followed him inside. Four classic cars glowed under the fluorescent lights. The El Camino, a deep navy blue, was parked in the last bay.

"I'm a bit of a collector," he said, expression sheepish. "I know it must seem like a rather indulgent hobby—and it is—but to me, these cars represent a piece of history."

"Is that an Aston Martin, like the ones in the Bond movies?" Smitty asked, pointing at a cherry-red convertible with a caramel top.

"Yes. She's a beauty, isn't she?" The man nodded with a smile. "I bought that car in 2001. It's the reason I built this garage." Cancini's hazel eyes swept over the windowless garage. Large fluorescent lights hung over each car. A workbench at least fifteen feet in length ran along the far wall. Shiny tools hung from hooks, and car manuals sat on the bench next to a desktop computer and printer. Heating and cooling units had been installed at each end of the garage. "I spend a lot of time in here, probably too much if you ask my wife. She only puts up with it because, years ago, she thought it was good father-son time." He turned to Smitty. "Do you know much about cars?"

"A little," Smitty answered. "My uncle was a mechanic at a garage that worked on a lot of imports. I helped out sometimes."

"A good mechanic is worth his weight in gold," the man said. He pointed toward the El Camino. "Well, here it is." Cancini walked the length of the car while the man talked. "I bought this beauty at an auction about seven years ago, although it didn't look this good back then." He chuckled. "Took me months to restore, but it was worth it."

Ketchum rambled on about the engine and the seats, but Cancini had stopped listening. He stood behind the car, taking in the sweeping rear end and distinctive taillights. Mrs. Adkins could have been mistaken, but he didn't think so, and the color matched her description. He stepped closer and crouched down, bending his head to see under the bumper and around the exhaust. He pulled his phone from his pocket and took a picture.

Smitty asked a question about the horsepower, and the conversation ground to a halt. Ketchum rubbed his hands together. "Well, you've seen the car. Is there anything else I can help you with?"

Cancini stood up and shoved his hands in his pockets. "A witness identified a dark-colored '59 El Camino speeding away from the scene of an arson earlier this week."

Ketchum shook his head. "There must be some mistake. You can't think I had anything to do with that."

"Where were you between one and three a.m. on Monday morning?"

The man blinked. "You're not kidding, are you? It has to be another El Camino or maybe even another car." He looked from one detective to the other. "I was here. In bed. My wife can verify that."

"I'm sure she can, but we'll have to ask her anyway." Cancini nodded toward the car. "When was the last time the car was driven?"

Ketchum smiled briefly. "That's easy. Labor Day weekend. My wife and I took the car out for a drive." He reached out and caressed the hood of the car. "I try to keep the mileage down, but it was a beautiful day and I thought I'd take it for one more spin before the weather turned."

Smitty glanced once at Cancini, then asked, "So you only drive it in the summer?"

"For the most part. That's true with all my cars. I don't take chances in rain at all. Call it a quirk . . ." He shrugged as his words trailed off.

"So there hadn't been any rain or bad weather the last time you drove this car?"

"That's right."

Cancini frowned. "Odd then."

"What?" Ketchum looked at the car and back at the detective.

"There's something that looks a lot like mud spatter under the rear bumper on the passenger side."

"What? That's impossible." He got down on one knee and inspected the car. After a moment, he rose, his salt and pepper brows furrowed. "I clean these cars myself every week. I don't understand." He moved to the driver's door and opened the car. Sliding inside, he leaned forward to read the odometer. Getting out, he walked to the workbench and opened a notebook. He closed it and laid it gently back on the bench. He turned to the detectives. "Thirty-two miles."

"Sir?" Smitty asked.

"Thirty-two miles have been added. Somebody drove it after I parked it last September."

Cancini watched the man's face. His eyes hadn't left the polished exterior of the El Camino. V-shaped lines covered his forehead, and his mouth hung open. Cancini cleared his throat. "Does anyone have access to this car besides you?"

Ketchum's gaze returned to the detectives. "My wife, but she doesn't like to drive them. Besides, she was asleep with me that night."

"Anyone else? A friend? A mechanic? A relative?"

"No. There's only me and my wife and . . ." He spun around as though someone had appeared over his shoulder, his head panning the garage.

Cancini followed the man's gaze but couldn't find what Ketchum was looking for. After a moment, the man's head bowed and his shoulders slumped. He took a deep breath, then faced the detectives. "My son and I are not close. We were once, a long time ago. But something changed. I don't know when or how exactly." The lines in his face deepened and he seemed to shrink in size. "After he flunked out of school for the second time, I suggested the military. I hoped they could straighten him out. Lord knows, I couldn't control him." Ketchum looked over their shoulders, lost in a memory. "I thought for a while things were working out. He sent letters to his mother. She was happy. Then, about six months ago, he showed up at the door, dishonorably discharged. I don't know what he did—something to do with a fight, I think. The truth is, I didn't want to know. He only stayed a couple of days.

He spent most of the time here, in the garage with the cars. He drove each of them, and then he was gone. I don't know where he is now."

"Does he know how to access the garage?"

"Yes."

Cancini searched the wall behind Ketchum again. Car covers were folded on shelves. Cleaning mitts, soaps, and waxes were stacked nearby. Keys hung from five silver hooks. "Would he have access to the keys to the El Camino?"

The man jerked a thumb toward the silver hooks. "I keep the keys right over there. Anyone who can get in the garage can find the keys." He paused, then added, his words barely a whisper, "The El Camino was always his favorite."

Cancini pulled a folded sheet from the inside pocket of his coat. Opening the page to the copy of the crude drawing, he held the paper up for the man. "Mr. Ketchum, does your son have any tattoos? Maybe a tattoo like this?"

"I—I don't know. He might have." He swallowed, his voice shaking. "We don't see him anymore. We don't really know him." One tear slipped from the corner of his eye. "He's our only son." His chin dropped to his chest and his narrow shoulders shook just enough that the detectives remained quiet. "I'm sorry." Ketchum lifted his head again. "It's just hard, that's all."

"Take your time."

The man nodded. He wiped his face with a handkerchief and took several deep breaths. "I don't really know if my son took the car—only that it's been moved. I'm sorry I can't be of more help."

"Mr. Ketchum, with your permission, we need to have forensics go over the car as soon as possible. It's important to find out whether or not it may have been used the night of the arson.

Check the car for fingerprints. Debris in the tires. Anything that could help."

Ketchum rolled the handkerchief into a ball and stuffed it in his pocket. "I need to speak to my wife now. This is going to be quite a shock."

"Of course," Cancini said. "We can see ourselves out."

When he was gone, Smitty turned to him. "So we're thinking the son took the car and set the fire. Why? What's his motive?"

"Money. If I'm right, after his dishonorable discharge, he joined the Death Squad here. He was hired for the job."

"By Vega."

"Exactly."

"Makes sense, but the guy's not going to volunteer Vega as the one who hired him."

"I don't expect him to admit anything. First thing is to prove he drove the car the night of the fire."

Smitty walked around the car, leaning in. "That's not going to be easy."

"The son tried to wipe it clean, but he was either in a hurry or missed that spot." Cancini nodded toward the bumper. "Chances are there's not a single print inside that car other than Ketchum's from today, but we could still get lucky."

"How?"

"He might've forgotten to wipe the keys."

Smitty looked at him, face breaking into a grin. "Good thinking."

Cancini shrugged. "Yeah. Sometimes."

Chapter Sixty

CANCINI CHECKED HIS watch. It was past lunch. He sighed, disappointed. Sophia Vega would be gone by now. He'd hoped to be there, to speak to her himself, but between finding the car and Martin insisting on another one of his infernal meetings, it hadn't worked out. Cancini stretched his legs and stifled a yawn, barely hearing the captain.

"It comes back to the money." Martin held up a copy of Holland's bank account records and whistled through his teeth. He smacked a wad of pink gum and dropped the report back on his desk. "It's a helluva lot of money. People are gonna want to know how a priest had this much cash running through his account."

Cancini's head came up. "People?"

Martin shrugged. "People. The press. It's not like we can keep this quiet forever. I can see the headline now. Dead priest laundering drug money. Or maybe: Dead priest steals from the poor to give to the rich. We can't have that."

Cancini sat up straighter in his chair. His jaw tightened. "He didn't steal it."

"Well, what the hell would you call it then? That money didn't belong to him. He didn't earn it, and as of right now, we can't prove Vega put it there." The captain was technically right. They knew the money was being illegally funneled through Holland's account, but proving it was something else. "Besides, how do we know he wasn't the one using Vega?"

Cancini didn't answer right away. He'd wondered the same thing. There were too many things about Father Holland that bothered him, and the relationship between Vega and Holland was one of them. Longtime friends? Partners? It was possible, but he didn't think so. The e-mails and Father Joe's memories painted a different picture. "We don't, but the e-mails support the theory that Vega or someone who worked for him hacked Holland's account and used it to funnel the money."

"Have the e-mails been authenticated?"

"We're working on it."

"Good. I want Vega, but I want it to stick."

Cancini nodded and stood.

"Can we prove motive with the e-mails?" Martin asked.

"Threats were made. We still have to prove Vega was the source of the e-mails."

"Let's think about this." Martin leaned back in his chair, folding his arms behind his head. Cancini sighed and sat down again. "If we assume Holland knew the money was Vega's, why'd he take it? He had to know the danger. Why do it?"

It was something the detective had considered as well. "At first, I think maybe he was angry. Then, when he calmed down, he decided he could get even and do a good thing at the same time. So he planned, moved the money, then set up the foundation. Pretty smart, really."

"Yeah? Well, if he was so smart, how'd he end up dead?"

"He ran out of time."

Martin stared.

Cancini licked his lips. He had a few ideas, but none he could verify yet. "Look, I'm thinking he had some kind of plan to deal with Vega. I think he thought he could convince him somehow to forget about it."

"No one forgets about that kind of money."

"Maybe not, but—"

Both men turned toward the knock on the door. Smitty stuck his head in, nodding at his partner. "I need to see you for a minute."

Cancini stood. "I'll check in with you later."

"I have meetings all afternoon," the captain said. "Let me know if anything breaks. Stay on Vega."

He raised a hand and followed Smitty down the hall. "Thanks, partner. I could really use some coffee."

Smitty passed the coffeepot, looked over his shoulder, and headed to the garage stairs. "I need to talk to you."

Cancini followed him down. A chill in the air seeped into his bones, and his stomach turned. "What is it?"

"Father Joe is missing."

Chapter Sixty-one

"Mrs. Vega, I wouldn't bother you, but I know you met with Father Joe this morning at my apartment." The lady pursed her lips and looked away. "You heard about the fire at the church?" She nodded once. "Father Joe has been staying at my apartment, under police protection." Her caramel-colored eyes opened wide and her red lips parted. "He asked me to call off the guard so that he could meet with you." He paused, his voice soft. "Did you come to my apartment this morning?"

"I—I didn't know it was your apartment. He just said he was staying with a friend."

"That was true. The friend is me." He brushed his hand over his head. "What time did you arrive at the apartment?"

"A few minutes after eleven."

"How long did you stay?"

"About an hour. He's such a lovely man, you know. We talked and then he went downstairs with me and walked me out."

"To the street?" Cancini had placed the guard outside the building in the Laundromat across the street. The officer reported that the lady had left just after twelve. She'd come out of the building alone. He'd waited five minutes, then gone inside and returned to his post outside the apartment door. At one, a delivery man had brought Father Joe's lunch. The guard had knocked on the door and there was no answer. He'd knocked again but heard only silence. Inside, the apartment was empty.

"No. Just to the door." She smoothed her hair, touching the pins at the base of her neck. "Is everything all right?"

"Did you see whether or not he came out of the building after he walked you out?"

"I . . . I don't think so. It was chilly outside so I stopped for a minute at the front door to put on my gloves. I looked back at Father Joe and he was standing at the elevators, waiting. He waved good-bye."

"Did you see him get in the elevator to go back up to the apartment?"

"I saw him get in the elevator, but I don't think he went up."

"He got back out?"

"No. I think he went down. The down arrow was lit." The lines between her painted brows deepened. "Is something wrong?"

"Not at all." Cancini blinked, thinking. Each apartment was assigned a storage space that was in the basement. It was only accessible from inside the building through the elevator, but there was an exit at the rear of the building. It could be unlocked with a keycard. He'd stationed the officer in front of the building and had a second tailing Mrs. Vega. Damn. He'd never considered the basement. "He just missed a meeting," he told her. Cancini stood and touched her on the shoulder. "I'm sure everything's fine."

"Detective?" Looking up at him, she twisted a handkerchief between her fingers. "I know you can't tell me anything, but thank you so much for investigating the murder of Father Holland. It's just so horrible, so sad." Her voice cracked and she covered her mouth with her hand. "I'm so sorry. It's just that I've known Father Holland since he was a boy. He and my Carlos were friends in school."

"I'm sorry for your loss, Mrs. Vega." He sat down again. "Your son and Father Holland. Were they still friends?"

"I don't think so. My Carlos is not a religious man. He's a good man, mind you, but he doesn't go to Mass." She blinked. "It's just awful, isn't it? Carlos came by that morning to check on me, brought my favorite cheese pastry. He does that, you know. Anyway, we were sitting here having coffee together when Angel Marquez called. She's the one that told us. Said there were police all over the church, and Father Holland had been shot in the face. Is that true, Detective? Was he really shot in the face?"

"He was shot, but I'm not at liberty to discuss the details, Mrs. Vega." She nodded, her face somber. "How did Carlos react to the news?"

"He was devastated, of course. He went all white and could barely speak for a minute." Her eyes shimmered with tears. "Then he said he had to go."

"Have you spoken to him about it since?"

"Oh yes. He called to see how I was doing and asked me to let him know about the funeral arrangements. He went to the Mass of Transferal with me. I told him how much it would have meant to Father Holland." She bit her red-stained lips. "I know he would have wanted Carlos to be there." She breathed in and out, her voice steadying. "I still can't believe it. I told Father Holland how proud his mother would have been of him. He was such a sweet man. Thanked me for giving him a place to stay when he was just a boy. He'd run away from foster care after his mother died, though I didn't blame him one bit. I don't know if you knew that about him."

"I did."

"Anyway, I always pretended I didn't know why he was there, but I knew. He needed to be around family, not strangers, and we were the closest he had left." The tears spilled from her eyes. "I even pretended I didn't know he lived with us. I never asked questions. Carlos took care of him mostly, and then one day, he was gone."

"Do you know why he left, Mrs. Vega?"

"Not really. He was eighteen I think, though."

"How did Carlos take it?"

She shrugged and sniffled. "I think he was okay. Carlos had a girlfriend and the boys didn't spend as much time together. Neither of them talked about it, but maybe they were already drifting apart."

"Do you know where Father Holland went when he stopped living with you?"

"No, he disappeared as suddenly as he'd arrived. I didn't see him again until he came back to take over St. William." She half smiled. "He'd grown into a man by then, so handsome and strong. A man of God."

"But as far as you know, after Father Holland came back, he and Carlos weren't friends again."

"I don't think so. Carlos said he wasn't comfortable in the church. Wouldn't go with me. Breaks my heart. But Father Holland told me not to worry about it, that God would see the good in Carlos. We prayed together for him."

"When did you do that?"

"The day before he died. That's why I know Father Holland would want Carlos there. He told me how much he loved him and that even though they were no longer friends, they were still family." She tried to smile again. "You understand? Family is everything, and we always take care of family." The tears flowed now.

Cancini handed her a tissue and waited. "Why did you want to see Father Joe?"

"About the foundation." She reached behind her and pulled out a large manila envelope. She handed it to Cancini. "This is why."

He slipped the document from the envelope. The words swam in front of him, a blur of legal jargon, but he picked out charitable trust, restrictions, and board of trustees. His head pounded. "How did you get this?"

"Father Holland gave it to me on Saturday after the evening Mass. He asked to speak to me, and that's when"—she paused and blew her nose—"he gave it to me." She pointed at the papers. "The last page is why he wanted to see me."

Cancini flipped to the last page, a single document declaring Sophia Vega a trustee of the foundation. He sifted through the pile and found four additional trustee documents. Father Joe, the St. William finance committee chair, an attorney, and Father Holland.

Cancini sat back against the soft cushions of the sofa, the pages in his lap. He'd been right. Father Holland did have a plan, a way to keep the money and stay alive. He'd planned to use Sophia Vega's involvement with the foundation as insurance. Had the plan backfired, or had it just been too little, too late?

He cleared his throat. "Did Father Holland tell you how much money was in the trust?"

"Yes. Quite a large sum. I almost fell out of my chair when he told me. He got very excited when he told me all the great things he hoped to do with it: the repairs to the church, expanding the outreach program, so many good things."

"Did he mention where the money came from?"

"An anonymous donation. Can you believe that? A blessing, he called it. A gift from God, I said." She spoke the words with no guile and no trace of suspicion. "That's why I felt it was such an honor that he chose me to serve on the foundation. I told him I didn't think I was worthy. I'm old, I said. But he told me he wanted my experience, my dedication to the church." She leaned forward. "I think he just wanted to thank me for all those years ago."

He held up the envelope. "Do you mind if I borrow this? I'll have it sent back as soon as we've made a copy."

"Of course you can." The lines between her heavy brows deepened. "Do you think it's important?"

"Probably not," he said evasively. "Just covering all our bases." She nodded. "Mrs. Vega, did you and Father Joe discuss anything else this morning? Father Holland? Carlos?"

"He asked me about Carlos's business. He owns several chicken restaurants now. Chicken del Rey? Have you heard of it?" Her voice echoed with pride. He nodded and knew instantly Father Joe had been right. Mrs. Vega didn't know about the illegal activities. "Silly name, I know, but the rotisserie chicken is wonderful. It's quite busy for lunch and dinner. You would love the food."

Cancini tucked the envelope under his arm and got to his feet. He'd come for information about Father Joe, and instead learned something about Father Holland. While he didn't doubt that Sophia Vega might make an excellent trustee for the foundation, he felt sure her dedication to the church had nothing to do with her appointment. "Thank you, Mrs. Vega. I appreciate you seeing me today."

"Please tell Father Joe thank you again for meeting with me today."

Where was the old man? He wasn't answering his phone. No one had seen him. Fighting to keep his voice steady, Cancini took the hand she offered and did the only thing he could—lie. "I will, Mrs. Vega. I will."

Chapter Sixty-two

CANCINI STOOD WITH his feet apart and his hands shoved in his pockets. In front of him, the large whiteboard was a maze of names and lines and dates. Crime scene photos and pictures were taped on the wall around the board. Father Joe's face, lined and innocent, stared back at him. Damn. Cancini's chin dropped to his chest and his hands curled into fists. Where did Father Joe go? He raised his head again to find Jensen hovering, waiting. Cancini sighed. "Have we got anything?"

"Not much. No sign he's been back to his apartment or the church," Jensen said. "I talked to the foreman cleaning up the damage at the church. He said he hadn't seen anyone that fit Father Sweeney's description. Just a few curious onlookers."

Cold fingers of fear crawled up Cancini's spine. Father Joe hadn't been seen in more than six hours. He grabbed a fax from the top of his desk and handed it to Jensen. "This is a list of the sick from his parish. Let's find out if he's making rounds. Two of those names are men at Holy Memorial. He could be there." He paused, took a breath. "There's a Bible study that was scheduled for seven o'clock. It's probably still going on now, and we need to find out if he's there. It's been moved from the church while they clean it up. The address is on the bottom of that page. Also, I want someone at tomorrow morning's Mass if he isn't located before then."

Jensen glanced at the list, started to say something, then held his tongue. "I've got it."

Cancini's attention was drawn back to the board. He needed to find Father Joe, but he also needed to find Holland's murderer. He didn't want to think about how one action could affect the other. He nodded toward his partner. "What've we got on the El Camino?"

Smitty opened a file folder. "Small amount of residue and gravel under the bumper are consistent with the gravel from the driveway at the front of the church." He looked up. "You were right. The inside and the rest of the outside of the car were wiped clean. But the key did contain a partial. We're running it now to see if it matches Ketchum's son."

"But we still haven't found Junior?"

"His apartment is empty. One of the neighbors in the building said he hadn't seen Ketchum since last Sunday. Told me he usually plays music so loud he bangs on the wall to make it stop, but since Sunday afternoon, nothing."

"Anything else?"

"The neighbor said Ketchum has a tattoo on the inside of his forearm." Cancini shivered. "A tattoo of a skull and dagger."

Chapter Sixty-three

Sunday, February 21: The Day of

MATT SLIPPED INTO the sanctuary, taking a seat in the last pew. On the altar, six women and two men of varying ages practiced the week's communion anthem. It was a small choir but better than having none at all. Their voices rose and fell with the tempo of the old piano, and he smiled, letting the harmony wrap him in the warmth of the message. After they finished, he stood and exchanged pleasantries as they filed past him. When the last of the choir was gone, he glided down the aisle to the altar. He fell to his knees, his eyes on the plaster sculpture of Jesus on the cross. Clasping his hands together, he prayed. "I believe in God, the Father Almighty; Creator of Heaven and Earth." He bowed his head, and the words he knew so well fell from his lips. He followed the Apostles' Creed with the Our Father, three Hail Marys, and finally one Glory Be. Each prayer was said one after the other, his voice soft as a whisper.

He raised his eyes again to the cross hanging high on the wall.

The blood at the hands and feet of Christ had faded from red to brown. Even in need of repair, Matt could not deny the beauty and forgiveness in the face of Jesus. Matt reached up and removed his clerical collar. He laid it gently on the floor. He moved his lips again.

"Lord Jesus, I come to you as a man, not as a priest." He inhaled, his chest expanding as he settled his nerves. "Help me to know if I'm doing the right thing, if I've finally gotten it right. I just don't know." He shook his head, and his voice trembled. "I've made so many mistakes. There are so many things I'm not proud of. Am I doing the right thing now? Am I good?"

He thought of the woman who'd brought him into the world, the woman who'd done her best in spite of her weaknesses. She'd taken care of him until she couldn't. As a young man, he'd been compelled to reverse the order and take care of her instead. It wasn't a conscious choice or even one he'd questioned. It was the way it had to be. Even now, he missed her face, her voice, her smile. She'd been weak, but her love had been strong. Before she died, they'd had a good day, trekking through the National Zoo. He thought he was too old by then but went anyway. Walking through the grounds, they'd pointed at the animals, shared a bag of popcorn, and laughed. Her sunken eyes had glowed in the bright sun, and for once, her sallow skin had looked more porcelain than paste. She'd reached out and held his hand, and they walked that way for the rest of the day. His embarrassment had faded with each squeal of joy, each warm glance.

He was a teenager by then, tall and lean. She'd stood on tiptoes and planted a warm kiss on his cheek. "You are a good boy, Matt, a good person. Don't let the rottenness in the world take that away." She'd stepped back and cocked her head. "Promise me, Matt."

He'd held on to her hand, not wanting to let go. "Promise you what?"

"Promise me you'll never lose that goodness. Hang on to it. Don't ever let it go."

"Okay," he'd agreed, ready to tell her anything that day.

"No." She'd gripped his hand tighter. "You need to promise."

He'd hesitated. The light in her eyes had burned, and there'd been an urgency in her voice he hadn't heard before. "I promise," he'd said finally.

She'd smiled, but the joy of the day had faded away. His hand had slipped out of hers and they'd returned to Barry Farm. The next day, she'd OD'd.

Had he kept his promise? He couldn't be sure anymore. Was there still goodness in him or only a distorted sense of what was good? He sighed and wiped away the tears. He picked up his collar and got to his feet. He needed to prepare for the evening Mass. The image of Jesus looked down on him, and he crossed himself. "Help me, Jesus."

Chapter Sixty-four

BRONSON'S SHADOW FELL over Cancini's desk. "I gotta talk to you, boss."

Smitty watched the exchange, light brows arched. Cancini stood and gestured to both men. "In the conference room." He shut the door behind the group. "What is it?"

"The wife, Erica Harding. I just got a hit from the Fairfax emergency room."

"Shit." Smitty paced, his face reddening with each word. "What is it with that asshole?"

Cancini waved a hand and pulled out a chair. "Calm down. Let's hear what Bronson has to say." Smitty sat and crossed his arms over his chest. Cancini patted him on the shoulder. Tensions ran high and they were all well past exhausted. He nodded at Bronson again. "Go on."

Bronson shot a wary look at Smitty. "I did like you said and asked all the ERs in the area to let us know if they had any new admissions for Mrs. Harding. Fairfax called. She came in three hours ago. They treated her for a broken wrist and sent her home."

"Not that it matters, but what was her story?" Cancini asked.

"Fell down the stairs. The nurse confided—off the record—Mrs. Harding had been in before."

Cancini rubbed his hand over the stubble on his chin. "How many times?"

"Three. Two last year and again today."

Falling down the stairs was suspicious enough, but adding in two previous ER visits counted as excessive by anyone's standards. Still, broken bones didn't tell the whole story. The lady had tried to hide bruises on her arms and neck with makeup and a sweeping hairstyle. Something ugly was going on in that house. If the man could break his wife's bones, what else could he do?

"Where's Harding now?"

"Still at work as far as I know."

Cancini pushed back his chair. "Pick him up."

Bronson opened and closed his mouth. "On what charges?"

"None. We just want to talk to him." He shoved his hands in his pockets.

Smitty's cell phone buzzed. He held up a hand, nodding as he listened. He covered the phone with his hand and mouthed, "They got Ketchum." He listened again. Cancini waited. The cool air in the room prickled at his neck, and he shifted his weight from one foot to the other. Smitty hung up. "Picked him up about twenty minutes ago outside his apartment building. They're bringing him in now."

Cancini licked his lips, considering the questioning ahead. "Can we get the ladies from the church in for a lineup? I want to know if he was the man at Mass the night Father Holland was murdered."

Smitty moved toward the door. "On it."

Bronson hesitated, his high forehead creased. "Boss? You still want me to pick up Harding? I can stay here if you need me."

Smitty was right. Things were happening, and with a positive ID from the parishioners, they might be able to connect Ketchum to Father Holland and the fire at Father Joe's church. Still, Harding had hurt his wife. Again. He couldn't let that go. Cancini clapped the younger man on the shoulder. "I do need you, Bronson. I need you to pick up Harding now."

Chapter Sixty-five

"I HAVE NOTHING to say." Ketchum Junior lifted his chin and turned away.

Cancini studied the young man in front of him. Medium height but powerfully built, he rested his hands on the table as though ready to spring out of his chair at the slightest provocation. The short haircut he'd worn for the military was long gone, his stringy hair falling to his shoulders. He had his father's square chin and straight nose, but his eyes were ice-gray, wary, persecuted. Metal studs decorated his black leather jacket.

Cancini dropped his gaze and turned his attention to his notepad. He wrote for several minutes, and the silence in the room lengthened. Smitty, Martin, and a lawyer from the district attorney's office waited on the other side of the glass.

Ketchum stood up. "This is bullshit. You have no reason to bring me here. I have rights. I haven't done anything."

"Sit down."

The man glared at the detective and crossed his arms.

"Suit yourself." Cancini read from his notebook. "Tuesday evening, you broke into your father's garage and stole his El Camino. At approximately one a.m., you drove the car to Maryland Drive and placed some accelerants at the rear of the church. You were seen leaving the scene by a neighbor." Cancini looked up. "Arson is a crime, Mr. Ketchum."

"You can't prove any of that."

"I don't have to prove it. That's what the prosecutor is for. I just need enough evidence to arrest you, get you off the streets and behind bars."

The man's face paled, but he recovered quickly. "I'm not going to jail."

"You are. Arson is a felony offense, punishable by up to twenty years. Add in breaking and entering and grand larceny, and you could spend the rest of your life behind bars."

The man laughed. "Breaking and entering? Even if I did borrow my dad's car, that's my house. I can go anytime I want." His upper lip curled. "Please."

"You don't live there. Your parents kicked you out because they didn't want you there. You came onto their property during the night and stole one of your father's cars. That's breaking and entering."

"You don't know what you're talking about. My dad will never let you get away with that shit."

"Oh? Are you and your father close?" Cancini drank from his cup, letting the words hang in the air. "We can place the car at the scene of the arson, and there were traces of accelerant in the back of the trunk. Your father keeps a record of the miles on every car. Did you know that? He didn't drive the car. There's only one set of keys, and only three people who know about them. Your parents and you. Do you really think one of your parents is going to take the rap for you on this?"

"They don't have to. You still can't prove anything."

"By itself, it's suggestive, circumstantial, but you made one very simple mistake."

"You must be talking about someone else. I don't make mistakes."

"You wiped down the inside of the car, the steering wheel, the door handle"—Cancini paused—"but you didn't wipe down the key." Ketchum blinked, his face pale again. The fingerprint was only a partial, but Ketchum didn't know that. "That makes it a slam-dunk." Cancini closed his notebook. "You were at St. William for Sunday Mass recently. You came in with another man just before communion. Several parishioners can identify you."

The man had regained his composure and shrugged. "So what? I went to church. That's not a crime."

"But I think you were there for the same reason you started that fire."

"I don't know what you're talking about."

"You're part of a group of specialists, aren't you? It's known by a few different names, but I believe Death Squad is the most well-known."

Ketchum laughed. "Do you believe everything you hear, Detective?"

"You perform jobs that require your special talents, if you will, for those who can pay." The man folded his arms again. "What was the job when you went to Mass? Was it a warning? Did you come back and shoot Father Holland?"

The man snorted. "I didn't shoot anyone."

Cancini lifted one shoulder. "How do I know that?"

The man shook his head. "I didn't off that guy."

"Then who shot Father Holland?"

"How the fuck should I know? You're the detective."

Cancini closed his notebook. "I guess I got it wrong."

"You got that right."

"We know you set that fire, Ketchum, and as soon as we get a warrant for your apartment, you will be spending the rest of your days behind bars. You can help yourself if you cooperate." Ketchum's eyes drifted to the one-way window. "You didn't just decide to burn down St. Ignatius or go to St. William that night. Someone hired you, paid you to target that specific church, the same way Father Holland was targeted. I want to know who that someone is."

The man stared, the fight draining from his body. The tough edge slipped away, and his face slackened. "I want a lawyer."

Chapter Sixty-six

"IT'S NOT ENOUGH." Assistant District Attorney Emma Lawrence spoke in the same clipped tone she used in the courtroom. Precise. Direct. "You can't charge him with murder."

Martin groaned audibly, his face drawn.

Silent, Cancini recognized she was right. They had a dozen witnesses who could place Ketchum in the church a couple of hours before Holland was murdered, but every one of those witnesses also saw him leave before the Mass ended. Even if they suspected his attendance was a threat, being there wasn't a crime.

She swung around to face Cancini. "Tell me again how the fire is connected to the murder of Father Holland."

"Father Sweeney knew both Holland and Vega when they were boys. He stayed close to Father Holland and was his confessor."

Emma chewed her lower lip. "You think Holland told this Father Sweeney about the money and where it came from in a confession."

"Yes."

"And you think Vega knows it."

"Yes."

"Can you tie Vega to the money?"

"Not in any way that will hold up in court. Not yet."

She nodded. "What about Ketchum? Can you connect him to Vega?"

"We're doing the best we can," Martin said.

"Good. There's nothing more I can do. I'll present the request for a search warrant as soon as Judge Koon is finished in court." She stood and looped her bag over her shoulder. "Ketchum's lawyer knows the deal if they decide to play."

"Humph." Martin grouched. "The way this case has gone, how likely is that to happen?"

She shrugged. "Honestly? Not very." She looked at Cancini. "Nice bluff, but a partial print and his military experience is not enough to beat reasonable doubt. If his lawyer's any good, he'll tell him to take his chances. We might be able to indict him on the fire, but a conviction is a long shot without more evidence. If we get the warrant, it better be worth it."

Martin threw his pen down on the desk. "Damn." After she left, he gnawed through two toothpicks in succession, ignoring the packs of gum on the desk. "Heard anything from Sweeney?"

Cancini swallowed. To focus on the investigation, he'd tried to ignore the lump of dread growing in the pit of his stomach, but with each passing hour, it was getting harder. There'd been no word on Father Joe. "Not yet."

"He's probably holed up with one of his priest friends. Don't they do that?"

"Sometimes." It was possible he'd spent the night with a friend, but it didn't explain why Cancini hadn't heard from him.

"He'll turn up." When the captain's wife called, Martin pushed the toothpicks away, and Cancini ducked out.

Smitty waited at his desk and handed him a large cup of coffee. "Ketchum is downstairs in holding. His lawyer just left. Are we gonna charge him?"

Cancini took the cup. "Thanks. Don't know yet, but Lawrence doesn't think he'll take the deal. She thinks his lawyer will roll the dice. My gut tells me he'll keep his mouth shut for now."

"So, what do we do?"

"We wait. In the meantime, I'm gonna take a run at Harding."

"Can I join you?"

Cancini eyed his partner. "Normally, I would say yes, but you haven't been yourself about this guy. Earlier, when Bronson told you about the broken wrist, you let it get personal." The lanky detective's narrow shoulders sank down into his chest. "Tell me I'm wrong. Tell me I've made a mistake."

Smitty's white-blond head fell to his chest. He sighed, letting out a long breath. "You're not wrong."

Cancini glanced around the squad room. Every detective's face wore the wrung-out expression of long hours and no sleep. Ketchum was the carrot, but Vega was the prize. Harding was something else, a different kind of depravity. "Do you want to talk about it?"

Smitty lifted his head. "Not right now. Later."

Cancini looked away. Bronson had put Harding in the small conference room farthest from Martin's office. Had Harding broken his wife's wrist? It appeared to be a pattern, but that wasn't Cancini's biggest problem with the man.

"Cancini." Martin's anger vibrated in his beet-red face. The compassion from earlier had evaporated. "Why the hell is Bronson sitting in a conference room with Sonny Harding? Did I not make myself clear? I come out of my office to find Bronson taking food to this man, a man who is not supposed to be here." His chest heaved with each word. "Goddammit, Cancini. This is the kind of shit I'm talking about. We've got a suspect. We need to be focused on bringing in that suspect."

Cancini pressed his lips together and breathed in and out through his nose. The only sound came from a cell phone chirping and distant voices being carried up the stairs. He felt the eyes of every detective in the squad room. "Turns out Harding doesn't have an alibi for the time of Holland's murder."

"So? What does that have to do with Vega?"

"Vega's smooth, Captain. If we get an indictment, his lawyers will throw suspicion elsewhere. Harding is violent. He didn't like Holland. Bronson is working to eliminate Harding as a suspect to protect the case against Vega. Call it insurance."

Martin blinked, opened his mouth, and closed it again. "Insurance, huh?" He glanced at Smitty. "This sounds a lot like bullshit."

Cancini shrugged and slipped his hands into his pockets. "I'm just covering all the bases, Captain, the way you would want."

Martin scowled, then checked his watch. "Shit. I've gotta go. The mayor wants a personal update on the case an hour ago." He pointed a finger at Cancini's nose. "We'll finish this when I get back."

The sound of Martin's steps as he stomped down the stairs echoed across the room. The murmur of voices rose again, and Cancini pulled his hands from his pockets, uncurling his fingers one by one. If nothing else, Martin was consistent. In Cancini's mind, the man had no imagination, no instinct, but he'd gotten just enough right over the years to move up the ladder. He made a better captain than detective. Still, Cancini didn't like the suggestion he wasn't doing everything in his power to find Holland's killer. That rankled, burned.

"You know, it might've been bullshit," Smitty said, tone approving, "that whole business about insurance, but it does make some sense. Eliminating Harding makes the case against Vega more solid."

Cancini shrugged again. What Martin thought mattered less than whether he got some answers. Harding's flimsy alibi bothered him. He looked up at his young partner. "Can you keep the personal out?"

Smitty returned his gaze and nodded once.

"Good. Let's go." He picked up his notebook and slipped it into the pocket of his worn leather jacket. He pushed open the door to the conference room, Smitty at his heel, Martin already forgotten.

"Mr. Harding," Cancini said with a grim smile. "Glad you were able to come in today."

Chapter Sixty-seven

Sunday, February 21: The Day of

MATT WALKED DOWN the aisle behind the altar boys, his pace slow and measured. The candles flickered in the late-afternoon light and he stood erect. The last notes of the processional faded away, and he raised his hands and his voice. "Let us pray."

The first reader's voice droned on, and he lowered his eyes. Underneath the cassock, his heart pounded, and sweat trickled down his back. Would his plan work? He had no idea. Sophia had promised to speak with Carlos at the first opportunity, but there was no telling when that might be and no guarantee the man would listen. Long ago, there would have been no doubt. The Carlos he'd grown up with would have walked on fire for his mother. Matt remembered Carlos as a boy who would have done anything to protect her, to keep her safe. But they were both just boys then. His mind drifted back to the day he'd landed on Carlos's doorstep, no money in his pocket, no bags.

Carlos had scratched at a pimple on his face and tossed him a blanket. "Sorry, man. That's all I got."

Matt had caught the thin fabric in his hands and fingered the scratchy wool. "It's okay," he'd said. "I can sleep in my hoodie, too." He'd cleared his throat. "Thanks for letting me crash. I just couldn't go to that place, to those people."

Carlos had flopped into a faded brown chair, his long legs spread apart. "No problem. If I was you, there's no way could I live with anyone but my real mom. It's just not the same. It's like some kind of fake people trying to be your fake mom and dad. No way. And your mom was cool, too. It sucks."

Matt had swallowed the lump in his throat. "Yeah."

"You can stay here as long as you want, you know."

"I'm not going to school. No one can know I'm here. Not even your mom."

Carlos had rubbed his hands across his thighs, and his face had clouded. "I get the school thing, but my mom lives here, too. Gonna be tough to keep you a secret."

"I can't go back." Matt had heard the quiver in his own voice.

"Sure, man, I get it." Carlos had leaned forward, his elbows propped on his knees. "You can help me if you stay."

"Help you?" Matt's hands had tightened on the old blanket. "Are you running again?"

Carlos picked at the loose strings hanging from the torn knees of his jeans. "Some, but I've got get my own crew now, too."

"Your own crew? Wow." It had been only a few months, and things had already changed. His mother's death still fresh, he'd turned away, hiding his tears.

"It's just weed, man, and if I don't run it, somebody else will.

That's the hood and we both know it. Shit, I'd rather the money go to me than some other asshole."

Matt's head had dropped into his hands. It was just business. No one knew that better than he did. Hadn't he been a runner, taking money from users even while his own mother was sinking further and further into her own abyss? He'd rocked back and forth while Carlos had talked.

"Look, you don't have to. You can stay anyway. My mom won't know. She works all the time. You can sleep on the floor in my room. She don't come in there ever, and if she does see you, we'll just say you're visitin', but she won't ask. She's too tired all the time anyway." He'd taken a breath. "That's why I gotta run my own crew. I gotta make some serious cash and change things. I don't want my mom livin' in Barry Farm forever. Hell, I don't want any of us living in this shithole." He'd paused again. "People fuckin' die here." Matt's head had jerked up, mouth hanging open. Carlos had looked him straight in the eye. "It's the only way out. You of all people know that." A heavy silence had settled over the teens. "I've got a plan. You used to have a plan, too. Remember?" Matt had nodded once, uncertain. "It's no skin off my back, man, if you don't wanna run, but you could earn some cash."

Matt told himself it would be for only a little while. He would leave when he'd had enough, when he had a plan of his own. He'd looked up. "What about your mom?"

"She'll be cool with you poppin' in and out. We'll say you have a guardian or something and you're staying here sometimes 'cause we're such good friends and all."

"That's not what I mean. Does she know? About the running?"

"Fuck no. Did your mom?"

"I don't know." He'd remembered how she kept pressuring him to be good, to do good. "Maybe."

Carlos had leaned forward, his expression a mix of fear and determination. "Well, not my mom. Ever. It's between you and me. You got it?"

Matt had sighed. He'd understood. Sophia Vega was a God-fearing woman. She went to Mass every day. She worked hard for low wages just to put food on the table. She didn't drink, and she didn't take drugs. She wouldn't understand. "I got it."

Father Holland looked up as the second reader finished, the past slipping away. The congregation rose to sing. He moved toward the pulpit, his robes brushing the threadbare carpet. His book lay open to the Scripture. At the end of the song, he looked out at the expectant faces and said a silent prayer. When he was a teenager, Carlos had included Matt in his plans, pulled him along. After the stabbing, Matt had left, no longer able to ignore the life he was being drawn into day after day. He'd made a new life. Carlos was supposed to leave him alone, but he'd broken his promise. Matt hadn't asked for the money. He hadn't asked for any of it, but there it was for the taking. Now he had his own plan.

Chapter Sixty-eight

SONNY HARDING WORE a heavy jacket, a flannel shirt, and loose-fitting jeans. Even seated, his bulk filled the small conference room. Cancini slipped out of his jacket and took the chair opposite Harding. Smitty took the chair at the farthest end of the table.

"It's a bit warm in here. Maybe you'd like to take your coat off?" The man's nostrils flared with each breath, but he didn't move. "Your choice." Cancini crossed his legs and leaned back. "I understand you didn't go to work today, Mr. Harding. Is there a reason for that?"

Harding faced the institutional gray wall, eyes averted.

"Take your time, Mr. Harding. I have all day."

The man blinked. His massive shoulder moved an inch, maybe two. "Just taking the day off."

"So you could follow your wife?" Harding's skin reddened. A minute passed and his hands gripped the table. "Did you follow her to the hospital, Mr. Harding?" Cancini leaned across the table, his voice soft. "After you broke her wrist?"

Harding's knuckles whitened. Sweat dripped from his temple and trailed down to his chin. His jaw rolled through gritted teeth.

Cancini shrugged and read from his notebook. "Your wife appears to be extremely accident-prone." A light sheen of perspiration covered Harding's face, but his expression remained unchanged. "According to several folks at the church, you're a little possessive. That's understandable, of course. She's a very attractive woman." Harding flinched. "Very attractive," he repeated. Harding's hands curled. "I also understand you've gotten into a few scuffles—one at work, another at a bar where you had to pay for damages." Harding's face froze. "Taking all that into account, you can see how I might have a few questions about your wife's accidents." The man's hands clenched and unclenched in his lap. "Would you like to explain your behavior?"

Harding's head sagged and rolled from side to side. "No, no, no, no."

Cancini shot a questioning look at Smitty. His partner shook his head.

"Mr. Harding? Are you saying you don't want to explain?"

The man lifted his head. "I can't." He came to his feet, jerking his head from side to side as though physically erasing something from his mind. "I need to go."

"We're not the only ones who might be interested in your wife's accidents. I'm trying to give you the opportunity to clear things up."

Harding's breath whistled through his nose.

"Mr. Harding?" Cancini asked. "It's time to tell the truth."

His hands fell to the table, and he leaned forward, his breathing heavy. "If my wife says she fell, she fell."

Cancini's jaw tightened. "Did she fall on her own, Mr. Harding, or did she have some help?"

Harding's eyes bugged, and his fist crashed against the table. The untouched sandwich rolled to the floor. Smitty jumped to his feet, his right hand pushing back his jacket to reveal his weapon.

Cancini uncrossed his arms, his face steely. "I'd like you to sit down, Mr. Harding."

"I'd rather stand."

Cancini's face darkened. "Sit down."

The man held Cancini's gaze a moment longer, his barrel chest visibly rising and falling. His breathing quieted, and his color returned to a more normal hue. With a napkin, he wiped the sweat from his forehead. "I know my wife would never accuse me of doing . . . doing what you've been saying. Why am I here?"

"Your wife doesn't need to accuse you, Mr. Harding. All we need is a doctor's report, anything that makes her injuries appear suspicious enough to investigate." He paused, letting the words sink in.

"I would never intentionally hurt my wife. I love her," Harding said, his voice only a whisper.

At the end of the table, Smitty snorted. Harding glanced at the young man once, started to say something, then dropped his chin to his chest. Cancini had heard abusers claim love before. He'd heard denials followed by teary apologies and empty promises. Often, there was even a kernel of truth in those apologies, just before it started again. Cancini changed tacks. "Just for the sake of argument, let's say we're not here to talk about your wife's long list of accidents. We have a few other questions."

"What questions?"

"I don't think you were entirely honest with us about where you were on Sunday night, the night Father Holland was murdered." The large man shrank in his chair. "I've got witnesses who say you were seated at the bar at Wild Wingos Sunday evening and not home with your wife. Is that true?"

Harding sucked in his breath. "Yeah, I was there. I like to watch the games now and then. They have those big screens TVs. Erica's not a fan, so I go there sometimes . . ."

"And?"

His eyelids flickered and he sighed. "And I like to put money on the games. Erica doesn't know about that." He looked from one detective to the other. "She doesn't need to know that, right?"

"Not if you tell the truth about where you were."

A moment passed. Harding nodded once.

"How long were you at the bar?"

"Until about six-thirty or so."

"But the game didn't end for another hour. Why did you leave early?"

Harding shrugged. "I figured I was going to lose. No point in sitting there and watching it anymore."

Cancini noticed that Harding hadn't mentioned the call from Goins. "Where did you go when you left?"

Harding licked his lips. "I was upset about the money, so I drove around for an hour, maybe more. I don't really know. When I calmed down, I went home."

"What time was that?"

"Eight. Maybe a little after."

"Was your wife home?"

"Of course. Where else would she be at eight o' clock on a Sunday night?" Cancini studied Harding's face, but could read nothing. According to the private detective, Erica Harding had been dropped off at Ballston. Her husband also knew his wife had been at the mall. What was the man not telling them?

"I don't know, Mr. Harding. That's why I'm asking you."

The man waved a hand. "She was home. Look, I didn't tell you about being at the bar because I didn't want Erica to find out about the gambling. She wouldn't approve, and it has nothing to do with her."

"Where is your wife now?"

"At work. I dropped her off after she saw the doctor." He checked his watch. "I need to pick her up soon." He stood again. "Can I go now?"

"Mr. Harding, would you say you and your wife are close?"

Harding frowned. "We've known each other since we were kids."

"Since you were kids," Cancini echoed his words. "That's a long time. Have you always been together?"

A vein near the corner of Harding's eye throbbed. "No. We broke up a couple of times. You know how high school can be." He forced a smile that looked frozen on his face. "I think she might've dated some. I'm not sure."

Cancini's pulse quickened. The man was lying. Cancini guessed Harding knew exactly how many men his wife had dated and exactly who they were. "How did you feel about that? About her dating other men?"

"It was her business," Harding said, his tone flat. He wiped his hands on his flannel shirt.

Following Erica's every move was not a new thing. Cancini suspected Harding had done it all his life. "What about you? Did you ever date anyone other than Erica?"

Harding's brows crinkled. "No. I loved her. I can't remember when I didn't."

Cancini nodded. He recognized this to be the truth. "The breakups were her idea?"

"She just needed time." A shadow crossed over his face as he spoke. "But she always came back to me. Always." He got to his feet. "Can I go now?"

"In a minute. One more question, Mr. Harding."

The man rocked on his toes. "Yes?"

"Do you know if your wife confided in Father Holland about her accidents or your marriage or anything else?"

Harding stiffened. "You would have to ask her about that, Detective."

"I will."

His face drained of color. "She's still pretty upset. It might not be a good time."

"I'll keep that in mind." Cancini raised a hand. "Oh, and Mr. Harding? Don't leave town."

"Something odd about that marriage," Cancini said after Harding was gone. His fingers drummed the conference room table.

Bitterness tinged Smitty's words. "You mean besides the fact that he beats her, follows her everywhere, and has been obsessed with her since they were kids?"

Cancini cocked his head to one side. All that was true, but there was something else, something he was missing about the man and his wife. Sadness? Pain? "Besides that. There's something weird."

Smitty's phone buzzed. He listened, stood, and whooped. "She got the warrant for Ketchum's apartment."

Head pounding, Cancini grabbed his jacket from the back of the chair. Harding and his issues would have to wait.

Chapter Sixty-nine

"CANCINI?" JENSEN HELD up a clear bag with a gun. "Found this hidden under the mattresses."

Cancini pulled a pair of plastic gloves over his wrists. He took the bag from Jensen and turned it over in his hands. "Jensen, you and Bronson take this to ballistics. I need to know if it matches either shooting."

Doubt crossed the younger man's face. "It's late. No one will be there."

Time was running out on how much longer they could keep Ketchum in holding. They needed an answer now, and Cancini couldn't worry about whether some analyst could work after five. "I don't give a damn what time it is. Call someone. Anyone who can get the job done. Do you think you can handle that?"

Jensen backed away, taking the bag with him.

Cancini glanced around the apartment. The living room contained a sofa, a TV, a single coffee table, and a bookshelf piled high with gun magazines. A box spring and mattress filled the small bedroom. The drawers in the battered dresser hung open. Ketchum's clothes and shoes had been dumped onto the floor. Officers picked through the piles, item by item.

In the bathroom, a gray film covered the bathtub and floor. A musty towel hung from a hook on the door. Cancini emptied the medicine cabinet and sifted through the bottles of aspirin and tubes of ointment. Nothing. He closed the cabinet door and stared at the cracked mirror over the sink. They needed that gun to match one of the shootings. They'd found no evidence of accelerants. They had no physical evidence tying Ketchum to the fire or the murder. The El Camino was circumstantial, and his lawyer knew it. No prosecutor would dare take that flimsy evidence before a judge. Without a ballistics match, they would have to let him go.

He pulled his phone from his pocket. He'd left six new messages for Father Joe. None had been returned. No one had heard from him in twenty-four hours. It wasn't like the old man to disappear without a word. Cancini's stomach clenched. Where could he be?

"Cancini!" Smitty's voice rang out. "I got something."

Cancini found his partner in the kitchen crouched over a pile of fast-food bags and cigarette butts. In his hand, he held up a white slip of paper.

"It's a gas receipt," Smitty said as he rose to his feet. He handed it to Cancini. "For five dollars of gas. The same volume as the gas can found partly melted by the fire."

Cancini took the receipt between his gloved fingers. "Could be another explanation."

"Don't know what that could be. Ketchum doesn't own a car or a lawn mower or anything else that needs five gallons of gas."

"He might have bought gas for a friend."

"On the same day as the fire? The receipt has the time stamped on it. Ten-forty p.m."

Cancini's neck tingled as he handed back the slip. "Good work. Bag it."

Chapter Seventy

CANCINI PULLED OUT his chair and yawned. The folders on his desk were divided into two piles. The first, he'd scoured. The second, he'd left for the night. After less than four hours of sleep, he was as refreshed as he could be. A large pot of coffee would have to make up the difference.

The remaining files were not thick, but with each page, his confidence they would find something tying Ketchum to Vega diminished. Ballistics had matched the bullet from the drive-by shooting to the gun they found in Ketchum's apartment, and he'd been formally charged. It was something but not nearly enough. Unless they could add the arson, Ketchum would make bail and be back on the streets in a day, two at the most. There was no reason for Ketchum to give up Vega. It wasn't worth the risk. Cancini sighed and stretched his arms over his head. His bones creaked and he settled wearily back in his chair. He opened a file. Shit. Maybe they wouldn't find anything, but he wouldn't give up. Vega was in this up to his neck. Somehow. Someway.

An hour later, he sat up straight. In his hand, he held a payroll report from a Chicken del Rey. Through an ongoing IRS audit prompted by the FBI, Talbot had gotten his hands on copies of recent payroll reports and sent them over. Focusing on the daily printouts, he scanned several more. There it was again. Twice Ketchum had been paid by Vega's restaurant. He checked the hourly wage. It was well above minimum wage, and the hours were nearly full-time. It wasn't a huge sum of money, but the second payday occurred the day after the fire. Was this evidence that Vega was funneling blood money through his restaurant chain?

Smitty strolled in with a greasy bag of biscuits in his hand. Cancini noted the dark circles under his partner's eyes and the blond stubble that peppered his chin and upper lip. Smitty nodded toward the clock on the wall. "You're in early. Did you get any sleep at all?"

"Some."

"Uh-huh." He set a wrapped biscuit on Cancini's desk. "How long have you been here?"

"Long enough." Cancini waved the payroll report in the air. His young partner raised a light eyebrow. "Ketchum told us he was unemployed, right?"

Smitty unwrapped his biscuit. "That's what he said. His dad was paying the rent."

"According to this, he was working for Chicken del Rey. I've got two copies of reports that show he was getting paid for a full-time management job."

"What?" A bite of biscuit fell out of the young man's mouth. He reached for the report, scanned the page, and found Ketchum's name. "We've got him."

"It won't be that easy." Cancini shrugged. "He'll have an explanation, but it proves a connection."

"What proves a connection?" Martin approached with a stack of newspapers under his arm.

Cancini briefed the captain on the payroll report and the payments to Ketchum. "We can use this as leverage with his lawyer. See if he might be more willing to play now."

"I'll get Lawrence down here ASAP." A few more detectives made their way to their desks. The precinct slowly came to life, all focus back on the Holland investigation. Martin rubbed his chin. "Why would Vega take that kind of risk? Why would he use his restaurant to pay a hired gun? Doesn't make sense."

Cancini agreed. He'd been thinking the same thing. "You're right. This is sloppy for Vega. The only explanation is he's cash-strapped. He's got creditors that need to be paid. Maybe when Holland cleaned out the half mil, Vega's cash flow took a hit."

"What about the money he was socking money away in that German corporation?"

"Landon hasn't been able to trace the money from there. Could be that it was going back out again or isn't easily available. Or maybe Vega's just greedy and no one else knows about it." He stood up and paced behind his chair, reports clutched in his hand. "I'd like Landon to go through all these reports again—find out if there are any other suspicious payments. If we get lucky, fraud might be enough to bring Vega in even if Ketchum refuses to cooperate."

"Good thinking." Martin pointed at the whiteboard. "Any ties to Holland yet?"

"Not yet. Ketchum is still our best bet, but only if he talks.

Landon is still digging into the e-mails but we've got nothing that shows any recent contact between Holland and Vega."

"What about that receipt for gas?"

Smitty spoke up. "The gas station has cameras, but they don't work. Nothing there and Ketchum paid in cash. None of the cashiers remembers seeing him so far, but we're going to hit the station again, see if they recognize the El Camino."

"All right. I'll get Lawrence to squeeze Ketchum's lawyer. Maybe if he thinks he's going to do some serious time, he'll give up Vega."

Cancini remained quiet. Ketchum might turn, but it would take more than a payroll report and a gas receipt. The ballistics report was still the most solid evidence they had, but the gun was stolen and Ketchum was claiming he found it in the street.

Martin, walking away, stopped and asked, "By the way, who's paying for Ketchum's lawyer? That guy can't be cheap."

"We checked with his parents," Smitty said. "They don't know anything about it. His office claims he's doing pro bono work. It's another angle where we can try to find a connection to Vega."

Martin pursed his lips. "Good. We need a goddamn break in this case."

"Cancini." The dark-haired detective wheeled around. Jensen held a slip of paper in his hand. "Your friend."

Cancini's heart thumped. "What is it?"

Jensen handed him the scrap of paper. "They located his cell phone."

Chapter Seventy-one

CANCINI CHEWED ON his lower lip, his muscles tense. He couldn't stop his mind from going to dark places, thoughts he didn't want to think.

"It's in a bodega," Jensen had said. "The tracking software gives the address where the phone is located."

Cancini, coat in hand, hadn't waited to hear more.

Ten minutes later, they had almost reached the location. Cancini gripped the phone in his hand. Jensen had sent a follow-up text, one that sent chills up and down the detective's spine.

No activity on the phone since Tuesday.

Smitty turned off Benning Road, turned twice more, and pulled over. "Do you see what I see?"

"I see it." At the end of the block, two doors down from the bodega, was a Chicken del Rey.

"Can't be a coincidence," Smitty said, his voice tight.

Quiet, Cancini climbed out of the car. The wind howled, and he shivered under his thin coat. Cars crawled past them as commuters headed toward the beltway or the Baltimore-Washington

Parkway. A smattering of folks hurried along the sidewalks, rushing to a metro or bus stop.

Cancini scanned the block. A take-out pizza joint was nestled between two brownstones. A "For Lease" sign hung in another window. Only the grocery appeared to be open. He ducked inside. A bell jingled until the door slammed shut behind them.

"Damn, it smells good in here," Smitty said.

The warm odors of oranges, cinnamon, and coffee hit them in the face. Cancini's stomach growled. The biscuit Smitty had brought him was still sitting on his desk, uneaten and cold. A middle-aged woman stood at a long counter watching both detectives. Behind her, in the small kitchen, Cancini spotted a man with hunched shoulders prepping foods. He moved toward the cashier.

Introducing himself, he pulled out a photo of Father Joe. "Do you know this man?"

She leaned in. "I've seen him before. He's a priest that comes to St. William sometimes." Her hand flew to her mouth. "Oh my God. Has something happened to him?"

"No, no," he said quickly. "We're just trying to find him to ask him some questions." He could see his answer didn't fully alleviate her suspicions, but he didn't have time to waste. "An unrelated matter."

"It's Father Joe, right?"

"Yes, ma'am." Smitty stood next to him. "Have you seen the father in the past few days? Maybe he came in the store for something?"

She shook her head. "No. Not that I've seen."

"Does anyone else ever work the cash register? Anyone else that might have seen him?"

"Just my husband and my daughter." She waved a hand behind her. "Jorge?" she called. His head came up and he shuffled up to the counter. "This is my husband, Jorge. He comes in early to make coffee and pastries." She pointed at the picture. "They want to know if we've seen Father Joe in the store this week."

He wiped his hands on the apron tied around his waist and leaned toward the photo. "Nope. Not this week. Not ever." He turned away.

Cancini looked back at the woman. "What about your daughter?"

"Sorry. She's been out with the flu all week. It's just been me and Jorge."

The bells jingled again, and a young couple came into the store, arm in arm. Cancini combed each aisle, searching behind items and under the shelves. Smitty went to the front windows where two small tables were placed. He scanned the windowsill and around the tables. He shook his head once when they returned to the front counter.

"Were you looking for something?" The cashier placed her hands on her hips, eyebrows raised.

"A cell phone," Cancini said. "Father Joe's was stolen, and we wondered if you had found it here."

The bells rang again. "No." She tilted her head to see the door.

"Do you mind if we look around? Check the bathroom and the kitchen?"

She hesitated, then stepped back toward the kitchen. She spoke rapidly, the words Spanish and mostly unintelligible to Cancini. Jorge glanced over his shoulder and shrugged.

Smitty nodded toward the single restroom in the corner of the store and disappeared. Cancini headed into the kitchen. Jorge worked at a shiny counter in the center of the room. An oversized refrigerator and freezer sat against the back wall. A sink, oven, and battered cabinets hung against another wall. Opened boxes loaded with dried goods and cans filled metal shelves. He moved to the open boxes, searching through the contents. More boxes were piled in the corner, unopened. He shifted them, inspecting the floor around and behind them. A trash can sat at each end of the silver counter. The one closer to Jorge held the morning's trash: coffee grounds, an empty flour bag, and fruit peels. The other was empty.

He looked up to find Jorge watching him. "Where do you take the trash?"

The man nodded at a door next to the freezer. He spoke with a heavy accent. "Dumpster in the alley."

Cancini crossed the kitchen and pushed the door open. He stepped outside to a narrow alley and saw a large Dumpster to his left. Jagged shards of glass littered the ground, and "No Parking" signs hung from the fence. On the other side of the fence, several squat, concrete buildings lined the block. Plywood and plastic sheeting covered several windows, and faded graffiti stained the walls. To the right, behind the pizza restaurant, sat a smaller Dumpster. Cancini went back inside.

"There are two Dumpsters in the alley."

Jorge looked up and came over to the open door. He waved a butcher knife in the direction of the larger Dumpster. "We use that one."

"Does anyone else use it?"

"Chicken del Rey."

Cancini's jaw tightened. "Anyone else?"

"Who knows? Some of the neighborhood punks, maybe some

squatters." He indicated the run-down cinder-block building. "Punks," he said again and spit on the ground.

The pit in Cancini's stomach grew. A wind blew up and closed the door. "How often does the city empty the Dumpster?"

"They come on Tuesday mornings." His wife came into the kitchen, and Jorge returned to chopping, no longer interested. Smitty came in behind her.

"That was two days ago," Cancini said. The Dumpster hadn't been emptied since before Father Joe had disappeared. He glanced at Smitty then back at the woman. "Would you mind if we took a quick look in the Dumpster, see if the phone is in there?" He didn't need her permission but figured it was better that way. And if there was anything—or anyone—to find in there, he didn't want it to be someone else who found it.

The front bells rang again, and she waved a hand in the air. "Do what you want."

Outside, both detectives pulled on plastic gloves. Smitty used a pair of milk crates to hoist himself up and looked over the opening to the trash bin. Cancini's nose wrinkled at the odors of discarded and rancid food. He shivered and looked up and down the alley. The weather had been cold all week. The smell could have been worse.

"I'm going in," Smitty said.

Cancini nodded. The phone had been traced to this address, and neither Father Joe nor the phone was in the store. The Dumpster was the last place to search. Cancini wanted the trace to be wrong. His heart thudded in his ears and he bowed his head. Over the noise from the street, he heard Smitty moving and pushing his way through the bin. After several long minutes, his partner's head appeared over the top of the bin. "Just trash."

Cancini exhaled and bent over at the waist. The words were all he'd needed to hear. His heart slowed, and he breathed in and out. Just trash, but they still needed to find that phone. "I'm coming in."

A half hour later, Cancini's hand closed around a hard, rectangular item. Covered in grease, it slipped from his grasp. "Damn." He dug further, found it again. Holding it up, there was no doubt it was a cell phone. He shivered again. Father Joe wouldn't have thrown his cell phone in the Dumpster. Had it been accidentally swept into the trash? Cancini wanted to believe that was possible, but the lump in his stomach and the cold fear in his heart told him otherwise. Someone else had thrown that phone in the Dumpster. Maybe someone who didn't want Father Joe to be found.

Chapter Seventy-two

"WHAT'VE WE GOT?" Cancini leaned in, his face close to Landon's.

The young man tapped his computer screen. "The phone definitely belongs to your friend. It matches the number he gave us. I verified it with the phone company."

"What about activity in the last forty-eight hours?" Cancini steadied his breathing.

"Mostly incoming only. I've got a handful of calls and texts." Pointing at the spreadsheet, he said. "There were several calls made to the phone by you. I've highlighted those in blue."

Cancini nodded. He'd called the number at least two dozen times in two days.

Landon touched the screen again. "These are the rest listed under recent calls. Most were made before Tuesday. This one is from Sophia Vega and the others look like they are related to church business. This one is your father, right?" Cancini looked at him. "It's in his contacts." Cancini squinted at the screen, reading the time of the call. Close to two o'clock on Tuesday. Landon changed the screen. "And here's a short list of texts, four to be exact, again mostly church business."

"Father Joe doesn't like texting."

Landon pushed a button and another screen came up. "He must have gotten over that."

Cancini studied the screen. He pointed at an unidentified call. "What's that?"

Landon glanced at him. "I had to do a little tracking but I found the source." He paused. "CDR, Incorporated."

Cancini shifted in his seat and his heart skipped a beat. He knew that name. "Chicken del Rey?"

"Yep."

Cancini pulled his phone from his pocket and called the number.

A pert young voice answered the phone. "Chicken del Rey. How can I help you?"

"Can you tell me which location I've called?"

"Southeast."

"Thank you," he said, and hung up the phone.

The Southeast store had a large office in the back. Talbot had told them Vega frequented that office on a regular basis. His blood ran cold and he looked away. Father Joe had called the Chicken del Rey number just past noon. That would have been right after he'd met with Sophia Vega. The last outgoing call was to Cancini's father two hours later. That was followed by the list of incoming and outgoing texts. He squinted at the screen. "Is this ten-thirty p.m. Tuesday?"

"Yes," Landon said. "That's the last outgoing message."

"Who did he text?"

"This one was a little more difficult, but it's also a CDR phone.

It's listed in a group of company phones for employees. According to their office, they aren't specifically assigned. Just available, and no one keeps track of them." Cancini picked up his phone to dial again, but Landon laid a hand on his arm. "I already tried a bunch of times. The phone's been disconnected."

"There's nothing after that last text?"

"Nothing," he said. "I'm sorry."

Cancini stared at the list, his stomach swirling. He'd been holding out hope the old man had left the apartment building on his own and been unreachable out of stubbornness. But even if he could convince himself of all that, he also knew Father Joe would never let him worry unnecessarily. There'd been no note and he hadn't taken any of his clothing or his medications. Wherever he'd gone, he'd planned to return. Cancini's head pounded and every nerve ending in his body screamed. He closed his eyes and pinched the bridge of nose. There were too many questions and not enough answers, and the ones he did have weren't comforting.

He focused on Landon again. "Did this CDR number ever try to reach him?"

"Not that I can see."

"Had he ever texted that number before?"

"Not that I could find."

Cancini took a deep breath. "Show me the text."

Landon pushed a couple of buttons, and a piece of paper shot out of his printer. He handed the page to Cancini.

I know what you've done. We need to talk. I'm coming to you.

The fingers of his hand curled around the printed page. Mind numb, he shoved the balled-up paper in his pocket. "Thanks, Landon." Evidence or no evidence, Father Joe's safety was the only thing on his mind, and his only lead came back to Vega.

Chapter Seventy-three

Sunday, February 21: The Day of

MATT HELD THE scrap of paper between his fingers. Inside, a number had been written in heavy, black ink. His stomach fluttered. He'd found the note slipped under the door of his office after the evening Mass. Had the man with the tattoo visited his office during the Eucharist? It would be easy enough to do. The doors weren't locked. Even though there was no name next to the number, he knew. Carlos.

He fell into the chair and waved his fingers until the trembling stopped. The man with the tattoo had shaken him more than he'd realized. When the last parishioner had left, his body had gone cold. He'd hurried to his office and closed the door. Now, he slipped the paper in his pocket and hurried to the corner market. Using the old pay phone on the wall, he dialed the number. Carlos picked up on the second ring.

"Yes?"

"It's me." An icy silence filled the line. "I'm not going to return—"

"Then we have nothing to discuss." The line went dead.

Matt hesitated, then dropped in more coins. He spoke as soon as he heard his former friend pick up the line. "Carlos, don't hang up." The words rushed out. "I spoke to your mother yesterday—"

"You did what?"

Matt could feel Carlos's anger pulsing across the line. "After services. I asked her to stay so I could discuss something with her. Something important." He gripped the phone and concentrated on his words. "I wanted to talk to her about the money and all the good we could do. She'd like to help."

"What the fuck are you talking about?"

Matt pressed the phone to his ear. His heart thudded in his chest, and he touched the cross around his neck. "She wants—"

"You told my mother about the money? I will fuckin' kill you."

"No. It's not what you think. I didn't tell her about you or . . . your business." A calm came over him, and the words slowed down. "We talked about the foundation money for St. William."

"I don't give a shit about some stupid-ass foundation money. I want my money."

"You're not listening. Your money is the foundation money. That's why I can't return it. I used it to set up the foundation. There are trustees and a lawyer. Every dollar that goes in or out has to be accounted for."

Seconds ticked by, and Matt waited for Carlos to understand. It didn't matter. "I don't care where it is or what you're calling it. Get my money back. You're running out of time."

"I can't. It's too late."

"Then you're a dead man."

"Carlos, talk to your mother. Please."

"Goddammit! I told you to leave my mother out of this. She's not part of this, and if I find out you said one fuckin' word to her, I swear to Christ, I will fuckin' kill you myself."

"Carlos, talk to Sophia."

"Fuck you, Matty."

The line went dead again. Limp, Matt let the phone drop from his hand. He walked back to his office, sinking into his chair. He struggled to breathe, weakness taking over his body. After a moment, he raised his head, eyes coming to rest on the picture of his graduation from seminary. His heart quieted then. He reached up, touched the cross he wore around his neck, and prayed. His pulse slowed, and his strength returned.

"Amen," he said aloud.

Calmer, he knew he needed to get back to the church and close up for the evening. He pushed away from the desk, the slip of paper still clutched in his hand.

He sank into the front pew, his cassock fanning out below his feet. An exhaustion stole over him, but he looked up to the cross. He would not give in. He would help the people of this church and he would give them back their community. No matter the cost.

Chapter Seventy-four

"Judge Koon won't sign the warrant." The words, delivered in a
monotone, matched the blank expression on Martin's face.

"Shit," Smitty said, and flopped back in his chair, arms folded
against his chest.

Cancini couldn't blame Judge Koon. The warrant for Ketchum
had made some sense. A warrant to search Vega's home and computers could be risky. She knew Vega's reputation and his access
to legal advice. And what did they have to back up the warrant
anyway? A missing priest, a text to a corporate cell phone, and a
payroll stub for Ketchum, a man who had not yet been convicted
of a crime and wouldn't talk. It wasn't much. It wasn't anything,
but they needed that warrant.

"She's not the only judge in town," Cancini said. His eyes itched
with grit and exhaustion. "What about Simpson?" he asked. Judge
Simpson didn't mind playing a little fast and loose. More importantly, he abhorred street gangs and drugs.

"I'll talk to Emma," the captain said.

Cancini watched him walk away. He was dead on his feet;

his neck and shoulders ached. He was no closer to arresting a suspect for the murder of Holland, and worse, Father Joe was still missing. They'd been able to keep it out of the papers so far, but they wouldn't be able to for much longer. He stared at the whiteboard and the lines connecting Father Joe and Father Holland. Another line connected both men to Sophia Vega. That line stretched to her son, Carlos Vega. He stepped closer to the board and blocked off an empty corner. He wrote the hours of the day, beginning with the last hour Father Joe was seen. One by one he filled in the phone calls and texts Father Joe had made and received on Tuesday, the day he disappeared. In his pocket, his phone buzzed.

"Dad? Everything okay?"

"I didn't get my lunch."

Cancini frowned. The nurse should have been serving dinner at this hour. "Isn't Jada there?"

"Of course she is. Thanks to you, the damn woman never leaves. She's always fluffing and hovering. You know how I can't stand that, and when she does leave, the other one comes." Cancini's chin fell to his chest and he counted silently to ten. His father kept complaining. "I don't know which one of them is worse. Maybe the one at night. She wears enough perfume to choke a horse. Doesn't she know I can't breathe?"

"I'll talk to her," Cancini said. He glanced over at Martin's office. The captain had his own phone to his ear. "Is there anything else, Dad? I'm on a case."

"Father Joe didn't bring my lunch today, and he's not answering his phone. Do you know where he is?"

Cancini's shoulders sagged. He'd been wondering when this question would come. "No, Dad. I don't. Maybe he forgot about lunch and his phone battery died." He hated the lie, but didn't know what else to do.

"Humph. He wouldn't forget." Cancini's fingers tightened around the phone. "He told me he'd bring me barbecue today. When he didn't come, that lazy Jada made me one of her nasty tuna sandwiches. I was really looking forward to that barbecue."

"When did he tell you that, Dad?"

"I don't know. The other day. What difference does it make?"

"It doesn't." Cancini spoke the words carefully. "I'm just wondering if it was Tuesday. I saw him then, too. Was it Tuesday, or maybe it was yesterday?"

The old man clucked his tongue. "You've never just wondered anything in your life, son. What's really going on?"

Cancini sighed. His father's mind wasn't entirely addled by oxygen yet. He debated how much to tell him. "Someone tried to burn down St. Ignatius a few days ago. You might have seen that in the paper. Father Joe's been laying low. That's why you probably didn't see him today."

"Laying low, huh? That doesn't sound like Father Joe to me." Cancini heard the clicking of the oxygen machine in the background. "Does this have anything to do with the murder of that priest at St. William?"

"I can't talk about that case, Dad."

His father was silent, the only sound the terminal clicking. When he spoke again, his voice was soft. "He was here Tuesday. He comes every week because he knows I can't stand staring at these walls all day. We played a game of chess and then he left."

"Did he say where he was going when he left?"

"Said he was going over to St. William to take care of some business."

"Did he talk about going anywhere else or seeing anyone else?"

"Nope. Just that. Then he said he'd be back Thursday with my barbecue. It's Thursday."

Cancini looked up to the ceiling. "I'll have some sent over."

"Don't bother. I don't want it anymore. I'm not an idiot, you know." The old man's voice cracked, and Cancini's eyes stung. "Find him. Please."

Chapter Seventy-five

CANCINI STOOD OUTSIDE the heavy doors of St. William and pulled his overcoat tight, the damp air seeping into his bones.

Smitty shifted his weight from one foot to the other, his hands jammed deep in his pockets. "Why are we here again?"

Shoulders hunched against the cold, Cancini glanced over at the empty parking lot. "Gotta do something. I can't sit around waiting for that warrant another minute."

"Judge Simpson promised to review it before six."

"We'd already have it if Landon could find who sent those e-mails to Holland."

"That's a big if."

"Probably." Thunder rumbled in the distance. "Father Joe came over here after he visited my father. Might as well find out what he was doing."

Smitty pulled open the door and waved a hand. "Lead the way."

Cancini stepped through the vestibule and peeked in the empty sanctuary. Cold candles and dying flowers sat on the altar. While Masses had resumed, the church remained without a resident priest. They passed through the sanctuary to the Commons. The church office door stood open, soft music spilling out.

Erica Harding swiveled around in her chair, her broken wrist pressed against her side. She switched off the music coming from her computer. "Detectives, I wasn't expecting you today. Is everything okay?"

Cancini nodded toward her arm. "Maybe I should be asking you that."

"Wh-what?" She looked down at the soft cast around her wrist and forced a laugh. "Oh. That. It's just a sprain. I slipped on some ice."

Smitty coughed and stared at the ground, his face red. They both remembered she'd used the stairs as her excuse at the hospital. Aloud, Cancini said, "Sorry to hear that."

"Thank you." She sat up straight in her chair, a pink cardigan draped over her shoulders. Her hair, pulled back into a ponytail, accentuated her arched brows and sculpted cheekbones. Her makeup, subtly applied, almost masked the faded bruise at her jawline. "What can I help you with, Detectives?"

"Were you working on Tuesday?"

"I was. That's normally my day off, but with Father Holland gone, I've been coming in to cover the office and trying to get things ready for whoever is coming in to say Mass this week. The diocese is doing their best, but I'm afraid it's going to be at least another couple of weeks before a new priest is assigned to St. William."

"Have you heard about Father Joe's parish?"

Her smile faded. "Yes. I saw it on the news. Why would someone do a terrible thing like that?" She flushed, and her lower lip trembled. "Why does anyone do terrible things at all?"

"Did Father Joe talk to you about the fire on Tuesday? He mentioned he was coming by the church."

"He did come by. He was so sweet to do that, checking to see how we're doing over here, but we didn't talk about the fire. Mostly, we talked about Father Holland and how hard everyone is taking it." She raised a hand and swiped at a tear. "It's been difficult, you know. Without him, the numbers are already dropping. I mean, Sunday was still busy enough, but the daily Masses are mostly empty."

"Was your husband here that day?"

She frowned. "What day?"

"Tuesday."

"Does that matter?"

Cancini shrugged. "Just wondered. He hangs around the church a lot."

Tears gone, she glanced at the door. "He wasn't here."

"How long did Father Joe stay?"

The line creasing her brow deepened. "Ten minutes or so. After we talked, I saw him go into the sanctuary. I don't know how long he was there. I assumed he was going in to pray, so I left him alone. When I went in later, he was gone."

"What time would you say he went into the sanctuary?"

She touched her finger to her chin. "A little before three, I think." The phone rang, and she turned away.

Smitty's head came close to Cancini's ear. "What do you think?" he asked.

Cancini shrugged. "It would be like him to come by and check how things were going. Even though he'd been shot and his own church had been burned, he would've put others first."

"You say that like it's a bad thing."

"No, it's not that. He went to see my dad. He came here. What I can't understand is why he left the building in the first place when he knew it wasn't safe."

"You said he was going stir-crazy. Maybe that's all it was."

Cancini shook his head. Erica was still on the phone and typing into her computer. "No. He didn't like it, but he understood why he had to be there. It was something else."

"Vega."

Cancini didn't say anything. Father Joe had called Vega's restaurant and texted a CDR number. He hadn't been seen since.

"Gentlemen?" Erica stood. "I'm getting ready to close the office for the day. Is there anything else I can help you with?"

"Did Father Joe happen to mention where he was going after he left here?"

Her ponytail swung. "No. Should he have?"

"Just wondering," Cancini said. "Was anyone else here Tuesday afternoon?"

"Father Renwick came to say the evening Mass, but that was about an hour and a half later. We've been on a very lean staff here—especially lately."

Cancini watched as she turned off her computer and straightened her desk with her right hand, the left held against her side. "I hear they're forecasting an early snow tomorrow. You might need to get a new pair of boots." He paused a beat. "I wouldn't want you to slip or fall down the stairs again."

She looked up sharply. "Thank you, Detective. Maybe I'll go shopping tonight."

"You do that."

"Have a nice evening, Detectives." She began to tidy her desk, closing drawers and stacking papers.

"Speaking of shopping," he said, his hand on the door. "I understand you and your husband were not home together the night Father Holland was murdered."

"That's not true. We were together."

"Later, but not the whole night. Weren't you both out earlier, separately?"

She flushed pink. "My husband told me you asked him about that. Sonny had gone out to watch some game. I don't care for sports, so he does that sometimes."

"And you?"

"I decided to run a personal errand."

"What was the errand, if you don't mind my asking?"

Her eyelashes fluttered and she looked down at her hands. "I was planning to buy a nightgown, a negligee. I thought my husband would like it. I was going to surprise him."

"Did you?"

"Did I what?"

"Surprise him?"

"Oh." She blushed again. "No, I couldn't find anything that he wouldn't have, um, disliked, and the mall was getting ready to close. Guess it wasn't good planning on my part."

"You took a cab to the mall."

She nodded. "I do that sometimes."

"You told the cabdriver to wait for you, but you never came out."

"I took the subway home. Please don't tell my husband that. Sonny doesn't really like me to ride the subway. There are strangers standing next to you or sitting next to you . . ." Her voice faded away."

"Why didn't you just take the cab home?"

"I didn't like the way the driver was looking at me." She gave a rueful laugh. "Maybe I'm becoming as suspicious as my husband, but I didn't trust him. I took the subway and walked. It's only a few blocks. Sonny came home early and we were home the rest of the night, just like we told you." Her fingers trembled as she smoothed her hair. "My husband is on his way to pick me up."

Smitty cleared his throat and leaned in toward Cancini. "It's almost six."

"Right," Cancini said. "Thanks for your time, Mrs. Harding." She nodded mutely, and Smitty followed Cancini back through the sanctuary. They paused in the vestibule.

"No way that lady has that many accidents. Why does she keep protecting him?" Bright pink spots appeared on his pale cheeks. "I saw it with my own sister, but I still don't get it."

Cancini clamped a hand on Smitty's shoulder. He didn't blame him. He was equally bothered by Harding's possessive behavior and volatile temper, but whatever was going on there would have to wait. "Now isn't the time. As much as we'd like to do something about it, we came here to track Father Joe."

Smitty opened his mouth, closed it again. He pushed open the door and buttoned his coat. "This weather sucks," he said. "Feels like it's been raining and cold for days."

His young partner was right again. Cancini spotted a bright red umbrella propped in the corner near the door. He was tempted to borrow the abandoned umbrella, thought better of it, and followed Smitty outside.

Sleet hit the windshield and slowed traffic to a crawl. They rode in silence for several minutes. Cancini, mind racing, scratched at the stubble on his chin. Cold rain dripped from his hair down the back of his neck. "Why would Father Joe try to see Vega at night?" He laid his head back against the seat, letting the words tumble out. "And why would he go alone? He knew Vega was a suspect. He knows how dangerous the man is. Why would he take the risk?"

Smitty parked and glanced up at the precinct. He made no move to get out of the car and let his hands rest on the wheel.

Cancini slammed the dashboard with the palm of his hand. "Dammit! I feel like I'm missing something." The car heater whirred and the sleet tapped on the foggy windows. "Sorry," he said. "I'm just frustrated. We're running around in circles and we've got nothing tying any of this together. We've got a mountain of maybes."

Smitty drove for several minutes before breaking the silence. "Where do you think he is?"

Cancini stared out the window. Gray skies darkened the streets, matching his mood. "I wish I knew."

Chapter Seventy-six

CANCINI ROSE FROM the hard cot and arched his back, the stiff muscles screaming in protest. Gritting his teeth, he splashed cold water on his face and stared at his reflection. His skin, ghostly under the single light, itched under two days of stubble. The whites of his eyes were stained pink, the fragile blood vessels burning and swollen. He washed his face a second time, dried with paper towels, and slipped on a clean shirt. Pulling his phone from his pocket, he checked for messages or an alert from Missing Persons. No word on Father Joe. His shoulders drooped and his head fell to his chest. A phone ringing in the squad room jolted him out of his inertia. Grabbing his items, he left the locker room.

The Vega file sat open on his desk, dozens of pages spread fanlike across the surface. He sighed again. Simpson hadn't signed the warrant. He'd wanted to, but claimed he needed more than an unanswered text and conjecture. Cancini swallowed the bile that rose in his throat. Vega was dirty, more than dirty, and no one could do a damn thing about it. They'd applied pressure during the night, brought in the usual informants, grilled as many sources as possible. In every case, it was the same. Twitchy fingers. Shifty eyes. No one would talk. Some claimed ignorance, others clammed up. None could hide their fear.

Searching for anything that tied Vega to Father Holland or Father Joe, Cancini combed through the file, reading everything two and three times over. Around him, the precinct filled slowly. Voices, hoarse with exhaustion, too much coffee, and too many cigarettes, echoed across the jumble of desks. He swallowed some aspirin and held his aching head in his hands. Smitty set a bagel and coffee on his desk.

"Good morning, boys," Martin said. The smell of spearmint clung to the captain's clothes. "What've we got?"

Cancini's cell phone rang, and he snapped it up. "Yeah?"

A woman's voice came across the line. "Well, hello back to you, Detective. How are you, this morning?"

"Fine, Emma," he answered automatically. Smitty sat up straighter, and Martin leaned forward. "And you?"

"Better than fine and you're about to be, too."

He made notes as she talked, the pounding in his head forgotten. Hanging up, he leaned back in his chair.

"Well?" Martin asked, chomping hard on a fresh stick of gum.

"Ketchum rolled."

Martin and Smitty exchanged a look.

"He's willing to take a plea to charges of arson and assault. The ID on the El Camino from the gas station pushed him over the edge. That with the ballistics match on the drive-by, the payroll report, and the receipt. Maybe he just couldn't stomach the idea of jail. Either way, he's willing to testify that Vega paid him to set the fire and take a shot at Father Joe."

The captain clapped his hand on the desk. "Holy shit. I knew it. I knew we'd get him."

Cancini shook his head. "We don't have him yet. Vega will lawyer up, and all we've got is Ketchum's testimony and a payroll report. And Ketchum won't cop to the murder of Father Holland."

"Why not?" Smitty asked.

"A couple of reasons. First, his lawyer knows we don't have any evidence tying Ketchum to the murder scene. The gun used in the drive-by isn't the same as the one used to shoot Father Holland, and there are dozens of witnesses who saw Ketchum leave the church before the Mass ended. Second, according to Lawrence, Ketchum says Vega only asked him to scare Holland. His story is that if Vega hired someone to shoot the priest, it was someone else."

"That doesn't make sense. Why would he hire someone else? Had to be Ketchum," Smitty said.

Cancini paced the floor in front of the whiteboard. Smitty's logic sounded right. Why would Vega hire one thug to scare Holland and another to shoot him? Would he risk expanding the circle of those threatening the priest? "Lawrence said Ketchum was adamant he had nothing to do with the murder." Cancini shrugged. "For what it's worth, she believes him."

Martin puffed his chest. "Since when do we start believing hired killers?" Cancini and Smitty remained quiet as the captain's voice pitched higher. "Ketchum will say whatever he needs to say to avoid a capital murder charge. No way we're letting him walk on that one even if I have to sit in on the goddamn plea deal myself." He paused to catch his breath. "It doesn't matter right now anyway. Simpson will sign the warrant this time, and the arson and assault are enough to question Vega." He wagged a finger at Cancini. "Find him and bring him in."

Chapter Seventy-seven

VEGA'S LAWYER CAME to her feet when Cancini entered the room. Watching him, she laid one hand on her client's shoulder and smiled. "I'll allow you five minutes of this charade, gentlemen," she said, her voice soft but firm. Chocolate-brown eyes looked over horn-rimmed glasses balanced on the end of a wide nose. Her dark hair, prematurely streaked with gray, was pulled back into a twist. Still smiling, she touched the collar of her white blouse and fingered a single strand of pearls. She placed her card on the table and pushed it toward Cancini.

He leaned forward to read it. Sylvia Morris.

"Shall we get started?" she asked.

A bored-looking Vega stared at the one-way glass. If he was angry, he hid it well. Cancini dropped a thick file onto the table, the sound like a shot. Vega's dark gaze slid to the file and then to Cancini, one heavy brow arched. "Is that supposed to scare me?" The left corner of his mouth turned up in a smirk. "You're going to have to do better than that, Detective."

The lawyer touched his hand. "Gentlemen, you are fortunate

we even agreed to come in today. Your time is running out." Vega smiled wider.

Cancini took the chair across from Vega. He let the seconds tick by, his fingers drumming the file. He glanced back toward the glass. Martin and the D.A. were watching. "Mr. Vega, we'd like to ask you a few questions about your relationship with Gerald Ketchum."

Vega's brows drew together. "Ketchum? Do I know him?"

Cancini opened the file and pulled out the payroll reports. He spread them across the table. "Your company paid him twice recently. I assume you know him."

"A lot of people work for me at my chicken stores," he said with a shrug. "I can't remember all of them."

"What does Mr. Ketchum do for you?"

He shrugged again. "I told you. I can't remember all of them."

"This employee has a very distinctive tattoo. Skull bisected by a dagger. Three drops of blood."

"So?"

"Have you ever seen anyone with that tattoo before?"

"I see lots of tattoos."

Sylvia tapped her watch. "Two minutes."

Cancini picked up the pages and replaced them in the folder. "Ketchum, the employee you can't remember, has been paid in excess of five thousand dollars in the last few weeks. That's a lot of money. You sure you don't know what he does for you?"

"I said I—"

"Mr. Vega has already answered that question, Detective." Morris squeezed his arm, and Vega's mouth clamped shut. She cocked her head to the side. "Obviously, Mr. Vega cannot possibly know every employee personally. He owns the restaurants, which means he doesn't deal with the day-to-day business. He hires people to do that."

"Mr. Ketchum has admitted he shot at a priest," Cancini said, switching directions. "He also confessed to setting fire to a church. I assume you saw the stories in the paper."

"We all saw the stories, Detective, and those are terrible things. That being said, my client has already told you he doesn't know this Ketchum." The lawyer tapped Vega on the shoulder, and they both stood. "Your five minutes are up. If you have any additional questions, please call my office, and I'll be happy to set up an appointment."

"Sit down, Mr. Vega. We're not done here."

Sylvia's head twisted, and her placid expression turned steely. "Really, Detective? My client has answered your questions, and I have yet to hear a valid reason he's been asked to come in here."

"Is a charge of solicitation to commit murder and arson in the first degree reason enough?"

Vega laughed, the sound a sharp cackle that sent a shiver up Cancini's spine. "Solicitation? What the fuck is that?"

Sylvia raised a hand, and Vega's guffaws faded to a snort. "I think he means hiring someone to commit murder."

Vega's scowled at the large pane of glass, his smile gone. "This is bullshit."

Cancini motioned to the file. "I've got a few more questions."

"I don't have to answer your questions."

"You're right. You don't. You've got your lawyer to hide behind." Vega's upper lip curled, and he took a step forward.

Vega's lawyer placed a hand on his forearm and pulled him back. "Are you prepared to arrest my client today?"

"Depends on how he answers my questions."

"And if he chooses not to answer—which is his right?"

"I'd have no choice but to place him under arrest." Cancini's case was flimsy—even with Ketchum's testimony—but they didn't know that.

Vega's chin jutted forward. "You don't have shit."

"You don't know what I have, Mr. Vega. Unless you have some pretty good answers to my questions, I plan on locking you up."

"I'll be out before dinner, asshole."

"Have someplace to go? Is it the Amberjack Club or the Bang-Bang tonight?"

"You think I don't already know you been following me? You think I give a shit? You've got nothing, and we both know it. You arrest me and I'll be eating surf and turf and dancin' with some fine ladies before you can figure out what the fuck just happened. You just keep jacking off, asshole. We're outta here."

Cancini kept his voice steady, his body still. "It's a Friday afternoon." He stared hard at Vega. "These are felonies, Mr. Vega, and it's supposed to start snowing soon. No judge is hanging around late today. Even your lawyer can't change that. If I arrest you, you're in till Monday, like it or not." Cancini raised one shoulder and smiled. "You can answer my questions or not. Your choice."

The lawyer's mouth opened and closed. Her gaze drifted to the one-way glass, then to her client. She nodded once and shrugged. "You have one man's word and a payroll report. We both know that's not enough to hold my client, Detective, but"—she smiled again and pulled out a chair—"we're feeling generous today. A few more questions. That's all."

After they were seated again, Cancini asked, "How long had you known Father Holland?"

Vega's started. "Is that what this is about?" He gave a single shake of his dark head, and the gold around his neck flashed under the lights. "I knew him when we were kids. So what?"

"You were close when you were young, weren't you?"

"Everyone hung around back then. It was Barry Farm, man. You had to fuckin' stick together."

"But not anymore?"

"Didn't have anything in common, man. You know how it is."

"Did money have anything to do with it?"

Vega laughed out loud. "Shit. Matty never had any money. He chose a life that made him poor. I'm a businessman. Like I said, we didn't have anything in common anymore."

"So you hadn't been in touch with him recently, through e-mail, or on the phone?"

"We weren't friends anymore, but we weren't enemies, either. I might've called him or e-mailed him. I don't really remember. My mother went to his church. She loved the man."

"Father Holland wasn't the only priest you knew."

He shrugged again. "So? I was raised Catholic."

"Did you know Father Joe Sweeney?"

"You know I knew him." He sat forward, his hands spread on the table, ready to push away. "This is a waste of time. I don't feel like talking anymore."

"Did you see him Tuesday?"

Vega's lawyer leaned over and whispered in his ear. He raised a shoulder and faced Cancini. "Yeah, I saw him. He wanted to talk."

"About what?"

"Why don't you ask him?"

"I want to hear your version."

Vega held Cancini's gaze, then shook his head. "I got nothin' to say, man."

Cancini's heart thumped in his chest. "What time did he come by your house?"

"My house? He didn't come by my house. He met me at one of my restaurants, the Southeast store."

Cancini tensed, the muscles in his shoulders rock-hard. That store sat on the same block where they'd found Father Joe's cell phone buried in a Dumpster. "What time?"

"How the fuck should I remember? Why don't you ask him?"

"It was late," Cancini said.

"What are you talkin' about?" His black eyes bugged. "Wait. I do remember. It was the fuckin' middle of the day. Shit, I even offered him lunch."

Cancini hesitated. Vega had admitted meeting with Father Joe earlier in the day, yet denied seeing him that night. "What did you talk about?"

Vega's lawyer cleared her throat and shook her head. Vega nodded. "Nothing important."

Cancini struggled to keep his voice even. "Did anyone else see him talking to you?"

"The whole damn restaurant saw him talking to me."

"What time did he leave?"

"I don't know. One? One-thirty? I'm not a fucking clock."

Cancini rubbed his palms against his pants. He'd seen the text. *I'm coming to you.*

"After he came to the restaurant, he texted you again that night. Did you respond?"

"I don't know what you're talkin' about. I didn't get any text."

"Are you sure?" Cancini handed Sylvia a blacked-out phone log with the single number highlighted.

Vega squinted at the sheet. Cancini almost missed the twitch at the corner of Vega's eye. "That's not my number." He pulled a phone from his pocket. "This is my phone. I don't know that number."

Cancini didn't look at the phone in Vega's hand. "It's registered to Chicken del Rey."

His lawyer held a hand to her mouth and spoke into his ear. Vega frowned and shook his head. "It could be one of my phones for the business, but I don't use that phone. I don't even know where it is."

"We can get a warrant for the phone records, Mr. Vega."

Vega's voice rose. "I told you I don't know where that phone is. Coulda been stolen."

"We can get a warrant to search your house, your computer. We can see who you've e-mailed, who you've called." Vega cast a questioning glance at his lawyer. She frowned, but said nothing. "Did you know you can never really wipe a hard drive clean, Mr. Vega? It's not just hackers who can find bank accounts and steal money these days. We've got some fine hackers of our own right here in the police department. I wonder what they might find on your computer."

Vega lurched to his feet, pushing the table into Cancini. "Then why don't you fuckin' do that?" His arm swept across the table, and papers flew from the folder. "We're done here," he said with a sneer. "Unless you plan to arrest me."

Cancini made no move to stop them. After, he joined Martin on the other side of the glass. "Well? Was it enough time?"

Martin nodded. "Judge Simpson signed off on the warrant ten minutes ago. Smitty's waiting for you."

Chapter Seventy-eight

VEGA ANSWERED THE door, a scotch in his hand. Not bothering to hide the contempt on his face, he turned on his heel. Cancini followed him to a white living room: white walls, white sofas, and white tables. Only a red and gray rug in front of the fireplace provided any color.

The lawyer stood near the hearth, the warrant clutched in her hand. The soft lines of her matronly face hardened. "Smooth, Detective. While my client was busy cooperating, you were stalling for time to get a warrant. Don't think I'm going to forget about this."

"I wouldn't expect anything else," Cancini said. He watched as forensic analysts carried every electronic device out of the house. In other rooms, drawers were turned inside out, contents dumped in piles. Vega flinched with each thud.

Tossing back his scotch, he turned to Cancini. "What do you want?"

"Did you kill Father Holland?"

"No."

"Would you tell me if you did?"

"No."

Cancini moved to the open doorway to find Smitty trotting down the stairs. His young partner kept his voice low. "No one else here. As far as we can tell, there's no sign of him, but we'll keep looking." Cancini let out his breath. He hadn't really expected to find Father Joe in the house, but knowing he wasn't there did nothing to shrink the pit in his stomach. He nodded once, and Smitty disappeared again.

Vega crossed to the bar and poured another drink. When he spoke again, his words slurred. "I never wanted Matty to die."

"Carlos. That's enough," the lawyer admonished, features taut and body tensed.

Vega flopped down onto the sofa, glass balanced on his chest.

Cancini sat opposite him, heart racing. "What do you mean you didn't want him to die?"

"We're not doing this," the woman warned.

Vega ignored her. A melancholy seemed to settle over him. "Matty was my best friend for a long time, a long fuckin' time. I miss those days." Cancini waited. "We did everything together. He had it tough with his mom, you know. She took the pipe, other stuff, but she was a sweet lady. Matty tried. When his mom OD'd, they took him away, tried to stick him with some lame-ass foster family. He stayed in our crib for a while." His voice dropped off.

"What happened to him after that?"

Vega drained his scotch, eyes hooded. "He left. Couldn't handle the life here, you know. Just wasn't in his blood."

"Like it was with you."

Vega issued a harsh laugh. "Nice try, Detective. Matty just wanted outta Barry Farm. We all did."

Cancini had learned enough to know this was probably true.

"I didn't see the priest thing comin', though. Finally shows his face again and he's wearin' the collar. Couldn't fuckin' believe it."

"You used his bank account to launder money."

"Don't answer that," Sylvia said.

Cancini waved a hand. "It wasn't a question."

Vega stretched out and rested his head against the back cushion. Footsteps and crashing noises came from the top floor, and the lawyer jumped. Vega sighed but appeared more bored than alarmed.

Hands on her hips, the lawyer asked, "Are you done yet?"

Cancini focused on the reclining Vega. "Why don't I tell you a story?"

Vega's gaze fell on him and slid away again. "Suit yourself."

Cancini sat forward. "Goes like this. There's this local boss, has a pretty good business going—drugs, some gambling, prostitution—but decides he needs a fresh way to funnel some cash. He realizes he has the perfect target in an old friend that happens to be a priest. Who'd suspect a priest of laundering drug money, right? Everything's going great until the priest finds out. Does the priest confront his old friend or go to the police? Neither one. Instead, he decides to turn the tables on the boss and steal the money. He studies the deposits and withdrawals, finds a pattern, and waits. When the time is right, he empties the account, then shuts it down." He paused. A vein at Vega's temple throbbed. Otherwise, he remained motionless. "How'm I doing so far?"

Vega shrugged. "Make a good movie."

Cancini leaned in closer, his words no longer a third-person story. "Maybe you didn't know it was Father Holland who took the money at first. Probably came as quite a shock, a priest stealing from someone like you." Vega's face darkened. Cancini kept talking. "He'd gotten the better of you, stolen your own money right from under your nose. The real problem, though, is that he refused to give it back. You play nice at first. He'd been your best friend once, right? But as more and more time goes by, you get madder and madder. Not only has he stolen from you, he's making you look bad."

Vega's nostrils flared, but he remained silent.

"Enough." The lawyer stepped closer to Vega. "This is absurd."

Cancini ignored her. "You sent e-mails. They started nice enough, but then you had to start threatening him. You didn't just want your money back by then. You needed it back. Your businesses—your illegitimate businesses—rely on cash flow, and a half million is a lot of cash."

"You're damn right it's a lot of cash—a whole lotta fuckin' cash." Vega growled, face pinched.

"You send Ketchum around a few times to scare him. It works at first. Father Holland grows anxious, can't sleep. He sees a doctor for anti-anxiety pills. But still, he won't back down, won't give you your money. You give him a deadline to return the money. Tell him if he doesn't, he's a dead man." Cancini paused, thinking about Vega's earlier comment. "You don't want to do it, though."

Vega sat forward, his head in his hands.

"Instead of turning over the money, Father Holland puts it into an untouchable trust with only one beneficiary, St. William Catholic Church. He leaves you no choice. You have a business to run. You have a reputation."

One minute passed. Two. Vega staggered to his feet. At the bar, he filled his glass to the rim. He waved his fresh drink in the air, splattering brown drops on the carpet. "Join me?"

Cancini shook his head.

"Sylvia?"

"No, and I think you've had enough."

"The fuck I have," he slurred.

Smitty joined them in the living room, his face grim. He leaned in toward Cancini. "We've got the laptop that sent the e-mails." A pair of handcuffs dangled from his long fingers.

Vega eyed the silver cuffs, face slack. He swallowed his drink in one long gulp and wiped his mouth with the back of his hand. Smitty stepped forward. Vega raised one hand and turned toward Cancini. "It's a good story, Detective, except for the ending," he said slowly, all trace of slurring gone.

A cold sweat broke out under Cancini's shirt. "What's wrong with the ending?"

"You're the fucking detective," Vega said, tone mocking. "You figure it out."

Chapter Seventy-nine

MARTIN'S FACE GLOWED as he made the rounds of the precinct, slapping backs and pumping his fist. The arrest of Carlos Vega was the biggest thing to have happened in his career, the biggest thing to have happened in most of their careers. Cancini stood apart, mood dour. They were no closer to finding Father Joe than they'd been before they'd brought Vega in, and Vega hadn't said another word after the arrest. Cancini knew if the lawyer was telling the truth, he wouldn't anytime soon. Vega had nodded at Cancini as he was led out, chin upraised, dark eyes filled with an unspoken challenge.

It's a good story, Detective, except for the ending.

Cancini shook the nagging words from his head. They'd pulled multiple computers and tablets from Vega's house and offices. Nearly apoplectic with glee, Landon had spent twenty minutes going on about ghost drives and IP addresses and servers. It only mattered to Cancini as long as it held up in court. Either way, they'd arrested Vega for solicitation to commit murder and arson.

He should have been relieved at the arrest, satisfied, but instead he felt vaguely restless, uneasy.

Bronson hung back from the informal celebration, his face pinched and pasty. With a sigh, Cancini edged closer to the younger detective. "What's wrong, Bronson?"

The stocky man shrugged. "Nothing."

Cancini had no patience for Bronson's petulance, but he also recognized he was the source of it. "Bronson, you stayed on the Hardings, just like I asked. It's my fault you weren't at Vega's arrest. I'm sorry. I owe you one."

Bronson raised his eyes to meet Cancini's. "Thanks."

Cancini leaned against the wall, his arms folded. "Well, did you find anything interesting on the Hardings?"

"Yeah. Don't know what it means though."

Cancini checked his watch. Martin's press conference wouldn't take place for another hour. "I've got a few minutes. Shoot."

Bronson pulled out his phone. "You know the Hardings are from the same town, went to high school together." Cancini nodded. "What I found out is that right around the time they graduated, she accused another kid—a college kid—of rape. The police charged the kid, but it never went to trial."

"Why not?"

"Not enough evidence. The kid denied it. Insisted she'd pursued him and they'd dated for several months. When he tried to end it, he said she went ballistic and came up with the assault accusation."

It could have been true or not. Cancini had heard it all. "And the husband knew about this?"

"The whole town knew, and from what I heard, believed Erica's story. Even though the charges were dropped, the kid was suspended from school anyway. He moved away. Haven't found him yet."

If Erica's story was true, she'd suffered a horrible attack. "How old was she when this happened?" Cancini asked.

"Seventeen."

Cancini was quiet a moment. "Are you thinking this is why Harding is so protective of his wife, because she'd been raped?"

Bronson shrugged. "I thought so at first, but then I got to thinking, the guy hits her. Doesn't seem all that protective to me."

The only domestic abuse cases Cancini had worked were the ones that ended in tragedy. He frowned thinking of the beatings that culminated in shootings or stabbings, families left broken and shattered. Emotions ran high in those cases and sometimes swung from wild anger and jealousy to deep remorse and self-loathing. Other times, there was no remorse at all. Where did the Hardings fit on the spectrum? "No, it doesn't," he said.

"There's something else." Bronson consulted his phone, then spoke again. "The Hardings got together again after that, went to college together. Then in their senior year, during the middle of the semester, one of Erica's professors gets fired. The story was that he was fired because he'd been sleeping with one of his students and his wife found out. The professor tried to end the affair and the student went to the administration to complain he'd taken advantage of her. The student took out an ad against him in the school paper, plastered signs all over campus. Pretty nasty stuff."

Bronson looked at him expectantly and Cancini's skin prickled. "Erica was the student?"

"Yep."

"And after that?"

"The professor was fired, his wife left him, and his kids abandoned him. Guess he was pretty sorry after that."

Cancini tapped his foot on the floor. "What about Erica?"

"Far as I can tell, she went back to Harding again and they got married a year later. No other incidents I could find after that. Just Harding's temper and following his wife."

Around them, the precinct grew quieter as the celebratory mood was replaced by the reality of paperwork and the vetting of evidence. Martin disappeared into his office, presumably to prep and primp for the press conference. Cancini bowed his head in thought, images of Erica's bruises and injuries flitting through his mind. If what Bronson had learned was true, Harding was the one man who'd stayed by her side, supported her even when she entered into other relationships. And yet he was also the man who showed his love with his fists. The lines in his forehead deepened. If he'd thought their relationship strange before, he sure didn't know what to think now. "What's your take, Bronson?"

The detective snorted, the sound a high-pitched whistling. "The only thing I know is if I had a woman like Erica Harding, I'd hang on. For one thing, she's hot as hell, and for another, I wouldn't want to cross her. Not that I blame any of those guys. Shit, a woman like that, I'd ride it as long as I could, too." Cancini stared hard at the younger man. Bronson shrank back against the wall. "Sorry. It just came out."

Cancini let it go, unfolding his arms. His head ached. Erica Harding had never fit the mold of mild-mannered church secretary. Still, a woman who took beatings didn't seem consistent with a woman who screamed rape and plastered posters of straying professors on telephone poles. That woman didn't sit there while her husband beat her. She fought back. The hair on the back of his neck rose.

I wouldn't want to cross her.

Cancini's gaze shifted to the large window facing the street. Wet snow mixed with freezing rain fell from the sky, hitting the ground in sheets. By mid-morning, the streets would be covered.

What was the nature of the secretary's relationship with Father Holland? The lunchtime visits. Harding's jealousy. What did it mean? As a teenager and then college student, Erica Harding hadn't taken rejection well. She'd made the men who'd left her pay and pay dearly. Had Father Holland let her down?

Cancini touched the glass, the cold sharp against his hand. Outside, the light faded to gray, the sky and sidewalk blending to one. A portly man emerged from a building across the street, huddled under a red and white umbrella. He sucked in his breath. Father Joe? The man broke into a trot, and Cancini's shoulders sagged. He blinked, watching the man turn the corner, the bright red of the umbrella gone.

I wouldn't want to cross her.

His head shot up. "Jesus Christ." He raced to his desk, his heart knocking into his chest.

"What?" Smitty asked, his eyebrows high on his forehead.

Cancini shrugged into his coat. "No time to explain. Let's go."

Chapter Eighty

Tuesday, February 16: Five Days Before the Day of

MATT WANTED DESPERATELY to wipe away her tears, take her in his arms, and hold her. What man wouldn't want a woman so beautiful, so warm? What man wouldn't want to run his fingers through her silken hair and breathe in her musky scent? And she needed a hero, or at least he'd thought she did for a while, but even knowing the truth didn't matter. When she sat close to him, he held his breath. When her knee touched his, his heart raced and he felt things he thought he'd forgotten. But he wasn't just any man. He was a priest. His rules were different. His commitment did not lie in the fruits of the flesh but in God. He repeated the words in his mind even as she fell to her knees, her face in her hands. He looked away, ashamed. He hadn't meant to hurt her.

"I'm sorry," he said after a while.

"Stop saying that," she begged. Dark mascara trailed down her cheeks, and the red lipstick she wore appeared to darken against her porcelain skin. "I get it. You don't want me. You think I'm awful."

"You know that's not true. I don't think you're awful." He hesitated. "And I do want you, but I can't. We can't."

She swallowed a sob. "Because you're married to the church."

"And you're married to Sonny."

"Right. And that would be a sin." She didn't bother to hide her resentment. "And we don't want to be sinners, do we? The great and wonderful Father Holland can't be found to be a sinner, now can he?" Matt blinked. Erica held on to the kitchen counter, climbing to her feet. "Some of us only sin when it's in our best interest." Her lips turned up. "Isn't that right, Father?"

He slowly shook his head. "I don't know what you mean."

"Don't you?" She splashed water on her face, wiping away the smeared makeup. She flicked at the damp tendrils curling at her cheeks. "You think I'm a sinner, don't you?"

He let out a long breath. "None of us is without sin, Erica. You know that."

"I know the verses as well as you do." He stiffened. "No offense," she added quickly. "But if we're all sinners, what difference does it make which sin we're guilty of? God knows we're going to sin and forgives us. He does forgive us, right?" She angled her head to one shoulder and smiled.

He half smiled, unsure where she was going. "I suppose he does, but there is confession and repentance."

"Right. Of course. What I was wondering, though, is which is the greater sin, Father? Adultery or"—her lips twitched as she spoke—"or stealing?" A vein at his temple twitched and his smile faded. "No answer, Father?"

"I don't think there's a ranking system on sins," he said finally.

She waved a graceful hand in the air. "Exactly what I would have expected from you. No answer at all." He stepped back from her. "But as long as none of us is without sin, what difference does it make if we add one more?"

"You know it doesn't work that way, Erica. You're twisting my words."

"Am I? I didn't mean to."

He sighed, looking over her shoulder. The sun had settled over the rooftops. Her husband would be home soon. He needed to leave. He felt her eyes on him as he drew himself up to his full height. "I have to get going," he said. "Are you going to be okay?"

She rubbed at an angry purple bruise that covered the inside of her forearm. "That's your question? I've devoted myself to you for more than two years. I've been there for you in every way you needed." Bitterness dripped from her words. "I've pledged my love to you, and you've taken all of it. Everything I had to give, and you ask me if I'm going to be okay."

His hand came up, fingering the cross hanging at his throat. "I've been your friend, Erica. You make it sound . . . dirty."

She laughed, the sound harsh to his ears. "Oh please. You're no different than any other man. You stare at my breasts, rub your leg against mine. You smell my hair, smell my perfume. You get off on my attention." His face flamed, but he didn't flinch. "You've imagined what it would be like between us. Same as me." She closed the space between them, pressing her body close to his. "I've been waiting so long." Her hands slid up to his shoulders, squeezing. He froze, his hands hanging at his sides. She leaned in, her lips brushing against his neck. He shivered, willing his body to be strong. With both hands, he gently pushed her away.

"What you say is true. I haven't been without sin. I should have put a stop to this . . . this flirtation a long time ago."

"Flirtation?" She raised her chin, eyes challenging him. "Then why didn't you?"

"I'm weak," he said, the words soft. "I thank God we never crossed the line. It has to stop now. It's not good for either of us."

The lines of her face hardened, and her tone was icy. "You're choosing St. William over me."

"I've chosen to dedicate my life to serving God."

"Then you've chosen God over me. It's the same thing. I'm not important to you. I'm nothing."

He raised his hands, palms upward. "I don't know what you want me to say."

She stepped forward, the space between them barely more than a few inches. The tears, long gone, had been replaced by a cold glare. "I want you to say the truth."

Chapter Eighty-one

CANCINI BURST THROUGH the doors of St. William, pausing only long enough to pick up the red umbrella in the corner, exactly like Father Joe's umbrella. In the sanctuary, he walked up and down the aisles. He inspected the confessionals. Nothing. He hurried to the office, where he found Erica typing at her computer.

Startled, giant eyes looked back at him. "I wasn't expecting you today, Detectives." She folded her hands on the desk. "I'm finishing the bulletin for Sunday, but I have a few minutes. Is there something I can help you with?" Cancini circled the small room and opened the door that led to Father Holland's office. She jumped up from her chair and followed him. "What are you doing?"

Without answering, he left the inner office as quickly as he'd entered it. Cancini returned to the Commons that led to the sanctuary, Erica trailing after him. His gaze settled on the long hall at the back of the Commons. Doors on both sides of the darkened hall stood closed. "What are those rooms?"

"Some offices, conference rooms, classrooms." She raised a

hand and pointed. "There's a kitchen at the end of the hall. What's this all about anyway?"

"You wouldn't mind if we looked around, would you?"

"I—I guess not."

Cancini opened each door one by one, his heart pounding under his coat. Each room was as she described. Desks and file cabinets, conference tables, chairs arranged in circles. Inside each room, he opened cabinets and closets. Erica stayed close, her questions nonstop.

"Did something happen I don't know about? What are you looking for? Maybe I can help you."

Silent, he closed one door after another. His breathing quickened. He came to the kitchen at the end of the hall. He flipped the switch, banishing the shadows. White counters and cabinets glowed under canned lights. The air smelled faintly of bleach and lemon. The drawers and cabinets held dishes, pots, and food. He yanked open the refrigerator. Nothing out of the ordinary. He slammed the door shut. His head pounded with doubt. He'd been so sure.

Wordless, he returned to the office, where Smitty waited. He clicked on Erica's computer, and up came the bulletin.

"What are you doing?" she cried, hands on her hips. "It's taken me all afternoon to work on that."

Smitty took her by the arm and pulled her gently back from the desk.

Cancini opened the drawers one by one. Pens, folders, a key ring. In the bottom drawer, he saw her purse. He closed the drawer, searching the rest of the office. Erica's coat hung from a rack in the corner. A framed photograph of the pope hung on the far wall next to the bulletin board. Father Holland's wish list of projects was still pinned near the top. He'd seen nothing out of the ordinary, nothing to indicate Father Joe had been there any longer than the secretary had already said. He held up the red umbrella in his hand.

"This umbrella was here yesterday. Do you know who it belongs to?"

She frowned. "People leave umbrellas here all the time. I usually put them in a lost and found box." She pointed to a box under a table. He saw two other umbrellas inside. His chin dropped to his chest and he took a deep breath, fighting the despair that threatened to overwhelm him.

Smitty cleared his throat. "Thank you for your time, Mrs. Harding. That will be all for now."

"That's it." She put her right hand on her hip, her face flushed in anger. "You come in here and search the whole place. You even go through my desk, and that's it." She spoke faster, louder. "Thank you for your time," she imitated. Watching, Cancini realized this was the woman Bronson had described, the one who lashed out when she felt wronged. "Don't come back here again," she hissed.

Smitty flinched, physically taken aback at the change in the church secretary. "This is the scene of a murder investigation," Smitty said after regaining his composure. "We'll come back whenever it's necessary."

"Then solve the murder, and get out. Now." She slammed the door behind them.

Cancini leaned against the wall in the Commons, hands shaking. He blinked and slowed his breathing. How could a priest just disappear?

"Are you ready?" Smitty asked, voice soft.

"In a minute." Above them, a bell chimed in the steeple, breaking the silence and echoing through the building. He looked up, drawn back to the dark hallway. The bell rang a second time and a third. He passed door after door, stopping in front of a large wooden credenza topped by a tall hutch. He motioned to Smitty. "Turn on that light at the end of the hall, would you?"

The fluorescent came to life, brightening the hall. Cancini stepped back from the credenza and looked down at the floor. Black scratches marked the floor for several feet in the direction of the Commons. The credenza had been moved. A shadow on the wall above the marks showed him where the credenza had once been. He glanced back toward Erica's office and licked his lips. Holland's wish list of items. The obvious things he remembered. Steeple, windows, parking lot, but there was more, wasn't there? And then it came to him. The basement. The church had a basement. But where? He looked back at the credenza, and his heart fluttered. With his hand, he reached behind the hutch, feeling for it, stopping when his bony fingers hit on the molding.

"Smitty."

"What?"

"There's a door."

Cancini placed both hands against the credenza and pushed. The furniture slid easily, revealing the basement door. He tried the handle. Locked. His stomach lurched. There had to be a way in. He glanced back down the hall to the Commons. It was nearly six. Sonny Harding would arrive any minute to pick up his wife. He pulled his gun from his holster and broke into a trot.

Erica sprang to her feet when the door swung open. "I thought I told you to leave."

"Move," he said, gun trained on her. She backed away from her desk, full lips set in an angry line. He yanked open the drawer and pulled out the key ring. Cancini looked over at Smitty. "Don't let her out of your sight."

Unlocking the door, he found himself at the top of a narrow staircase. He fumbled for the light switch and flipped it on. Nothing. He pulled a penlight from his pocket and picked his way down the stairs. With each step, he inhaled the odors of mold and must. Sweat beaded on his forehead. Waving his light, he could just make out a cavernous room to his left. Cobwebs hung from the ceiling, brushing his head and shoulders. Broken tables and chairs, layered with dust, were piled up in the large space. He moved closer, shining his light into the corners. A rat scurried along the floor and disappeared behind a sea of cardboard boxes. "Shit."

On the other side of the stairs, he found a long hall lined with doors, similar to the one upstairs. Sweat trickled down his neck and under his collar. He took a deep breath and tried the first door. Boxes filled the room, stacked from floor to ceiling. Against the far wall, he spotted trash bags, chewed and soiled. He closed the door and stood outside the next door. Cupping his hand around his mouth, he shouted, "Father Joe?" His words bounced back, the silence a stab to his gut. He opened the next door and the next. Boxes, rusty tools, and broken tables filled the basement rooms. The darkness wrapped around him, the air cold and damp. He banged on the next door, pushed it open, and called his old friend's name again and again. Then it came, a sound too low to distinguish, and he rushed from the room. Waving his light in the direction of the noise, he saw three doors, the last padlocked.

Hands shaking, he tried one key after another. None worked. He wiped the sweat from his brow and pounded on the door. He put his ear against the wood. The sound came again, muffled but louder. Knocking? Scraping? He didn't care. Someone or something was on the other side. He threw his shoulder against the door again and again, but it wouldn't budge. He leaned over, his chest heaving. "Goddammit!"

Straightening, he pulled out his gun and aimed at the padlock. The shot reverberated through the empty basement, and the broken lock clattered to the floor. The door swung open. "Father Joe?" His light scanned the room until he found him, sitting slumped against the wall, tape plastered across his mouth. Dried blood stuck to his head, darkening his cheek. The old priest's eyes found his before they closed, his body sliding down the wall to the floor. Cancini rushed to his side and sank to his knees. Mumbling the words to the only prayer he could remember, Cancini dialed 911.

Chapter Eighty-two

"Can I see her?" Sonny Harding sat across from Cancini, his shoulders hunched, his face gray.

"Later." The dark-haired detective flipped the pages of his notebook. "When did you know your wife had murdered Father Holland?"

The man shivered. He gazed at the floor, licking his lips. "I didn't know. I don't know. I mean . . ." He looked up. "We never talked about it. She hasn't been herself lately."

"You're still protecting her."

"I've always protected her. I'm her husband."

"We found the gun she used in the back of your closet. Do you know where she got that gun, Mr. Harding?"

He shook his head slowly.

"In the box with the gun was a pair of gloves. One of them still had traces of Father Holland's blood on the fingertip. Your wife is going away for a very long time."

Harding sat mute.

"We know she went to St. William that night to murder Father Holland. What we don't know is why."

Harding sank further down in the chair.

Cancini tapped his pen against the page. "She hurt herself, didn't she?"

Harding's head rolled from side to side. "I tried to stop her," he said finally. "I couldn't understand it, but she wouldn't listen to me. You don't know how she is. She's so strong, so beautiful. I wanted to protect her from herself, but she wouldn't let me." He twisted his hands in his lap. "I love her so much."

"Why do you think she would hurt herself, Mr. Harding?"

"I don't know."

"Did you ever think she might have wanted people to feel sorry for her? She might have wanted people—people like Father Holland—to believe her husband was abusing her?"

"I never touched her." His face contorted with each word. "I would never do that. Never."

"I believe you, Mr. Harding." Cancini paused. He thought he understood Erica's reasons, what drove her to injure herself, to murder Father Holland, but he needed to be sure. "I'm asking if maybe your wife hurt herself to get attention. Maybe to get Father Holland's attention?" Cancini leaned closer.

"Mr. Harding?"

"Maybe. Probably. She talked about him a lot. She was excited for her job every day. I know I wasn't. I hated going to work. But not Erica. She just seemed to love it more and more . . ." His voice drifted away.

Cancini kept his voice low, his tone soft. "She loved Father Holland more and more?"

Harding nodded, mouth clamped shut.

"Were you jealous, Mr. Harding?"

The man blinked several times. "Jealous? Not the way you think. Erica would never leave me. I know that."

"Then why did you have your wife followed? Why did you drive her to work when she could have taken the subway? Why did you hang around the church when you weren't working?"

He shrugged. "To protect her." Cancini glanced once at Smitty. The blond shook his head.

"Protect her from who?"

Harding picked at his fingers. "It's hard to explain."

Cancini leaned forward. "Try."

The man shrugged, his eyes vacant. "Erica thought she was in love with Father Holland." He bowed his head. "Maybe she was. She thought he loved her, too."

Cancini arched one dark eyebrow. "She told you all this?"

"Not in so many words. She hinted. She wanted me to know. I saw her flirting with him sometimes. She didn't try to hide it. She knew I'd never leave her. I couldn't. She's the only woman I've ever loved." He took a deep breath. "I figured I'd wait it out—like I did before."

"Like when you were teenagers and you broke up?"

Harding nodded.

"She dated someone else."

"Yes, but she came back to me."

"You told us that before. We did some checking around," Cancini said. Harding's skin turned ashen. "We know about the rape and the professor." Harding picked at his fingernail, pulling at the skin until it bled. "That boy didn't rape her, did he?"

"No."

"Why did she accuse him then?"

Harding blinked. "He'd hurt her. He didn't love her like I do." He looked down at his hands. "The Bible is the only book Erica reads. Did you know that? She can quote the whole thing."

Cancini's body went still. He'd known a man like that, a man who'd taken the Bible in the most literal sense and used it to justify the murders he committed. He was convinced God spoke to him through the words and pages. Cancini spoke slowly, "The boy hurt her so she needed to hurt him back. An eye for an eye?"

"No." He gave a shake of his head. "Maybe. You don't know how she suffered. She prayed and prayed after that."

"And after the professor lost everything—his job and his family—did she pray about that, too?"

Harding looked up, his voice shaking. "You don't understand."

Cancini slid forward, his hands on his knees. "You're wrong, Mr. Harding. I think I do." He paused. "I think it would it be fair to say your wife doesn't handle rejection very well. In fact, she's likely to take revenge against anyone who rejects her. Isn't that right, Mr. Harding?"

Harding rocked back and forth in his chair.

"You said she loved Father Holland. I believe that's true. She did her best to make him love her back. Because he was a priest, she knew it would be harder and take longer. She was patient. She hurt herself to gain his sympathy and his attention. It almost worked, too. But in the end, he couldn't do it, wouldn't break his vows for her." Harding's shoulders shook, his face wet with tears. "Father Holland rejected your wife, just like the others, and he died for it."

Epilogue

CANCINI LET THE breeze blow open his coat, savoring the unusually mild weather after the rain, sleet, and snow of the last several days. Julia hooked her arm through his and laid her head against his shoulder. The moon shone bright overhead, and the stars twinkled in the dark sky. The case was over, and she was home for a long weekend. He draped his arm over her shoulder and slowed his steps.

"What will happen to Vega?" she asked as they walked.

It was a good question, and one he'd wondered himself. Vega had a good legal team, led by the matriarchal Sylvia Morris, but Ketchum's testimony looked credible. "Probably get the minimum, but he'll be off the streets for a few years anyway. If Talbot can prove the money laundering, he'll go away for longer. The German authorities are cooperating. It could take a while though."

"You got the murderer and the gangster." She cocked her head and smiled up at him. "Pretty good, Detective." He didn't know what to say, so he said nothing. "What will happen to his organization?"

"Someone will move up. Vega had two or three lieutenants, but it won't be easy for any of them. There's liable to be more competition among the gangs with Vega gone, more jockeying for territory and product. The FBI and the local gang department are planning to use this case to make a wide sweep before it gets violent. In a weird way, Father Holland's murder might have some positive effects. The church gets renovated. The community gets cleaned up. Vega's off the streets." Cancini paused. "He would have been happy, I think."

They walked on in silence. The door to a neighborhood tavern banged open, and a couple staggered outside. Laughter and blaring music filled the air. When the door slammed shut, the night was quiet again. At the corner, Julia asked, "Who's going to take over at St. William?"

"Still temporary for a while, but Father Joe tells me they've selected a new priest. He should be starting in a month or so. The old coot even says he'll be helping out over there as soon as he has all his strength back."

She stood still, concern etched in her face. "Really? Is that a good idea?"

"According to him, it's a great idea."

"But I thought he was still on bed rest."

"He is, but not for long if he has anything to say about it." Cancini sighed and wrapped his arm around her again. Father Joe had been half dead when he'd found him. Weak and dehydrated, he'd been locked in that dark basement for three days, no food and only the water Erica brought him. He wouldn't have lasted much longer. His recovery would be slow. He was an old man already dealing with a gunshot wound and a bad heart. Cancini swallowed and forced the memory of his fear from his mind. It was over now, and Father Joe was safe and under a doctor's care. "He's stubborn. He'll be up and about sooner rather than later."

"I'm not sure that sounds like a good thing."

He glanced down at her. There was no criticism in the expression she wore, just a warm curiosity. He thought maybe she was right. He would always be worried about the old man, but he couldn't help admiring his courage and his strength.

"I'm just glad he's going to be okay," he said.

Julia squeezed his arm. "Me too." A minute passed. "I still don't understand why he went to see her, though. Why wouldn't he come to you?"

"Misguided faith." Cancini shook his head. "Father Joe believes in forgiveness. He wanted to give Erica a chance to confess her sins. Same reason he went to see Vega. He knew everything, wanted to offer them both reconciliation. Vega turned him down flat." He breathed in the fresh air. "Because he was Father Holland's confessor, Father Joe knew Holland had been struggling to keep his vows. He'd been counseling him, helping him. Father Joe thought he was doing the right thing by going to Erica. Instead, she realized he knew what she'd done. All of it."

"You mean about the faked injuries?"

"That, and Father Joe also figured out Erica knew more than she'd let on about the money, the foundation. As the notary, she'd seen the documents. Father Holland may not have realized how much she understood until it was too late, but before that, they were close. He'd even confided some of his past to her in private moments. She used that to steer attention away from herself toward Vega. She sent the text to Vega's holding company and threw Father Joe's phone in the Dumpster. It's still not clear how she got the number, but she might talk in time."

"Smart lady. And very sick."

Cancini nodded. He'd been a detective for more than two decades and had never seen anyone do the things that Erica had done to herself. He wouldn't be surprised if psychiatrists used her as a test case.

"I hope you don't mind all these questions," Julia said, her blue eyes darker under the night sky.

"You're a reporter, Ms. Manning. I would expect nothing less."

She laughed until her face grew serious. "So, how did Father Joe know it was Erica that had shot Father Holland in the first place?"

"He didn't until Sophia Vega came to see him. She told Father Joe that her son knew about her role in the foundation, talked to him about it at almost the exact time Father Holland was murdered. She was not only his alibi, but Father Joe understood Vega would never have Father Holland killed after that. He would never do anything to hurt his mother. That left Erica."

"Wow." Julia's hair swung with a shake of her head. "It's crazy."

Cancini agreed, although he thought perhaps that was understating the case. Erica Harding would plead temporary insanity, and he realized, in spite of a solid case against her, she could win. Even crazier, he suspected her husband would stay by her side until the end, unable and unwilling to break the hold his wife had on him.

Julia came to a stop, face turned toward the gray brick building in front of them. "Isn't this your place?"

"This is the one." His stomach fluttered and he hesitated. For the first time, the timing seemed right. Since his wife had moved out, no other woman had stayed the night. No other woman had been important enough or touched him in the way that Julia had. He reached down and brushed the hair from her face. He traced the line of her cheekbone to her lips. "Are you sure?"

She sucked in her breath and raised her hand to his chest. He pulled her close, and she whispered. "Yes, Detective. Very sure."

Acknowledgments

FULL CONFESSION: THE tiny idea that grew into this novel came from a story I'd heard many years ago involving a stately and well-liked priest who'd had great success growing his parish. After a few years, one of the parishioners became infatuated him. She began to come around more often than necessary, write him notes, and ultimately resorted to what might kindly be described as low-level stalking. Obviously, the woman wasn't homicidal, no one was murdered, and the situation resolved itself when the priest moved to another city and church. No harm done. Still, the story stuck in my mind.

When I began writing *The Last Sin*, I set out to explore both the notion of "a woman scorned" and the humanity of the priest. Young and handsome, Father Holland is not without sin. It made me wonder. Does that make him less of a "good" man and priest or more of one? Ultimately, however, each reader must decide for themselves.

During the writing of the novel, I leaned on a pair of priests to fill in some of the blanks for me when it came to the sacraments and many of the rituals. I will always be grateful to them for their help. Any mistakes in this story as it relates to Catholicism are strictly mine.

As always, I am indebted to those kind souls who were willing to read and critique an early draft of *The Last Sin*. Thank you to Donna McGrath for your pages of notes and spot-on comments. As an avid mystery reader, you can be counted on to tell me what worked and what didn't. Thank you for that.

I also need to thank Cameron Murphy, my beautiful daughter, for acting as both beta reader and sounding board. You are always available to listen to plot points and your skills with a red pen are appreciated. It is a gift to get an honest critique and edit delivered with humor and kindness. I love you.

Finally, to my loyal beta readers, Kate Melia and Maria Gravely, thank you for always jumping in and for loving the story in spite of the obvious warts. Whole paragraphs and personality traits died necessary deaths after your sharp critiques. And thank you also to Beth Rendon for listening and being there.

Even after two, three, four revisions, a writer can wonder. When I did finally deliver the finished manuscript to my agent and publisher, I held my breath. Time went by until the enthusiastic reception I received from my agent, Rebecca Scherer, made my day. Thanks, Rebecca, for that and for always being there when needed. Thank you to Chloe Moffett, my editor, who helped turned the manuscript into a tighter, better novel that I'm thrilled to have as the third in the Detective Cancini series. Thank you also to HarperCollins/Witness Impulse for the support along the way.

Writing is hard work. While it's different for every author, the multiple revisions between the first draft and submission can be even harder. Thank you to my husband, David, for your patience and understanding during all the hours it took to finish *The Last Sin*. More importantly, thank you for your sense of humor and making me laugh out loud every day. Thank you again to Cameron, and to my other amazing children—Thomas, Luke, and Meredith—for your support and flexibility. I know how lucky I am.

Finally, I am very grateful to the readers and mystery lovers who picked up *The Last Sin*, *Stay of Execution*, and *A Guilty Mind*, as well as to all those who've asked for more. Happy reading!

If you liked *The Last Sin*,
keep reading for an excerpt from
another Detective Cancini Mystery
by K.L. Murphy

STAY OF EXECUTION

Available now wherever e-books are sold

Chapter One

SHADOWS DANCED ALONG the cinder-block walls. A light shone through the tiny window in the door, then moved past as the guard made his rounds. The prisoner lay still while the steps faded, then rolled to a sitting position, rusty bedsprings squeaking under his weight. His head jerked up toward the door. He waited before standing, bare feet hitting the cold, concrete floor.

In a few days, a week, it would all be over. No more guards. No more looking at the same walls twenty-three hours a day. No more crap food. No more of this godforsaken hellhole. He would go home, where he belonged.

On the far wall, a steel container served as his toilet. The stench of old piss stung his nose, but for once, he didn't mind. How quickly things had changed. Maybe he should've been surprised, but he wasn't. Hell, he'd been expecting it for a long time. Some would say he was lucky, might even call his release a miracle. Shit. Maybe it was a miracle. After all, it wasn't every day a man on death row got handed his walking papers. Not that he cared much about cheating death. So what if he wouldn't be executed tomorrow, or next month, or next year? He would still die eventually. Everyone does.

He knew how it would go. The lawyers would show up in their tailored suits and Italian shoes, all smug with their accomplishment. There'd be backslapping, and people he'd never seen before asking what he needed. No one had done that in a long damn time. He ran a hand over his heavy beard. They'd have clothes in his size, a suit and a tie. A barber would give him a haircut and shave. They'd clean him up. It was part of the deal.

He understood his role. His lawyers had shown him the newspapers. The governor himself had weighed in. None of the lawyers could understand why he wanted to go back home. His family was dead. He had no friends. Yet his return would not go unnoticed. There would be a press conference and cameras. It was reason enough.

In the semidarkness, he lay shirtless on his cot. A bead of sweat dripped from his temple to his ear. He'd have to be on his best behavior. Everything he said and did would be watched. Reporters would follow him for a story. The injustice, they'd say. The outrage. An innocent man had suffered, and now his ordeal was over. But they didn't know anything about injustice. They didn't know anything about him. He'd been inside for a long time, and the years had not passed quickly. He had unfinished business now, scores to settle. Everything was about to change.

Chapter Two

DETECTIVE MIKE CANCINI sat up with a start. For the third time in a week, he'd dozed off in the hard hospital chair. He shifted to look at the old man lying in the bed. The rise and fall of his father's sunken chest kept time with his snores. Tubes ran from his arms to the green lights on the monitor. His pulse was steady and his blood pressure read normal.

The television cast a soft light across the room. Cancini stood, stretching his stiff limbs. He used the remote to click to the nightly news. His eyes went back to the old man. His father looked so pale. What little hair remained was snow-white and combed back. Dark bruises dotted the thin skin of his arms where doctors and nurses had poked and prodded. If it weren't for the snoring, Cancini would wonder. He shook away the thoughts. His father had always been stronger than he looked. Strong and stubborn.

"In a surprise move today," a TV reporter said, "the governor has granted a writ of innocence to Leo Spradlin, the man once known as the Coed Killer."

Cancini's head whipped around. He moved closer to the screen.

"Mr. Spradlin, currently housed in solitary at Red Onion State Prison, was convicted of the rapes and murders of five women, all students at Blue Hill College. Sentenced more than twenty years ago, Mr. Spradlin was scheduled for execution later this month." Behind the reporter, a camera panned the dreary prison campus, the highest security facility in Virginia. "A statement from the governor's office and the attorney general indicated that new DNA evidence exonerates Spradlin."

Cancini's temple throbbed. A headshot of Spradlin appeared in the corner of the screen. The man's hair was longish now, not short the way he wore it back then. A heavy beard covered his chiseled face, but his pale blue eyes were the same, clear and cold as a winter night.

"Lawyers working for the newly innocent man had this to say."

The picture switched to an attorney in a gray suit. "Leo Spradlin is a grateful man tonight." The lawyer stood on the steps of the state capitol, microphones shoved under his chin. "He is particularly grateful to the governor for hearing his case. As many of you have already heard, DNA evidence that had previously been used to help convict Mr. Spradlin has been reexamined using more current technology. That same evidence now proves beyond a shadow of a doubt that Mr. Spradlin is not the Coed Killer. Mr. Spradlin is also immensely grateful to the Freedom and Justice Group and men like Dan Whitmore." He paused, nodding at the short, squat man standing to his right. "Finally, he would like me to thank all the friends and family who stood by him through this long ordeal and for their strong faith in him."

"What friends? What family?" Cancini muttered. His long fingers tightened on the remote. No one had stood by the man. Spradlin had alienated anyone and everyone who might once have cared for him. Not just during the original trial. Through count-less appeals and hearings, no one ever appeared on Spradlin's behalf. Cancini should know. He'd never missed a single one.

The reporter returned to the screen. She nodded. "The gov-ernor's office also issued the following statement: 'In an effort to right this terrible miscarriage of justice, Mr. Spradlin will be granted a full pardon along with his writ of innocence and will be released within a matter of days.'"

A heat rose in Cancini. He'd heard rumblings the DNA evi-dence was getting another look, but he hadn't given it much thought. It was true some of the evidence in the murder case had been circumstantial, but the DNA evidence—such as it was at the time—had been convincing. The jury had deliberated less than two hours. What had changed?

The newswoman shuffled papers. When she spun to the left, the camera followed. "And on Wall Street today, the Dow Jones took a tumble. Stockholders were warned to brace for another market correction."

Cancini hit the mute button, shaking his head. The sheets ruf-fled behind him. He squared his shoulders, meeting his father's gaze.

"What does it mean? Is it true?" His father sounded tired, his words barely audible.

The detective swallowed. "How long have you been awake?"

"Long enough. Thought that was your case."

Cancini winced. It wasn't a question. He put the remote back on the nightstand, then tucked the blankets under the old man's spindly arms. His father's hands, blue with puffy veins, lay flat on the bed.

"Well?"

Cancini didn't answer, unable to wrap his head around the reversal. He rubbed the stubble on his chin. How could a man as guilty as Spradlin suddenly be innocent? That case had made his career, started him on the road as a homicide detective. Did that mean everything was built on a lie? If it was, he knew what his father would think. His son was a failure.

"I don't know anything, Dad. I only knew they were looking into old evidence. Not this."

"You said he was guilty. He went to jail."

"He went to jail because a jury convicted him. They thought he was guilty. We all thought he was guilty." He grabbed his jacket and glanced once more at the monitors. Everything appeared normal. "I've gotta go." He started toward the door. "I'll try to come by tomorrow night."

"Michael?"

"Yes, Dad?"

The old man's eyes, still sharp, glowed like shiny coins at the bottom of a murky fountain. "Did you make a mistake?"

The detective swallowed his resentment. His father wouldn't be the only one to ask. Had he made a mistake? The governor seemed to think so. But if Spradlin was innocent, who was guilty? After the arrest, the murders and rapes had stopped. Coincidence? Cancini didn't know if he could accept that.

"I don't know, Dad. I'm not sure."

"Then get sure."

Chapter Three

JULIA MANNING LOOKED over tortoiseshell readers and peered at the digital clock. After midnight again. She shifted in the worn leather chair, pulling her legs to her chest and resting her head on her knees. It would be another sleepless night. She had no one to coax her to bed, no one to pull her close during the night. She lifted her chin. Damn him.

Holed up in her office, she felt the emptiness of the large house echo throughout the halls. She'd carved out a workspace from the smallest room, barely larger than a closet, but she loved it anyway. Behind her, a wall of shelves overflowed with books and papers. Her collection of knickknacks and pictures from childhood hung on the walls and cluttered the battered desk. It was a mess, but it was hers.

"How can you stand it in here?" Jack had asked one day, leaning in the doorway. His eyes had swept across the room to the furniture crammed in corners and the stacks of old magazines. "Doesn't it make you claustrophobic?"

"No," she'd answered honestly. It didn't and never had. Although the space was small, the window overlooking the backyard made it feel larger, and the light that shone through all day made it bright and warm. "It's comfortable."

Jack had not seemed convinced. "When Marta comes next time, you should have her clean in here." He'd waved a hand toward the junk spilling from the bookcase and said, "It smells." He'd left quickly, as though the foul odor he'd detected might follow. At the time, she'd laughed. Curled up now, she was no longer amused. Then again, blame comes in all shapes and sizes. Laying it all on Jack would be too easy. She couldn't deny she'd begun to spend more time in her office. It hadn't happened all at once, but they had drifted away from each other. Still, she wasn't the one who'd brought other people into it.

Blinking back tears, she picked up the oversized manila envelope perched on the corner of her desk. It was heavy in her hands, thick with the background research she'd requested. A story of this magnitude came with expectations and a whopping amount of history. Julia rifled through her desk for an empty spiral notebook. She pushed up her glasses and studied the first several pages, photocopies of old newspaper articles.

Little Springs Gazette
November 8

Late yesterday, the body of a young woman was found at the edge of the Thompson River. Three hunters, guests of the Powhatan Lodge, discovered the woman's remains. The deceased has been identified as Cheryl Fornak, a sophomore at Blue Hill Christian College.

Julia skimmed the remainder of the article. She picked up her tea, sipping the lukewarm liquid. "Cheryl Fornak," she said out loud. She'd had a friend named Cheryl in college. They'd been close for a while, even sharing an apartment the first few months after graduation. They'd drifted apart when Cheryl got engaged and followed her fiancé to Texas. In her notebook, Julia wrote the number one, and next to it, the girl's name, her age, and the date of her murder. On a separate line, she wrote down the names of the police chief, the town, and the college.

She flipped through the next few pages. After the autopsy, the case had been classified as a rape and murder. Days and weeks had passed with little progress in the investigation when a second girl was found.

Little Springs Gazette
December 5

Early yesterday morning, the body of a second young woman was found nearly ten miles outside Little Springs. A truck driver headed to Blue Hill Christian College spotted the woman, identified as Theresa Daniels, lying on the shoulder of 81 South. The police and a college spokesman confirmed that the young woman was a student at the school, a senior biology major. Authorities revealed that the death would be listed as a homicide. The autopsy is expected to begin as early as today.

It has been almost one month since the body of Blue Hill Christian College sophomore Cheryl Fornak was discovered on the banks of the Thompson River. Dozens of students and local residents have been interviewed in connection with the case. However, the investigation has stalled, and the police have declined to name any suspects in Fornak's rape and murder. Police would not make a statement regarding any connection between the two deaths.

A spokesman for Blue Hill issued this statement, "We are stunned by both murders. Nothing like this has ever happened in the history of our school or in the history of this town. Our highest priority is to protect our students. In light of the second murder, we have instituted a curfew and all school buildings will be locked down by campus security at eleven p.m. each evening. Where it is possible, the faculty will reschedule evening classes."

Manny Fulton, the mayor of Little Springs, attended a town meeting at the high school last night and addressed the murders. "Chief Hobson and the rest of the men are doing their best to find out what has happened to these young women. The best thing we can do is cooperate in any way possible and help them do their jobs so we can all sleep better at night."

Julia shifted in her chair and finished her tea. Her notes were a jumble of names and dates. She drew a line connecting the names of the dead girls, adding the words, "one month." Julia returned to the articles. A third young woman was found just before Christmas break that year.

Little Springs Gazette
December 7

Shocking the town and Blue Hill Christian College, a third victim was found in the early hours of the morning by campus security. The body of Marilyn Trammel, a freshman, was spotted in a Dumpster behind the campus center. Onlookers who saw the naked body pulled from the trash bin reported seeing dark welts and dried blood. Police would not elaborate on the extent of her injuries, only indicating that the woman had probably been dead less than six hours. This murder comes forty-eight hours after the discovery of the slain Theresa Daniels and a month after that of Cheryl Fornak. Although all three victims were students at Blue Hill, there does not appear to be a connection among the three women. They did not share classes, dormitories, or sororities. One source admits that police are stumped. When asked if each of the victims had been raped and how each was murdered, the police spokesman would not comment.

Michael Hudgins, dean of student affairs, announced the immediate cancellation of all classes and exams. "In light of recent events and the ongoing investigation, we are suspending exams until after winter break. Campus will officially close at five p.m. tomorrow, and all students are expected to vacate college housing."

Julia tapped the notebook with her pen. Only two days between the second and third murders and the first body to be found on campus. The first two girls were found miles from Blue Hill. The third was clearly a departure. Was the killer growing bolder or more reckless?

Julia rifled through the next set of articles. Although there were no murders over the Christmas break, there was also no apparent progress in solving the first three cases. The lack of an arrest was bad for the town and worse for the college. Some students—mostly girls—had applied for deferrals, opting not to return for the spring semester. The town had invoked a curfew of ten p.m. and had brought in additional police from neighboring towns. Still, the killer remained at large.

Julia dropped the pages in her lap, thinking about the dead girls from Blue Hill. No doubt their parents thought they were sending their teenage daughters away to a safe place, a college with strong Christian principles and no city crime, a place where they could grow up and get an education. But Cheryl Fornak, Theresa Daniels, and Marilyn Trammel didn't get to grow up. Head bowed, Julia continued to read. Within days of the students' return, another girl was found, and then another. Five college girls. All raped. All dead. Shivering in the air-conditioning, Julia rubbed her arms.

In an unprecedented move, the college had announced the immediate suspension of the semester. She read the statement from old papers.

The safety of our young women and all of our students is at the forefront of this decision. We cannot, in good conscience, ask the students to remain on campus until this situation has been resolved.

The FBI had been brought in after the fourth murder, spearheading the interviews with every male student enrolled at the college. With a serial rapist and murderer on the loose, the Little Springs town council was forced to invoke "sunset" curfews. The media dubbed the murderer the Coed Killer, a name that stuck.

Rumors of vendettas against the college and the town spread like wildfire. Fights broke out among locals as suspicions ran high. Businesses suffered and still, no suspects.

Julia circled the dates of all the murders. The timeline was curious. Had the killer had second thoughts after the first? Why the long gap and then increasingly smaller ones? Over the break, they'd stopped. Did that suggest the killer was also a student? After Christmas, he hadn't waited long to strike again and then again. After the semester was suspended, the murders appeared to stop. Then the police arrested Leo Spradlin.

Julia sifted through the stack of research for pictures of the victims. She placed the photos in a row. Five girls smiling at the camera, all young, all pretty. There was nothing obvious linking them, no common physical traits that she could see. According to the articles, they had different majors and different friends. Yet they'd all known Spradlin—a one-time student at the school—a fact he'd never denied. She set the pictures aside and picked up Spradlin's mug shot. He was young, barely older than college-age himself. Attractive, with dark hair, he had a strong chin and a straight nose. It wasn't hard to see how a young woman might have wanted to be alone with him. She squinted at the black and white photo that was more school portrait than mug shot. His hair was combed and he was neatly dressed. He looked directly into the camera. She held the picture closer, trying to read his expression, but saw nothing. No fear. No anger. No remorse.

Now he would be a free man. His impending release had already made a big splash across Virginia. It was a story that promised to get even bigger, fueling the death penalty debate and causing increased speculation about the governor's political agenda. The release was one thing, the aftermath another. If Spradlin wasn't the Coed Killer, who was? No newspaper could resist this story. The *Washington Herald* was no exception.

Julia turned the page in the notebook and wrote a list of questions. Rereading the short list, Julia hoped she knew what she was doing. She was not the first choice among the staff, and she knew it. Conroy was the star reporter at the paper, and he wouldn't miss this story for the world. But Jack owed her. If he wasn't going to be a great husband, the least he could do was help her rebuild the career she'd let slip from her grasp.

Now that she had the story, she had to do something with it. She picked up the picture of Spradlin again. He'd spent two decades in prison for crimes he didn't commit. Was he bitter? Angry? What would that do to a man? She shook her head, stacking the pages and sliding them back into the large envelope. Spradlin was going back to Little Springs after his release. His lawyers had announced he would hold a press conference the day of his homecoming. The town would be flooded with press, publicity-seekers, and gawkers.

Julia knew a story like this attracted all kinds. She also knew most stories die after a few days. And that was precisely her strategy. She would attend the press conference like the others and position herself for an interview. But when the others were gone, scurrying after the next headline, she would stay. She was in it for the long haul. She was in it for the story of her life.

Chapter Four

THE NIGHT WRAPPED around him like a soft blanket, comforting and soothing. He lay on top of the covers, his body still, letting the darkness seep into his thoughts, his dreams. During the day, he pushed it away, but at night, he embraced it. Eyes wide, he stared at the bare ceiling. After a while, he could see the girls again. He breathed in, nostrils flaring. The memories were all he had.

They'd fought like hell. In vain, of course, but back then, even he hadn't understood his strength or the depth of his needs. The first one, Cheryl, had been especially difficult. He thought most often of her. Swinging her arms and kicking her legs, she'd tried desperately to fight him off, but was the first to learn he was not to be underestimated. What she couldn't have known was that the fear in her eyes only fueled his desire. With each girl, his hunger grew. Their screams and their tears gave him a rush that made him forget everything but the ecstasy of the moment. When they closed their eyes to shut him out, he would jerk their heads, forcing them to watch, to see him as he really was. Since that first night, he'd fallen asleep replaying those beautiful images.

He smiled, his loins hot. It had been such a long fucking time, but now it would be different. The release was big news, and the homecoming was fast approaching. He'd been told there would be press, regional and national. A story of this magnitude was bound to stir controversy. He didn't give a shit. The words "guilt" and "innocence" were thrown around, but few understood how they worked, how closely they were intertwined. One could not exist without the other.

He closed his eyes, holding on to the image of Cheryl. He'd left her in the woods, buried under leaves and sticks, her white skin smeared with mud from the river, her blond hair spread out like a fan around her twisted head. Even dead, her eyes had looked back at him, round and gaping. Nothing could ever erase that beautiful picture. Nothing. And now he'd been given a gift. The Coed Killer would be back.

About the Author

K.L. MURPHY was born in Key West, Florida, the eldest of four children in a military family. She has worked as a freelance writer for several regional publications in Virginia, and is the author of *A Guilty Mind* and *Stay of Execution*. She lives in Richmond, Virginia, with her husband, four children, and two very large, very hairy dogs. To learn more about the Detective Cancini Mystery series or future projects, visit www.kellielarsenmurphy.com.

www.witnessimpulse.com

Discover great authors, exclusive offers, and more at hc.com.